Celestial Navigation

Celestial Navigation

A Novel

Jonathan R. Lewis

This book is a work of fiction. All dialogue, all incidents, and all characters are products of the author's imagination, and any similarities to real persons, living or dead, are coincidental.

Copyright © 2022 by Jonathan Ridgely Lewis
All rights reserved.
ISBN: 979-8-218-11219-6

Edited by Allison Felus
Cover and interior design by Jonathan Hahn
Cover Art by Daniel Bellitsky / Shutterstock

Printed in the United States of America

For Philip (1958–1999)—
the brightest, the boldest, the bravest, the best.

Contents

1	Meteors 1		18	Transit 141
2	Wavelength 5		19	Spectrum 151
3	Conjunction 15		20	Perigee 163
4	Altitude 23		21	Apogee 175
5	Velocity 30		22	Eccentricity 186
6	Alignment 36		23	Limb 198
7	Fusion 42		24	Occultation 210
8	Luminosity 51		25	Inclination 221
9	Orbit 56		26	Panspermia 232
10	Halo 63		27	Retrograde 243
11	Eclipse 70		28	Nebula 254
12	Collision 81		29	Space-Time 264
13	Gravity 89		30	Quasar 276
14	Ellipse 98		31	Wormhole 287
15	Maelstrom 108		32	Zenith 298
16	Barycenter 120			
17	Supernova 129			*Acknowledgments* .. 310

1
Meteors

"A particle of rock or dust that burns away in the Earth's atmosphere."

The Vikings set off on their voyages across open ocean with little more than the sky, the horizon, and the currents of the waves to guide them to their unknown destinations. During the day, they used a rudimentary sun dial that would find their bearings by tracking the sun's passage across the skies as the hours passed. On dark overcast days, they used a sunstone, which the Norse sagas suggest was a crystal, to detect polarized light coming off the sun even when it lay hidden behind the thickest clouds. It was easier navigating by nightfall when they merely had to look overhead at the stars to chart their course. On occasion, a meteor would streak across their field of vision, causing excitement amongst their crew.

The more superstitious of them might see the shooting star as an ill portent. Others would take it as a good omen. They did not know that a meteor was simply a piece of intergalactic debris, garbage really, hurtling across the universe. As its rock mass hit Earth's atmosphere, the meteor began the process of ablation, becoming superheated and starting to burn up and break apart as its descent accelerated. These shooting stars, then, were neither an omen for good nor for ill. They were just rocks, and they were utterly random.

Early in the morning of Tuesday, July 15, 1958, Aleksander Kulik saw a shooting star in the night sky over Louisville, Kentucky, and chose to consider it a good sign for the birth of his fourth child. A few hours earlier, the contractions had begun, and his wife Leighton calmly announced, "Zan, it's time." He walked to the black telephone hanging on the wall of the kitchen and looked at the two phone numbers taped next to it. He first dialed the doctor to let him know that they would be heading to the hospital and to arrange to meet him there.

The second call was to the neighbors next door. The line was busy, so Zan hung up and waited exactly ten seconds before dialing again. He got a busy signal again, so he walked out of the house and across the backyard to knock on their kitchen door. The wife, Barbara, opened the door almost immediately and knew why he was there. "I'm taking Leigh to the hospital. Can Pamela come over?" Her daughter Pam babysat the Kulik kids, and she was now hogging the telephone, gossiping with a classmate. Barbara walked over, took the phone out of Pam's hand, hung it up, and ordered her to "go over now."

That handled, Zan walked back to his house, unlocking the car as he went. He grabbed his wife's packed bag, put her nicest housecoat over her nightgown and walked her to the car. At 9:00 p.m. on a Monday night, there was no traffic on the Louisville streets, so the seven-mile drive from their house in the Hikes Point area to St. Anthony's Hospital in the Highlands neighborhood took only twenty minutes. Nurses whisked Leigh off to the maternity ward, while Zan filled out paperwork and consulted briefly with the doctor.

He had several hours to kill, so he found the second floor waiting room closest to maternity, but a few other expectant fathers had already taken up residence there, pacing the floor nervously and chain smoking furiously. Fanning the smoke away from his face, Zan looked for another quiet spot to wait. Walking down the hospital corridor past the main stairwell, he noticed a propped-open door revealing metal stairs climbing four stories up to the top floor of the old brick building. The stairs led to a small room below the cupola over the hospital's front entrance. He climbed the ladder rungs embedded into the wall to make his final ascent.

It was late in the evening so the city below him had gone quiet. The sky was clear, and he had a great perch from which to watch the world below. As he rested his elbows on the railing, he looked up and spotted a shooting star that seemed suspended in air for the longest time. Zan said out loud to himself and the pigeons roosting in the rafters, "May this child always feel loved and have a very happy life." His fourth child, and third son, Caleb Ivan Kulik, was born at 3:12 a.m. that next morning.

For several weeks in July there was a great deal of space garbage burning up in the atmosphere over the Midwest. Just two weeks later, a shooting star heralded the birth of another child in the suburbs of Chicago, but that child's father would miss it because he was sound asleep in his bed at that very moment. His child would wait until much later in the morning before announcing his intention of making his grand entrance into the world.

James and Elizabeth Davies lived in Lombard, Illinois, a suburb twenty-four miles due west of downtown Chicago. Married while they were still in college, they started having children immediately. Although she was only twenty-two, Betty was already in her third pregnancy. Jim slept like a rock that night, but Betty began tossing and turning around 5:00 a.m. She finally gave up on getting any more sleep and went downstairs to the kitchen.

She packed overnight bags for the kids, made sack lunches for them and prepared breakfast. By the time Jim had come downstairs, fresh coffee was ready in the percolator. She announced that she was changing their prearranged plan for the day. She had already begun having labor pains, so it did not make any sense to her that they should wait the twenty minutes it would take Jim's parents to drive from Elmhurst westward to their house in Lombard, and then take an additional twenty minutes to drive right past her in-laws' house to get to Lincoln Memorial Hospital on the very same street where they lived.

They would take their kids with them and drop them off along the way. After calmly eating breakfast, Jim loaded everyone into their Nash Rambler, with three-year-old Jessica buckled into the middle seat, while eighteen-month-old Nicky sat on Betty's lap. After dropping off the kids with his parents, Jim deposited Betty with the maternity nurses. He headed to the waiting lounge to pace the floor with the other expectant fathers and smoke nearly a pack of cigarettes. His third child, and second son, Jacob Ewan Davies was born at 1:23 p.m. on Tuesday, July 29, 1958. If Jim had seen the shooting star that passed over his house the night before, he too might have hoped it a good omen.

2

Wavelength

"The distance between consecutive crests of a wave, serving as a unit of measure of electromagnetic radiation."

At nine months of age, little curly headed Cal Kulik began making gurgling and cooing sounds in his earliest attempts to communicate with the world. He would watch his parents intently as they talked together over the kitchen table or seated in their living room. Often, his father would notice the boy staring intently at them and wondered what he must be thinking. "Hey there, little man. What's on your mind?" Cal would giggle and smile and then go right back to staring. When Zan and Leigh were distracted with their resumed conversation, they failed to notice that Cal had started babbling gibberish in concert with them. If they stopped talking, he stopped. When they started again, he became vocal once more.

At Christmas when he was seventeen months old, Cal got a large stuffed animal, a bright yellow dog that his mother named Old Yeller after the Disney movie. Cal was still keenly watching the people in his world having conversations, conveying ideas to one another, interacting, asking, and answering. He would look at his family and then look at Yeller. He looked at them again and returned his gaze to the stuffed dog. Suddenly, a switch seemed to turn on in his brain and there was no stopping him.

The various words and phrases he had heard up until that point started to make sense. They had intent; they had meaning; they had purpose. From that moment, he began to talk. He never shut up in fact, delighted with the sound of his own voice. He talked all day long, but his parents quickly noticed something else. He would sing the words to songs he had heard on the radio or stereo hi-fi the night before. If he could not manage to pronounce a certain word, he would just switch to "na, na, na," approximating the melody with near perfect precision.

Jake Davies took a lot longer to begin talking. On his first birthday, his gift was a stuffed animal of the TV cartoon character Huckleberry Hound. The toy's tall blue body with bow tie, plastic face, and straw boater made him taller than the toddler. To see Jake carry this stuffed animal, that was as big as he was, made his grandparents smile at the ridiculousness of his efforts. However, it pierced his mother's heart to watch him struggle. Jake had respiratory issues and already had suffered through a prolonged bout of bronchitis in just his first year of life.

He lugged Huck around and hugged him, but the boy was always noticeably quiet. Giggling and smiling were easy enough for him, but making the sounds that little children make as they prepare to talk seemed to require too much effort, so he did not try. Whenever his sister and brother played roughly and loudly with their toys in the basement, Jake spent the evenings quietly sitting on the couch with his parents as they listened to the stereo. His mother played classical music, preferring the grand symphonies of Tchaikovsky and Rachmaninoff, while his dad would lose himself in the improvisations of a jazz trio. It sounded like just so much noise to Jake.

On one of his many sick days, Jake sat on the couch underneath a blanket with Huckleberry Hound by his side. Betty put a record on the turntable, and the shimmer of violins caught Jake's attention right before a man with a rich deep baritone began to sing the opening line of "Oh, What a Beautiful Mornin'." His ears perked up as the full orchestra gradually joined in. His parents owned the cast albums to several hit Broadway musicals, and this became the accompaniment to his childhood. He learned how to sing along with these records before he learned how to talk.

The Kulik children were all born exactly two years apart—Natalia in 1952, Aleksander in 1954, Edward in 1956, and Cal, the baby of the family, in 1958. Zan and Leigh had bought their modest ranch house brand new in 1953 and it seemed spacious enough when they only had three kids. By the birth of their final child, they were bursting at the seams of their small 1,100-square-foot home, sharing just three bedrooms and one bathroom. Their basement doubled the square footage of their home, but it was unfinished. It had only the washer and dryer, a laundry sink and a toilet exposed to the rest of the big open space.

As their kids got older and bigger, Zan first had to enclose that open toilet and sink, then added a shower stall, and finally subdivided the basement into bedroom spaces and a family room. The first to move down to the basement was their oldest son Alek, followed by middle son Eddie by the time their baby brother was born. Cal was just six when he joined his brothers down there. A basement door led outside, which allowed them access to the storage shed and fenced backyard that had a single large tree in the left corner and bushes along the back fence.

Meanwhile in Chicago, the Davies added another son, Shaun, to their brood; he was the last in line after Jessica, Nicky, and Jake, all of them born two years apart. The Davies' split-level, which they bought brand new in 1956, was barely larger than the Kuliks' ranch house, but it suited them better thanks to the five different levels that allowed them to spread out. The living room and eat-in kitchen took up the ground floor, with two bedrooms and a hall bath on the second level, and a huge bedroom and second bathroom on the top floor. The attic, up another level, served as out-of-season storage.

The unfinished basement became the kids' playground during the long Chicago winters. It often snowed by Halloween, and they might not see the ground again until after Easter. Their back yard only extended twenty-five feet past the kitchen door, but behind a row of lilac bushes was a plot of land belonging to the railroad company that ran train tracks a few hundred feet further back from their property. Every spring, Jim would mow a huge swath of that prairie grass, so he had room to add a swing set, kid's pool, and picnic table. Many a summer barbecue, birthday celebration, and pool party happened in that illegal backyard.

Whenever Jake's siblings ran around the yard, he often sat in a lawn chair and watched them, or he played quietly with his toys. On a warm afternoon in May when he was five, he was sitting on the front sidewalk playing with his building blocks. A garter snake slithered out from under the front stoop and stopped to sun itself on the warm concrete right between Jake's legs. He began screaming. Betty came running out of the house to see what was causing the commotion. She calmly lifted Jake away from the monster and grabbed the hoe that she always kept beside the front door. She flicked the snake into the flower bed, where she hacked it to death with ruthless precision. Clearly, she was a seasoned assassin, accustomed to this kind of casual slaughter.

Leigh Kulik had little interest in gossiping with the other neighborhood housewives, but she put forth her best effort, inviting them over for Saturday morning coffee cake. In the middle of their pleasantly dull conversation, Cal came crashing through the kitchen, yelling, "Mommy, look!" He presented his prize which flew out of his hands and landed on top of the coffee cake. The ladies jumped up, screaming as they ran out the front door. Leigh sighed and said, "Cal, why must you do that? I've told you to not bring creatures into the house." She tried not to laugh at her exuberant son, as she kneeled on the carpet to collect the garter snake that had slithered under her couch.

Each boy had a few casual male friends in the neighborhood, but they were more drawn to girls as their main pals. Jake had mousy Bonnie Griffith who lived down the street. Cal had pretty and petite Diane Brand who was right next door. At age six, Jake and Bonnie were using building blocks to make a house that they would have together one day when they were old and married. Bonnie knew nothing about load bearing supports and removed a couple of walls that were necessary to hold up the roof. When Jake told her that he did not like that and put the blocks back, Bonnie responded by smashing him over the head with a rock. The gash required four stitches. The course of young love sometimes hurt.

Diane decided that she would marry Cal someday. They were just six years old when she staged a make-believe wedding for them, complete with a backyard altar and a row of folding chairs for their imaginary guests. Diane wanted to enact every little moment of their big day, while Cal just wanted to be done with it so he could go climb a tree. After an hour of this nonsense, Cal decided he had had enough and pulled her toward the altar. He lifted her imaginary veil and gave her a very quick peck on the cheek. Diane shrieked, "No, that's not how it is supposed to go." She made it clear that only the girl gets to decide everything. "Now you've ruined it forever." She slapped Cal's face and ran into her house sobbing.

Every year, Jake suffered yet another bout of bronchitis. The relentless coughing racked his entire body and lasted for weeks. Even a mild cold had the potential to worsen into a more serious illness that caused him much breathing distress. While Betty and Jim were reluctant to dub him a "delicate" child, the family doctor did describe him as fragile and ordered allergy tests. Betty took him on the train to an allergist's office in downtown Chicago, where he laid on his stomach for six hours, staring out a dirty window at a brick wall and crying while a nurse scratched more than four hundred needle marks across his back to check for reactions.

When the list of allergies came back disproportionately long,

Betty and Jim moved Jake out of the boys' bedroom on the third floor and put his sister Jessie up there with Nicky and Shaun instead. Jake got Jessie's old bedroom all to himself, but Betty had to strip it bare of any personality. Jim removed the curtains and pulled out the area rug; Betty banned all stuffed animals and had to dust the room every day. Instead of the usual lunch that his sister and brothers got, Jake now took a lunchbox to school filled with a stinky sandwich (usually tuna or liverwurst), an apple, and a thermos of Hi-C, because he was now allergic to milk.

At the start of second grade, his teacher, Mrs. Abrams, was concerned with how much school Jake was missing. She recommended that his parents should let him join the school chorus. She felt strongly that singing might help with some of his breathing issues, and the family doctor concurred. From the first day, Jake felt like he had found his place in the world. He had a sweet voice, despite the fact that the rest of his family had no discernible musical talent. The Davies had a dog, a toffee-colored Rhodesian Ridgeback named Traeger, who howled along in unison from underneath the kitchen table whenever the family attempted to shriek out their discordant rendition of "Happy Birthday to You" several times a year.

Cal's family was more naturally musical. Each of the four kids played an instrument in the school band or orchestra, and they all sang in their school's choruses. Zan was Ukrainian and grew up knowing the dances of the old country and singing traditional folk songs. Ukrainian music is known for its full-bodied men's choruses, and Zan had a powerful tenor voice that could wring every ounce of emotion out of a song. Leigh came from an Irish background, and she was a walking encyclopedia of music. She loved to sing old folk songs, madrigals, and weepy Gaelic ballads, which were pretty but never seemed as exotic or as interesting as Zan's songs.

The Kulik family would have impromptu recitals in which everyone would sing or play an instrument or dance. Often, a song playing on the radio would prompt a spontaneous sing-along or an outburst of dancing. These sing-alongs were a frequent occurrence in the evenings, at summer backyard gatherings, during birthday celebrations, or around the table after Sunday dinner. Zan would turn on the living room stereo, then they would move the coffee table out of the way so the kids could sing along and dance to a favorite song on the radio.

His older sister Natalia studied ballet and gymnastics, so it was no surprise that Cal picked them up too. He was a natural talent, wholly unaware at how well he could do just about anything he set his mind to. Not only that, but he also had an ear for music and could repeat back whole passages of songs after hearing them just one time. His lovely young boy's singing voice might one day have the same power and range as his father's. His tireless energy and enthusiasm also made him a great dancer. And yet, Cal seemed entirely unaware of any of these talents, and he had no interest in performing other than as a passing family activity.

In the 1960s, it was customary for families to indoctrinate their boys as early as possible into the masculine culture of team sports. Both small for their age, Cal and Jake were too slight in stature to consider touch football, and too short to play basketball. Their parents' attempts to interest them in baseball did not last long. Jake thought it was great at first because all he had to do was stand there in the outfield and not run, which might cause a coughing fit. He eventually quit because he took a baseball square in the face, breaking his nose. Likewise, Cal told his friends he quit because he hated the long periods of standing around waiting for something to happen, neglecting to mention the baseline hit that rocketed into his balls.

Cal was not sure about team sports, because he had never spent so much time with so many other boys. He had two brothers, but that was family. This was a bunch of guys competing with one another to see who was the toughest, most male of them all. Who was the best, who was the biggest, who was the fastest, who was the brightest? He disliked sports' need for superlatives to declare one side the winner over the other. He was probably better than his teammates at everything, but he felt diminished in this forced group setting. Cal had far more energy to expend and thought it might best be used elsewhere.

Both boys wanted to excel at something, but it had to be where they only needed to challenge themselves, not compete with others. They came to discover gymnastics. Cal's family already frequented the American Turners facility, out on River Road along the Ohio River, to use the pool on hot summer days, but kids could also learn how to do acrobatics there. Hanging out there during his big sister Nat's practices, Cal would be off to the side trying to figure out some of the moves he saw the girls do. He landed on his head a few times, but he started picking up the moves without anyone telling him how. Gymnastics seemed a perfect fit for his boundless exuberance and limitless energy.

For Jake, it was his school principal who suggested it. The man worried that a doctor's note excusing Jake from any gym classes and his lack of activity during recess might possibly make the boy sicker and weaker in the long run. He recommended tumbling lessons, which were free to anyone in the school. The instructor was Mr. Bronner, one of the teachers who had been a competitive gymnast when he was in college. He wanted to share his passion for athletic discipline with the future Olympic gymnasts of the world. At the first lesson, Mr. Bronner demonstrated a cartwheel and told everyone, "Don't think about it; just do it."

Most of the kids collapsed in a heap or careened off into a wall. Jake had so much pent-up energy that he launched himself into one cartwheel that propelled him into a second, but he had a moment of panic, stopping upside down and yelling, "Help, how do I get down?" The teacher told Jake to just fold in half by dropping his legs. Jake was thrilled to have gotten out alive, but the instructor was amazed that this little beginner completed two perfect cartwheels and a handstand without realizing what they were.

Both boys became skilled at performing tricks, with cartwheels being the easiest, but soon learning aerials, round-offs, walkovers, barrel rolls, handstands, backflips, donkey kicks, and fence jumps. Jake could manage the short bursts of energy without coughing his lungs out, and he did start to get stronger. He just loved jumping around. Cal discovered his own well of strength and became so accomplished that he started training other kids when he was just ten years old. A year later, the City Parks and Recreation Department gave him his first after-school job, teaching tumbling to other kids both younger and older than himself.

3

Conjunction

"When two or more celestial objects appear close together in the sky."

After World War II, it seemed that every family wanted to achieve their own version of the American Dream. Whether it was reasonable or not, most people strived to have the exact same kind of life that they saw on television sitcoms every night of the week. Every woman was supposed to want to be as good a mother and housewife as Donna Reed or Jane Wyatt, while every man had a hard time living up to the model of husbandly perfection exemplified by Carl Betz and Robert Young. Every family strived to work toward the dream house, the nice car, multiple children, and the family dog. It was all about upward mobility.

Zan Kulik's life trajectory had a circuitous route that brought him to Louisville. Born in northwestern Ukraine in 1923, he was seven years old when his family immigrated to the United States, settling in Sacramento, California. When the Japanese attacked Pearl Harbor on December 7, 1941, he was like every teenage boy in America who suddenly became infected with wartime patriotism. He was just eighteen years old when he enlisted in the navy and served as a medic until the end of the war. He returned home to Sacramento, where he met Leighton, who was studying to become a teacher.

They dated for a few years during college and finally got married before either of them had graduated. Zan's job as an anatomy researcher kept them in California for a few years, where they started their family. Earning his medical degree, Zan could go wherever there was a hospital, so it was an offer for work as a physiologist that brought the family to Louisville, Kentucky, in the fall of 1953. Buying a modest ranch home for their growing family, Zan felt that he had achieved his American Dream. He was thirty years old.

Jim Davies had lived his entire life in the suburbs of Chicago, until he attended Miami University in Oxford, Ohio. It was at a drunken fraternity mixer that he met his future wife, Betty. For the twenty-year-old junior, it was love at first sight when he saw this tiny, pretty, eighteen-year-old freshman who cursed like a sailor. They had dated for two semesters when Jim popped the question to Betty before she could escape back home for the summer.

They had a small church wedding in Hammond, Indiana, where Betty's parents lived, right before heading back to school. Betty had assumed she would be starting her sophomore year, but her father told her, "You are now your husband's responsibility" and so refused to pay for any more college tuition. They were married in August, and she was pregnant two months later. To support his wife and soon-to-be-born child, Jim worked two jobs while remaining a full-time student. He did shelf stocking at Woolworth's on weekends and worked weekday afternoons and evenings at a uranium plant that processed nuclear rods. The workers sat on crates of radioactive material on the loading dock to smoke their cigarettes and eat their sack lunches.

After graduation, Jim took his wife and daughter Jessica back to the Chicago suburbs, buying a brand-new split-level home in 1956 and filling it with a few more kids. They upgraded to a larger home for the brief two-year detour they lived in Monsey, New York. When another job change brought him to Louisville, Jim was thirty-four, so buying their large Georgian colonial brick home felt like the fulfillment of his American Dream.

Neither Cal nor Jake knew exactly what their parents did for a living. Cal knew that his dad worked in a hospital and his mom worked in a school. Jake knew his father went to an office building, while his mother spent hours every day in a corner of the basement trying to work on her latest oil painting in between doing loads of laundry, nursing scraped knees, and making meals. Cal had lived his entire life in Louisville and knew no place else. Jake thought each new home was yet another adventure. Cal and Jake had no idea what upward mobility was, unless it had something to do with getting older and hopefully growing taller. Because as kids, they often got into precarious situations that always made their moms yell at them, "Do not make me get out of this chair."

From kindergarten, Cal's best friend was Griffin Taylor, who lived three houses down. He had the same dark curly hair as Cal, but the similarities ended there. Griffin was an asthmatic little boy with horn-rimmed glasses and lenses as thick as soda bottles. His bad eyesight meant he frequently did not see fast objects hurtling toward his face, so his mother worried endlessly about him. If there was a stick in the yard or a stone in the driveway, he would trip over it. If he picked up a pair of scissors, he always cut himself. He even managed somehow to stab himself once, when his dad asked him to bring the hedge clippers and he tripped over his baby sister who was crawling across the backyard in front of him. Fortunately, it was only a minor flesh wound that barely broke the skin.

Griff's mother only stopped worrying about her son when he was with Cal. The two of them would sit quietly in the family room reading books, doing homework together at the kitchen table, or listening to the radio in Griff's bedroom. The problems came whenever they went outside and were away from Mrs. Taylor's protective gaze. When they climbed the tree in the backyard, Griff chose to perch on the one dead branch in the entire tree, and it broke off, sending him tumbling six feet to the ground. While riding their bikes on the street in front of their houses, Cal was showing off by letting go of the handlebars and shouting, "Look, no hands." Griff tried to match his friend's derring-do by riding his bike blindly, saying, "Look, no eyes." He slammed face first into a mailbox.

Their friendship did not end suddenly one day from rancor, disagreement, or disinterest; it just petered out because Griff was exhausted. Most of the time, he just wanted to sit and hang out, while Cal was like a child's windup toy that never, ever ran down. Cal's next best friend was Tony, who he knew from grade school. They hung out together for a couple years without ever developing common interests. Tony hated to read; he had no opinions about much of anything; he called himself a jock but hated going outside. All Tony wanted to do was listen to rock music. He was the exact opposite of Cal, who quickly became bored with him.

Cal came about his boundless energy naturally. Everyone in his family was physically active. His parents loved biking and hiking; his older brothers played sports, and his sister did gymnastics. With four kids, Zan and Leigh could not afford to take expensive vacations, staying in hotels and eating every meal at restaurants, so they took them camping instead. They loaded up the station wagon and tried to visit as many state and national parks as they could get to on their yearly vacation. To witness their arrival gave the impression of a clown car exploding. Kid after kid would spill out, followed by mountains of supplies to last them the trip's duration.

When the Kulik kids were all small, it was fun to all pile into one large family tent. As the kids got older and bigger, however, the extreme proximity to one another became fractious. The solution was to bring even more supplies, including several smaller tents that made it look like Goldilocks was camping: the Papa Bear tent slept Zan and the two older boys; the medium Mama Bear tent was for Leigh and Nat; and the Baby Bear tent was for Cal, who did not want to share. Situated around their campfire and Coleman stove, Zan joked that they were just like the Kennedy family with their very own family compound.

They went hiking in the woods, swimming in lakes, fishing, running, canoeing, kayaking, climbing trees, and making as much noise as possible. The Kuliks roughed it, and it was out in the wilderness that Cal was in his element. He decided early on that he would have been happy to spend every minute of his life outdoors. Unfortunately, the camping trips became such huge logistical nightmares for a family this size, to the extent that, if everyone was being honest, they would have admitted to dreading their annual summer trips. They decided to make their vacations easier by building their very own log cabin.

After purchasing a building kit from *Popular Mechanics* magazine and a hilly plot of land, Zan thought this cabin could be their home away from home. Just thirty-five miles southeast from their house, the location was right outside of the Taylorsville Lake State Park. They were able to find a sloping lot that was right on the edge of a protected forest preserve, so there would not be many neighbors. They started building in March 1970 and enlisted everyone they knew to help. Their progress oftentimes looked like a colony of ants busily scurrying over a mound of earth on some inexplicable mission that only other ants could understand. The building was chaotic and fun, and it took two-and-a-half years to complete the cabin.

The Davies family also went camping when the kids were little for the same reasons. However, Betty Davies was not as inclined to rough it. She was a short woman, under five feet tall, so the idea of hiking in the woods, clamoring over downed trees and across slippery rocks, seemed less like fun and more like dangerous activities that might kill her. Instead of trying to corral their four children into a single tent, it made more sense to her that they should rent a cheap cabin where they could eat inexpensively and occupy the hours swimming and boating or sitting around a campfire, roasting marshmallows.

When they lived in Chicago, they would drive the seven hundred miles from their home to the cabin Betty's Uncle Al owned on a small lake outside of the town of Andes in upstate New York. Jim would leave early in the morning and make the entire drive in a single day, arriving after dark. Betty had taken a flat sheet, added elastic bands to fit it securely to the backside of the car's front seat, and sewed pockets of felt to the sheet to store plenty of items to keep four, young, rambunctious kids distracted on the long twelve-hour drive. There were pockets for crosswords, seek-and-finds, paperback novels, comic books, a comb, pencils and pens and paper, games, cards, sliding puzzles, and maze games.

When they moved briefly to Rockland County, New York, in 1966, they continued to spend their next three summer vacations at Uncle Al's cabin, but the drive to the Catskills was a lot shorter and so seemed like less of an adventure to Jake. Once they arrived, the kids would dash upstairs to claim their bedrooms, dumping their suitcase or backpack in the doorways to prevent anyone else from usurping their space. Once they had swarmed the place and settled in, everyone would sit quietly on the screened porch facing the lake and listen to the sounds of nighttime before heading up to bed.

Every day began with family breakfast, usually just cereal out of a box and semi-cold milk, but occasionally the kids awoke to the smell of frying bacon and scrambled eggs. It was a real treat if Jim heated up the griddle to make pancakes or French toast. Once the meal had been devoured with crumbs flying six feet in every direction, Betty started the hour-long countdown until the kids could go jump in the lake. Dressed in their swimsuits with towels draped over their shoulders, all four of them would inch away from the kitchen breakfast bar and sidle toward the couch. After a few minutes, the brood would saunter onto the screened porch. As they tried to sneak out the side door, Betty issued her usual stern warning, "Don't even think about it. It's not time yet."

Finally, Betty gave the all-clear, and Jessie, Nicky, Jake, and Shaun fell all over one another, racing down the yard and out onto the dock to leap into the always chilly water that never seemed to warm up in the mountains' summer. A boys' camp was down the shoreline to the left of Uncle Al's cabin, and a girls' camp lay directly across the lake. At dawn, the boys' camp played a robust rendition of reveille over their P.A. system. In an auditory game of one-upmanship, the girls' camp instead blared "I Enjoy Being a Girl," and Jake could not help but to sing along, unaware, or unconcerned that it was only 6:30 a.m. His family probably never hated Rodgers and Hammerstein as much as they did when each day was dawning over Perch Lake.

Lazy days consisted of swimming out to the floating raft, sunning in lawn chairs, rowing around the lake, walking along the shoreline, reading books on the porch, taking naps in the hammock, and pigging out on hamburgers and hot dogs. Jake loved to climb trees, and he found a large maple tree with long pendulous branches at the edge of the water a few cabins down. He thought he could make like an acrobat and swing from a branch to cannonball into the water. He did not know the lake there was only two feet deep. On his first leap, he badly sprained his ankle. He decided from then on that he was not Tarzan.

With the move to Louisville, though, Jim decided that upstate New York was probably just too far away. Future summer vacations would have to happen closer to their new home, so Jim bought a pop-up camper. He should have consulted with Betty, who felt that camping was no vacation for her since she would have more work to do than if she just stayed home. She had hoped that their camping days were behind them. The pop-up camper got used several times in the first few years before it ended up permanently languishing in their side yard next to the garage.

4

Altitude

"The angular distance of an object above the horizon."

The Davies' first house in Lombard had two mature maple trees on the left side of the front lawn. When Jake's asthma would get the better of him, he would rest in a lawn chaise watching his siblings play on the grass while he would gaze up into the leaves. One tree was down by the road and was of little interest, but the tree closest to the house intrigued him. He noticed the lowest branch was only about five feet off the ground with higher branches climbing past the side of the house to overhang the steeply pitched roof.

Jake pulled the chaise underneath the tree, jumped up to the nearest branch, swung his leg over, and pulled himself up. He climbed until he was about forty feet off the ground and above the highest peak of the roof. He ventured a little too far out and fell off the branch onto the roof. Relieved of his weight, the branch snapped back fully six feet over his head and out of reach, offering no escape from his precarious perch. He just sat there waiting for someone to notice him. Their neighbor across the street, Mrs. Griffith, happened to step out her front door, saw Jake on the roof, and bolted across the street.

Betty came running out of the house with Mrs. Griffith's screaming, looked up at her son, and ordered, "Jake, you stay right there," as if he were planning on going anywhere else, or could. The fire truck came screeching down their street with siren blaring, a source of much excitement for the other kids. A fireman slung Jake over his shoulder and carried him down the ladder. The rescue team chuckled at the daring seven-year-old's accidental adventure, while Betty cried and kissed his cheek as she smacked his rump a few times.

The fire department was not as amused the second time it happened a month later. This time, one of the rescuers produced a chainsaw, as if by magic, or perhaps remembering what happened last time. They cut off the offending tree limb. Three weeks later, an undeterred Jake wrangled the wood ladder out of the garage, placed it under the now-lowest branch and climbed up the tree to land on the roof yet again. This time, the fire department cut down the tree.

When the family moved to Monsey, New York, the four kids uttered a collective cry of dismay when they saw their new house for the first time. The developer of this new suburban neighborhood, about an hour north of New York City, had bulldozed all plant life to erect the modest split-level and two-story homes. The entire landscape was a desolate wasteland of dirt and rocks. The house was colorful, with gleaming new red brick and a bright, pretty, yellow aluminum siding. The yard was brown.

Betty planted flowers along the front porch to give the house some curb appeal. Jim planted sod and several saplings in the yard that first summer, but it would be years before any trees grew large enough and strong enough to hold the weight of even the smallest, most emaciated child. Jake found an apple orchard adjacent to their street and was always shooed off the property by the caretaker, who feared he was damaging the trees as well as eating all their profits.

Upon the family's arrival in Louisville, Kentucky, Jim took a circuitous route through the city to help get everyone acquainted with the area. Riding in the car along Eastern Parkway, the kids marveled at the cathedral-like ceiling formed by the old growth trees that lined the boulevard. They had never seen trees so big or so much green. Everywhere they looked, every neighborhood, every street, every house was shaded and protected by a canopy of leaves overhead.

Jim veered left onto Fleming Road and drove up the hill to offer a dramatic reveal of the house that was their new home. It was a grand Georgian colonial red-brick structure on a sloping lot that looked to everyone like a mansion. What Jake noticed first were the trees—the one-hundred-foot-tall Sycamore in the back, the two Black Walnuts flanking the side yard, and, in the front yard, Basswood Lindens, a blooming Dogwood and Magnolia, and a weirdly deformed-looking Crabapple tree. Jake thought he had moved to a magic forest.

Cal's neighborhood on the eastern edge of Louisville came into existence during the early 1950s when an old farm transformed into hundreds of cookie-cutter tract houses. Every house looked the same in shape and size and varied in appearance only so much as the exterior had either pale red brick, which looked more of a ghastly bubblegum pink, or aluminum siding in the wide variety of tones from beige to tan. In the left corner of each backyard stood exactly one stubby Yellowwood tree barely twenty-five feet tall that hung over the fences where four back yards met in perfect ninety-degree angles.

Cal made his first attempt at climbing his lone backyard tree when he was just five years old. He wriggled up to the very top branch and remained there for most of the day, amazed at his own ability to climb to a height that no human had ever managed before. He was thrilled to have hidden himself away. Leigh called out his name three times to get him to come in for dinner, but he waited until the perfect moment when he knew she was looking in his direction to make a dramatic leap from the tree to the ground.

As he got older, he loved to climb the tree with a paperback novel in hand and wedge himself between branches and read for hours. He was so comfortable up there that the gentle sway of the tree and the rustle of leaves often lulled him to sleep. He knew he had to do something different when he almost fell out of his perch while napping. The next day, he collected wood from the backyard shed and built himself a small platform at the junction of three branches so he could read, nap, and while away the day. He tried to get his mother to let him take his sleeping bag up there to spend the night, but Leigh always refused, concerned that he would break his neck in the dark.

A classmate, Peter, was bragging about the tree fort he had built at his house, so Cal just had to see it. Peter's house abutted the woods along Beargrass Creek, so the trees were far older and larger. Peter and his brother had built a tree house with walls, windows, a roof, and stairs leading from one level to the next. Duly impressed, Cal went home, determined to have an equally impressive structure in his own backyard. On Sundays, he snuck into a nearby construction site and took junk lumber from the garbage pile. With walls and a roof on his tree platform, he kept adding to the ramshackle structure every weekend for the next year.

It grew so large that the neighbors could hardly see the tree for all the lumber poking out between every branch and twig. The structure hung over not just Cal's backyard but three others as well, and everyone thought it an eyesore and worried that it would blow down in a strong windstorm. Trying to be polite about it but wanting it gone, the neighbors started tossing objects at it, hoping to knock it down. At first, the Kuliks would find an errant beachball in their backyard. It soon progressed to a brick, then a basketball, a few lawn chairs, and even an outdoor grill.

Cal's impenetrable fortress withstood the neighborly onslaught until Mr. Grant next door climbed on a ladder and took a sledgehammer to the portions hanging over his children's swing set. Finally, the neighbors ganged up on him, insisting that Cal had to dismantle the tree fort, although his dad, Zan, allowed him to keep the original platform. It just was not as much fun for him this way, and he was annoyed that no one else thought his fort was cool.

He started looking farther afield for the next tree to conquer. He rode his bike over to Cherokee Park and picked the largest one he could find to climb. These bigger, taller, sturdier trees provided him with a natural scaffold to cradle him, so he would not even miss his rickety platform. Most days, he spent hours looking upon people strolling through the park from his hidden spot, happy to think that no one would ever find him.

The only tree Jake could climb in his yard was the Maple, at the top of the driveway, because the lowest branch was just a few feet off the ground. The Sycamore was the most majestic tree, but the lowest point of access was fifteen feet above the screened porch roof. The Black Walnut trees also had high limbs. A previous owner had trimmed up the two Basswood Lindens in the front yard so they would not obscure the pleasing view of the front of the house. The Dogwood and the Magnolia were purely decorative, with brittle branches not meant for the weight of intrepid climbing children. The Crabapple had hundreds of closely bunched tendrils that shot up from every branch, making it difficult for even a squirrel to navigate, much less a ten-year-old human.

With only the one tree to climb, Jake grew bored of the same exact view after six months. He hopped on his bike and rode over to Cherokee Park, found a stately White Oak standing sentinel at the top of a hill. He dropped his bike next to another bicycle abandoned at the tree's base and began climbing. It was early April, so the tree's full foliage had not yet come in. Jake preferred it this way. It allowed him to peek through the leaves but afforded camouflage, hiding him from the rest of the world.

It was a full ten minutes before Jake happened to glance around at the tree he was in and suddenly noticed a pair of eyes looking down on him. A voice said, "Hey there." Startled, Jake almost jumped out of his skin and very nearly fell out of the tree. He pulled back, letting go of his branch and losing his balance. As he started to tilt backward, the kid above, swung down, hanging from his knees, and grabbed a fistful of Jake's t-shirt. The voice said, "Could you please grab a branch? I don't want you to fall." Jake did so, and the curly-headed boy hoisted him up to safety.

Seated across from each other on the same branch, Jake tried to calm himself and catch his breath. "You scared the crap out of me. I didn't know anyone was up here."

Cal responded, "You threw your bike down next to mine. That should have given you a clue."

"But why didn't you say something?

"I like the quiet."

The two boys fell into a brief silence, not knowing what to say. They scrutinized each other with quick glances, hoping the other would not notice. Cal liked how the sun streamed through the leaves and seemed to bounce off Jake's straight blond hair, which formed a helmet around his face. Jake thought Cal had the blackest hair and darkest eyes he had ever seen, but a closer look and glimmer of sunlight revealed it to be a much warmer, dark brown. They chatted awkwardly about anything that came to mind, so as not to let the conversation die down, when Cal decided, "Let's go find another tree."

They rode off together until Cal found what he was looking for. It was another White Oak with higher branches, requiring both to lean their bikes against the trunk, stand on their banana seats, and swing themselves up. They found a perfect swirl of branches that formed a circular staircase all the way to the top, nearly eighty feet off the ground. They leaned against the trunk, each straddling their own branch, but so close together that their arms overlapped, and just talked all afternoon. Finally, Cal said, "It's getting late. I got to get home for dinner."

They descended quickly and hopped on their bikes. As Cal sped off, he shouted over his shoulder, "That was fun. See you later." Jake yelled, "Hey, what's your name?" Cal was already too far away and never heard the question. Every Saturday after that, Jake returned to those two trees in Cherokee Park, hoping to find that curly dark-haired boy again. He hoped the kid would just happen to come back there, perhaps looking for him too. Six months later, Jake stopped going to the park and went back to climbing the Maple tree in his side yard.

5

Velocity

"The rate of change of an object's position with respect to a frame of reference, including time, speed and direction."

The two boys first met when they were ten years old, and it would be exactly a year before they would see each other again. It was April 1970, and they almost crashed their bikes. Cal departed Hogan's Fountain in Cherokee Park, zooming down the hill as fast as he could go, gripping his handlebars, his head thrown back, his legs kicked out to his sides. A dense hedgerow of Yew bushes obscured his view, so he did not see Jake on his bike zooming toward him in the opposite direction down another hill.

Jake's view opened suddenly, and he slammed on his brakes, fishtailing his bike at the last second so he only broadsided Cal's bike rather than t-boning him. Cal fell hard on his rump, so Jake rushed over, being the one to offer a hand-up this time.

The bikes undamaged and no bones broken, Cal asked, "Where you headin'?"

"Nowhere special."

"Can I come along?"

They meandered along the trails in the park and worked their way over to the train tracks beside Westport Road. They followed the tracks until they jagged to the southeast and seemed to disappear for nearly a mile, and then reappeared running parallel to another quiet residential street. Cal took the lead and together they rode as fast as they could, as if trying to cover the most ground in the least amount of time. They followed the tracks, zigzagging in every direction. After an hour and a half of riding seemingly in circles, Jake was utterly lost. By this point, they had ridden out of the city limits and into the next county.

They rode until they reached the town of La Grange, twenty-five miles from their starting point, and it seemed to be an utterly random destination. Cal raced up to an old diner that looked like the very definition of a "greasy spoon," skidded his tires as he slammed on the brakes, threw down his bike on the sidewalk, and calmly walked inside. Jake realized quickly that this is how it would always be with this curly-headed kid, who just did something, while Jake had to rush and catch up when he finally understood that he was meant to follow.

The aroma of charred meat, VO5 hairspray, and decades-old grease assaulted Jake's nose as he entered. His attention went to an elderly couple, sitting immobile in a banquette against the wall, looking as much a part of the diner as the vinyl bench and chrome table at which they sat. Jake might have thought them dead, or at least mannequins, had it not been for the swirl of smoke from the cigarettes they held over a plastic ashtray. Cal was seated at the counter and said, "Let's get lunch." He ordered a grilled cheese sandwich with dill pickles, chips, and a cola. Jake ordered the exact same thing, minus the pickles.

They ate quickly without saying a word and then got their drinks put into waxy carry-out cups with paper straws. They sat on a park bench under a tree along Main Street to sip their sodas. Jake's paper straw had flattened so he could not suck on it anymore, so he popped the lid, went to take another sip, and spilled most of his drink down the front of his t-shirt. Cal smirked but did not laugh and decided it would be best if he had an accident too. He pulled off his cup lid and splashed his soda down his front as well. "Stupid straws."

He pulled off his wet shirt and tucked it into the waist band of his shorts. Eager to earn the approval of this new friend, Jake did the same. They finished their drinks but stayed on the park bench, waiting for who knows what. After ten minutes of enjoying the view of absolutely nothing in La Grange's quiet little town center, Jake had to finally ask, "Why are we waiting?"

"You'll see," Cal responded, and as if on cue, they heard a train horn off to the west.

The sound grew ever louder and suddenly the concrete beneath their feet began to shake. Gates along every side street started to clang their warning signals and dropped down to prevent any crossing. Then as the ground seemed ready to shake apart, the headlight on a lumbering CSX cargo train appeared at the end of the block. Up until that minute, Jake had not noticed the train tracks in the middle of Main Street. He wondered out loud, "Why did they put tracks right there?"

The train had slowed to an unexciting two-mile-an-hour crawl through the center of town. Cal stood up and walked toward the tracks. Jake was so transfixed by the sight of Cal's naked back that he almost did not notice him walking into the path of the approaching train. Terrified that they would both be run over and wind up on the front page of the *Courier-Journal* for their stupidity, Jake paused for just a second and then rushed toward Cal, grabbing his arm and shoulder to pull him out of harm's way just as the engine passed them. Cal held his ground and blithely reached out to touch each train car, counting them as they went by.

Velocity

Jake was still holding on to Cal as he pulled him back to the curb. Cal draped his arm over Jake's shoulder, smiling at their bravery. "That was cool, huh?" They got back on their bikes and raced through countless neighborhoods, going as fast as they could but in no rush for the day to come to an end. Going nowhere in particular together had a special magic that day. Had one of them had an odometer, they would have been surprised to learn that they had ridden sixty miles. Cal led them to Bardstown Road at the Watterson Expressway, where they would separate.

Cal pointed to the east side of the expressway, "My house is this way. Gardiner Lane Shopping Center is on that side. Do you know how to get home from there?"

Jake assured him, "Yeah, I know where I am." With that Cal shot off like a rocket. Jake yelled, "Hey, wait a minute!" Cal circled his bike, smiled, and waved, but once again he was out of earshot. He turned away and rode off again, as Jake yelled after him, "But who are you?" They still had not gotten around to sharing their names.

The two boys would finally learn each other's names the following year, now two years since their first meeting. In the spring of 1971, both participated in the annual music competition conducted by the Kentucky Music Educators Association (though it was not really a competition in the sense that one person would be declared the big winner, and everyone else would have to content themselves with the ignoble rank of loser). The music students performed a solo with a musical instrument of their choice in front of a panel of adjudicators for a qualitative rating of "4 for Excellent," "3 for Good,"

"2 for Fair", and "1 for Needs Work." Cal wondered aloud if they ever gave a 0 score, meaning "You Suck." Both Cal and Jake had started playing the flute at ten years of age and had similarly obsessive approaches when they started to learn how to play, quickly memorizing their finger positions and how to properly use their embouchure to blow across the mouthpiece.

Their scheduled appointments fell within fifteen minutes of one another, so they waited together on the floor of the school hallway. When the monitor called out the next several players' names to "get ready," the boys finally had their introduction. Jake asked, "Do you prefer Caleb?" to which he responded, "Oh no, I'm definitely a Cal. And you?" "Everyone calls me Jake."

Jake was the more technical flute player, working primarily from his sheet music, never straying from the notes written on the page but also not bringing much feeling to his playing. Cal, on the other hand, was more emotional, feeling the music in such a way that he tended to embellish upon the composer's work, which was a big no-no for the judges on the panel. Jake performed a flute concerto by Telemann, while Cal did his own wistful rendition of The Doors' "Riders on the Storm."

With their performances finished, they ate their sack lunches together outside in the chilly air while waiting for their rankings. The judges appreciated Jake's traditional selection of music more, but Cal won them over with his creativity and daring. Both received a 3.5 rating for the year. Once they had their scores, Cal bolted. Jake now knew the other boy's name but still did not know where to find him.

Another year passed, and in May 1972, Jake and Cal ended up at the same gymnastic competition, held in Covington,

Kentucky, just across the Ohio River from Cincinnati. They attended different schools and so were on different gymnastic teams, but they wound up staying at the same motor lodge. From that Friday evening to Sunday afternoon, the two boys crossed paths at least fifteen times and always stopped to spend a few moments together. Although this was only their fourth isolated meeting, it seemed that they had known each other forever and all the gaps in time hardly mattered.

They had no direct competition with one another at the meet, since Cal had a couple years more experience. Jake could walk on his hands and do a few flips and tricks and that was about it. The disparity between their skill sets became apparent when Cal was showing off to some of his teammates and did a handstand on the fourth-floor balcony railing. He had no fear of the forty-foot drop to the parking lot pavement below, but his coach, Mr. Williams, pulled him from the railing and gave him a quick smack to the head for being reckless. After a memorable weekend glancing off one another yet again, Cal and Jake exchanged phone numbers. Over the summer, neither would work up the courage to call the other.

6

Alignment

"When planets occur in the same part of the sky and appear to form a straight line."

If the memorable experiences they had had from their previous chance encounters with one another were not enough to convince the boys that perhaps they were fated to meet, the universe seemed to be aligning to make sure that they would finally come together. The first factor involved their mothers, both of whom had become resentful parents. Leigh Kulik and Betty Davies had specific career aspirations and saw those dreams, if not thwarted, then at least delayed by motherhood.

Leigh wanted to be more than just a schoolteacher; she wanted to become a professor. With her two eldest children already off to college and her middle son set to go the following year, she decided to go back to school to get her masters and doctorate in music theory. She felt that Cal, at almost fourteen, was old enough to manage just fine without having his mom hovering over him all day. Enlisting the family's support to help her and each other out, she felt no guilt in doing something for herself, as it also would benefit her family in the long run. She made her decision and enrolled in the courses she needed.

Betty was not so proactive and simply left home that

summer. Jake had heard his parents arguing that spring about how Betty felt neglected as her kids were getting older and did not need their stay-at-home mom all that much. She wanted to paint and give herself the space to do that without interference or interruption. Jim suggested that she go off to her Uncle Al's cabin near Andes, New York for a few weeks. She loaded the car with her easel, canvases and oil paints and left the family to their own devices for the entire summer.

The second event to bring the boys closer together was the Board of Education's decision, in the summer of 1972, to start moving toward court-ordered desegregation of their public school system. It would be a few years yet before their full plan would be put into place, but this was the first step. The word "desegregation" was a flash point for many, so instead, the Board told the public that they were starting to redistrict students to deal with school overcrowding.

In Jake's neighborhood, Richmond Junior High was an enormous edifice built in 1900, while the modern Emerson High School was already too small even by the time it opened. One school could handle the number of students; the other could not. Emerson had an overflow that had to be housed in temporary classrooms inside long trailers lacking air conditioning. Richmond therefore became a three-year junior high for the seventh, eighth, and ninth grades, while Emerson became high school for just sophomores, juniors, and seniors. Most other schools in Louisville were two-year junior highs and four-year high schools.

Jake's father, Jim, felt that since his job was to provide for his family, then it was Betty's job to take care of everything involving their children. While she was not there, the official notice from the Board of Education that Jake would be bused to another school outside of their neighborhood got added to the pile of Betty's mail that sat unopened on the dining room sideboard for weeks. As the mail grew high and toppled onto the floor, Jim threw away the junk mail, set aside any personal correspondence she had received, and opened anything that looked important. When he read the busing notification, Jim decided it was time to bring Betty home. He called to tell her to pack up her things and meet him at the Albany Airport so they could drive home together.

Upon returning home, Betty left Jim to unpack all her art supplies from the car, while she headed straight to her unopened mail. She looked over the busing notice and remarked, "What the hell? This makes no damn sense." In redistricting the schools, the Board of Education had made an arbitrary decision that cut an invisible line right through their house. Jessie, Nick, and Shaun had bedrooms on one side of the line, and Jake's bedroom was on the other. Betty yelled to Jim, "It's only Jake who's getting bused."

Families could file for an exemption, and Jake stood a very good chance of being excused from the redistricting as he was the only one in his family designated to go. However, the exemption had to be filed by a certain date. His mother had not been there, so she missed the deadline. Betty fumed, "Goddamnit, Emerson is two blocks away, and they are busing him halfway across town to Bon Air. It's stupid." Bon Air High School was only four miles away.

With less than a month before the start of school, she made a mad scramble to try to get Jake that exemption. She dragged him to a few Jefferson County Board of Education meetings about this issue, as if his adorable blondness and small frame might compel sympathy that he needed to stay closer to home. Perhaps his very presence at those meetings might shame them into changing their minds. It did not, and Betty lost her cool repeatedly and yelled at anyone who gave her the time of day. The more she shouted at people, the more indifferent they became toward Jake's situation.

His parents had a lot of frantic whispered conversations around the house that month. Betty made many calls and screamed into the phone a lot. His folks considered this situation so dire that for several weeks they considered moving out of their neighborhood. They looked at a few houses and almost put in an offer on one on Alta Vista Way, closer to Cherokee Park. The house was in the same school district as their current home, just in an area not affected by the busing mandate.

Finally, Jim asked Jake's opinion, and he admitted that going to a new school scared him. He had already had enough trouble making friends who enjoyed the same pursuits as he did, and he worried that he would feel utterly alone. But ultimately, Jim decided that it did not make economic sense to move over this issue. Jake would take the bus to Bon Air, and Betty would continue to fight to get him switched to their nearby school as soon as possible. Betty was irritated that she would have to be the one to do this, and she got snippy with Jake as if it was all his fault.

Cal's summer was far less chaotic. His family did not take a summer camping trip again this year, because they were still building their cabin. Cal did not mind one bit, because he was out in nature where he felt most at ease. His love of climbing trees came in handy when Zan assigned him the task of shimmying up even the tallest, most difficult tree trunks and hand-cutting the lowest branches to improve the cabin's view of Taylorsville Lake. When they needed more lumber to make the railings for the wraparound porch, Cal would choose the poplar trees that could be cleared, organize their cutting, and set to work debarking the wood. He had just celebrated his fourteenth birthday.

Utterly fearless, Cal loved to stand at the edge of the roof overlooking the highest drop to the ground, darting quickly from one side to the other with the agility of a squirrel. One day while nailing shingles to the roof, he misplaced his foot and slid down the slope, unable to get a handhold before he slipped over the edge. His gymnastics training saved his life as he managed to grab a beam underneath, swinging himself onto the wraparound porch just below. The friends and crew working that day saw him tumble and dubbed him Tarzan.

Leigh would do her studying at the cabin, despite the construction swirling around her. She would set up her books, notebooks, and pens on the kitchen table, and she defied all attempts to distract her from her homework. If someone acted helpless wanting some food, she never raised her nose from her book and would silently point in the direction of the refrigerator. If someone asked a question, she simply ignored them. If they persisted, she would finally glance up from her work with a look that could kill. It was controlled chaos all summer, but the family was together working toward their shared goal of finishing the cabin, while Leigh worked toward hers. It was a happy time.

As summer ended, Zan sat with Cal and looked over his class list. Zan asked if he had any goals for the upcoming year. Cal responded, "I hope I make some good friends." While always friendly and polite with everyone he met, Cal had to work overtime to make people like him as much as he liked them. Zan knew his son could be a handful. With some kids, Cal was too energetic and wore them out. With others, Cal was too smart and grew bored with numbskulls. Zan assured Cal, "Good people will come to you."

After two weeks of trying to convince the Board of Education to grant an exemption, the Davies got confirmation that Jake would indeed be attending Bon Air High School in September, not nearby Emerson. It was the morning of his fourteenth birthday, and Betty started to make shrimp creole for dinner and German chocolate cake for dessert, Jake's favorites. As the day progressed, she bristled more and more at the idea that Jake would be at a faraway school, and she would probably have to play taxi driver all year.

Before he went to bed, she sat him down to have a heart-to-heart chat. She tried to make it sound like she was most concerned about her son's ability to focus on his work at a new school. Jake could tell, though, that she had decided that she was not going to drop him off or pick him up for all his usual after-school extracurricular activities. She emphatically stated, "No theater, no band, no dance, no orchestra, no chorus, no gymnastics." She might as well have told Jake "no breathing." Those were the only things that made his school experience bearable. It was going to be a very long, rough year.

7

Fusion

"The nuclear process whereby several small nuclei are combined to make a larger one."

Betty did relent on the "no band" rule before the first day of school. In the fall, all band members who would march at football games had band class during first period, followed by a special band members–only study hall. The band director could overlap into that study hall every day so as to maximize their time out on the football field fine-tuning their marching routines, so that he would not have to schedule extra rehearsals after school. This prompted yet another heated discussion between Jake's parents. Betty complained that she'd still have to taxi him to football games, but Jim said, "He has to have something he likes this year." When she would not budge on this matter, Jim gave in. "Fine, I'll take him to the games."

With his mother relieved of taxi duty, Jake got to take band class. On his first day at Bon Air, the school bus driver, Mr. Monroe, had not yet fine-tuned the new pick-up and drop-off schedule. Jake arrived an hour early to this strange new school, and he discovered that his homeroom would be the same as his first period class. Sitting on the tile floor outside the band room,

Fusion

Jake got bored waiting and decided to kill some time by walking on his hands down the hall.

Out of the corner of his eye, he saw someone else had joined him and was also hand-walking right alongside. It was Cal, so their reunion was upside-down. Nonchalantly, Cal said, "Hey there." Jake asked, "What's up?" Cal replied, "Us." Jake started to giggle, followed soon by Cal, and both boys fell out of their handstands into a laughing heap.

Seated on the floor with their backs up against lockers, Cal asked to see Jake's class schedule and discovered that they already would be sharing five out of six classes. Cal jumped up, saying "be right back," and off he ran. He was back within ten minutes, revealing he had gotten the office to change his schedule so they would have all their classes together. He asked, "You excited to start high school?" Jake was not sure. "I don't know anyone. I don't have any friends here."

Cal smiled, "Sure, you do. You have me." Their conversation came around to gymnastics, prompting a quick display of more tricks each could do. They were oblivious to the other students pouring into the band room as the bell rang. Their teacher, Mr. Ward, came out into the hall to bark at them, "Hey, you two twinkle-toes. Knock it off and get in class." Cal put his hands over his head and did a delicate little pirouette, while Jake did a jeté leap. They laughed at their own cleverness but were smart enough to stop abruptly before they reached the doorway, where anyone else could see them.

During first period, Mr. Ward passed out sheet music and told every section—brass, woodwinds, percussion—to look at a particular musical phrase. One by one, each student played their designated line of music so Mr. Ward could assign placement. Both having played the flute for four years, Cal and Jake placed high, with Cal taking First Chair, Second Seat, and Jake being First Chair, Third Seat. It was no surprise to them that there were no other boys in the flute section. The next hour was a cacophony of toots, blats, whomps, and plops as the band made their fumbling first attempt to play Michael Jackson's "Rockin' Robin."

Even though goody-two-shoes Sandra Willard had made First Chair, First Seat, she could not finesse the opening line of the song. Only Cal and Jake could manage to play the fast, trilling arpeggio of "tweedily deedily dee." While the rest of the class stumbled through the song, they hardly missed a note. Mr. Ward said, "Nice work on the trill section, guys." The boys turned to each other and smiled carefully, but they froze when the teacher added, "Appropriately flutey fruity." The rest of the period they dared not look to the left or the right, afraid to breathe and wanting to sink into the floor.

For their second period band-only study hall, they spent the next hour out on the football field without their instruments. Mr. Ward went from band teacher to drill sergeant, running everyone through the basics of "marching." It was nothing more than high knee lifts and stormtrooper goose-stepping while turning left or right or diagonally. The students were wandering all over with no spatial awareness of where they were on the field or in relation to anyone else out there. Whenever the drill sergeant's back was turned, Cal would do a backflip, followed immediately by Jake's roundoff. They giggled through the entire period. The other students were utterly terrified, thinking those acrobatic tricks were something that they too would have to master before the first at-home football game.

On that first day of high school, they spent nearly every minute together. They walked from one class to the next, close enough to feel like they were bonding with one another but not so close that their arms would touch. They were being cautious that the other kids did not think they were too friendly. Upon entering a classroom, they looked for two seats next to each other and grabbed those whenever possible, or at least sat close by if not. They skipped the cafeteria at lunchtime to sit together in the library. Even though they uttered not a word, prune-faced, beehived librarian Mrs. Hartnett was more annoyed at their repeated note passing to each other than the loud giggling of a bunch of twittery senior girls in the corner.

Every day at school unfolded the same way. They talked quietly so as not to draw attention and be as anonymous as they could be. They became adept at communicating silently with one another through head tilts, smirks, and eye rolls. The only thing that they did not do together was go to the boys' room when they had to pee. That would have been just a little too much familiarity, and the other kids would have noticed how inseparable they were becoming. At the end of each day, they would give each other a big smile as they headed toward different sides of the school, Cal leaving by the west door to walk home and Jake going out the east door to board his bus.

As much as they might have wanted to spend more time together after school, they both had afternoon jobs. Jake rode the bus, rushed home to throw his school stuff in his bedroom, grabbed his *Courier-Journal* apron and ran the mile to work. He sold newspapers on the corner of Bardstown Road and Douglas Avenue in front of the Twig and Leaf Diner, an after-school job he had held since he was ten years old. His bundle of sixty newspapers would be waiting for him, and it only took an hour to sell out, so he could get home in time for dinner.

Cal ambled on his mile-long walk home but then switched into high gear, hopping on his bike and racing at top speed for a couple miles along busy streets and through dangerous intersections to get to his job at a nearby community center. He taught one, sometimes two, hour-long gymnastics classes to Louisville's budding acrobats and death-defying aerialists between the ages of six and twelve. From September to May, he taught tumbling; in the summer, he gave swimming lessons. Zan always said that his son Cal was half monkey, half fish.

Despite a full week of classes together, Cal and Jake wanted to spend all weekend with one another. They arranged where they would meet, what time, and what they wanted to do or where they wanted to go. On nice days, they rode their bikes throughout the city; they climbed trees; they hiked; they climbed over the open frames of houses under construction in new developments. On rainy days, they hung out at the Oxmoor Mall; they sang along to tunes on the radio in Cal's basement bedroom. Or they went to the movies, which became their favorite thing to do together.

They loved going to the Uptown Theater on the corner of Bardstown and Eastern Parkway, a faded single screen theater that fell on hard times when it could not compete with the multiscreen cinemas popping up in every mall. The Uptown pulled in audiences by showing double features of second-run movies on the weekend for just one dollar. Their movie pairings were deranged. One week, they saw *Night of the Living Dead* and *Fitzwilly* with Dick Van Dyke. The next week, it was Julie Andrews in *Thoroughly Modern Millie* followed by *The Tomb of Ligeia* with Vincent Price. *To Sir, with Love* and *Destroy All Monsters. Diamonds Are Forever* with *The Singing Nun.*

At the start of the school year, Jake had begun folk dancing. He had seen a local TV news story about a group that met once a week at the University of Louisville. One interviewee mentioned that everyone was welcome to come and dance. Jake asked his parents if he could go one week to see if he liked it. Since he was being bused to school that year, he had to forego the dance and music lessons he would have normally taken. His father, Jim, thought folk dance could fill that void for him and would be a good hobby to occupy some of his free time.

Betty drove him for the first few weeks, but Jake said that he would love to ride his bike there every week so she wouldn't have to drive. The circuitous route from their house in the Highlands area to the U of L would have required a couple of bus changes via Louisville's lousy transit system, so Jim made sure to add extra reflectors to Jake's bike wheels and bought a powerful headlamp for the handlebars and a sturdy bike lock. With their warning to stay on the sidewalks and take the side streets, he rode the five miles to folk dancing every week, rain or shine, in the fading light of early evening or after dark.

A married couple had founded the folk-dance group a couple years earlier. Freya was exuberant and had a welcoming smile, while her husband, Len, sported a goatee, flattop haircut, and horn-rimmed glasses that made him look slightly sinister to Jake. Since he had been taking dance classes for a couple years and had performed in a few musicals, Jake picked up the dances quickly and never forgot the steps once learned. His gymnastics meant he could do tricks, which would be great for the Ukrainian dances. Within a month, he had proven that he was a good dancer and that he intended to keep coming. Len pulled Jake aside and invited him to join their performing group. He accepted, without even thinking about asking his parents if it was okay.

He was the only teenager in the performing group, so Freya dubbed him "Young Jake" to differentiate him from an older group member also named Jacob. No one would have ever confused the blond fourteen-year-old for the fortysomething pudgy accountant, but everyone quickly adopted the nickname. Trying to chat with the adults, Young Jake asked what school they went to. Freya's eyes got wide, as she sputtered at the question. "How old do you think we are?" In the self-absorbed way of a teenager, Jake assumed that they were all his age. Gray-haired Marie laughed. "That's the nicest compliment I ever got."

Jake did not have many friends his own age, though. He certainly was not finding any spending so much time with the folk-dance group or at the community theater where he had done musicals for the past four summers. The Louisville Lyric Theater had cast him as Winthrop in *The Music Man* when he was ten, despite his confused first singing audition for them.

Even though he sang in school chorus and had learned how to read music for playing the flute, Jake did not quite comprehend that the musical notes on a staff of sheet music corresponded to whatever key he was supposed to be singing in. Jake had picked "Oom-Pah-Pah" from *Oliver!* for his audition, without paying any attention to the song's key. He sang the first line a full octave higher than what was written on the page, and it sounded like screeching even to his own untrained ears. A chestnut-haired lady, affectionately called Moms, was the musical director and called out to the pianist to lower the key. On his second attempt, Jake found the key had plummeted several octaves lower, so he was making sounds more akin to a foghorn or a dying moose than singing. Moms ran up onstage and took the time to help him find the correct notes. On his third attempt, Jake was much better, though far from perfect. However, the director, Francis, and the balding choreographer called Pops were charmed by Jake and thought it was hysterical that a ten-year-old boy was doing a saloon song sung by a hooker.

For the four years he had worked with the Lyric Theater, Moms and Pops became like surrogate parents to Jake, protecting him as the only nonadult company member and chaperoning him amidst the ribald backstage antics of the older actors. The Lyric Theater only did one show annually, during the summers, but they kept their regular actors' enthusiasm high throughout the rest of the year by holding social gatherings that were a combination of backyard barbecue, cast party, talent show, and sing-along. Now that he'd started high school, Jake was finally old enough to join in on the fun.

Moms and Pops were hosting this one at their house, and as the showtunes started inside, Jake saw a curly-haired kid escape to the backyard to sit underneath a tree to read a paperback. Jake followed him and was surprised to discover it was Cal. "Hey there. What are you doing here?"

"Um, it's my house. I live here." It turned out that the trim woman and bald man Jake knew only as Moms and Pops were Leigh and Zan, Cal's parents.

"I'm confused. I thought your mom was a teacher and your dad a doctor. Why are they working with the theater?"

"Well, Mom teaches music, and Pops used to be a dancer when he was a kid, so it's not that big of a stretch."

Leigh had wanted to introduce Jake to her son, unaware that they already knew one another from school. When she could not find either of them, she looked out the kitchen window and was happy to see Cal with a big smile on his face, engaging in animated conversation with his new friend. They spent the entire party outside, to the exclusion of everyone else. Zan saw how quickly the boys had bonded, so he hoped that here finally was someone who could keep up with his unstoppable son.

8

Luminosity

"The amount of light emitted by a star."

Just four weeks after the start of the fall semester, Bon Air had its first at-home football game. Jake almost missed getting there in time. His dad had to work late at the office, and his mom had made plans to have cocktail hour with the ladies from Welcome Wagon. His folks had inconveniently forgotten his football game, so Jake would have to find his own way to Bon Air that Friday evening. The entire afternoon leading up to the game seemed to move in slow motion.

On the way home, his school bus had a flat tire, so everyone had to get off while the driver changed it. Jake tried to leave and walk home rather than wait, but Mr. Monroe yelled at him to stay put. "I'm responsible for your safety until you get back home. If you leave and something happens to you, I lose my job. Sit!" The tire change took almost an hour. Dashing at full speed from home to the Twig and Leaf, he found his bundle of newspapers had not arrived yet. When the delivery truck finally got to him, he was already two hours behind schedule. Instead of sitting down and leisurely waiting for drivers to honk their horns to signal they wanted to buy a paper, Jake was aggressive, dodging cars in the busy intersection to sell out as fast as possible.

He raced through the back door in the kitchen to find his mother had only just gotten home. She had yet to start dinner. "We will eat in a little bit." Jake panicked. "Mom, I have the game. I have to get to school by 7."

"Well, I can't take you. I have to make dinner."

"But I can't be late. The whole band marches to the field at 7:30."

"Oh, they won't mind if you're a little late." Jake knew his mother did things in her own sweet time. He ran upstairs to his bedroom, rolled up his band uniform, and stuffed it and his flute case into a knapsack. When he got downstairs, he found the kitchen empty. Betty had gone to use the bathroom. Jake grabbed a Twinkie and an apple for his dinner and sprinted out the kitchen door into the garage. He jumped on his bike and sped off to Bon Air. He would face his mother's wrath later.

Cal was very methodical for a teenager, cramming so much into his life that he always had to stay on top of his schedule. The gymnastic lessons he taught started and ended precisely on time. He knew exactly how many minutes it would take him to ride his bike from the community center back home and how long he could practice his flute. He knew when dinner was happening and the amount of time needed to walk to Bon Air for the game. Whereas Jake was panting and sweating from his mad dash, Cal was almost serene as he helped him get ready more quickly by setting out his uniform and instrument while Jake ran to the toilet.

With only seconds to tie his shoes and grab his piccolo before the band lined up in formation and marched from the band room toward the field, Jake was practically crying in frustration. Cal whispered, "Hey, don't worry. You made it. I hope we don't screw this up. My family is coming." His parents supported Cal in everything he did. They were there for his marching band in the fall, and they cheered him on at every gymnastic meet and swim competition. While an observer might have thought that Cal was the golden child or spoiled with attention, his parents had always supported all their kids in the same way.

Jake did not think his own parents were equal in their support. Jim and Betty encouraged their kids to pursue activities that interested them, but they did not feel the need to attend every single event. They went out of their way to cheer for Nick and Shaun at almost all their soccer games, but they were off the hook when it came to Jessie, whose volunteering for Red Cross did not require an outward show of support, except for the occasional verbal encouragement. As for Jake's musicals, Betty and Jim went to his first performance as Winthrop in *The Music Man*, but neither came to see him in any of the shows he did in subsequent years.

At the weekly football games, both were no-shows, because Jake was only in the marching band and not one of the actual team players. Since they never went, they also never drove him to the games as they had promised. The following Friday was the same panicked dash to get back to school in time for the game. Since discovering that Leigh and Zan were Cal's parents, Jake at least had someone there to acknowledge his efforts. Leigh inquired about Jake's parents, hoping to finally meet them. "Oh, they couldn't make it. They are usually very busy every Friday."

Cal told his parents about Jake's usual Friday frustrations, so the next day, Leigh called Betty to invite Jake to sleep over with Cal on future Friday nights, to make it easier for him to attend the at-home games. He would still go home after school to sell his newspapers but then would bike over to the Kuliks' and eat dinner there. Afterward, the two boys could walk to school together for marching band, and Jake could stay over until late Saturday morning, when he needed to get back for his newspaper job. Betty confided, "He's always in such a rush on those nights. That would help a lot. Are you sure it won't be inconvenient?" Leigh expressed her admiration for Jake. "He's such a sweet kid, and he and Cal are the best of friends." This was news to Betty.

Their first sleepover happened the following weekend. It was a warm night in late October, so following the football game the boys climbed the one tree in the Kulik backyard. Cal had trimmed some of the upper branches so he could stargaze from his platform. "You get a great view from up here, and it's clear tonight. We should be able to see a lot."

They lay down head-to-foot so they could both fit, though the rickety wood platform was so narrow that the combined width of the boys' hips still left one butt cheek apiece hanging off opposite edges. As Jake wondered if he could avoid falling off, Cal scooched his body up closer to Jake's feet, so they fit a little better with a few more inches of space. Jake continued to bobble on the edge of the precipice, so Cal reached out and gently held on to his friend's arm.

"I used to have a better fort up here, but Pop thought it was getting too big. I still love coming up here."

Jake now wanted a tree platform in his yard. They lay silently, content with each other's company and intent on the stars overhead.

Jake said, "I guess I understand now why they're called twinkling stars. They're winking at us."

Cal was also a science nerd, in addition to everything else he knew. "Well, not really. Starlight bounces through different layers of the atmosphere, so a star seems to twinkle when its light moves through hot and cold layers, maybe caused by pollution or gas."

"Gas? You mean like a fart?"

Cal snorted, "You idiot." They giggled for a long time.

Jake added, "I like my explanation better."

The basement bathroom separated Cal's bedroom from those of his brothers. If they talked quietly, they would not have to worry about disturbing anyone. Cal's room was more than twice as big as Jake's. His bed and bedside table sat in one corner, while his desk, music stand, flute, and bookcase took up another corner. The rest of the room had a lot of what looked like junk to Jake, including a gymnastics floor mat, fishing pole, life jacket, boat paddles, and a large wall map. Hanging from the rafters was a ten-foot kayak.

His room was devoid of personal photos or posters. Dim light came from an orange lava lamp and a handmade lamp that held a bulb underneath three large bird feathers. It was in this semi-darkness that they tried putting off going to sleep. Cal leaned over the edge of his bed, so he could chat with Jake who was on a sleeping bag on the floor. They were a little too loud, because a foot stomped on the floor overhead, signaling it was time for them to shut up and go to sleep. Cal rolled off his bed, and sidled up next to Jake, so they could continue talking in whispers. At some point, they fell asleep there, with their heads sharing the same pillow and their foreheads pressed together.

9
Orbit

"The path of a celestial body as it moves through space."

Cal was the only person Jake looked forward to seeing at school. It felt like the rest of the world did not know of his existence. Due to a clerical error at the Board of Education, Jake became the Invisible Student who fell through the cracks. He was still on the roster at Emerson High School, even though he did not attend there. On the day of Emerson's yearbook photos, his name was on the list for an appointment, while at Bon Air, he was just listed as a "temporary transfer." On picture day at Bon Air, he nevertheless came in with his blond hair neatly combed and wearing his nicest sweater-vest, only to find that his name was not on the list of students. The photographer refused to take his photo.

In his neighborhood, kids knew he did not go to their school, so they could not bother being friendly with him. Even his own siblings were always running off to be with their friends and not including him. At Bon Air, he lived too far away, so the other students seemed to write him off, thinking he would probably never hang out with them. He was a nice kid, friendly, and confident in his own way, but no one seemed to care. He felt like a nonentity. He had only Cal.

A visitor to Bon Air might have gotten the impression that Cal was the most popular guy at school. He always had a smile on his face, was genuinely excited to be there, and was gregarious enough that he tried to mingle with everyone. It was all an act, a confidence and bravado that he projected but did not feel. Every minute of his day involved his internal calculations on how he had to behave, what to say, and the way he should say it. He figured that even if what he had to say was not particularly witty, a smile or a laugh would go a long way to convince the other person of his affability.

He had just enough swagger to be tolerated by the dumb jocks. He was cute enough to charm all the swoony teenage girls. He was smarter than most everyone else, fitting in comfortably with the math and science nerds. He performed with the marching band, orchestra, and chorus, making him one of the fine arts kids as well. From one period to the next, he was always adapting his personality to fit with whomever he was near. The only time he could be genuine was with Jake.

Their school days started with Band and ended with Chorus. Music was a strong bond between them. Cal loved Top 40 radio; Jake loved Broadway musicals. If they were not listening to music, then they were performing it. Or they talked about it, dissected it, expressed how hearing it made them feel. Whenever Cal mentioned a current hit he liked, Jake hummed a melody, sang a lyric or two, and asked, "that song?" Then Cal would start singing along in harmony.

Jake was not a natural singer. He always had to work hard to hear harmonies. Cal could do just about anything he set his mind to do, so singing seemed easy for him. His speaking voice had already started to drop, even though they were both the same age. Cal was quickly developing a tenor voice; Jake was still a boy soprano. Even as his voice got lower, Cal retained his ability to sing high notes, albeit still lower than Jake's stratospherically high voice.

If Jake started to sing, Cal invented a harmony line to sing along. If the tables were reversed, however, and Cal started singing first, Jake was nervous that he would not exhibit the same ease or skill. Oddly, though, singing with him was the only time that it felt effortless for Jake. They thought that they made beautiful music together, although people within earshot might have begged to differ. Most times when they sang, they were utter goofballs, making up their own lyrics and slipping into their falsetto voices to sing up an octave higher than the song was written. They laughed more than they sang.

Jake loved the sound of Cal's speaking voice because it had a resonance that he lacked, as well as this playful singsong quality to the way he would say things. Jake would take a deep breath and try to lower his speaking voice to sound just like Cal, but the attempts to sound more masculine were laughable. Jake hated that his high voice sounded so much like a girl's, but Cal said that they would not be able to harmonize as beautifully as they did otherwise.

Both boys tried to fit in with the other guys in their class, but it was easy to see how physically different they were. They were both at least a half foot shorter than the other ninth graders. Some guys were pushing toward the six-foot mark, and some even had hair on their chests. Jake had barely passed the five-foot mark and weighed only a hundred pounds. Cal was only an inch taller, but his mop of curly hair gave the impression of a few additional inches in height. Jake's family doctor once said that he might be a late bloomer. That assessment did not comfort Jake in the immediate moment.

They must have seemed an odd pair to the other students. Cal's very dark curls were in sharp contrast to Jake's floppy blond hair. Neither participated in nor had much interest in the school's team sports, which seemed a prerequisite for every red-blooded American male, except them. They attracted scorn and abuse from the older, bigger boys, because they always seemed happy, bouncing around with their boundless energy, singing to themselves, and going about their day with smiles on their faces. They could not understand what they had done to deserve such ill treatment.

Both boys experienced the occasional physical confrontation, which always surprised them. Cal handled it better with his quick thinking. When someone tripped him deliberately, sending his books flying, Cal turned it into a trick, rolling into a somersault and then jumping up to do a series of cartwheels. He always laughed like he had meant to trip like that. The bullies quickly realized that they were not going to get the reaction they wanted from Cal, so they stopped provoking him.

Jake's high voice and shorter height marked him as an easier target. When he got tripped, he scurried to gather up his books and tried to slink away before things turned violent. It seemed this little blond kid carrying a flute case was good for a laugh, so Jake endured trips, slaps, shoves, and punches. A guard on the football team, Mike Crumpler, came up behind Jake and slammed him hard against the locker. "Damn faggot." Jake did not know how to react, and tears welled up in his eyes.

Cal was nearby and jumped into action before Jake started crying. Cal needed to teach Jake how to handle this kind of conflict so he could survive it in the future. He walked up to Mike and said, "Hey, man. This guy is cool, and you need to see this great trick he can do." Cal grabbed Jake by the arm and yanked him down the hall away from Mike. He whispered, "okay, ten tight round-offs." Jake judged the distance, "Yeah, I think I can do that." Cal warned, "You better be sure, because if you hit this guy, he's going to kill you."

Jake took a deep breath, prepped, and then launched. Cal ran alongside to spot him as Jake did these full-body flips hurtling toward his target. Mike's eyes widened as he watched this small kid, who he thought was a pushover, turn into a wild cyclone hurtling toward him. Jake stopped on a dime within a foot of the guy, who nearly jumped out of his skin. Cal calmly stated, "A lot of muscle on this kid. His legs could crush your skull." Mike backed off.

Cal grabbed Jake's arm, spun him around quickly, and hustled him out of sight. As they turned a corner, Cal started laughing and jumping up and down. "Oh man, oh man, that was so good." Word got out about Jake's little demonstration of physical prowess, and the jocks at least hesitated before they challenged him again. No one at Bon Air ever tried to confront him face-to-face after that, but they still elbowed or shoved Jake aside daily while walking between classes. He frequently found ugly bruises whenever he undressed for bed.

Jake learned that he was not entirely helpless but still planned how he could hide out from the hormonally fueled jocks, just in case. He knew that sitting quietly in the principal's office was a haven, so he made friends with all the ladies behind the counter and the janitors. He was on a last-name basis with all of them, respectfully using Mr. Curtis, Mrs. Adams, Mrs. Klein, and such. They returned the courtesy, only half-jokingly referring to Jake as Mr. Davies, because he was so courteous to everyone. Every single staff member at Bon Air knew who he was, liked him, and looked out for him.

Cal was cagey and knew how to navigate the jungles of high school. He could be cautious, always scanning his environment and looking for threats. If ever a situation grew too tense, he knew how and when to remove himself. In those moments, he was like a small animal trying to avoid becoming prey to a hungry predator. Cal could gauge the mood of any room. He knew instinctively if he could approach someone, when to make his move, what to say. His social skills were akin to that of a seasoned politician, or at the very least a teenager who knew how to break into any clique.

Cal and Jake knew that they would always be safe in the library. Head librarian Mrs. Hartnett was an old-fashioned martinet who wielded her power and her wooden ruler over all who entered her domain. She did not take guff from anyone, even the hormonal boys who had sprouted up to over a foot taller than her. She would lean with one fist on the table and her other shoved into her ribcage, glowering until a noisy talker would notice her presence and finally shut up. She did not hesitate to slap a shoulder, smack a wrist with her ruler, or grab an unruly miscreant by the ear to drag them out into the hall.

Mrs. Hartnett did not allow any whispering, and she was not too fond of note passing either, although she forgave that from Jake and Cal because she had come to know that they were two of the nice kids. They would find a faraway corner to study in, and she never had to give them a second thought. Occasionally, she would even smile at them. From the first day of school on, Cal and Jake always sat next to one another on the same side of the table, always facing toward the library door. Both had seen too many gangster movies and knew to never allow an enemy to sneak attack from behind.

This was the only environment at school that they felt they could control. With a spiral notebook open between them, Cal moved his left hand underneath to cautiously graze Jake's right pinkie. When Jake did not jerk his hand away, Cal felt comfortable enough to rest his hand there, both content in the surreptitious touch. They always hid those cautious caresses underneath a notebook, a binder, or an encyclopedia. They seemed desperate to have that physical connection, as perhaps an unspoken way to tell the other, "hey, I've got you."

When Bon Air redesigned their library the year before, they replaced the seven-foot-tall wooden bookcases that lined every wall with enormous steel shelves. With the new configuration, two rows of shelves came together at a right-angle, creating a dead zone in the library's farthest corner. Jake discovered this little hideaway when he was running from another taunting by Mike. Jake grabbed the underside of the top shelf and vaulted over the heating duct to get into this compact space.

Looking for a reference book, Cal heard crying and peered around the shelves to discover Jake on the floor. Cal wiggled into the hideaway and scooched next to his friend. Shushing him so they could remain undetected, Cal offered his hand. They sat there quietly, holding hands until Jake calmed down. Whenever one of them was upset about something, this corner in the library was where they would always go. It became their secret spot.

10

Halo

"A circle of white or colored light around the sun, moon, or other luminous body caused by refraction through ice crystals in the atmosphere."

Gym class was a special kind of hell for Jake. He would have to suffer through it three days a week for two full semesters. Since football was too physically dangerous for students not built for the sport, and baseball had the potential for fastball injuries (something that Cal and Jake had each experienced), Physical Education class consisted mostly of track and calisthenics. Their gym teacher would instruct them on proper body form when running for an hour nonstop around the school property. Or he drilled them through a circuit of jumping jacks, squat thrusts, push-ups, sit-ups, and whatever body weight exercise passed for stretching.

On rainy days, the class would stay indoors to play basketball or the medieval torture known as dodgeball. These were prime opportunities for the bigger guys to unleash aggression on their smaller classmates. As an extra cruelty, the teacher added in the extra element of rope climbing. The last two people standing would have to race up the ropes and touch the ceiling girders to win. He specified that no one could throw a ball while someone was off the ground climbing the ropes. Someone always forgot, got excited, or simply ignored these instructions. Jake and Cal were usually the last two and frequently came out on top.

After ninth grade, Jake would never have to deal with gym class again, so for now it was best to grin and bear it. What he hated most was the perverse rule that a bunch of teenage boys, already prone to competing with one another in every way, had to get naked and shower together, even if they had hardly broken a sweat during class. The beefier boys, the football jerks, the baseball jocks, and the basketball players (who already towered over everyone else) had all gone through puberty, so they were not shy about showing off their personal assets to one another.

They strutted around the locker room, sans underwear, dicks swinging, snapping wet towels at each other, punching arms, slapping butts, and even grabbing an opponent in a naked full-body squeeze like Greco-Roman wrestlers. Jake wondered if he could squeeze his small frame into one of the half-sized lockers just long enough for everyone else to finish up and clear out of the locker room.

Cal had no such shyness. Like their classmates, he got naked within seconds and joined in on the clowning around, showing off, and showering. After toweling dry, he got back into his clothes with the relaxed tempo of a reverse striptease. Cal felt comfortable in his own skin and, if this is what he had to do to fit in with all the other guys, then he was game. He loved being free from the constraints of clothing against his body.

Louisville was still having mild weather the Friday night just before Thanksgiving. It was not warm, but it had not yet gotten cold enough for a heavy coat. After that night's game, they returned to Cal's house and climbed up to the tree platform before bedtime. The leaves had changed colors but had not fully fallen from the trees yet. They stood together and looked up at the stars for a moment before Cal began to shed his clothes. He pulled off his sweatshirt and hung it on a branch. He undid his belt and let his jeans fall to the platform. Finally, he bent over to take off his underwear and socks. He stood there naked in front of Jake. "Your turn."

Jake was incredulous. "It's freezing."

Cal was not having it. "No, it's not. It's above 50."

"But that's still cold."

"Oh, come on. Just for a few minutes."

Jake laughed and started undressing, although as slowly as he could. Cal became impatient, or else he was getting cold himself. Cal hurried Jake along by helping him shed his clothing faster than he was doing it. Off came the sweater, the t-shirt, the sneakers. Then Cal shoved his hands onto Jake's butt to push down his pants and underwear. "Take off your socks too."

The two of them stood there naked, but Jake preserved his modesty by covering his crotch with his hands. He did a little dance, hopping from foot to foot to try to keep a small measure of warmth circulating through his body. Cal said, "You don't need to hide from me. We have the exact same equipment." Jake reluctantly lowered his hands. They were indeed the same in all their naked attributes, virtually the same height, same weight, same size.

"Now, doesn't that feel great? Just feel the air against your body. Feel the cold." Cal raised his arms over his head and pulled his head back to look up at the night sky, as if in benediction to the heavens. "This is what freedom feels like. Don't you love it?"

Jake did love it. "It feels amazing, but my toes are getting numb." Cal sidled up next to his friend and put his left arm over his shoulders. Both were now shivering, so they wrapped themselves into a bear hug, sharing body heat and feeling the nakedness of the other's body. There was no space between them, and they stood there a little while longer, enjoying the sensation of their flesh pressed together fully for the first time. It was Jake who broke the hug, but just because he wanted to be warmer. Neither felt uncomfortable with what had transpired between them. It felt genuine and unforced.

They dressed quickly to go back inside the house, only to get naked again the second they had closed the door to Cal's bedroom. The furnace turned on, and Cal paused. "Feel the air on your skin. Feel the warmth." Jake laughed. "You goofball." The two of them giggled as quietly as possible as they fell to the floor tickling one another. They were very physical with one another. Part of it was the typical rowdiness of teenagers—laughter led to poking, which quickly turned into grabbing, which progressed to rolling around on the ground. But it was also a need for closeness. Neither hesitated to put an arm over the other's shoulder or around his waist or even offer a gentle touch to the face.

If they might have felt awkward out in the real world with other people, they felt no nervousness, uncertainty, embarrassment, or inhibitions when they were together. It was in their individual physicality that they felt most comfortable. They were lean in the way that teenagers can be. They had outgrown any baby fat and had moved past the stage of being skinny kids. Gymnastics and dance had defined their bodies. Few other kids their age could match them.

Jake loved how dance pulled and stretched every sinew in his body, how he could let go of every tension. He was ecstatic the first time he understood the mechanics of a dance step that had him whipping his head around to spot a location on the wall during a fast spin. Cal was keenly aware of his body moving through the air, how he had to do a deep knee bend to push off the ground, arch his spine, and stretch out his legs to complete a back flip. He loved the sense of accomplishment each time he landed on his feet instead of his rump.

Cal was developing a more defined musculature faster. Jake could already see the definition of Cal's pectoral muscles from his flat stomach, and ropey muscles were forming in his shoulders and back from all his outdoor activities. Jake was in great shape, and he had not an ounce of fat on his body, although he lacked definition. Cal was starting to have a young man's body. Jake still looked like a boy. Jake kept wondering when puberty would show up and finally work its magic on his body.

It did not matter to Cal, because he could not take his eyes off Jake. With golden hair the color of straw, hazel eyes, a sweet smile, and a compact body, Jake was what people called a beautiful boy. Similarly, Jake wanted Cal's gorgeous mop of very dark curls. His eyes were a warm toffee color; he had prominent cheekbones and blindingly white, perfectly straight teeth. His chin had a dimple that was apparent when Cal's face was at rest, which was not often, and disappeared altogether whenever he was smiling, which was all the time. Cal wished that he was cuter, but Jake thought he was perfect.

With the radio turned down low, they prepared to go to bed. Cal had put the sleeping bag down on the floor for Jake, like he always did, but he wanted to keep the feeling of closeness between them. Cal climbed into his twin bed, folded back the covers, and patted the mattress. Jake crawled into bed beside him without hesitation. It was at this moment that both boys understood their bond. They had never met anyone else who liked all the same things. They had the same energy and spirit. As he started to drift off, blissfully happy with their naked bodies entwined, Cal thought, "He is the other half of me."

On Saturday morning, they awoke to sounds of footsteps overhead in the kitchen. Keenly aware of each other's nakedness, both woke up with boners. Jake reached out to hold Cal's erection, staring intently at his face the entire time. A huge smile spread across his face, as Cal touched Jake. Their first-time attempt at mutual stroking ended abruptly as they heard Zan coming down the basement stairs. They rolled out of bed quickly and jumped into their pants and t-shirts so they could go have breakfast with Cal's parents.

They rode their bikes over to Seneca Park for a little fun before Jake had to go home for his newspaper job. As they sat on the hill watching a chilly autumn breeze ripple through the quickly dying grass, they talked about superficial matters, like Casey Kasem's Top 40 that week, what TV shows they liked, their favorite foods. They fell into a brief silence, wanting to know more personal stuff.

Cal broke the ice. "Is there a girl you like?'

Jake laughed uncomfortably. "No. How about you?"

"Not yet."

After a pause that went on just a few seconds too long, Cal asked, "Is there a boy you like?"

Jake hesitated even longer. "Yes."

"There is? Who is it? Tell me."

"It's you, silly."

"Well, of course you like me. We're friends." Cal held his gaze.

"Well, Cal. How about you? Is there a boy you like?"

Cal looked down at his hands. "Only you."

Jake responded sarcastically, "Oh, because we're friends?"

"Yeah, something like that." Cal gently poked Jake in the ribs, tickled him, and they started wrestling.

They rolled several feet down the hill before they came to a stop with their arms and legs locked together and their faces only a couple of inches apart. They were perfectly happy to stay entangled like that for several minutes. They chuckled as they pulled apart to sit cross-legged on the grass once more. Jake looked away and would not face Cal for a few minutes. Cal waited patiently. When Jake turned back to him, he had tears in his eyes.

"Hey, what's the matter? I didn't hurt you, did I?"

Jake shook his head. "No, it's not that. I'm happy I have you because I don't have any friends."

"Oh, there must be other people who like you."

Jake shook his head. "Not really."

"You're my only real friend too. I try, but it's hard to make friends."

Jake debated whether he should tell Cal this: "There is one person who gives me a lot of attention, but I don't know if you could call us friends."

"That sounds mysterious. Why can't you be friends?"

Jake added, "It's weird. He's older."

"Like a sophomore?"

Jake scoffed. "No, like much older."

"Like a college student?"

"He's a grown-up like my parents." Jake did not say anything more.

"It sounds like Jakey-boy has a secret. Is it a good one?"

Jake began shaking his head. "I can't tell anyone. I like it, but I don't think I should be doing it. I guess it's a bad secret."

The boys grew quiet. Now, it was Cal's turn to cry. He reached out for Jake's hand and held it tight, as he revealed ever so cautiously, "I have a bad secret too."

11

Eclipse

"The total or partial blocking of one celestial body by another."

Their association began innocently enough. Cal first met gymnastics coach Brad Williams when he was just ten years old. Cal had been lurking on the sidelines of his sister Natalie's gymnastics practices since he was seven. He would attempt to do the tricks he had seen the girls do on the mat, at first landing on his head more than landing on his feet. Gradually, Cal was able to hold a position long enough to figure out how he could then progress to the next move so he could complete a trick. Within six months, Cal could do a reasonable approximation of whatever the girls did. In two years, he was more expert at those moves than his sister's teammates. By the time he was ten, Cal was helping the younger kids work out their tricks at the activities center where his family swam and took lessons. That is where Brad took notice of budding gymnast Cal Kulik.

Brad Williams cut an imposing figure, with a booming deep voice, wavy chestnut brown hair, and a square jaw with a cleft chin. He was not that tall, just five foot eight, but every inch was packed with muscle from his years as a competitive wrestler between junior high and college. He could never find clothes that gave his body room to breathe. He never wore a shirt and tie because his neck was too big for the collar. His biceps stretched out short-sleeved arm holes and taxed the tensile strength of long-sleeved seams. If he wore a t-shirt, his massive chest threatened to explode out of its cotton constraints.

His huge thighs pulled so much on his slacks that the fabric would bunch up his crotch painfully. He had to practically shoehorn his bulbous butt into the seat of his pants. Unable to buy clothes that ordinary men might have worn, Brad opted for comfort, so his personal uniform became a pair of drawstring sweatpants and a polo shirt left untucked at the waist. People who knew him well could not remember seeing him wear anything else. Just look for a muscular tree trunk in sweats and a polo, and that was Coach Williams.

He had no experience doing gymnastics himself, but he understood the human body. His college kinesiology training came in handy working with young gymnasts. He could explain how to stretch, lift, flex, bend, arch, prepare, and launch so they could take flight on the mat, but he was incapable of doing the very things he taught. He was strong enough to hold a kid upside down in a pose or a handstand until they could maintain it themselves without getting hurt. One afternoon, he spotted Cal doing just the same thing. However, Cal could also demonstrate the trick perfectly if the younger kid could not get it.

Brad was amazed to learn that Cal was mostly self-taught and was now so skilled that he could do more, and knew more, than most of the coaches and trainers. Williams might have had the fitness degree from college, but Cal had the experience. Brad offered Cal a part-time job assisting him with lessons whenever he was available. Cal accepted, and the two started spending two afternoons a week together. The following year, Williams was instrumental in getting Cal a regular after-school job teaching gymnastics with him through the city's Parks and Recreation district.

For three years, the relationship between them was purely professional. When Cal turned thirteen, things changed. With Cal now a teenager, Brad felt less need to be so careful with the boy. Prior to this, Brad had never touched Cal. It started with Brad placing a hand upon Cal's shoulder to give him a quick, firm squeeze before promptly removing it. The next time he did it, the hand would stay there for an almost imperceptible moment longer. Another time, the hand would slide down to the shoulder blade, making a circular rubbing motion and ending with three strong pats on the back.

At the end of each gymnastic lesson, Brad's hands would make small advances around Cal's body, as if trying to see how far he could go. Eventually, the hand moved to the small of Cal's back, which quickly progressed to putting his arm around Cal's waist. He used the excuse of making small talk so he could stand close, holding onto Cal longer. The teenager never thought anything untoward about this touching because he liked Coach Williams. They were colleagues; they were friends. A shoulder squeeze, a pat on the back, an arm around the waist was just a show of appreciation, right?

For an entire year, Brad's physical contact with Cal happened in such small incremental moves as to be almost in slow motion. Once Cal had celebrated his fourteenth birthday and nothing bad had come of his advances, Brad started becoming more forward. After one particularly grueling day of demonstrating the basics of backflips to twenty different kids, Cal pulled a muscle in his lower back and could not stand up straight.

Coach Williams had training in Structural Integration, a technique known as Rolfing, employing deep manipulation of soft tissue to realign the body's myofascial structures. He offered a massage to work out the kink in Cal's back. He pulled the boy's shirt off over his head and helped him get onto a stretching table. Brad pushed his fingertips deep into the area of pain. Cal grunted at the increased pressure. Then Brad moved his hands sharply at a ninety-degree angle, and there was an audible pop. Cal sighed heavily and started to roll off the table. Coach pushed him gently back down onto the table. "Not done yet."

He expanded to a more general massage across the whole of Cal's back and then worked his way lower. Without asking for permission, he grabbed the waistband of Cal's gym shorts and pulled them below his buttocks. Brad's big hands applied strong pressure to every inch of Cal's firm bubble butt, as well as massaging deep into the groove between his ass cheeks. Cal could not help moaning. It felt amazing and he did not want it to stop, but Brad ended abruptly, announcing it was time for them to leave for the day.

Every time after that when they worked together, Coach Williams felt he had earned the right to touch Cal without the excuse of a massage. When they were alone in the office or workout room, he would cup his hand around a buttock and just hold it there while they talked. Coach often pulled Cal in very close to chat, holding onto the boy's waist with a firm grip. A muscular arm thrown over Cal's shoulders became a more frequent occurrence.

The gym had a small locker room and adjacent communal shower. Once they closed for the day and had locked the doors, Coach insisted that Cal shower, finding something to straighten up in the locker room at that exact moment so he could observe. Eventually, Brad started showering at the same time, continuing their conversation while naked and standing barely three feet from one another. Brad brazenly displayed his sculptured physique for Cal as he lathered up.

Cal started to wash his back, so Brad stepped closer. "Here, let me help with that."

"Oh, that's okay. I can do it." Cal was flexible enough that he could reach his own back. The coach, however, had such large biceps and tight deltoids that his arms could not stretch that far around his body. Brad asked, "Well, can you do me?" He turned his back to Cal, who stepped forward, took the soap, and lathered the coach's back. "Not too fast. Get the soap everywhere."

When Brad turned back around, he was sporting a large erection, which he started stroking. "Come on, Cal. You too. It will feel great."

Cal was not shy, but he had never done this in front of someone else. Nevertheless, he did not feel threatened by Coach's request and started touching himself until he too was aroused. Their small talk over, the only sounds were the water streaming from the shower heads, their increased rate of breathing, and the final moan of pleasure when both climaxed at almost the same moment. From that day on, they always showered and masturbated together.

Cal did not know how he would react if Coach attempted to do anything more, but he felt sure that he would never have to find out. Brad seemed satisfied with the situation, appreciating each other's physiques as they jerked off together. Cal still thought of Brad as a friend, but sometimes he felt nervous whenever they were together. Then high school started, Cal became close to Jake, and suddenly he began to feel very confused.

For Jake, it began with babysitting. Once he turned thirteen years old, he had crossed that magical milestone wherein the neighbors suddenly thought he was old enough to watch their children. Most of the mothers in the neighborhood preferred to have girls babysit; the fathers did not care. Jake was responsible, bookish, and most reassuring of all, not wild, so he was perfect for babysitting. He had several families, but his favorite was the Blakely family, because the father was kind and attentive toward him. Meanwhile, his wife mostly ignored Jake simply because he was not a girl.

The Blakelys seemed like the picture-perfect, Irish Catholic, All-American family, and Mark and Becca usually had a date night on the weekends. Jake would go over about 6:00 p.m., just as Becca finished feeding two-year-old Adam so she could go upstairs and get ready. Mark would come back in from his evening jog, wearing tight gym shorts and a tank top covered in sweat. He would run upstairs to quickly shower, change, and still make it downstairs before his wife, who took forever getting dressed. He would call up to her, "Honey, we have to go."

During those protracted waits, he chatted with Jake like they were the best of friends. He never talked down to him, as most adults did to kids his age, but instead treated him as an equal. He asked Jake about school, marching band, his newspaper job, his friends. Becca, on the other hand, would barely say a word as they left the house. Following her out the kitchen door, Mark smiled and winked at Jake as if to say, "Sorry about my wife."

In August, Becca gave birth to their daughter, but something happened right as Jake started high school at Bon Air. Close to dinner time, the phone rang in the Davies' house. It was Mark, telling Betty that he had an emergency and asking if Jake could come over right away and babysit Adam for a few hours. Betty ordered Jake to grab his homework and then walked him out the kitchen, through the garage, and up the driveway. They lived across the street and two doors down. Mark had come outside to wait for Jake, and Betty waved at him to signal her concern.

Jake did not know what the extent of their emergency was, but his mother had told him that Becca had something called the "baby blues." While bathing their newborn daughter, Becca had let go and simply watched as the infant's head slid below the water. Mark had been home, rescued the baby, and called an ambulance, whose staff was required to report the incident. The police jailed Becca for a couple of days, until a judge ordered Becca to undergo eight weeks of psychiatric evaluation. Mark's sister Christie had also given birth to a daughter within a few days of Becca's delivery, so she agreed to take the Blakelys' baby girl and nurse her while Becca was indefinitely detained.

On the nights he babysat for them, Jake usually would make small talk with Mark, asking what movie the couple saw or how the evening with Adam went. On this night, Mark returned after three hours and rushed upstairs right away to look in on Adam. Perhaps he wanted to assure himself that the other member of his family was still safe. As he pulled out his wallet to pay Jake his five dollars for babysitting, Mark started sobbing. Jake liked Mr. Blakely a lot and did not know what to do because he had never seen a grown man cry, so he gave him a hug.

Jake reached across and put both his hands on Mark's left forearm. While he continued to sob, Mark absentmindedly rubbed Jake's right shoulder in reassurance. Jake mimicked this action and began to rub Mark's left arm in the same way.

However, Jake was small, a full foot shorter than Mark, so his arms were not around his waist or his hips but rather several inches lower. Jake's innocent rubbing meant that his arm was moving up and down against Mark's crotch. He got an erection.

Jake had done some exploring with other neighbor kids in the bushes behind their houses, so he knew this erection meant Mark was getting excited. Jake broke the hug and placed his right hand on the erect penis trying to burst out of Mark's pants. Jake started stroking him, and it took Mark a moment to realize what was happening. He stopped crying almost immediately and gently said, "Hey, hey, no, we can't do that." It was neither an angry rebuke nor an order to stop, just a gentle suggestion that Jake should not be doing that.

Jake burst into tears. "Please don't tell my mom I like that."

Mark kneeled, dried his tears, smiled, and then gave him a swift kiss on the cheek. As he stood up, Jake came in for a hug again, and both did that hiccupping of breath that comes after a good hard cry. Mark pried Jake loose from his death grip, patted his shoulder, and walked him to the end of his driveway. Every time Jake babysat for them, Mark watched from his driveway as Jake crossed the street. Jake flicked the light over his garage door a couple of times to signal that he was safely inside.

The next morning, Mark called Betty and asked if Jake could babysit probably every night, for perhaps a month or longer. Betty said that if her son kept up with his homework, then it would be no problem. She assured Mark that her son would be happy to help him out. That evening, Jake watched Adam for a few hours before Mark came home. Once again, he ran up to check up on his son. As they stood in the kitchen, there was no crying this time, but Jake still came in close and put his hand on Mark's crotch again. He got hard quickly and this time he did not tell Jake to stop. He did not say a word and just let the boy touch him for a few minutes.

"Okay, that's enough," Mark said as he readjusted his pants. Jake grabbed his homework off the dining room table, and then the two of them walked to the end of the driveway. As they parted, Jake once again begged, "Please don't tell my mom." After a slight pause, Mark responded, "No, it's our little secret." On the third night, Jake once again stroked Mark through his pants. He moaned softly and then his whole body shuddered. They walked to the street curb.

"Don't tell my mom."

"Our little secret."

That became their regular good-night exchange. Repeated every night, Jake was giving Mr. Blakely permission to go further. The following night, Mark ran upstairs to check on Adam and took a few minutes longer than usual. Mark had changed his clothes and came down again wearing gym shorts. Jake got him hard again, but he wanted to really touch him, not his clothing. With the shorts, Jake just had to tug at the waistband to see him. They looked at each other as Jake held Mark's erect penis for the first time without his clothes in the way. Mark moaned, started to shudder, and quickly grabbed a dish towel off the kitchen counter seconds before he exploded.

"Don't tell my mom."

"Our little secret."

After four nights of letting Jake play with him, Mark changed it up by taking charge. He changed into sweats again and pulled Jake into the half bathroom just off the kitchen. Standing face-to-face, Mark undid Jake's belt, unhooked his pants, and unzipped his fly. He put his right hand down the front of Jake's pants and began to stroke the boy for the first time. The pants and underwear slid to the floor. With his left hand, Mark pushed down his sweats as well. He stroked himself as he stroked Jake until both ejaculated. He kissed the top of Jake's head. The two of them laughed as they tried to turn around with their pants down around their ankles so they could wash their hands together in the sink.

Every night together, they tried something new. Mark's movements toward Jake were so finely calibrated that each new discovery was a prelude to the next thing. Once he had mastered hand jobs, Jake learned about how to receive and then give blow jobs. If Jake did not understand the mechanics of how something worked, Mark demonstrated it first on the teenager, who was then eager to return the favor. After jogging one evening, Mark went to take a shower before they played. Jake peeked up the stairs as Mark walked nude from the master bedroom to the hall bathroom. It was the first time that Jake had seen him completely naked. Mark closed the bathroom door.

For a few nights, they played this cat-and-mouse game with the bathroom door. The next night, Mark caught Jake looking up the stairs at him as he walked to the bathroom, so he just smiled down at the boy. He left the bathroom door ajar. The following night, Mark left the bathroom door wide open, and Jake crept quietly up the stairs, so he could peek in. Mark was standing in the bathtub with the shower curtain pushed aside, and Jake flinched when he realized that Mark would see him peeking. Mark motioned Jake to come in. "Close the door and lock it." He motioned to the boy to join him, and Jake started to step into the shower fully dressed. "Take off your clothes, silly." Mark pulled him into the shower. It was the first time the two of them had gotten completely naked together.

Within two weeks of beginning to fool around, the handsome, fit, twenty-nine-year-old neighbor was fucking Jake. He was just fourteen years old. The boy did not feel rushed, or forced, or used, because Mark was kind and always gentle with him. Mark was never aggressive and never once demanded Jake "do this" or "try that." He let Jake's own curiosity determine what they did and how soon they did it. When they got undressed, Jake would just crawl all over him. If Mark desired something, he did it to Jake first. It was never just about his pleasure. He wanted Jake to experience it too.

Jake felt that Mark was like a teacher, showing him things that no biology class or sex education would ever give him. He had no idea how or why or where Mark learned all these amazing tricks to share with him. It did not matter. All Jake knew was that Mark had always treated him kindly, and this sweet-natured, gentle man became a beast in bed. Jake loved it. Although Jake had been the instigator, he did have a vague awareness that they probably should not be doing these things together. He seemed to understand that he should never tell anyone, even though Mark never demanded secrecy. However, Mark awakened something in Jake, and he could hardly wait to go share it with Cal.

12
Collision

"When two celestial bodies come into contact, merging into a single entity."

Cal and Jake had now revealed they each had a secret, but they were afraid to say anything more. Each boy knew to what they were referring, but neither revealed the adults' names. They did not want anyone else to know, and they did not want to get these men into trouble. So, the boys never spoke of specifics, and they never hinted any further about their secret relationships. But they both sensed what the other was going through. It did not have to be said; they just knew.

As a result, they were very tentative with one another, not timid, but very careful not to be too aggressive. They had shown mutual romantic and sexual interest, but they did not want to scare the other off so they could not rush it. They were learning a body language of touch and response that became their silent way of asking questions and providing answers. Cal might casually slide his hand along Jake's arm. If Jake returned the move, it was okay to proceed or go further. Jake liked to come up behind Cal to gently grab his bicep. Cal would respond by draping his arms around Jake. They thrived on their shared sense of touch.

They usually had sleepovers at Cal's house, but Jim felt that Jake should return the favor and invite his friend to spend the night. They stayed at Cal's after the football game, and then the next night Cal had his first sleepover at the Davies' house. It felt like an amusement park to him, because it was more than twice as large as his house. Cal loved the 1939-built Georgian Colonial for all its little rooms that served as different hang-out spots—the small sitting room with two chairs and a TV, the long screened-in porch where Jake's family ate and played games, the empty family room where they played with their dog Traeger.

If Jim and Betty's cigarette smoking ever bothered Cal, he did not show it. Plus they could simply move to a spot further away. It was an excuse for the two friends to seek out private time. On weekend nights, Jake's siblings were usually out and about, so it was only the two of them, along with Jake's parents. While the basement family room was also Betty's art studio, the room was devoid of activity most of the time.

The boys went downstairs and unhooked Traeger from his chain. The ninety-pound Ridgeback was starved for attention and plopped down between Cal and Jake. The three of them lay together on the floor, silently for a while, with not a word needing to be said, or softly cooing endearments to the dog. In petting Traeger, their arms touched, and they spent as much time caressing one another as petting the dog. If anyone interrupted them by coming downstairs, they only had to move their arms to not be discovered touching.

After Traeger signaled that he was done by returning to his corner, Jake and Cal put on their coats and went outside to sit on the front lawn. They stretched out on the grass and took in the scent of musty decay from the hundreds of thousands of leaves that had fallen from the many trees in the yard. They watched the interplay of light from the streetlamps flickering among the now-empty branches. They listened to kids playing in their yards until their mothers screamed for them to come inside and couples chatting while taking their evening stroll around the block. They did not need to talk; they were just taking in the world.

They went back inside, collected Traeger from the basement, said goodnight to Jim and Betty, and went up to Jake's bedroom. They set up the room for appearances, with the sleeping bag on the floor for Cal, but Jake still locked the door. Traeger settled down on a large floor pillow on the carpet. It was Cal's first time sleeping over and he noticed the window in the small walk-in closet. When he saw the roof right outside, Cal opened it and climbed out.

"What are you doing? My dad won't like it."

"It's okay, Jake. I just want to look at the stars for a while. Come out and sit with me."

Jake looked toward his bedroom door and glanced down at Traeger, who was snoring away in the corner. The coast was clear, so he grabbed the blanket off his bed and followed Cal onto the sloped roof. They pulled the blanket over their bodies and lay back to look up at the night sky. Jake's pinkie reached out to Cal, so they linked fingers. It was like a pinkie swear that little kids would do, an unspoken promise that this bond between them would be forever.

Jake said, "The stars seem brighter tonight."

"Probably the cold air and no pollution."

"Are you looking for a particular star?"

Cal said, "I always look for Polaris."

"I never heard of that one."

"It's what everyone calls the North Star."

"Why not just call it that?"

"Polaris is a much cooler name, don't you think? They call it the North Star because it is positioned almost directly above the North Pole, so it seems to be fixed in the sky."

Jake added, "I like that no matter where you are in the world, you can always find it overhead."

Cal corrected him, "Well, you can find it if you are in the Northern Hemisphere. I imagine sailors in the old days must have used it when sailing across the ocean. It is a constant reference point, like the moon."

"You are such a nerd."

"If ever we are far apart, just glance up and know that I will also be looking at the North Star with you."

"I like that idea. Nice to know we will always be under the same sky. I mean if we are both in the Northern Hemisphere." Jake sighed. "I'm not sure I understand the science behind that."

Cal added, "I read that astronomy is more math than science."

Jake laughed. "Well, that explains why I don't get it. I'm not great with math. I mean, I have a checking account and my dad taught me how to balance my checkbook, but other than that, I'm hopeless."

"Whatever the science, it's a poetic thought."

Jake rolled his eyes and laughed. He was beginning to think his best friend was an alien from outer space.

They went back inside, got undressed, and climbed into Jake's bed. The house had gotten quiet; Traeger's snoring had gotten louder. Cal focused on the sound of Jake's slowed, gentle breathing as he drifted off to sleep. Cal did not like to think of being apart from his best friend, so he pulled Jake into a tight hug to make sure he could not and would not get away. Cal was comforted by the feeling of their naked bodies together, and so fell asleep.

Collision

They got up at 5:00 a.m., dressed quickly, and hopped on their bikes. It was Sunday morning and Jake had to sell his newspapers early. The bundles of newspaper sections had already been dumped on the sidewalk, and they made quick work of stuffing the sections together. At 6:00 a.m., the Twig and Leaf opened, so they bought hot chocolate to keep warm, and the first car honked its horn. Most Sundays, Jake spent at least five hours sitting on the ledge outside the diner waiting for the next car to show up or running to the curb more frequently once church services let out.

With Cal helping, Jake sold out his supply of one hundred newspapers before 10:00 a.m. Flush with the coins weighing down his *Courier-Journal* apron, Jake bought the two of them breakfast in the Twig and Leaf. The manager Marty always needed cash for the register and bought Jake's coins so he would not have to lug them around all day. Jake and Cal were done early enough that they decided to ride their bikes a mile down Bardstown Road to catch the noontime matinee at the Uptown Theater.

The week's double feature was *The Vikings*, with Kirk Douglas and Tony Curtis, and *The Trouble with Angels*, starring Rosalind Russell. Both had seen the nuns-at-boarding school comedy, but *The Vikings* was new to them. The adventure had opened in theaters the summer of 1958, just weeks before they were born, and it was a big hit. As kids, they had missed the network TV premiere of the movie because they were not much interested in the subject matter at that time. Since then, Cal had read the novel on which the film was based, so he was excited to finally see it. Jake liked whatever Cal liked.

After two hours of clanging steel, teeth gnashing, snarling, grunting, and scenery chewing, they were let down by their own expectations. Instead of a rousing action adventure or even a compelling examination of Viking history and culture, what they got was a tepid romantic potboiler as Douglas and Curtis fought over Janet Leigh as the damsel-in-distress. Ernest Borgnine scowled and growled through the whole thing, pitching his dialogue at an ear-piercing roar.

Cal's immediate reaction: "Well, that sucked. The book was better."

"The love story was so boring. Who would want to read about that?"

"Well, the book had a lot about Viking history, and none of that was in the movie." Cal went into a detailed description of Viking habitats and how they navigated the oceans on their voyages from Norway to England and Scotland, and beyond to Iceland, Greenland, and North America. He talked about how they used a sun compass with a vertical pointer to cast a shadow on a horizontal surface. On cloudy days, they used a crystal to refract sunlight through the cloud cover.

Jake's eyes crossed at all the information. "Why do you know so much about Vikings?"

"I like this stuff. I find it interesting. I want to do some sailing on the ocean someday, and we can learn a lot from the Vikings."

Jake had more questions about the acting. "Can there be people as crazy as Ernest Borgnine? Why were they shouting so much? They must have thought we were all deaf."

Cal agreed that it was not very good. "Oh well, I can always read the book again." Jake did not understand why his friend would ever want to relive this.

After two-and-a-half years of construction, the Kuliks' cabin was finally finished. It was not fancy but rather a beautifully rustic home-away-from-home. The main room had a cushy couch and two wingback chairs facing the stone fireplace, with a round table for meals or games near the porch door. The kitchen was small with just a refrigerator, sink, and small stove and oven. Under the sleeping loft, there was a compact private bedroom for Leigh and Zan and the cabin's only bathroom. An extensive porch wrapped around the cabin on three sides.

On the first Saturday in December 1972, Leigh and Zan invited the theater company members to spend the afternoon and evening at the cabin. Leigh had called to ask Jake's parents for permission, which they granted. Jake was the only teenager in the acting troupe, but he did not feel out of place because Cal was there. The furniture was moved aside so everyone could dance to the radio in front of the fireplace; some sang; everyone ate; Cal played his flute. The adults drank booze and some smoked cigarettes out on the porch. Jake thought it a most agreeable way to spend the day.

The day of celebration continued into the late evening. The older friends drove home, while some of the college-aged guests had sleeping bags to sleep out on the porch, and a few even brought tents to pitch on the sloped lot. Leigh arranged that Jake would spend the night with them, but Jake had left his sleeping bag at home. It was probably still sitting in the garage right next to the kitchen door. Leigh told Jake not to fret. He could share Cal's sleeping bag. When his mother said this, Cal poked Jake's back several times to secretly convey his excitement.

When they went to bed, Jake tried not to crowd out Cal, so he was half out of the sleeping bag, but it was cold, and he was shivering. Cal pulled Jake into his body to get him warm and then zipped them up in the sleeping bag. They whispered and giggled a lot. After about an hour of being so close, Cal gave Jake a peck on the cheek. Jake locked eyes with his friend, and he raised up to return the kiss. It started as just a quick brushing of the lips, but after a moment Cal attempted the kind of kiss that he saw in the movies. It was a little clumsy. Jake learned how to kiss from Mr. Blakely, so he thought he better take the lead on this.

Jake got an erection and could feel Cal getting hard too, so he smiled and quickly rolled over. Cal came in close to spoon and pushed his erection against Jake's butt, separated only by the thinness of their underwear. Cal knew it would be okay and started grinding. Jake rolled onto his stomach, so he would only have to turn slightly to kiss Cal again.

They wrestled off each other's underwear inside the zipped-up sleeping bag. Cal rolled on top once naked, rubbing against Jake's butt until he ejaculated. After he grabbed his discarded underwear to wipe off, he whispered that it was now Jake's turn. Once Jake was done, they lay in each other's arms until they were ready for a second round. This time, they were face-to-face. It felt so much sweeter being able to kiss one another while rubbing furiously until they felt the hot splash against their stomachs. Cal thought he could die happy at that moment. Jake wondered if this was what love felt like.

Within two weeks, their first semester of high school ended. They had a full month before they had to return for classes. Jake got Cal a Christmas present. He came up with the idea of making a neck choker of love beads with a small amulet carved with the Viking symbol of Yggdrasil, the mythological Tree of Life. It seemed like the perfect gift because they first met in a tree. Jake called the Kulik house and asked Zan when he could see Cal. Zan told him: "I'm sorry, buddy. Cal has gone to Alabama to go canoeing with friends. He'll be back in time for school." Jake was shocked. "What friends?"

13

Gravity

"The pull of matter on all other matter in the universe, a fundamental force in the cosmos responsible for pulling structures like stars together."

Cal's family was very outdoorsy, going camping, swimming, hiking, and fishing. Cal had gone kayaking before, but it was classmate Brent Cooper who helped Cal develop a keener interest in boating. Brent had grown up going on vacations with his parents and older brother Tim to northern Alabama. In December, the Coopers decided to take an off-season trip to do some canoeing down the lazy Flint River. Brent invited Cal to join his family, and they headed off right after Christmas Day.

With high temperatures only in the mid-fifties, it was a chilly excursion, but Cal loved the long hours of silently floating downstream and vowed to do it again soon. When he returned to school, it was all he could talk about. Jake had never heard Cal express any interest in canoeing before this, and he was jealous that he did not get to share that experience with him.

Cal asked, "Do you like canoeing?"

"I guess so. I went out in a canoe once when I was in the Cub Scouts."

Cal was disappointed in his friend's lack of enthusiasm. Jake sensed this and quickly added, "But I'd love to go with you sometime."

Cal smiled at that and continued talking and talking and talking about his little vacation with Brent. The question that was on Jake's mind was: "How do you know this guy?" Brent Cooper had come to Bon Air in the same redistricting that brought Jake there. Jake had just never noticed Brent before. He was another one of the loners and lost kids like himself who did not really fit into the high school hierarchy and floated on the periphery of all the class cliques. These outsiders always fascinated Cal, which is probably why he became close to Jake and had now befriended Brent.

This was someone else who offered something new and different for Cal, but this sudden friendship felt like a threat to Jake. From the moment they returned to classes, Jake noticed how Cal's time and attention were now divided between himself and Brent. Jake went to the library over lunch break only to find that Cal was eating in the cafeteria with Brent. When bully Mike Crumpler gave Jake a particularly cruel tongue lashing in front of several classmates, Jake ran to the secret corner in the library. Cal did not show up to comfort him this time.

Cal considered switching his first period class. With football season over, marching band turned into orchestra class. Many band members, particularly the drummers and many of the brass players, opted out of orchestra, but most of the woodwinds usually made the switch to join with the string players to perform classical music. Cal did not dislike classical music, but he preferred the catalog of current Top 40 hits that marching band played. The music teacher had a habit of going over difficult melodic passages many, many times until the class got it right. Cal thought he might die of boredom. But he would suffer through it for now.

The big change to their routine was the lack of Friday night football games, which meant Jake and Cal no longer had a good reason to continue with their weekly sleepovers. Happily, Cal still wanted to spend time together, so he always pushed his parents to let Jake come with them out to the cabin at least once a month. Jake filled in the gap and made sure that Cal slept over at his house at least once a month as well. It was no longer a weekly get-together, but it was better than nothing.

It was important to Jake that he continued to have these chances to be with his best friend. He had been sexualized early, and he did not want to suddenly stop exploring that curiosity. What he did with Mr. Blakely is what he wanted to do with Cal. For two months in the fall, Jake had been going over to the Blakely house every night. Then Mark's grandparents came to stay with him and Adam, while Mrs. Blakely was away being cured of whatever malady she suffered.

Jake's unrestricted time with Mark had come to an end. Mark had promised that they would still get together, but it could not be as frequently now that he had family visiting. Jake would see these strangers in the front yard playing with Adam or taking the toddler around the block on daily walks. With these interlopers staying, Mark started varying his usual routine, taking his daily jog much later in the evening.

One night, Jake stood on the grass by the street, looking over toward the Blakely house. He gasped when he realized that Mark just jogged past him. He stepped into the light of the streetlamps and waited for him to complete another lap around the block. Mark stopped when he saw Jake standing there. Jake tried to keep it together, but he started crying when they were face-to-face. He confessed to missing him. Mark too missed their trysts, so he suggested they meet at his office some day after he had finished working.

Jake went to folk dancing every Tuesday night on the U. of L. campus. Mark's law firm was just three blocks away. On those folk-dance nights, Jake quickly grabbed a sandwich for dinner and left home earlier. Mark had the only first-floor office with both an inside entrance and a door to the outside. Jake could enter unseen by others in the building and exit without anyone ever knowing he had been there. His nondescript office had a large steel desk and a row of bookcases against the back wall. Behind a wooden door, there was a wide side room, almost a hallway, leading from his office to a private full bathroom. There was a couch in that room where he would take naps. He installed a deadbolt on the inside of that door, so he could prevent anyone from barging in on him.

Jake showed up at 5:30 sharp and knocked on the outside door. They tore off each other's clothes and fucked furiously on that musty, ugly floral couch for more than an hour. Following a quick rinse-off in the shower, Jake gave his neighbor a peck on the cheek and left for folk dance. They did this every Tuesday night. Jake had loved having sex every night of the week at Mark's house but sneaking out to his office to do it just once a week now started to feel like they had something to hide. It felt wrong.

For more than a year and a half, Cal had been okay with the arrangement he had with Coach Williams. Jerking off together in the gym showers felt exciting and sexy. Cal continued to allow it, if the Coach kept his distance; Brad, however, kept trying to push his luck and wanted actual physical contact between them. Instead of the mutual masturbation, Coach wanted the teenager to jerk him off. In the same way that he knew how to wriggle out of a tense situation at school, Cal could squirm away whenever they got too close in the shower. He chuckled and smiled to make it seem that he felt comfortable, even when he did not.

Brad went too far when he came up behind Cal and started grinding against his butt. He wanted more; Cal did not. When Cal firmly pushed away, the Coach grabbed Cal's neck roughly to pull him closer. Cal shoved back and shouted as loud as he could, "NO." Coach backed off, and Cal bolted out of the locker room. The next day, they were back to the old arrangement, but with a lot more caution between them as they showered and stroked. Brad knew he could never expect more than this. Cal was now on his guard. What had been fun and naughty now felt ugly and dangerous.

Cal felt utterly confused. He loved being naked and loved touching his own body. He admired Coach's muscular physique as a model of athletic perfection for which he too strived. If he was being truly honest with himself, Cal would admit to getting exciting whenever he looked at Coach's nude body in the showers. However, Cal felt that Coach had expectations of him that he himself did not want and did not encourage. It felt like entitlement, that as an adult Brad was somehow allowed to do whatever he wanted with someone much younger.

He was not so conflicted about Jake. Their dynamic was never that of forcing one's will and desires upon the other. It had no expectation. Theirs was a bond of trust. Coming together after even a short time apart, they felt a joy at seeing each other again. There was no stopping the broad smiles that spread across their faces, a reflection of the comfort, anticipation, and affection they felt for one another. With Mark and Coach, it was a matter of two adults taking what they wanted from the teenagers. Between Cal and Jake, it was act of giving between two friends who were eager to explore and to please.

Every time they went to the Kulik cabin, it was the same arrangement. With the sleeping loft all to themselves, they spread out both sleeping bags side-by-side so they could move between them easily. They were quick to get naked up there because they did not worry about anyone walking in and surprising them. They were overhead, and the ceiling had too low clearance for most of the full-grown adults to stand up. Someone would have to climb up the tall, steep ladder to check on them, which no one ever did.

By now, Jake was a sexually experienced teenager, thanks to Mark's expert tutelage. He did not know that Cal was not as experienced, so he kept thinking his best friend would ask to try new things together. Cal had Coach and Jake had Mark to let them know what to do. Without the adults to guide them, though, the teenagers were clueless as to what could happen next. They shared everything together and they understood each other, but they were too shy to express those desires out loud. They wasted a lot of time waiting.

Finally, Jake decided it was time for more. They were so excited to be alone together again that both practically shivered with anticipation. Jake almost whispered, "Wanna fuck?" He always thought of Cal as this sweet guy, so he was worried that it would have seemed crass to express it so bluntly. The words never left his mouth, but they were naked. Both boys got hard. Jake wanted it; Cal wanted it too. Entwined in one another's arms, Jake decided to try something new.

He rolled over on top of Cal and gave him a long, deep kiss. Jake kissed his neck and his throat, and Cal giggled as Jake started kissing down his trim torso. He wiggled further down between Cal's legs. Jake looked up and winked; Cal gave him a look that conveyed deep affection, surprise, and more than a little trepidation. What was he doing? And then Jake put Cal's erect penis in his mouth and started sucking him. Cal gasped, but he quickly gave in to the sensation and started running his hands through Jake's blond hair. After he finished, Cal pulled Jake face-to-face for another long kiss.

They spooned; they cuddled; they touched; they kissed; but Cal did not return the favor. On subsequent visits to the cabin after that, Cal always liked getting a blow job, and yet he never offered to do the same for his friend. Jake started to wonder if he had gone too far. The rubbing, the stroking, the kissing, all of it might just have been two boys playing, but putting his mouth on Cal's genitals might have been too homo. He began second-guessing everything about their physical closeness. Was Cal just experimenting? Jake knew he was different from most of the other guys their age, but he thought Cal was just like him. The one-way blow jobs made him nervous that maybe Cal was not.

At school, they were friendly but careful not to seem too close to one another. Around their families, they were more boisterous but still cautious. It was only when they were alone together that they could let down their guard and show what they felt for each other. It was a physical expression, a shared sense of what the other person was wanting and expecting at any moment. But they never said those feelings out loud. They never mentioned love; they did not talk about sex. Cal seemed content with that; Jake was concerned.

Just as Cal and Jake did not talk about their feelings with each other, they also forgot to share their plans for the summer, both assuming that they would be spending a lot of time together as always. After the Memorial Day holiday, they had a dull four-day week of nothing—no homework, not much class participation—before school whimpered to a close on June 1st. At the end of every day, Jake would wait in the hall to say good-bye to Cal before they went to their separate exits to go home. Cal's new friendship with Brent distracted him enough that he often forgot to meet Jake, who then had to run to catch his bus when he realized that Cal was not coming.

At the end of that last Friday of their school year, Jake had planned for the two of them to talk briefly about what they wanted to do over the summer break. Cal was again a no-show. He expected to get a phone call at some point over the weekend, but the phone never rang. Jake waited as long as he could stand it and then caved, calling the Kulik house. Zan answered and engaged Jake in a conversation about their upcoming summer musical. Jake had little interest in discussing that at that moment.

"Where's Cal?"

Zan sighed at Jake's abrupt change of subject. "Off on a big adventure. I expect he will be gone all summer."

What? Why did Cal not tell him this? Jake was so upset that he did not know if he should cry or scream in frustration. "Where'd he go?"

"He and Brent and a couple others are biking along a lake."

Why was he not invited? Jake and Cal spent most of their free time on their bikes and he would have loved to go away for the whole summer with his best friend. If he were thinking more clearly, Jake might have remembered that he had told Cal he would be doing another show with the Lyric Theater company, like he did every summer. It was his favorite performance thing he did, and he looked forward to it every year. But Jake would have gladly given up his annual opportunity at musical comedy glory, if he had been given the chance to be with Cal.

What had changed between them? They had been so close, and now with the arrival of that damn Brent guy, he had to compete for Cal's attention. He felt pushed down into second place. He felt forgotten, dismissed even. Not being included in this newest adventure was bad enough, but Jake also wondered if Brent and Cal were exploring not just the great outdoors together, but each other as well. Jake tried his hardest to be mad at Cal, but he felt more defeated and scared.

14

Ellipse

"The eccentricities of an oval-shaped orbit (an ellipse) will bring planets closest to the sun at times, before sending them to the farthest point away at other times."

With Cal, everything became a bigger deal than it needed to be, and far more complicated than anyone else wanted. The original plan was for Brent, Cal, Brent's older brother Timmy, and Timmy's girlfriend Susan to camp out somewhere near Lake Cumberland, the biggest reservoir in Kentucky. They would spend their days riding their bicycles on the backroads and kayaking on the lake's many fingerlike inlets. Cal had more ambitious plans, though, and convinced the others that they should circumnavigate Lake Erie, one of the smaller Great Lakes, on their bikes. It was only eight hundred fifty miles all the way around, which Cal reasoned they could easily accomplish in ten days.

Brent and Timmy's parents, Al and Shelley, had planned to take the boys to a cabin in the mountains of western Pennsylvania for the summer. They could still do that while the boys and their companions biked Lake Erie and would be close enough if anyone needed assistance. So Al put the four bikes in the back of his pickup truck and Cal rode with him, while the brothers and Susan rode in the station wagon driven by Shelley on the six-hour drive from Louisville to northern Ohio. Al and Shelley deposited the kids and their bikes at a cheap motel on the west side of Toledo.

Cal was annoyed to be staying in the motel, because he thought the whole point of this trip was to be outdoors. He wanted to camp, but the other three overruled him, arguing that they would rather be comfortable on the night before their grueling bike trip began. The next morning, Cal roused everyone bright and early at 6:00 a.m., eager to get started. In the weeks before the trip, Cal had devised a way to attach a large plastic milk crate to the top of everyone's bike rack, which extended over their back tires. Before they set off, Cal showed the others how to fit their pup tents, bed rolls, and backpacks into their individual milk crates.

Biking through Ohio proved to be more problematic than anticipated. The largest population centers in the state were clustered along Lake Erie, with interstate highways and state roads putting traffic in their way along the entirety of their planned route. Northern Ohio turned out to be remarkably ugly, with little that would qualify as nature or the great outdoors. Once the quartet passed the eastern edge of Toledo, the landscape become somewhat prettier, with a view of the lake and enough greenery, but it was still littered with too much evidence of humanity taking up space that should have been left to wildlife. At least, that was Cal's opinion.

Sandusky was a nice-looking town, and they spent the night there, even though they had biked only fifty miles that first day. Their route took them on city streets right by the lake, where they could see Cedar Point amusement park's roller coasters rising above the skinny island just across the water from downtown. Timmy and Susan wanted to stop to ride the Blue Streak, but Cal insisted that they keep going. They argued the pros and cons of going to Cedar Point, even as they continued biking well beyond it.

They spent the night at a campground far east of Sandusky, while Timmy and Susan still fumed about the roller coasters. They could only carry minimal supplies and equipment on each bike, including food, so their paltry first supper was a can of tuna split four ways and a tube of crackers. They ate without saying a word. Susan was the first to break the silence: "Cal, who died and put you in charge?"

Cal was still a month away from his fifteenth birthday, so he was the youngest in the group. Timmy and Susan were both eighteen and just about to head off to college, so they did not like this kid telling them what to do. Cal responded, "I'm not in charge, but this trip was my idea and I planned everything. I'm just trying to keep us on track."

Timmy added, "Well, it's a vacation, and you're supposed to have fun on vacation. If someone wants to stop, then let's stop. We're not in a rush."

Cal had to tell them that he had promised his parents he would be home in time for his birthday in mid-July. Brent piped in, "But that's more than five weeks away. You said this trip would only take ten days."

"Well, it will only take ten days if we keep moving and stay on schedule. This is something big. It's not about sightseeing; it's about completing the journey."

Their constant grumbling upset Cal, so he removed himself from the group. He walked to the edge of the campground to be alone. He glanced up just as a meteor streaked across the night sky. "Hey, Jake, look at the . . . " He did not finish the sentence, because he suddenly remembered that his best friend was back home and not there to share the moment with him.

The second day started better than the last one ended, as everyone had gotten a good night's sleep. Breakfast consisted of peanut butter spread on chocolate-covered graham crackers. Susan rummaged through Cal's backpack to find the maps. "So, what's the plan? Where are we headed today, and how many miles do you expect us to cover?"

"We need to get through Cleveland before we're done today. It's only sixty-five miles. Traffic is too heavy for us to travel on those downtown streets after dark, and some of the neighborhoods are not safe."

"Sixty-five miles? That's a lot."

Cal warned, "The big day is tomorrow, probably the farthest we need to cover in a single day. We're building up our endurance."

Susan looked to Timmy. "Why do I feel like I'm going to die before we even get close to finishing?"

They were making good time for the first hour until they reached the western suburbs of Cleveland. There was nothing beautiful about the shoreline here, a depressing fifty-mile span of chemical plants, oil tankers, cargo ships, train yards, and garbage dumps. They had to stop every few blocks for stop signs, red lights, and traffic jams. Lake Erie even smelled bad, like a million rotten eggs cooking on the surface of the water in the summer sun. They reached a consensus and agreed to take a more southerly route away from the lake. Timmy and Susan were even more discontent by the time they reached their camp site east of Cleveland.

The next morning, Susan announced that she was probably going to quit after the day's ride. Timmy was not happy. He thought this was something fun and romantic the two of them could do together before they went off to separate colleges in the fall. The more Timmy tried to convince her to keep going, the more Susan yelled at him to shut up. If the two of them led the pack, they slowed down to argue with each other. When Brent and Cal took the lead, the bickering lovebirds fell far behind. Cal kept circling back to ask them to pick up the pace, to which Susan screamed, "Oh fuck off, Cal."

Cal had enough of dealing with this whiny girl, so he kept pushing them harder. Day three had taken them over a hundred miles, all the way to Erie, Pennsylvania. As promised, Susan got to a payphone and called Timmy's mom, Shelley, to come and rescue her. The boys resumed their ride the next morning, once Mrs. Cooper had driven off with Susan. By the time they had accomplished the ninety-five miles to Buffalo, New York, it was Timmy's turn to bow out. He was mad at Susan for bailing, but he was angrier with Cal for pushing too hard.

The three guys had a quiet, tense final evening together, camping next to an auto junkyard. Timmy agreed to bike the final twenty-five miles to Niagara Falls as encouragement to his younger brother, but by lunchtime, just as they were about to cross the border, Brent decided that he too had to stop. "This was supposed to be fun, but it's too much work."

Cal tried to convince him to keep going. "I wanted to get us past all the ugly stuff quickly. The lake is supposed to be a lot nicer on the Canadian side." But it was a no-go, and Brent and Timmy made the phone call to their parents together. Cal knew that the Coopers would insist that he too must quit the ride since the others had dropped out, so Cal said good-bye quickly and walked his bike over the bridge into Canada before anyone could stop him. He hoped Mrs. Cooper would not call his parents, who would surely insist that he come home right away.

Hopping back on his bike, he hugged the banks of the Niagara River until he found the road he needed to return to Lake Erie. As he had hoped, it was prettier on the Ontario side.

After an hour of riding at a grueling pace, he reached Crystal Beach, a pretty village with a great sand beach that almost enticed him to stop for the night, but he wanted to keep to his schedule. He made a serious miscalculation when he found out that he could not cross the Grand River at Port Maitland as planned, so he had to detour twenty miles inland.

It was a happy accident because the sleepy town of Byng looked like a place where he might want to live someday. The neighborhoods had cottages and ranch houses nestled in the trees; the roads were gently sloped through dense deciduous forests, and it was so quiet. Cal did not hear the usual cacophony of traffic that had accompanied him every minute of the trip so far; all he heard was birdsong and the sound of water. Situated along the banks of the Grand River and dotted with many lakes and marshes, Byng had a large conservation area, and it was there that Cal found a campground just off the main road by a large pond.

He had felt comfortable being by himself all day after the others had left him at Niagara Falls, but as night approached, he started to feel nervous about being alone in a strange, new place without anyone else to keep him company. After pitching his pup tent, he wandered over to the communal bonfire and looked at the people there roasting marshmallows and chatting. A four-year-old boy rushed up to Cal and demanded, "Hold my truck for me."

The boy's six-year-old sister followed and said, "I need you to watch my bear for me, so I can go over there," as she pointed to some indefinite area over her shoulder.

Cal told her, "I would be happy to, but I need to know your bear's name."

"His name is Pooh. Don't make him mad. He might eat you."

Cal laughed but stopped immediately when he noticed a woman looking at him. "Hi, I'm Jeannette. That's Billy and Annie. I'm their mom. Are you staying here with your parents?"

Cal had to think quickly. "No, our car broke down and they stayed back in Port Maitland until it gets fixed."

Jeannette frowned at that. "How old are you, honey?" Cal lied again and said that he was seventeen. She did not believe him. "Are you running away?"

"Oh no. My friends and I are taking a long bike trip."

She wanted to make sure he was okay. "You said you were here with your parents."

"Well, we're riding our bikes and camping out, while my parents follow along in the car. They prefer to stay in hotels."

"Where are your friends, then?"

"Um, back in town with my parents."

Jeannette encouraged Cal to hang out with her, husband Pierre, and the two kids. When she went to put the kids in their sleeping bags, Cal thought that it was time to go back to his tent.

The next day, he paid two dollars to rent a canoe for the entire day so he could explore the waterways. Close to the campground, it was too noisy, with children squealing nonstop and the grown-ups laughing uproariously at anything and everything that anyone did or said to them. So Cal rowed in the opposite direction, away from the campground, to commune silently with the river and marshes. The gentle sounds of his paddle dipping in the water, the breeze through the trees, and the trills of the birds overhead lulled him into a tranquil state, in which he had no awareness of time, the distance he had traveled, or the exertion upon his body. He pushed away any thoughts that might distract his mind from the simplicity and beauty of this moment. He was mindful of the space he took up in the world, and his surroundings. He felt serene.

He loved the place so much that he decided to stay for a few days, but at the bonfire that night, Jeannette grilled him once again. "Take me to your parents, Cal. I want to finally meet them."

Cal hesitated just long enough to figure out something to tell her, and it was clear to Jeannette that he was not being honest with her. "Honey, this is not right. You're all alone. You need to tell me what's going on."

"Okay. I was doing a long bike ride with my friends, and their parents dropped us off and were waiting to hear from us. Susan dropped out first; her boyfriend Timmy quit next; and then his brother Brent also quit. I wanted to keep going."

"It's not right. Do your parents know you're out here by yourself? You're so young. Now, tell me how old you are, really."

Cal lied to Jeannette once again. "I will be seventeen in July." He knew without a doubt that she would freak out if she learned that he would only be turning fifteen in a few weeks.

"What you are doing is dangerous. Let me put the kids to sleep, and we are going to call someone for you."

As soon as she herded Billy and Annie into the tent, Cal left. He walked back to his pup tent, packed up his bike, and moved to the furthest corner of the campground away from busybody Jeannette. He did not bother setting up his tent again, but rather just slept in his bedroll, so he could beat a hasty retreat in the morning and continue his ride unimpeded by any further interference.

Just after dawn, Cal took off on his bike. He completed sixty miles of lakefront before 11:00 a.m. when he reached his next destination, the sand spit at Long Point. A storm moved through the area, with heavy rains, strong winds, and lightning. Cal had hoped to rent a kayak to go out on the inner bay or even out onto Lake Erie on the windward side of Long Point, but the storm made the waters too choppy. Although Cal might have tried anyway, the boat rental shops were closed due to the bad weather. He spent the entire day reading a novel under a park picnic shelter as it poured.

The following day, he blazed along one hundred miles of roadway to Rondeau Park, another wildlife area on a peninsula jutting out into the lake. The seven hours of riding was a long stretch without conversation or camaraderie. Once he pulled into Rondeau's campground, he walked his bike to the common barbecue and firepit area. Cal needed some company. He chatted with Karl, who was camping with his wife Francine and their three kids and thought he would hang out near them.

He changed his mind when Francine turned as maternal and nosy as Jeannette had been. "Are you out here by yourself? Where are your parents?" Cal did not waste another moment there, hopping on his bike and riding down the peninsula, deeper into the park, and further away from anyone else. Before dark, he found an abandoned trail down a hillside to a secluded, deserted beach and set up his tent there. He stayed for two full days, stripping naked to swim and walk around the boulders along the shore, and not getting dressed again until it was time to leave.

He had only one more full day of exploring along the lake, riding to Amherstburg to stay the night, before tackling the blended metropolitan nightmare of Windsor and Detroit across the border. He hated how the big cities seemed to take over everything. Even the views of the lake were made ugly by the industry that obliterated the shoreline—factories, power plants, enormous cargo ships. He rode all day until he was far away from the city and found a wilderness area, an hour south of Detroit, where he could camp.

He spent the next ten days meandering through southeastern Michigan, western Ohio, and eastern Indiana, in no rush to return home to Louisville. Over the course of three-and-a-half weeks, he had biked twelve hundred miles, accomplishing the adventure of a lifetime. When he finally walked in the kitchen door of his house, Leigh and Zan greeted him with hugs and kisses and a casual "nice to have you home." He was never so glad to see someone else in his life.

15

Maelstrom

"The effect of looking at a faraway galaxy with its irregular spiral of glowing gas and reflective dust swirling toward a central radius."

Jake was despondent when he found out that Cal had vanished on him again for what he believed would be the entire summer. He kept distracting himself with responsibilities and activities. He and his brothers mowed neighbors' yards in the mornings; he sold his newspapers in the afternoon; he babysat in the evenings. On the weekends, he was in rehearsals for *The Sound of Music*, a show which he was not excited to do. He loved the movie, but the stage musical was a snooze. Fortunately, the Von Trapp children had plenty to do, so he was never bored.

During rehearsals, he befriended Billy Keller, who had gone to the same schools with him since fifth grade, including being bused together to Bon Air. They had not spent much time together. Billy volunteered for the backstage crew at the theater. His parents were very strict Southern Baptists, so while Billy said he would have liked to audition for the musical, he would have never gotten up the nerve to do it. Most likely, his parents would not have allowed it, anyway. Billy told Jake, "They think singing and dancing will lead to wild sex orgies."

Jake was incredulous. "It's a musical, and Maria is a nun, for chrissakes."

"Please don't swear. It only proves their point." Jake rolled his eyes.

Billy was a smart guy, but he was an odd duck. For a fourteen-year-old, he was ridiculously tall, at least eight inches taller than Jake. He had jet black hair, dark irises that merged with his pupils to make his eyes look like black marbles, and a ghastly pallor that made his skin almost translucent. Every article of clothing hung off his scarecrow body like a tarp. Everything he said came out in a barely audible whisper. Jake went over to Billy's house just once that summer, and every moment was weirder than the last. Billy must have been a late-in-life child, because Billy's parents looked far more senior than most other families, and his sister was sixteen years older.

Billy invited Jake to hang out, but Jake was shocked to see that there was not a television, a record player, or even a radio anywhere in the house. They were not allowed up to Billy's bedroom without supervision. If they sat in the living room, Mrs. Keller was in the room with them, listening to every word they said. Billy had never watched TV, had never gone to a movie, and did not listen to Top 40 radio. It was difficult for Jake and Billy to find something to say to one another.

If they commented on a schoolmate's behavior, his mother would admonish them. "Every tree that does not bear good fruit is cut down and thrown into the fire." Speaking on something they heard from someone's else mouth prompted a lecture on the danger of malicious gossip. They could not even discuss entertainment stuff, because the Kellers prevented pop culture from infecting their household. Talking about things that they might like to do brought about a matronly sneer, perhaps deemed as "ungodly" to want anything they did not already have or did not need.

When Jake mentioned that the manager of the Twig and Leaf diner gave him free hot chocolate on cold days when he was selling newspapers, Mrs. Keller chimed in with, "Do not give dogs what is sacred; do not throw your pearls to pigs. If you do, they may trample them under their feet, and then turn and tear you to pieces." Jake was not sure of what her point was in saying that, but he thought it had something to do with accepting charity. He did not know if she took that out of the Bible or a horror movie. It drove the boys out to the backyard.

They sat on the grass, and his mother screamed that Billy would ruin his nice plaid polyester pants. He was not allowed to wear shorts, even on the hottest days of the year. When he sat on a lawn chair, she ordered Billy to "get out of the sun. You'll burn your skin." When they sat on the bench swing in the shade, she demanded the two boys sit further apart. From twenty-five feet away, she shouted, "You shall not lie with a male as with a woman; it is an abomination." Jake was pretty sure that the entire neighborhood could hear her. He never went back.

Jake thought it might be better if Billy came over to his house instead, but he was wrong. Whenever Jake put a record on the turntable or switched on a radio station, Billy asked him to turn it off so they could talk or work on homework. He would not pet Traeger, innocently announcing that dogs were dirty. He did not ride a bike; he would not climb a tree; he did not even like to take walks. His strict parents had turned Billy into a timid boy and effectively ruined him for life. They had nothing in common. He remained friendly with Billy at the theater, even if they could hardly manage a conversation, but they stopped trying to spend time together.

Jake rekindled a friendship with Noah, another neighborhood kid, with whom he had been close in his first two years in Louisville. Noah's mother had been as obsessively watchful as Billy's mother was, which Jake found oppressive. As Jake had become more active with his music, dance, and theater stuff, Noah had gotten involved with the school's baseball team, and they had grown apart. Noah was another social outcast and spent most of his time alone. They bumped into each other one evening, when Jake was walking Traeger, and Noah was taking an after-dinner stroll around the block with his parents.

Noah invited Jake to join him the next day at the Lakeside Swimming Club, a huge pool facility built into an old rock quarry. They got into their swimsuits and instantly separated, with Noah heading to the diving boards so he could cannonball and drench everyone within a twenty-foot radius. Jake sat down in the wading pool to watch Noah make a fool of himself. Coming up behind Noah on the diving board was Cal, only recently returned from his biking trip. Just as Jake was there on a guest pass from Noah, neither did Cal's family have a membership to Lakeside. He was there as a guest of Brent, who invited Cal to go swimming as an apology for quitting the Lake Erie ride.

Jake just sat there in the wading pool and watched Cal dive a few times. He looked away, hoping Cal would not notice him as he walked by. Jake heard water splashing behind him, and suddenly he was there. Cal asked, "What are you doing in the baby pool?" Jake had to admit that he was not good in the water. He had gotten water stuck in his left ear when he was nine years old, which led to a very bad infection and a long hospital stay. He worried about it happening again, so he rarely submerged his head after that and so never learned how to swim beyond a frantic dog-paddle.

"Well, let's get it so you are comfortable in the water."

Jake was not having Cal's chumminess at that moment. He was still mad at him for going away and not telling him. "Oh, that's okay. I'm fine right here. You go do your thing with your friends."

"You're my friend. I want to be here with you. Let me teach you how to float. Please." He stood up and held out his hand to Jake, and he did not let go as they walked to the shallow end of the big pool. Jake was surprised that Cal allowed this momentary public display of contact between them. As they walked into chest-high water, Cal gave him a few quick tips on breathing to expand the lungs so his body would be more buoyant.

"Now, lean back into my shoulder and stretch your legs straight out in front of you. I will support you under the back."

Jake did as he was instructed, even though he had to let his ears drop below the water's surface. He felt Cal's left arm underneath him with his outstretched palm in the small of his back. Cal instructed, "Now, take a deep breath. Keep the air in your chest but switch to breathing in and out of your nose. And relax."

Before letting go, Cal came in close and whispered, "I'm so sorry. Don't be mad at me." Jake relaxed enough that Cal did not need to hold him up any longer. Before he took his arm away, Cal caressed Jake's butt quickly. Jake was floating. Cal leaned back to float alongside him. They linked pinkies so they would not float away from each other, and they stayed in the water together until their fingers and toes had pruned. Cal invited Jake to come to the cabin that weekend, since it was his birthday.

As they sang happy birthday to Cal, his mother Leigh learned that Jake's birthday was just two weeks later. She arranged to have Jake come over to the house that week, so she could have a cake there for both boys to celebrate their fifteenth birthdays together. Leigh invited Jake's parents to come, but they were busy and declined the invitation, as usual. Leigh was irritated at that. The rest of the summer was a return to normal for Cal and Jake, going to movies, riding their bikes, climbing trees, swimming, and spending all their free time together.

Sophomore year was not much different from their freshman year. Jake was now a teacher's aide for English, Humanities, and Chorus, while Cal was studying harder for National Honors Society. While they only had four classes in common, Cal and Jake were back in the marching band, sleeping over on game nights, hanging out together a few times a week in the library during lunch break. Twice a week, Cal ate lunch with Brent in the cafeteria. Jake did not mind, because that separation made Cal want to be with him even more when they were not at school. Their intimacies together never diminished.

Cal had a swirl of emotions about Jake. He never defined what it was that he felt. He worried that they spent too much time together, so he planned the long bike trip for a change of scene. Once he had that distance, all he could think about was getting back home to Jake. He worked overtime to endear himself to people, but then longed for solitude. Come close, now go away. It was different with Jake. There was an emotional pull between them, and that scared the hell out of Cal. He could be the most fearless person, but when something emotional scared him, he ran away from it.

Christmas break arrived, and Cal was off again on another adventure that did not include Jake. This time, Cal, Brent, and

Timmy went to Panama City, Florida, to go kayaking. Jake had once again bought Cal a Christmas present, a wristband compass for his various journeys. He threw it unopened into his sock drawer, alongside the Tree of Life gift from the previous Christmas that he never got the chance to give. The day after Christmas, Jake was so upset he opened the presents and kept them for himself, even though he had no use for a compass. He now thought the Tree of Life necklace had been a silly, sentimental idea. But he forgave Cal; he always did.

Weather in Louisville was usually mild during the winter, but 1974 started with out-of-ordinary extremes. It had been much colder than usual from New Year's Day to March, and it snowed three inches on March 23, three days after the official start of spring. Cal and Jake had been bike riding on that Saturday morning when the temperature plummeted by almost twenty-five degrees in two hours, and they got caught in a sudden snowstorm. They had a snowball fight, skied on their sneakers down a hill, and tilted their faces skyward to feel the snowflakes melting against the warmth of their skin.

The snow was gone by the next day, and it got up to eighty degrees the following week. A powerful low-pressure system developed over the North American Plains States, while a warm front near the Gulf Coast surged north, bringing with it unusually moist air. The two systems collided, setting off a string of powerful storms. On Monday April 1, Campbellsburg, Kentucky, just northeast of Louisville, had most of its downtown business district destroyed by an F3 tornado.

Two days later, a large-scale trough extended over most of the contiguous United States. The Gulf Coast warm front had dissipated and then redeveloped northward over the Ohio River Valley. On the afternoon of Wednesday, April 3, the skies exploded. At 3:25 p.m., a tornado touched down at F5 intensity in Brandenburg, Kentucky, just forty-five miles southwest of downtown Louisville, killing thirty-one people, leveling houses, and wrapping cars and pickup trucks around telephone poles and tree trunks.

An hour later, Louisville saw two funnel clouds form at the same time. The first touched down to become an F4 tornado in the far southwest corner of the city. The second funnel cloud formed over Louisville's Standiford Field Airport, touching down just over the Watterson Expressway on the Kentucky Fairgrounds and hopping over I-65, where it flipped over several vehicles on the highway. It touched back down in the Audubon neighborhood where it demolished an elementary school before beginning its swath of destruction through the city.

At that very minute the tornado started, Jake was standing on the corner of Bardstown Road and Douglass Avenue selling his newspapers for the afternoon. He looked at his watch, confused by how quickly it had gotten dark outside, thinking he had somehow lost track of the time. Sunset was not until about 8:00 p.m. Then Jake looked up and saw roiling clouds racing across the blackened skies. A strong gust of wind tore ten newspapers out of his hands and sent them flying down the block.

A police car roared into the intersection, with lights flashing and siren blaring. A cop leaned out of the passenger side, yelling, "Get inside. Get off the street." The cop car sped away to warn people further down the block. The diner manager Marty was standing at the entrance and yanked Jake inside. Everyone crouched down behind the lunch counter, and Jake peeked over the edge in time to see the huge trees across the street bend in half and explode. The tornado hopped over the diner and their intersection, touching down again just four buildings away to continue tearing up the block.

Five miles away, Cal was finishing up a gymnastic lesson for seven-year-old Ruthie Mills. Her mother, Deidre, showed up at the appointed time to collect her daughter, mentioning to Cal and Coach Williams, "Bad weather out there. We've got to get home." Coach tried to convince Deidre that they should take shelter in the basement below the gym, but she insisted on getting out of there. Then the sirens started to wail. Coach got Cal downstairs, and then the lights went out. They waited there in the dark for a half hour until the all-clear siren went off.

Coach wanted Cal to stay until they were sure it was safe, but Cal decided to leave so he could be at home. He had locked his bike to a sapling in front of the gym, but the wind had snapped the tree in half and threw his bike, undamaged, onto a dumpster. As he was racing home, a sudden downdraft flattened Cal, knocking him to the ground and scooting his bike slowly across the sidewalk away from him. The tornado had passed Jake's location, continuing its southwest to northeast path across the county, past Cal's location.

The rain was torrential, and Cal was soaked by the time he put his bike in the backyard storage shed. No one else was at home. His parents were still at work and would not be back for another hour. That would be under normal circumstances, but Cal could not know yet how splintered trees, downed telephone poles, and live electric wires in the street would impede their progress from only a few miles away. Cal got his transistor radio so he could hear whatever news was being broadcast about the storm. He sat there alone for five hours.

Cal's parents finally made it home by 10:00 p.m. and they ate a cold dinner by candlelight while listening to news on the radio. Jake's younger brother Shaun got caught on the other side of the tornado path, so he did not return to the Davies' house until the next afternoon. The F4 tornado extended twenty-two miles through the city, destroying over nine hundred homes, damaging thousands of others, making roads impassable, and leaving much of the city without electricity for days. The historic Cherokee Park had three thousand mature trees flattened, debarked, and splintered into millions of matchsticks.

Schools were closed for the rest of the week. Cal could not reach Jake on the telephone, so he rode his bike over to find his friend. They hugged tightly when they saw each other. Cal said, "I heard on the radio that Cherokee Park is a mess. We have to go." They dashed off on their bikes, changing their route every few blocks as they lifted their bikes over debris or navigated around flipped cars. The road entrances to the park were blocked by sawhorses and police cars. That did not deter them, as they knew all the bike paths and walking trails in and out. Once they found a way into the park, they did not recognize a thing about it.

The once-green, four-hundred-acre park looked like an upside-down *Alice in Wonderland* nightmare. As they entered, they saw a juniper shrub still rooted into the ground but stripped bare of its greenery. Right next to it was a hydrangea bush uprooted, yet with every single flower still attached. They found a massive Sycamore tree lying on its side. A Magnolia tree stood upside down, resting on its crown of branches with its root system sticking straight up in the air. Every white and pink petal lay on the ground immediately to the east of the tree, looking like a bloodstained carpet. The air smelled of sawdust from all the blasted wood.

Cal and Jake knew every corner of the park, but nothing looked the same and they could not get their bearings. Park benches and picnic tables were missing; park signs were ripped out of concrete and thrown into the creek. Natural landmarks were hidden by debris or blown away. They walked their bikes through the destruction for an hour until they found what they were looking for. The rock retaining wall that always served as their location marker hid behind a line of yew bushes thrown onto the bike path. The wide sloping hill, usually an open space, was littered with branches, garbage cans, trash, several flipped cars, and even a squashed delivery truck.

At the top of the hill, there should have been a stately, two-hundred-year-old White Oak tree. In unison, both dropped their bikes and stepped forward in shock. The tornado had probably blown straight through the tree, breaking it off and twisting the trunk almost ninety degrees so that it looked like pulled taffy. The rest of the tree was nowhere in sight. They pulled together in a hug and cried. They had always climbed that tree whenever they rode their bikes through Cherokee. This tree was where they first met each other five years earlier. Now it was gone.

With most of Cherokee Park closed for months to make repairs and do massive replanting, Cal and Jake took to riding their bikes over to the Collings Estate, a former tobacco plantation and horse farm just across from the city zoo. They rode on the natural dirt trails through the dense overgrowth until they came upon a gravel road and a groundskeeper's turnaround behind two metal poles and a heavy chain. It was easy enough to bike around the poles, and from the tire tracks, it was clear that many cars had done the same thing.

They stopped to climb a broad-limbed Maple tree. Below

them, they saw hikers come through the woods, walk up to the illegally parked cars, glance in the windows, and climb into the passenger side of the front seats. Cal and Jake watched as these young men did the same things to the strangers in the cars that the two of them had done together during their sleepovers. Cal laughed knowingly but wanted to get out of there. Jake wanted to stay to watch everything.

16

Barycenter

"The common center of mass about which any two or more bodies of a gravitationally bound system orbit."

In the summer of 1974, the city of Louisville inaugurated its annual Heritage Weekends, as a buildup to the nation's upcoming bicentennial. It took place on downtown's Belvedere Plaza beneath the twin towers of the gaudy Galt House Hotel with its fancy revolving restaurant. The multicultural weekends celebrated the diverse communities of the city, featuring booths selling traditional foods, drinks, and memorabilia, and hosting two full days of ongoing live performances. Jake's folk dance group became an integral part of each country's celebration.

For Ukrainian Weekend, Freya and Len made Jake their featured soloist doing all the gymnastic tricks. In truth, he was the only one young enough to physically manage the high kicks, leaps, splits, flips, and fast turns required of the Hopak dance. Cal came to watch Jake dance, and they were hanging out together with Jake's parents, when Mark Blakely walked up to offer congratulations. He had come with friends to check out the Heritage Weekend, not knowing that Jake would be performing. While he would normally not show any public display of affection, Mark gave Jake a quick hug and said, "Great job, Jake." He looked over nervously at his parents and Cal to see how they reacted.

Cal told Jake that he had a summer job in Chicago. His father's old military buddy, Rada Bondarenko, ran a summer sports camp for kids in the Park Ridge suburb. Jake was upset that Cal would be gone for yet another summer. He believed it had something to do with an incident at the cabin just a month prior. The boys had been shirtless, sitting on the edge of the porch. Jake was fascinated by the development of Cal's physique and his prominent Adam's apple, which he did not have. He followed the contours of Cal's pectorals and abdominals with his finger, gently caressing his chest and torso, and Zan had seen him do this.

Zan walked up and gave Jake a hard smack to the back of his head, silently asserting that he should not be doing that. Then he smacked Cal's head as well, for allowing this to happen. Without saying a word to each other, Cal and Jake knew they had to be more careful being affectionate with one another, at least where anyone else could see them. Their only time alone together was when they were at the cabin or having a sleepover at Cal's place after the football games. They could not jeopardize this by irritating Cal's parents.

It felt like Zan was intentionally separating the boys. Cal left for Chicago on the following Monday and stayed with Rada's family, including his very clingy sixteen-year-old daughter Iryna, another counselor at the sports camp. Cal made no moves toward Iryna, and she never asked for permission. She grabbed hold of Cal's arm their first day together, and she just declared that he was her boyfriend. Cal went along with it and did not mind the attention, but he also did nothing to encourage her further. She never let go of him all summer.

Jake's summer musical was *Oklahoma!*, and he played the made-up role of Bert. There were no kids or teenagers in the show, so the director Francis created a chorus role to cast him as partner to Verna, the seventy-year-old actress playing Aunt Eller. Billy was working backstage crew again and mentioned how creepy it was to see him sidling up to Verna onstage. "Francis is making it look like you want to bone Aunt Eller." Jake had no idea that was how it was coming across, so he stopped putting his arm around her waist and made sure to always keep at least six inches of space between them.

Jake began to understand the effect he had on certain men. He was comfortable with his body and had no problem with nudity, as he and Cal frequently doffed their clothes to hike the secluded woods near the cabin. In the men's dressing room, the more effeminate cast members would demurely change into their costumes privately in the restroom. One man, Daniel Kinnen, liked to strip down to his underwear and strut around like he was hot stuff. With his concave chest and little belly, Daniel would hardly pass for beefcake. More like a double cheeseburger, extra-large fries, and a chocolate milkshake in Jake's opinion.

Jake was not shy and got undressed in front of them, standing naked while chatting casually before he had to stuff his crotch into his uncomfortably tight spandex dance belt. The men ogled Jake furtively, admiring his lean dancer's build and gymnast's strength. They thought that Jake was seemingly unaware of the attention he was attracting, but the teenager knew exactly what he was doing. Everyone understood that they could look but not touch, because he was a minor. In the tight confines of backstage, though, someone always managed to grab his ass or crotch under the guise of squeezing past him in the dark.

With only two heterosexual men in the large cast (playing the male leads, naturally), conversations in the dressing room almost always veered toward sex and sexuality. Daniel imagined himself a wit along the lines of Oscar Wilde or Dorothy Parker, but all he did was quote bitchy dialogue he had memorized from *Auntie Mame*, *The Women*, or any Bette Davis movie. He talked endlessly about the love of a good man, marriage, finding a soul mate, and the Hollywood romantic notions of undying devotion. Jake thought it kind of sweet.

Rodney Creighton, the once-handsome leading man who had since entered the portly character man phase of his acting career, was outrageously direct in his attempts to shock Jake, who was not yet sixteen years old. Jake listened to every explicit detail that Rodney could come up with, all the while making a mental note whether he had already done that with either his neighbor Mark or Cal. When Rodney came up with something he had not done yet, Jake tried not to register surprise and burned a reminder in his brain to ask Mark to show him how to do it.

With Cal gone for the summer and the sex with Mark happening just once a week, Jake missed being physical with someone. He rode his bicycle over to the Collings Estate to check out that cruising area. Instead of climbing the tree to watch, he started climbing into cars, finding the nicest looking man there that day, and seeing what developed between them. Jake went there a few times a week before he had to go sell his newspapers. The area eventually came to the attention of the police, who raided the wooded area one afternoon while Jake was in the backseat of a Buick Regal with a guy named Stan.

The cops could see that he was a minor, so they never charged him with any crime. Jake gave the police his father's work number, thinking he would rather face his father's temper immediately than his mother's ongoing wrath. The cops brought Jake into the waiting room, where Jim greeted him with a hard slap to the face. "What the hell were you thinking?" Jim grabbed Jake by the neck and pulled him out to the car.

On the way home, Jim's anger turned to concern. "You have to be very careful, Jake, or you are going to get killed." Jake was silent and cried. "Look, I am sorry I slapped you. I just don't know how to deal with this. Did someone make you do this?"

Jake's response was curt. "Oh, of course not. That's stupid."

"Don't mouth off to me. How did this happen?"

Jake thought a short, simple answer would be best. "I rode my bike over there to climb a tree, and I saw all these cars in the woods. I wanted to see what was going on."

Jim hesitated and considered not asking, but he had to know. "So nothing happened? You were just looking?"

Jake lied. "Nothing happened. And then the cops showed up. Are you going to tell Mom?"

"What? You really must think I'm stupid. She would be mad at you, but she'd make my life a misery over this."

"It's not your fault. You didn't do anything. It was all me."

"You don't know your mother as well as I do. She wants to always find a reason for something and an answer to every problem."

Jake was annoyed. "Oh, so I'm a problem that needs to be fixed?"

"Maybe. I don't know. But this can never happen again. Next time you want to climb a tree, go out in the backyard. We have plenty of them."

"So you want me a prisoner at home then?"

"Not at all, but your ass is grounded until I tell you otherwise. I just need you to understand that what you are doing is dangerous. You must listen to me."

Jake was grounded for two weeks. He did not listen and was back in the woods and the backseat of cars as soon as he had his freedom again.

Cal returned home at the end of August. He could now tell his parents that he had had a "girlfriend" in Iryna for the entire summer. He wondered if maybe that was what he should be doing. He pondered the possibility of not contacting Jake upon his return, letting the friendship wither away from disinterest. He missed his friend, though, so he called Jake two days later. Cal rarely allowed public shows of affection or physical contact between the two of them, but he was so happy to see Jake after three months that he could not help kissing him on the cheek and giving him a strong, long hug. Once again, Jake forgot about his disappointment and sadness over Cal's absence all summer.

Cal had a surprise. He had gotten his learner's permit right as school let out in May, and Rada had taught him how to drive a car in Chicago over the summer. His first day back in Louisville, he passed his driving test and had gotten a driver's license. Since his parents were working that weekend, Cal invited Jake to go to the cabin, just the two of them alone, and Cal would drive. They left on Friday morning, which would give them almost three full days together without parental supervision or interference.

During the drive, Cal talked about the Bonderenko family, their house, their dogs, Chicago, the sports camp. He never mentioned that he had had a girlfriend briefly, and he kept Coach Williams's existence a secret as well. Jake told him about *Oklahoma!* and his fellow actors in the cast, talked about his usual summer jobs, mentioned the movies that he wanted them to see now that Cal was back. Jake had still never told him about his ongoing dalliance with Mark Blakely, and he was certainly not going to tell him about the cars in the woods, or that the police picked him up for solicitation.

It was a sunny, humid day, so Cal thought they should go to the private swimming hole on their property down the hill from their cabin. A stream emptied into a natural depression underneath several pine trees, and Cal, his dad Zan, and two brothers had dug out the underbrush and shored up the sides of the natural pool with rocks. Since they would be alone all weekend, Cal stripped off his clothes and told Jake, "Follow me." Jake undressed and they ran naked down the hill.

The swimming hole was large, twenty feet across by thirty feet long, forming a hidden oasis nestled underneath the pines. The previous summer, Cal had added a knotted rope, draped over a low branch. He got a running start, grabbed the rope, swung like Tarzan, and let out a delighted whoop as he dropped into the shallow pond. Jake followed suit, and the water felt so cool against his body. He had never skinny-dipped before this, and the sensation felt amazing. They gently moved through the water, sat on submerged rocks, and warmed their taut, lithe bodies with the sunlight filtering through the branches. They spent all afternoon there.

Jake got the charcoal grill started, while Cal prepped the food they had bought at the grocery before leaving town. Their dinner was a teenager's summertime feast of cheeseburgers, smoked sausage, cole slaw, potato chips, and soda. Cal marveled at how easily the two of them worked in tandem, never needing to discuss something beforehand. In that moment, it felt like a perfect partnership. He looked over at Jake as he stood next to the grill, no clothes on, with his blond hair shining in the sunlight, and he felt a wave of emotion. Cal walked up behind Jake, wrapped him in a hug, and kissed his shoulder. Cal was trying to become more comfortable with bringing his feelings for Jake out into the bright light of day.

They watched the sun go down and the stars come out. They turned off Cal's transistor radio, so they could appreciate the calm of evening. The sound of birds quieted down, overtaken soon by the katydids' rhythmic pulsing, the crickets' high-pitched chirping, and the frogs' croaking. The stream trickling down to the swimming hole was the only other sound they heard, until a gentle breeze swayed the branches, silencing the insects. Once they had readjusted their positions, the bugs renewed nature's cacophonous nighttime symphony.

Cal scanned the sky. "It looks really hazy, so not many stars tonight."

Jake glanced overhead. "Wow. The moon is so bright behind the clouds."

"It's a full moon on Sunday night. A perfect way to end the summer."

"No stargazing for us tonight, so the moon will have to do."

"When I was in Chicago, you couldn't always see the stars because of the city lights. On nights like those, I looked to the moon. I'd imagine you looking at it too, wherever you were. It helped me feel like we were together."

"I guess, but I would have liked it better if you were here. At least you thought about me once in a while."

Cal looked at Jake, his face tilted up and bathed in moonlight. "I'm here now, and I always think about you."

"But wouldn't being together be better than the looking to the moon?"

Cal framed his response carefully. "Yes, of course, but those heavenly bodies are always constant. You can always rely on them being there."

Jake was annoyed. "Unlike friends who go away. You mean like that? I'm constant too. I'm not the one who runs away every summer."

"I'm not running away, but I can't let a good opportunity go by. You want me here with you forever?"

Jake wanted to yell "Yes!" He did not say it out loud. "I don't mind you going away. I just miss you. When you don't tell me, it's like you don't care how I feel, like you don't care about me." They were silent for a few minutes, Jake nervous that he had said the words, Cal taking in the criticism leveled at him.

To ease the tension, Cal hummed "When You Wish Upon a Star," knowing Jake would start to sing. They harmonized on that, then "The Second Star to the Right," "Blue Moon," and "Moon River." They tried to name all the songs they knew that had the words "star" or "moon" in the lyrics. The moon won that contest. When it was time to go to sleep, Cal started up the ladder to the loft. Jake asked if they could use the bedroom for a change. Cal agreed that sleeping in a double bed together would be a lot nicer than sleeping bags on the floor of the loft.

Once their youthful passion for one another was spent, Cal drifted off to sleep, happily entwined around Jake. Moonlight shone down on them through the bedroom window. Jake gazed up, taking comfort in the moon's presence. Jake imagined that Cal would always be somewhere looking up, maybe looking for him. Jake prayed that Cal would always be as constant as the moon.

17

Supernova

"A cataclysmic explosion caused when a star exhausts its fuel and ends its life. It is the most powerful force in the universe."

Jake's plan for his junior year was to keep such a low profile as to be virtually nonexistent. The principal's office thwarted that idea when they proclaimed the first five days of fall semester as Service Week, announcing over the intercom during home room all the teachers' aides and their various duties. It offered a road map to Jake's location at various points through the day. The library storage rooms for both Mrs. Asher's English class and Mr. Braddock's Humanities class were situated right across the hall from their classrooms. The teachers could see Jake from their desks, as he alphabetized countless paperback novels.

Chorus director Joseph Hamment had always thought Jake neat, organized, and responsible, so he had invited Jake to be his teacher's aide the previous year. It was a simple job, straightening the chairs, putting all the music stands at the same height, and collating sheet music to store in the room's large walk-in closet. Chorus was the last class of the day, so the students bolted as soon as the bell rang. Mr. Hamment stuffed his papers into his leather book bag and left soon afterward.

Cal was not taking Chorus class this year, so Jake was alone for the fifteen minutes that it took him to organize the room. Cal and Jake had always wondered why the school would put the arts wing right across the concourse from the gymnasium and sports wing. The jocks hated the artsy kids, and vice versa, so the only explanation seemed to be that this proximity put the marching band closer to the stadium for football games. Its location meant the arts wing was out of sight from the principal's office, teachers, and staff. At the end of the school day, the arts wing was deserted, except for Jake.

He had managed to remain mostly invisible, but the verbal taunts by football guard Mike Crumpler started up again with the new school year. Jake knew that the epithets homo, faggot, fairy, nelly, and sissy meant that he liked other boys, and since he was having sex with Mark and messing around with Cal, he knew it was the truth. Instead of denying those taunts, he simply ignored them. That self-awareness protected him to a certain extent, until the time that it did not.

Mike became angry that he could not get a rise out of Jake, no matter how hard he tried, how loud he yelled, how often he taunted. Jake refused to react, and it drove Mike nuts. Finally, he decided to do something about it. Thanks to that helpful Service Week announcement, Mike knew exactly where to go. As Jake finished straightening the Chorus room, he stepped into the storage closet to refile sheet music. Mike had waited to make sure everyone else was gone, snuck in the room, switched off the lights, and pushed a chair under the doorknob.

Jake was not aware that anyone else was there, until Mike stood in the doorway, blocking the afternoon sunlight streaming in from the west-facing windows. He shoved Jake hard into the shelves, yanked down his pants and underwear, and raped him. It was over quickly, and Mike turned Jake around to face him, hoping to see fear. Instead, Jake merely smirked and said, "Thanks," which unnerved Mike. What he could not know is that Jake had been having sex for over two years. Jake was experienced; Mike was an amateur.

The following Monday, he was back with the same routine of blocking the door, pushing Jake into the shelves, and going at it. Jake really did not mind, because Mike was tall, well built, blond, and good looking. Jake's refusal to sob, complain, fight back, or yell for help felt like permission to Mike, who came back every day for the next two weeks. He always seemed so macho around school, but with each day he became gentler, no longer digging his fingers into Jake's waist, and kissing him tenderly, if clumsily, on the back of the neck.

Jake knew what was going on. "I guess I'm not the only homo here." Mike got angry, but the slap he gave Jake was halfhearted. Jake pulled back and punched him with all his strength, cutting his right knuckles badly on the two teeth he knocked out of Mike's mouth. Jake may have been a fairy, and he may have been smaller in stature, but he was strong from six years of gymnastics. Mike was shocked and suddenly afraid of short, wiry Jake. He backed away and left, but his momentary fear turned to anger once he was a safe distance away. He never considered that maybe he deserved that punch for the outrage perpetuated on Jake.

Mike got his revenge by telling several of his buddies about this little blond faggot, all alone in the Chorus room, who needed to be taught a lesson. "If that little faggot wants it so bad, we should give it to him." That undefinable thing called "it"—that was all he could think to say, like he could not bring himself to say sex, fucking, dick, or penis, because that would be too faggy. He told his buddies when Jake would be alone, and he came up with a strategy: if the Chorus room door was closed, then someone was probably already in there, showing Jake the consequences for being a fag. Jake had only two days' reprieve until someone got up the nerve to try "it."

Kevin Badesch was a senior and a member of the swim team. He was also a drummer in the marching band, so Jake knew him, but they'd never exchanged two words, nor had there ever been any animosity between them. But as instructed by Mike, Kevin marched in, blocked the door, turned off the lights, and pushed Jake down to his knees. As he unzipped his fly, Kevin warned, "If you bite me, I will kill you." Dave Hindman, who was a junior and in J.V. football, pulled down Jake's pants and threatened, "If I get syphilis, I'm gonna kill you."

Bruce Mitchell was another senior, a tall basketball player, who was the only Black guy that Mike deigned to have in his inner circle. Bruce wanted not only a blow job but also to fuck Jake. He ended his prolonged session with "If you tell anyone about this, you die!" Jake missed his bus because of Bruce, had to walk the four miles home, then got to his newspaper job late, which delayed dinner and angered his mother Betty.

Matt Brown and Frank Adair were both juniors and wannabe jocks who were not good enough for any of the sports teams, including the track team, which usually took everyone. They also were not very good at fucking, fumbling with belts, zippers, their hands, their penises, without a clue of what to do and how to do it. That Bobby Nevin participated in this felt like a betrayal to Jake, because the senior had been friendly to him in drama club and speech team. Jake did not know that Bobby had to fend off his own rumors about being a homo and did this to deflect suspicion away from himself.

The seven jocks kept coming back to Jake in the Chorus room repeatedly from September to March. Jake stopped going to the Collings Woods for random meetings in strangers' cars.

One Tuesday evening, he was at Mark's office when Mark turned around quickly, causing Jake to flinch. He had no idea what Jake was going through at school, but he saw the quick flash of fear and tried to soothe him. "Hey, hey, look here. It's just me. I'm your friend. Are you okay?" Jake did not tell him, but the soft caress on his shoulder and Mark's gentle deep voice calmed him down enough that he came in for a hug, and then he was fine.

The experience also changed how he reacted toward Cal. At first, Jake thought that none of this would have happened if Cal had only been in the Chorus that year, but it was not his fault. Jake took to hiding out more frequently in their secret corner of the library, and he started organizing the Chorus room even before class had let out so he might get out of there sooner. Jake and Cal continued to do sleepovers on game nights, see movies together, go to the cabin, and ride bikes, but Cal noticed how much quieter his friend had become. When they were alone together, Jake was a lot more tentative, nervous even.

Jake had gotten used to the regularity of his Chorus room companions. He started think of it as a stupid game, trying to guess who would show up that day and then dropping his own pants before someone else did it for him. The seven jocks would take turns, until one day someone new showed up. Herb Steig was a senior on the baseball team, but he was not one of Mike's buddies. He must have heard their whispers in the cafeteria about Jake and decided to try "it" out. The first time, Herb could not get it up, gave up after a few minutes, and shoved Jake hard into the shelves before leaving. The second attempt ended the same way but with a punch to the back of Jake's skull.

On his third try, Herb still failed and lashed out in frustration, pushing Jake against the wall and punching his back, ribs, and head repeatedly. He turned Jake around to give him a knee to the stomach. Jake's pants had been pulled down around his ankles and he was cowering with his hands over his crotch. Protecting his midsection, Jake took a barrage of punches to the face and chest, crying out in pain as his clavicle broke and his nose snapped. Then he felt a stabbing pain in his left eye as blood vessels burst and the retina detached.

Herb jerked Jake around to face the wall again, and Jake felt something wooden hit his backside. Herb had grabbed Mr. Hamment's metronome and was shoving it into Jake's ass. Pressed up against the shelves, Jake was losing his vision quickly from his swollen eyes when his right hand grazed a folding music stand. With Herb distracted by the metronome, Jake was freed up enough to spin around quickly and jab the music stand's pointed end toward Herb's face. It made contact and Jake kept pushing hard. The metal punctured Herb's cheek and shattered one of his molars. He screamed. In that momentary reprieve Jake yanked the metal weapon out of Herb's flesh and used the music stand like a baseball bat, making loud contact with his head and face several times. Jake kept swinging wildly.

Jake could hear Herb's fearful, shocked cries and sensed his hesitation to continue, so he let out with the most guttural scream he had ever made. His ability to project his singing voice to the farthest reaches of large theaters came in handy at that moment, with the sound bouncing around the room, ricocheting down the hallway, and roaring out into the main concourse. Herb fled; Jake fainted. A janitor, Jicard Martinez, had been sweeping up trash from the concourse and heard Jake's scream. He helped Jake to his feet after he revived and pulled up the boy's ripped underwear and corduroy pants. Mr. Martinez half guided and half carried him to the principal's office.

As he limped into the principal's office, Mrs. Klein looked up from her desk and yelled for the nurse. Mrs. Adams urged him to sit on the bench until the nurse came, but she screamed when Jake turned around, revealing the blood-stained seat of his pants. The school nurse, Nancy Marshall, examined Jake's swollen eyes, bloody wounds, broken bones, and horrifying condition. She knew that she could not treat his injuries properly and called for an ambulance to rush him to a hospital.

Jim left work immediately upon getting word from the school and arrived at Baptist Hospital fifteen minutes after Jake got there. A doctor pulled Jim aside to let him know the extent of Jake's injuries. In his assessment, he added, "The rectal trauma might have been worse, had he not already been getting up on this horse for quite a while now." The smart-ass remark did not register with Jim, at first, so he asked the doctor to repeat it. The doctor was less confident in his sense of humor the second time he said it. Jim demanded, "Say that once more." The doctor was now cowed into embarrassed silence by Jim's fury.

Two police officers walked up just as the doctor's feeble attempt at comedy came to an end. Sergeant Ron Bushnell had heard the "horse" comment and said, "So this is a faggot that we're talking about. Probably got what he deserved." Jim never wanted to punch someone as much as he did this police officer. "This is my son. You will not talk about him that way." Betty had been weeding the flower beds in the front yard, so she did not hear the phone ring until the third call. She arrived a half hour after Jim.

The second officer, a towering column of muscle, stepped forward and took charge of the situation. "I'm Officer Rodriguez, and your son was assaulted by someone in his school. The doctor says he's in bad shape. Might I go in and ask him some questions to see if I can find out who did this?" Rodriguez had just three minutes in the room with him until Jake passed out from the sedation. But Rodriguez assured Betty and Jim, "We will look into this. Once we have a name, we can press charges."

Jim said yes, but Betty interrupted, adamantly insisting, "No, that is not going to happen." Since Jake's injuries included one that would be perceived as homosexual, his mother wanted this matter to end right that very minute. Sergeant Bushnell was already disgusted by this situation, so when Betty refused to press charges, there was nothing more for him to do. He simply turned on his heel and walked out. Officer Rodriguez assured Jim, "I'm going to take care of this, so it never happens to him again."

It was the Friday before the start of their spring break, and Jake had planned on going out to the Kulik cabin that weekend. When Zan and Cal arrived to pick up Jake that evening, Jim had to inform them of Jake's assault. Cal was so upset that they skipped the cabin, and Zan drove Cal to the hospital to visit his friend first thing the next morning. Jake was still heavily sedated, so Zan sat in the corner while Cal pulled a chair up to the bed so he could hold Jake's hand. Looking at his battered face, Cal started to cry. "Why would anyone hurt you?"

Officer Rodriguez walked in as Cal rested his forehead on Jake's hand, uncertain if the boy was praying at that moment or willing energy and strength into his injured friend. Lifting his head, Cal smiled through his tears when he saw the uniformed cop standing there. "Are you going to catch the person who did this?"

"I plan on it. Tell me about your friend. I want to hear about your friendship. I want to know all about you guys."

Cal told him about their favorite things to do together, the subjects Jake liked at school, their love of movies, and all the usual things that teenagers like to do, but he left out all the stuff about what they did together in private. He could not exactly tell the truth, because his father was right there in the room. Rodriguez had done enough interrogations to know when information was being withheld. He could see what Cal felt for Jake. He did not press Cal further. Before leaving the room, he came up behind Cal and gave a strong squeeze to his shoulders.

"The doctor says your friend will need to rest for several days but should get better. I know he can feel your love and support. Keep doing it."

Betty explained Jake's absence by saying he was spending his spring break at the cabin with Cal's family. She and Jim went to the hospital each evening after Jim finished up at work. Cal visited for at least two hours every day, until the nurses told him to go home. Officer Rodriguez came to sit with Jake every day as well, eager to question the boy about his attacker. Jake finally woke up on Monday morning, his nose rebroken and reset, his detached retina repaired, his eye patched, and his bruises turning from deepest purple to ugly brown.

Rodriguez was there when he awoke, and he began the process of befriending Jake and earning his trust. At first, Jake swore that he tripped down the stairs, which Rodriguez knew was untrue, because he had interviewed staff at the high school and knew where the janitor had found Jake. Gradually, Jake trusted the cop, telling him more every day but still not revealing his attacker's identity.

Finally on Saturday morning, eight days after the attack, Jake told Rodriguez the entire story, how he had been raped, the rotating roster of his abusers, the newcomer to the group that he did not know. The cop just shook his head in dismay but amazed by Jake's fortitude. The kid had endured six months of rape by eight different classmates, and he never told anyone. Jake did not want to tell Rodriguez even now.

The cop was enormous—six foot seven inches tall, two hundred-fifty pounds of pure muscle, and possessing the largest hands Jake had ever seen. But he was a gentle giant. With his enormous paws, he held Jake's hand, softly caressing the boy's palms as he asked for the names of his attackers. He wanted not just the last guy who beat Jake to a pulp; he wanted to know all of them. He leaned in, so Jake could whisper the names in his ear.

As he stood to leave, Jake stopped the cop who towered over his hospital bed. "Thank you, Officer Rodriguez. You're a very nice man."

"My name is Ricardo, but all my friends call me Rick. You can call me that. Rick, okay? See you soon."

"Okay, see you later, Ranger Rick." The cop thought that was one of the funniest things anyone ever called him. This kid was going to be just fine.

The hospital released Jake on Sunday morning, after a nine-night convalescence. At 11:00 a.m. that morning, Officer Rodriguez paid a visit to the Steig house. The doorbell buzzer went unanswered, so Rick opened the screen to pound on the front door. Eventually, Amelia Steig, Herb's mother, opened the door in a stupor, prepared to curse out whatever jerk was bothering her so early. She bit her tongue when she saw the huge, uniformed police officer standing there. Without invitation, he pushed past her into the dingy living room with the brown and yellow plaid couch and dusty window shears that prevented most sunlight from entering this cave. Amelia already smelled of bourbon and cigarettes, her stench either left over from the previous night or because she had gotten an early start that morning.

Rodriguez looked around, stepping into the dirty kitchen, and peering down the dim hallway leading to the bedrooms. "I need to speak with your son Herb now. Where is he?"

"Out somewhere. How the hell should I know?"

"Well, being such a good mother, I assumed you might know what he is doing. I need to talk to him about Jake Davies."

Amelia started yelling. "That sonofabitch! He hurt my boy. I'm going to press charges and sue his fuckin' family."

Rodriguez smiled at her. "And why would you do that?"

"He stabbed my Herb. He needed twelves stitches. He might lose a couple of teeth too."

Rodriguez ordered her to sit down. She glared at him in defiance, before she hurled her wide ass so forcefully onto the cushions that the couch might have considered pressing charges. "What Jake did was self-defense. It was your son who assaulted him. So Herb got what he deserved."

"That's a goddamn lie. Herb told me what happened."

"Well, ma'am. I'm very sorry to tell you that Herb lied. We have an eyewitness, who has already given a statement to the police. He will testify that he heard Jake scream, ran to the Chorus room, saw your son Herb running away, and found Jake bloodied, bruised, and unconscious."

"You don't know it was Herb."

"There was no one else around. The witness saw your son and discovered the crime scene. Maybe you should look at the photos we took of Jake at the hospital." He spread ten photos out on the coffee table. Amelia recoiled from the images, unwilling to touch them, and not quite believing her son could do this to someone.

"Is the boy okay?"

"He will be, but you will not be filing assault charges against him. If you do, I will be forced to show that it was your son, in fact, who was responsible. In a trial, any jury will put one and one together, and toss out your motion as frivolous and maybe even opportunistic. Your son will then be charged with attempted murder and face a long prison term. Are we clear here?"

Afterwards, the cop visited the Davies house to check on Jake and talk with his parents. He sat in the living room with Jim and Betty, while Jake lay on the couch with damp tea bags over his eyes to help reduce the swelling. Jim and Betty were concerned about their son going back to school too soon, but Rodriguez thought it crucial that Jake let the other students know that he was not going to be a victim. Together, they hatched a plan for the next day so Jake could move past this traumatic experience.

18

Transit

> "The temporary dimming of starlight, due to debris from a supernova or collision passing in front of a star, blocking some of its light magnitude."

As promised, Rodriguez met Jake in Bon Air's principal's office at 7:30 a.m. on Monday morning. Jake wore loose-fitting painter's pants and a turtleneck to cover up most of his injuries, although he still had traces of the bruises of two black eyes. The two of them talked about what they were going to do and how it was going to happen. As homeroom started, Mrs. Klein started the day's announcements over the intercom with a special message crafted by the officer. "Students, we have a special guest in school today. Please welcome Louisville Police Officer Rick Rodriguez, who will be promoting school safety."

Ranger Rick put a reassuring hand on Jake's back and gave him a smile. "Remember what we talked about. Be calm and be brave. I will be right there with you." With that, Rodriguez and Jake walked to his homeroom. Jake knew to step into the classroom and stand aside so the hulking Rodriguez could step into view. It had the desired effect as his height and build filled the doorway, blocking any exit. The officer asked Jake in a voice that everyone could hear, "Which one?" Without dramatics, Jake looked to the left side of the room and answered, "Blond hair, dark blue shirt, back row."

Officer Rodriguez pushed through the narrow space between desks, went up to Mike Crumpler, grabbed his shirt, and yanked him hard to his feet, dragging him into the hallway. Jake followed. His teacher knew about the plan and did not interfere; the students were stunned into silence. With his right hand positioned threateningly but carefully around Mike's throat, Rodriguez slammed him into a locker and leaned down, so they were nose-to-nose.

"I know what you did, asshole. If you ever say another mean thing to this young man, ever let anyone else harass him, ever touch him again, ever threaten him, ever hurt him, I will come after you. I will break you. Think of me as his personal bodyguard. Do you understand me?" Mike nodded furiously, and he was so terrified that tears poured from his eyes. Rodriguez did not allow him time to recover, pulling him back into the class in front of everyone else, and pushing him down hard into his desk chair. He then stood by the teacher, smiled, and addressed everyone, "Be kind to your fellow students," before walking out.

Officer Rick and Jake went down the list of names. At the start of first period, they went to Mrs. Friedlach's Algebra class and repeated the same intimidation tactics first on Frank Adair, then Matt Brown. In second period Gym class, Rodriguez strode onto the basketball court and confronted Bruce Mitchell. The other basketball players just stood and stared at the massive cop until he turned to them and said, "Go away." They turned tail and ran.

The cop and the kid did another twofer, pulling both Kevin Badesch and Bobby Nevin out of Mr. Haddon's third period

Geometry at the same time. Kevin was terrified, not so much at Rick's imposing stature, but rather knowing everyone would be talking about this and wondering why he was being singled out. Bobby burst into tears, partly out of fear but mostly grief, knowing that he had betrayed his friend Jake. By fourth period History class, Dave Hindman was expecting the worst. As Officer Rodriguez strode up to him, Dave peed his pants before he even got out of his chair, a fact the cop made sure to point out to the class.

By lunch break, gossip had spread through the school. Every single student knew about the police officer pulling guys out of classes, but no one knew the reason why. It's not like the rapists were going to tell all their friends about what they had done, or brag about it even amongst themselves. That was the beauty of Rick's plan for Jake. Good old-fashioned teenage embarrassment would prevent a lot of this from continuing or ever happening again. It was a campaign of shame that Jake could in turn use to his advantage.

Rodriguez and Jake marched into the cafeteria, with identical sack lunches and sat on a bench to eat. The lunchroom went silent as a funeral parlor as everyone stared and waited to see what would happen next. They chatted amiably, took their time eating, threw their trash away, and then walked right over to Herb Steig. The senior had nearly killed Jake, but Jake fought back so Herb was now permanently disfigured with an ugly deep dent in his left cheek. Rodriguez taunted the gangly, pockmarked Herb, "Hey, nice scar. Get up, asshole, and come with me." Steig thought he would play it tough and told the cop, "Fuck off. You don't scare me."

Rodriguez grabbed Herb's hair, shoved his head down for a quick smack against the table and into his lunch, and in one swift move yanked him from the bench, off his feet, and up against the wall. In full view of everyone, the cop subdued Herb with a strong hand on his neck and the other arm flattening him to the wall. Rodriguez whispered the same warning that he gave to the other seven, but he made one more promise. "If anything ever happens to Jake, and I mean, ever, then I will know it was you. I will make sure you go to prison where everyone will do to you what you tried to do to him." Now, Herb was terrified.

Cal was seated at the next table with Brent and watched all of this. He wondered how this would help Jake, who was now put more in the spotlight by the cop's bravado. How would he cope when the cop was not there? How would the students treat him? He had his answer the next day, when Jake confidently walked into the cafeteria to eat lunch, something he never did. Everyone scattered to get away from him, so he had an entire lunch table to himself. He went from being the artsy, musical-loving, dancing, singing, flute-playing outcast to being a pariah. At least for that one day. That was okay with Jake.

The only complication came not from Mike, Kevin, Bruce, Matt, Frank, Dave, Bobby, or Herb but from their girlfriends, who had been left in the dark about why a cop might be interrogating them. Rich-girl Denise and cheerleader Jane were so unrelenting in their demand for answers that they started calling their boyfriends Mike and Kevin babies for suddenly becoming so timid. The girls took up taunting Jake, which terrified their boyfriends since they assumed they would be the ones to suffer the consequences of the girls' actions. But since they also could not be honest with them, Kevin and Mike had no choice but to break up with them. The girlfriends moved on quickly, gave up harassing Jake, and found other targets to abuse, malign, and belittle.

The eight rapists had been put on notice by Officer Rodriguez, so no one could say a word to Jake. A few redirected their frustration toward Cal, although it was mostly venting. Between classes, Jake was taking books out of his locker when he overheard someone giving Cal a hard time. It was Herb, who poked Cal in the chest and said, "Don't bother wasting your time on that fairy," pointing in Jake's direction. Having once been rescued by Cal from a bully, it was now time for Jake to return the favor.

Jake slammed his locker loudly and rushed over, stepping within inches of Herb. He was no longer afraid. "Oh, since I'm off limits, you're going to beat up my friend now?" Herb wanted to punch Jake in the face so badly but knew he could not. Jake knew it too, so he yelled loud enough for everyone in the hallway to hear, "Everyone is going to find out what you did to me." It was like Jake turned off a switch. Herb's macho stance melted away and he seemed to shrink in size, remembering Officer Rodriguez's warning.

At lunch, it was Frank Adair's turn to show he had not yet learned his lesson. When Jake sat down at a table across from Cal, Frank started fuming. "Goddamnit, this twerp again. Why does this faggot have to sit with us?" Jake got up, walked around the table, and squeezed in next to Frank. He did not say anything; he just leaned close into Frank's face and stared. Frank became so uncomfortable that he got up from the table, tossed his lunch in the trash, and left the cafeteria.

As they walked to their fifth period Biology class, Cal was upset. "You know, you don't have to protect me. I can take care of myself."

"I know. I just want to make sure that those guys remember they can't do that stuff anymore. I'm not afraid of them, but I want them to be afraid of me."

"Just don't be a jerk about it. You could wind up being as much of a bully as they are." Cal walked ahead and did not speak to Jake for the rest of the day. The next day, Bobby, Jake's former drama club friend who participated in the rapes, cautioned Cal that everyone was now spooked by Jake and warned that feeling might spill over to him. It put Cal in the awkward spot of defending Jake while still acting like he could not care less. Cal dismissed Bobby's concern with, "He's nobody to me." Cal was unaware that Jake was ten feet away and heard their conversation.

Jake wondered if he was perhaps becoming a liability for Cal, so he decided to back off a bit to let him hang out more with his other friends. The rapes and the assault had affected Cal almost as much as it did Jake. Cal ached for his best friend, but he did not know how to handle this kind of attention. No one said anything nasty to him about their friendship, but Cal felt it was just a matter of time before someone figured out what they meant to one another. Cal did not know what to do, so he did nothing. Jake realized it was self-preservation, but Cal's response, or lack of one, hurt him.

Officer Rodriguez popped into Bon Air High School whenever he could, which was once every week or so. He made sure he was seen by students at the principal's office, in the hallways, in the cafeteria, checking in with Jake. He even sought out Mike, Kevin, Bruce, Frank, Matt, Dave, Bobby, and Herb to remind them of what they had done and his warning to them. It had the desired effect in sending the message that Jake was now and forever off limits. Jake could finally relax a little bit. Cal, on the other hand, felt more unnerved.

After nearly a week of getting the cold shoulder from Cal, it was Mr. Braddock's weeklong Humanities discussion of Religions of the World that got the two of them talking again. Cal had always been something of a nerd, loving arcane facts and trivia that most classmates thought boring or unimportant. Once, hanging out by their lockers and killing time with a few other students before the school day began, Cal had been excited to share something he had read in the library. The girls could not care less, rolled their eyes, and then started laughing at him, effectively drowning him out. Jake could see Cal was hurt, so he whispered, "Tell me later, okay?"

Cal did not throw his superior knowledge in other people's faces; he just got excited about things that held no interest for anyone else. Braddock's Humanities series covered all religions so that no one would feel left out yet did not spend too much time on any one of them in case parents worried the class was proselytizing to their children. Braddock talked at length about the so-called Big Five religions of Christianity, Judaism, Islam, Buddhism, and Hinduism, while also bringing in discussion of Taoism, Shintoism, Mormonism, and alternative belief systems.

It was Braddock's final lecture of the series on how astrology touched upon religious beliefs and yet became the foundation of the science of astronomy that fascinated Cal. Braddock waxed poetic about Babylonian, Greek, Egyptian, and Phoenician cultures and how they looked to the stars and planets to find meaning and purpose to life's chaos. The concepts of vast distances across space, constellations depicting zodiac signs or mythological figures, and the universe's constant cycle of birth, death, and rebirth were all heady topics that nearly made other students' heads explode. Cal, however, lived for this stuff, and he knew the only other person who would share even a modicum of interest would be Jake.

At the end of class, Cal ran up to Jake and started talking about the Egyptians' notion that solar boats traveled between the heavens and the underworld. In Egyptian mythology, the sun god Ra brought light to the world traveling on his solar barque named Mandjet, which translated as "the Boat of a Million Years." He loved the concept that consciousness did not end with death but continued into the afterlife. Jake was intrigued that the Pharaohs' builders likely designed the pyramids of Giza along the axis of certain constellations. Cal was so smart that he never simply repeated the facts he had heard or learned. Those ideas inspired flights of fancy, talking about concepts, beliefs, all the possibilities of the universe. Jake was the only one to play along with him.

Cal was a sensitive soul. They both were, and that was a huge part of the bond between them. Most high school interactions were superficial, based on the commonality of experience rather than a unique perspective. Jake was a walking encyclopedia of movie and musical comedy information, about which no one else cared. Cal wanted to talk about history, science, and nature, topics that bored most everyone else, and people tuned him out. Jake did not, so Cal felt validated by the attention paid to him. Cal inspired Jake to ponder ideas more deeply, rather than simply reciting movie trivia, and Jake helped Cal to be a little less serious. They broadened each other's perspectives.

The fear, grief, tension, and conflict of the past few weeks set aside, they needed to be alone together at the cabin that weekend. Dangling their legs over the porch, they were content to just sit and stargaze, not needing to talk but also wanting to make sure there were no hard feelings from the past week. The silence lasted just long enough to become awkward, until Cal dove right in.

"I keep thinking about Mr. Braddock's religions class this week. He told us so much that I didn't know before."

"My family doesn't go to church, so I'm not much into religion." Jake's comment almost stopped the conversation dead in its tracks.

"My family stopped going a few years ago, so I could care less. But Braddock helped me understand that a belief system often comes from both the culture and the time in which it started. I never thought of that. I always thought it was like some law that people just followed."

"I guess people just accept what they are told and don't question stuff. Have you ever noticed at church that everybody has this same stupid look on their faces? It's like smiling for a photographer, but no one's taking a picture."

Cal laughed. "Yeah, it does seem pretty mindless. Maybe they think God is watching, and they must show how much they love being there, so they can get into heaven."

Jake hesitated before revealing, "I don't believe in God anymore. I guess that means no heaven for me."

Cal moved closer so there was no space between them. He reached out to hold Jake's hand. "Why would you think you don't deserve heaven?"

"The God thing. Everyone thinks God and heaven go together. Since I don't believe in that, I guess it can't happen for me."

"What do you believe in, then?" Cal looked at his friend, hoping Jake would say something profound that he too could grasp.

"I'm not sure. I try not to think of it. I knew this kid, Dylan, who died when we were seven. He had diabetes. He seemed okay and then one day he just wasn't there anymore. He was gone. If there is a God, why would he allow that to happen? Why are we alive if it all just ends one day? Dying scares me. If you die, everyone thinks you go to heaven, but what happens if you don't believe?"

Cal agreed with Jake. "I'm not sure I believe in God, either. I sure don't believe we are going to float on clouds for all eternity. I like to think of Heaven as a place we get to create, someplace safe, someplace beautiful, where we get to reunite with the ones who loved us the most. When I die, I want to wake up on a deserted tropical island, where I can just be myself and do what I want. That's my idea of heaven."

Jake could see that kind of island in his mind. "That sounds very nice, as long as the sun is not so hot."

Cal chuckled because he knew how much Jake disliked heat and humidity. "In heaven, the weather can be perfect, just the way you like it. What's your idea of heaven, then, minus God?"

Jake pondered this for a moment. "This place. I love it here—the cabin, the woods, the stream, the quiet, you. I could be here with you forever. Second choice would be a grassy meadow in a mountain valley by a lake."

"Oh, that's good too. Wouldn't it be cool to sail off on the Egyptians' solar boats? I imagine a place where the sun goes down and the stars are coming out. The sea would merge with the sky, and you wouldn't know if you were sailing through one or the other. I think it would be heaven for us to sail away to someplace like that."

"You do remember that I still can't swim, right?"

19

Spectrum

"A condition that is not limited to a specific set of values but can vary, without gaps, across a continuum, such as the rainbow of colors in visible light after passing through a prism."

The school year was fast ending, which meant the annual frenzy of girls looking for dates to the senior prom. Half the senior class was already coupled as girlfriends and boyfriends, while the other half reluctantly paired up with the least objectionable date left over from the slim pickings. The girls outnumbered the boys by a slight margin, so the few remaining wallflowers had no choice but to look to the boys, who were juniors, as their last-ditch candidates to go with them to the prom.

Mary, Susan, Beth, and Laura were all seniors. They swarmed around good-looking, energetic, charming junior Cal, like a bask of crocodiles waiting for an unsuspecting bird to land upon the surface of their swamp. They were so desperate to not be left out of this rite of passage that they zeroed in for the kill. Beth tried being coy with "I was wondering what you might be doing on Friday, May 23." Without waiting for Cal's response, Mary dove in with "Has anyone asked you to the prom?" Laura was a little more direct but made a statement rather than asking him a question with "I still don't have a date."

Susan saw how poorly her friends had fared, so she blurted out, "Cal, please go to the prom with me, so I don't look pathetic." Cal accepted nonchalantly like it was no big deal, but Susan was as elated as if she had won a beauty pageant or a million dollars. Beth and Mary had to blackmail their brothers into going with them. Laura set her sights on Jake, a less desirable choice since everyone in school assumed he was a fag. Laura had a deeper voice than most of the boys, dressed like a mechanic, and walked like a linebacker, so there was nothing romantic about this temporary alliance. She did not give Jake a chance to turn her down. "I need a date to prom. You're going with me."

Jake wore a baby blue polyester tux with navy-tinted ruffled shirt and a clip-on bowtie larger than a paperback novel. Cal rented a burgundy crushed-velvet tuxedo with pleated shirt, fake diamond studs, and a floppy black bowtie. Not much dancing happened unless the girls dragged their unwilling dates onto the floor. But once the deejay started "The Hustle," which had begun its radio play only a month earlier, the dance floor filled. It was sheer chaos, with no set steps for anyone to follow and a lot of crashing into one another as everyone tried to do the five-step shuffle in every direction across the floor. Cal and Susan bumped into Jake and Laura just as the song came to an end.

As the final chord faded out, the deejay announced, "Next up is a romantic oldie, so fellas grab your girl and slow dance." No matter that it was Don McLean's "Vincent," a song about the artist Van Gogh's depression and suicide. It had a gentle guitar and McLean's plaintive singing voice, so everyone assumed it was a love song. Every girl's head dropped to her date's shoulder at precisely the exact same moment. Cal and

Jake often harmonized on this song, and they found themselves facing each other as they did a slow step-touch, step-touch side to side.

The lyrics were not sappy sentiment, but most people never actually paid attention to the words. Cal and Jake knew the lyrics, which painted imagery of the impermanence of nature's vibrant colors, expansive landscapes, and specific times of day. For them, the song was beautiful and sad, acknowledging that not everything is as it seems on the surface. It spoke not of love so much as it did the messy consequences of loving something, or someone, so much that it hurts. It was their story, their song.

For nearly four blissful minutes on that starry, starry night, the two boys lost themselves dancing together, but unable to touch, oblivious to the girls between them. Tears flowed as they looked fondly at one another and mouthed the words "for one as beautiful as you." The song ended, and they abruptly left their partners on the dance floor and bolted to opposite sides of the gymnasium so each could find a private spot to hide their emotions from anyone else.

Cal got an offer from Rada Bondarenko to return to Chicago and work for his kids' sports camp for the summer again; he turned it down. Brent invited him to spend a month canoeing in Alabama; Cal said no. His prom partner Susan wanted the two of them to date for real and kept asking him out; he turned her down repeatedly though always gently. Since Jake had had such a rough spring with the assault and his hospitalization, Cal did not want to leave his best friend again. Jake was elated that Cal was staying in Louisville, just for him. Jake opted not to do the community theater's summer musical as a result.

Cal continued teaching gymnastics with Coach Williams on weekday mornings, followed by giving afternoon swim lessons at the Jewish Community Center pool. Jake was mowing lawns in the mornings and selling his newspapers in the afternoons. Cal learned the Showcase Cinemas on Bardstown Road were hiring movie ushers for the summer, and they decided they could earn extra spending money doing something that indulged one of their favorite pastimes. They filled out job applications together and both got hired to work five nights a week.

When the theaters opened in 1965, there were just two theaters, each seating two thousand people, one of the earlier examples of giving moviegoers more than one choice. A third theater opened in 1968, and the owners added a fourth in 1970. These auditoriums had double aisles separating three sections and an ocean of red velvet curtains that dropped from the ceiling to the floor, seemingly going on for miles. In 1973, a large building with six smaller movie theaters opened, creating Louisville's first multiplex.

The ushers had to wear royal blue uniforms, with navy and gold epaulets, and a matching pillbox hat that strapped under the chin. The theater manager insisted that the ushers had to wear the hat at a jaunty angle. Cal thought they looked like dorky bellhops; Jake thought that they looked cute, and royal blue was his favorite color. Fortunately, the hats did not last long. It was summer and the ushers had to go outside to move between the theaters, and the felt-covered cardboard hats quickly fell apart in the Louisville humidity.

Cal preferred comedies, and he got to work the theaters showing *The Return of the Pink Panther*, *Monty Python and the Holy Grail*, and *The Apple Dumpling Gang*; they made him laugh at the slapstick, although the last one was more aimed at kids. Jake preferred the musicals, and he always requested to be in the theaters showing the rock opera *Tommy* or Barbra Streisand in *Funny Lady*. Even though they were not yet seventeen, they also got to see the R-rated *Shampoo* and *Rollerball*, which had opened late in Louisville and were still drawing modest audiences to the smallest theaters at the multiplex.

Then there was this little movie called *Jaws*, which opened on Friday, June 20. It was the first time that any movie had opened in so many theaters at once around the country, so the filmmakers obviously thought that they had something special. The Showcase Cinemas, though, felt that it was nothing more than a horror movie. They dumped it into Cinema Seven, which seated only two hundred people. The first weekend, that theater was full, and word spread quickly about this terrifying movie. The second weekend saw lines of people snaking around the theater promenade into the parking lot and several blocks down Bardstown Road. The Showcase quickly moved *Jaws* into Cinema One with its two thousand seat capacity. It became the monster movie hit of the summer.

Cal loved the movie, but Jake found the mysteries of the ocean truly terrifying, because he was still a lousy swimmer. Cal and Jake would hang out before and after their shifts, but Cal always requested to usher for *Jaws*, while Jake preferred the less dangerous pleasures of *Funny Lady*. Both saw their favorite film probably fifty times apiece that summer. Occasionally, Cal would sneak out of the auditorium once the movie had started and head over to the cinema where Jake was working. At the back of the theater, Jake was mouthing the words to the songs and dancing along. Cal snuck up on him, humming "baaaa . . . dum . . . baaaa . . . dum . . . bum bum bum bum bum bum bum bum . . . ba da baaaaah" and throwing his arms around Jake, who screamed during one of Streisand's quieter solos.

When they had started high school nearly three years earlier, Jake and Cal were small for their age, with Jake just a smidge above five foot tall, and Cal measuring five-foot-one. They grew in small increments, but Cal always looked taller with several inches of dark curls piled on top of his head. This summer, Jake shot up past Cal, with a growth spurt that added four inches to his height. He now stood five-foot-eight to Cal's five-foot-six, but Jake was annoyed that Cal's mop of hair still made him look taller.

Along with the added height, Jake's voice finally cracked and dropped a full octave in just a few short weeks. Cal had started to sing Cat Stevens's "Morning Has Broken," a song they both loved, but Jake could not find his pitch. He felt like everything he had ever known about how to sing suddenly vanished. Jake had never felt like a natural singer, so he always had to concentrate hard when harmonizing, while Cal made it look and sound easy. Now, he felt like he was tone deaf and would never be able to sing again.

Cal calmed him down and convinced him that the notes had not changed, nor had his ability to sing them. Jake had to simply get used to his new vocal register. So, they sang together more than they ever had before to give Jake the practice and confidence he needed. They sang quietly outside the theaters once the movies had begun. They sang while they rode their bikes around town. They climbed trees in the park and sang while precariously perched sixty feet off the ground. They sang while dangling their legs off the porch at the cabin or while skinny-dipping in the swimming hole.

Cal was a high baritone, or a bari-tenor, with a deeper resonance to his voice and the ability to still sing high notes. Jake was no longer a boy soprano and started to feel more and more comfortable now being a high tenor. Cal assured him, "We still make beautiful music together," and then deliberately sang flat to throw Jake off his harmonies. Jake punched his arm, and they giggled like idiots.

Since Cal was already teaching kids how to swim at the JCC pool, the center asked him to take lifeguard training and get his certification. Cal was like a fish in water, so it was easier for him than most candidates. He had to swim three hundred yards continuously using the breaststroke or front crawl, and tread water for two minutes using only his legs. The most difficult task was to complete a timed event within one minute and forty seconds that included swimming twenty yards, diving ten feet to retrieve a ten-pound object, return to the surface to swim twenty yards back to the starting point, and then exit the water without using a ladder or steps.

Most candidates had to train extensively to pass the certification process, but Cal looked at the requirements and knew he could do it right then and there. He passed on his first try. The pool managers were amazed because no one had ever done that before, and they agreed to let Cal become a lifeguard if he promised to get training in CPR. Cal studied for a week, went to four required classes quickly, and passed this test on his first try as well. He was a lifeguard the following week. The primary perk was that he had unlimited guest passes to give Jake so he could use the JCC pool.

Jake rode his bike over to the pool whenever Cal was working. Once his two-hour shift was over, Cal had a half-hour break in his rotation. He spotted Jake's blond hair when he walked into the pool area, so he knew where to find him. Jake still did not swim, but he knew how to float because of Cal, so he would just dog paddle into the deep end, roll over, and float all afternoon. Cal dove into the water and swam underneath Jake, grabbing his waist and scaring the hell out of him. Both had seen *Jaws* one too many times that summer.

Cal rolled over on his back and floated alongside Jake, linking pinkies as they always did so they would not drift apart. No one could see how they were linked; all anyone would see was two bodies innocently meeting in the center of the pool. Cal seemed to be nervous. "Hey, can we talk about something important?"

Jake had hopes about what that could be. "Okay, shoot."

"I met this girl." He paused, waiting for Jake's response. Jake said nothing, so Cal continued cautiously. "Her name is Nicole. I guess you could say she's my girlfriend."

Jake did a quick calculation in his head. Cal taught gymnastics and swimming, was a lifeguard, worked as a movie usher, and they spent all their free time together. He had to ask, "Jeez, when did you have time to find a girlfriend?"

"I met her at the pool. She's a lifeguard too. In fact, she's over there on the tower right now."

Jake immediately dropped his feet to tread water so he could look at this new adversary. What he saw was a perky girl who was just a little too confident in her blandly manufactured appearance and her rarified position in the world, lording it over all the other peons below her in the pool. "She has an awful lot of Aqua Net in her hair. She's going to be upset if she ever has to get her head wet and actually rescue someone."

"Don't be mean. She's a nice girl. You would like her."

"No, I would not. She seems fake."

Cal ignored the insults. "I want you to meet her. My birthday is next week, so my family is going to the cabin on Friday to celebrate. Come with us. You and I can stay once everybody goes home."

"What about Nicole? Won't she be staying with you from now on?"

"No, she has to work the next morning, and my parents are busy. So, we will have the place to ourselves again."

Jake agreed to go reluctantly, and it was as he feared. For six hours, Jake spent most of the day by himself, wandering around the cabin, sitting on the porch, walking through the woods, and lounging by the swimming hole. Cal's parents, Zan and Leigh, were too busy playing host. Jake did not know Cal's brothers or sister at all. Cal was preoccupied either flirting with Nicole or fending off her aggressive advances, Jake was not sure which. Jake had this weird emotional response, feeling both jealous and seriously confused. Did Cal suddenly like girls now? That did not stop them from messing around as usual as soon as the family and Nicole left.

Left alone, it was like the day had never happened. They went to the bedroom instead of the loft, but before Jake could start giving Cal his customary blow job, Cal did it on him for the first time ever. He had obviously been paying attention to Jake's technique all the time because he proved to be surprisingly adept at it. Jake held off for as long as he could, but eventually he exploded in Cal's mouth. Cal smiled as he went into the bathroom, where Jake heard him spitting into the sink, followed by gargling with mouthwash.

As Cal climbed back into bed with another broad smile on his smile, Jake nonchalantly said, "P-tooey." Cal burst out laughing and fell on top of Jake. They roared for a good ten minutes until Jake gave Cal the most intense blow job of his life. Cal was so turned on that an hour later he gave Jake another one, taking Jake's erect penis out of his mouth mere seconds before he blew his load. The stream trajectory was several feet, and Jake accidentally ejaculated straight into his own right eye, which was bloodshot for several days afterward.

Over the next two weeks, Jake kept thinking about Cal and his "girlfriend" Nicole. Was he trying on the idea of having a girlfriend to see if it fit him? Was it wishful thinking? It made no sense to Jake, and the more he thought about it, he was convinced it was not possible. Cal was always so busy. When would he have time for a girlfriend? Was Cal lying to him? Jake wondered if Cal had mentioned a girlfriend to see how he would react. If he had reacted worse than just being snide, would Cal have ended the friendship?

The situation was frustrating. Jake did not know what Cal wanted. It made him think there was something wrong with him, something lacking. He needed to feel that someone wanted him, so Jake started going to the cruising area behind the Collings Estate again. In his first week back after several months, the police raided the wooded area again, but Jake was more vigilant this time. The cops had kept their sirens off until the last possible minute, but they jumped the gun and turned them on before they had entered the woods. Jake only had to pull up his pants, leap out of the car, and run. Officer Rodriguez was part of the police detail and happened to glimpse a blond-haired figure dashing into the bushes.

Rick trotted down the trail and pushed into the underbrush. "Jake, where are you? Come here, please." Jake held his breath, wondering how this cop knew his name. "Jake, it's me,

Ranger Rick. I saw you, so I know you're in here. Please come out." Sheepishly, Jake stood up and walked toward Rick, keeping his head down. Rick gently lifted Jake's chin so he would look into his eyes. "Hey, you got taller. What are you doing here, buddy?"

"I come here sometimes."

"Jake, it's not safe to do that. You could get hurt."

"Yeah, my dad says the same thing."

"Well, your dad's a smart man. You should listen to him."

"Dad doesn't know what I'm going through. He doesn't know how I feel. He's not like me."

Rick smiled down at him. "Well, I am like you, so I do understand." He let that sink in for a moment. "I was just like you. Wanting to explore, curious about my body, men, sex. But you need to understand this could be dangerous. You might get in a car with the wrong guy one day. How old are you now, Jake?"

"I just turned seventeen."

"Age of consent is sixteen here in Kentucky, but seventeen makes you an adult in the eyes of the law. You could be arrested and charged with a crime."

"Wait. What crime?"

"Solicitation, male prostitution. You could be arrested just for being a homosexual." Jake instantly denied that he was. He had never even considered that he was, even though he had been taunted to that effect for years now. Oh hell, he did not know what he was. He was still trying to figure that out. "Jake, what I'm trying to tell you is that you can't let anyone know. You must be careful and hide that part of yourself away."

"That is so unfair."

"It is, but that's just the way of the world. You must go along with it."

The whole conversation took less than three minutes, during which Rick held onto Jake's shoulders. Jake put his hands on Rick's large biceps to cop a feel. He smiled up at Rick.

"Did I tell you it was my birthday?"

"Really, Jake? You are impossible. Come back and find me, maybe, when you're a grown-up. Now get out of here, and don't come back. I won't always be able to protect you."

He kept watch as Jake pulled his bike from the bushes and darted off in the opposite direction of the police raid. Riding home, it suddenly occurred to Jake that maybe this was the problem between him and Cal. He was careless, reckless even. Cal was simply trying to keep that part of himself private, to hide himself away.

20

Perigee

"The point in the orbit of the Moon or other satellite where it is closest to the Earth."

With the start of the school year looming, attendance at the pool dipped, so Cal's job as a lifeguard came to an end. The huge numbers of moviegoers plummeted, so their summer jobs as movie ushers finished on Labor Day as well. Jake did a quick inventory before his first class and felt relieved that he would not have to contend with most of his rapists anymore. Juniors Matt Brown and Frank Adair had moved away over the summer. Mike Crumpler and pants-wetter Dave Hindman were so chastened by Officer Rodriguez's warning that they turned heel and ran whenever they saw Jake coming in their direction.

Seniors Kevin Badesch and Bruce Mitchell graduated in May and could go through the rest of their lives pretending that some kid named Jake Davies never existed. The other two did not survive the summer. Herb Steig spent most of his time getting drunk at friends' houses and ended up wrapping his mother's car, and himself, around a telephone pole. Bobby Nevin could never get over the guilt he felt for hurting Jake, with whom he had been friendly in drama club and on speech team. Bobby took his father's gun and put a bullet in his brain.

Jake and Cal only had two classes together as they started their senior year, and Cal made the decision to not be in the marching band. He planned on graduating a few months early so he could embark on a kayak trip in April, so he had to focus on those classes that completed his academic requirements. Cal invited Jake to still spend Friday nights at his house after the football games as he always did, but he neglected to remind his parents. On the night of the first at-home game, Jake showed up at the Kulik house only to discover that Cal was out on a date with Nicole. Zan let Jake come in, but it was awkward having him hang around the house for a couple hours waiting for Cal's return.

After the following game, Jake hung outside Cal's house in the dark waiting to make sure he was home. He did not return from that week's date night until almost midnight. The next morning over breakfast, Zan announced, "You guys are getting a little old for sleepovers. I don't think this arrangement is going to work anymore." This was not a discussion; it was a decision. Cal agreed to switch his date night with Nicole to Saturdays, so he and Jake could still go to the cabin most Friday nights whenever Jake did not have a football game.

Jake felt like the universe was trying to separate the two of them, but Cal made up for the reduced time together by making nightly phone calls. They talked about everything and nothing—the day's classes, movies, news, trivia, ideas that intrigued them, their hopes for the future. They rarely talked about their feelings. One evening, Jake had been talking to Cal so long that Betty bellowed up the stairs, "Jake, get off the goddamn phone." Even Cal's mother Leigh became annoyed at how much he hogged the phone. It felt like they spent almost no time together anymore, but the phone chats were better than nothing,

The fall semester flew by, and Jake hoped that he and Cal might have some time alone over Christmas break, but Cal had already made other plans. At least he had the decency to tell Jake over the phone this time, instead of simply vanishing as he usually did. Cal's intention for his springtime kayak adventure was to travel the length of the Fraser River in British Columbia. He was looking for a partner to do the trip with, but he was willing to go it alone if he could not find a fellow kayaker to do it with him.

"But why won't you be here for Christmas?"

Cal said that he needed to train as much as he could. "I will be kayaking every day, all day on Cumberland Lake to get ready."

"Damn, the water is going to be so cold in December."

"It will be even colder in Canada in April, so that's part of the training."

Cal did call Jake from a pay phone while he was in Cumberland a few times, including on Christmas Day. Jake was elated that they had the chance to wish each other Merry Christmas, despite not spending it together, but then they never had. Returning to school, Jake got another disappointment when Cal revealed he would be there only occasionally. He was not taking any classes, but rather doing extensive testing and writing papers to complete his course work so he could graduate early. Jake had always thought they would get to complete high school together, but Cal finished up by March 10, 1976.

Jake got his neighborhood pal Noah to cover his newspaper corner, so he and Cal could spend the entire weekend together at the cabin. It was a somber occasion for both. They engaged in small talk and never got into personal topics. Hiking through the woods, they did not sing or laugh; they walked along silently. Even stargazing was superficial, not sparking their usual conjecture or comic banter, but rather a scientific lecture from Cal about a certain constellation.

Jake could not take it. "Omigod, please stop talking. You're just babbling about nothing."

"Well, I'm sorry I'm boring you."

"You are not boring me, but you are being strange. You are not the same. It's like you have forgotten how to just be yourself around me. What's going on?"

"I know you're upset I'm leaving early. I didn't want to get all heavy and serious on you."

"Oh, please. Get as heavy as you want because you couldn't make me any unhappier than I am already. Just talk to me."

"What do you want me to say?"

"How about 'thanks for being my friend'? How about 'I'll miss you'? Something like that would be nice, but only if that's true for you."

"Of course, it's true. You act as though I'm going away forever."

"Feels like it. This trip sounds dangerous, kayaking in the middle of nowhere. I'm afraid you won't make it back."

Cal reassured him, "I always make it, and I will come back. And until I do, you only have to look up."

"That again. It was a sweet, romantic notion when we were kids. Now that looking-up-at-the-moon thing just feels like another barrier between us."

"It's not a barrier. It's our connection, and I do look up and think about you doing the same thing."

"Well, that's nice, but it feels to me like you are running away again. Always running from me. I wish I knew why because it makes me feel like crap. And you always seem sad when we are together now."

"I'm happy with you, but I'm scared."

"Of what? Of me?"

"Someone finding out about us."

Jake stared at him, until Cal looked his way. "Find out what? What is this thing about us?"

Cal could not or would not give him an answer. Maybe he did not know. Jake was not even sure he knew. They spent the rest of their evening silently looking at the stars, their positions shifting across the night sky almost as quickly as their swirl of emotions.

Cal found a kayak partner by calling some boating clubs and sports groups. Kurt Trent was a thirty-year-old dentist who wanted to try something different and took a break from work. Kurt was a seasoned kayaker, so he would be an equal partner to Cal in terms of strength and endurance. They talked at length on the phone about supplies, provisions, and equipment, and made their plan. They spent two weeks kayaking together in southern Indiana and on the Ohio River to train. Once the details were all in place, they flew to Vancouver and took a charter to the small city of Prince George. It was easier and cheaper to buy kayaks there.

They set out on April 15, kayaking every day for more than a month, but the planned route was fraught with mistakes and peril. Melting snow from the Canadian Rockies caused flooding in some areas, and they had to rely on Kurt's fishing and Cal's hunting skills for their food since towns were too far away. Many days they simply went without dinner. When they reached Vancouver, Kurt was content to have survived and announced he was done. Cal continued by himself, exploring the inlets and islands just north of Vancouver for another month.

Cal promised to write Jake and post letters whenever he got to civilization, and Jake did receive two letters. In both, Cal relayed how much he loved roaming the wilderness, but he spent days gliding on a wide stream through a dense forest, alone with his thoughts and desperate for company. In the second letter he wrote, "There is such beauty here in every tree, rock, and ripple of water. It is profound and humbling. It is so quiet here that I try to embrace it as part of the world's natural order, but the stillness sometimes makes me want to scream. When I get like that, I sing one of our songs. I keep expecting to hear your voice singing harmony with me. I am alone here. I love it and I hate it."

As a senior, Jake finally got a chance to be in the senior musical. In previous years, he had played the flute in the orchestras for *The Boyfriend*, *Bye Bye Birdie*, and *How to Succeed in Business Without Really Trying*. Bon Air High School had a new drama teacher that year, and she did not know what she was doing. Instead of picking a classic musical, she chose the cheapest show in the copyright catalogue. The show was *Rock N Roll*, a knockoff of *Grease* with none of that show's wit, fun songs, raunch, or energy. Jake got cast as one of the two male leads, the lovable kook prone to getting into trouble and making a fool of himself.

It was hardly great art, but Jake had a blast. His character had most of the jokes in the show, got to belt out the four biggest musical numbers, and dance the jitterbug. He also had to kiss the girl who played his girlfriend in the show, which Jake was sure would prove his skill as an actor. In the chorus was Joslyn LaPorte, who went by just Jos. She became Jake's gal pal, and they hung out together during Cal's absence. Billy Keller worked backstage crew on the show, just as he had on all the musicals Jake did with the community theater.

Jos desperately wanted to see Elton John in concert when he came to Louisville in April, but she didn't have enough money to go. Jake had no interest, but he made a lot of money from selling newspapers, so he thought it would be a nice idea if he bought them tickets for her birthday. That was a big mistake. Having worked once, she pulled the same sobbing routine a month later when she wanted to see the female-led rock band Heart. All total, he spent about $160, or the equivalent of sixteen Broadway musical cast albums he would have rather had. Jos decided that Jake was now her boyfriend.

Tragedy hit their school that spring. Stoner Derek heard that sniffing No-Stick Cooking Spray could get you high, so he sprayed an entire can into a baggie which he then tried to inhale. He had a stroke, suffered brain damage, and was in a vegetative state. He died after his family turned off his life support system. Another classmate, Sam, jumped off the Buechel Bypass bridge into the path of an oncoming cargo train. And then there was Jake's theater friend, the poor, weird, lonely, miserable Billy Keller.

Jake knew Billy was like him, but Billy tried very hard to assimilate. No one was buying it, as there was no mistaking his true nature with his effeminate gestures, delicate sensibilities, and his aversion to doing anything physical or too manly. The other kids were merciless in their torture of Billy. A few students called him a faggot, but most thought "freak" and "ghoul" fit him better. During the last week of school, he came to school extremely agitated, pacing, talking fast, crying uncontrollably. A letter jacket jock called him a faggot, prompting a full-blown meltdown by Billy, who started shrieking and threw himself on the guy.

They landed on the floor with Billy on top. Billy was shredding the jock's face with his long fingernails and going for his eyes next. It took a couple of teachers to pull him off. The ladies in the principal's office knew Jake was friendly with Billy, so they made an announcement over the intercom asking Jake to come to the front desk. Jake tried to calm him down, and it took him an hour to get Billy to explain why he was upset. Billy had just learned that his much older sister was in fact his mother, and his "parents" were really his grandparents.

These same religious fanatics who railed against the sin of homosexuality and sodomy to Billy had been covering up that their daughter had been a prostitute and got knocked up by a drug addict who later died of an overdose. Billy's entire life had been a lie, and any prospects for his future looked bleak. Late that night at his house, Billy pulled down the retractable attic stairs, climbed up, tied a noose to the rafters overhead, slipped it around his neck, and jumped off the attic stairs. He wanted to make sure that his family found him hanging in the upstairs hallway the next morning. They held no public funeral for him.

Jake was upset about Billy, and Jos proved her insensitivity by blurting out, "One less fag in the world." Jake wondered how she would react if she ever discovered the truth about him.

Perigee

For most of the month of May, Jake kept dodging all his female acquaintances. He had no plans to ask anyone to be his date for the prom, and he had not intended to even go. Finally, Jos got tired of waiting for Jake and demanded to know, "Damn it, are we going to prom or what?" His unenthusiastic response was, "Um okay, sure." Jake wore a white dinner jacket, black tuxedo pants, and a red bowtie. Jos looked like a pregnant bride in her overly large off-white gown that hung voluminously from her ample breasts. The prom committee had booked a ballroom in the Galt House, bordering the Belvedere Plaza along the Ohio River, where Jake had performed with his folk-dance group.

Jos thought she would create a romantic moment following prom by going on to the Belvedere to dance. She held her hands up, waiting for Jake to take her in a waltz hold. He came in to put his arm around her waist and started whipping her around in a frenzied polka. Jos was not a good dancer and could not keep up, tripping over her own feet. Jake had broken the mood by not letting her get romantic, but she was undeterred. She lunged at him and tried to French kiss him. He pushed her away gently, but she kept trying to kiss him, forcing Jake to keep turning his head. He was annoyed and told her, "It's time to go home," walking toward the parking garage, not waiting to see if she was following him or not.

That boundary he did not plan on crossing got knocked over by Jos, and it became the prevailing theme for the rest of his last summer at home. She started getting all weepy that he was leaving soon for college. She had known him for barely three months, but she kept wanting to talk about the future. What future? He was going away, and they would not see each other again. Jos started spending a lot more time at Jake's house and tried very hard to ingratiate herself. She tried to not take herself too seriously while doing just that, laughing easily without quite getting the jokes made at her expense, and making herself right at home when she was not always welcome.

Jim was always cordial to her, if not really wanting to get to know her. Betty, on the other hand, became close to this emotionally needy, extravagantly moody girl, practically adopting her as the second daughter she never had. Unfortunately for Jake, this meant Jos invaded his territory, and he could never get away from her. If he wanted to quietly read a book or listen to music, Jos plopped down next to him to talk. Uncomfortable with silence, she felt that dead space in a conversation meant something was wrong, so she never shut up.

In just a few short weeks, Jos became a black hole that sucked all the energy and fun out of Jake's home. Listening to sad music, talking about her home life, bemoaning the state of the world, everything, in fact, overwhelmed her in a flood of showstopping tears and loud crying. There was no escape from the nonstop personal melodrama she generated. Jake had to take a break from her and walked out the front door to lay on the grass and look up at the stars.

He and Cal had talked about the moon being their connection, but Jake had never actually talked to his friend this way. He counted the twinkling stars, found the North Star, and then focused on the pale crescent moon overhead, visualizing Cal in his location letting the moonlight caress his face. Jake began to talk to Cal, finally saying out loud all the things that he wanted to say to him but never had the courage to do. Jos intruded upon Jake's private moment with his faraway friend. She lay on the grass beside him, snuggled close, and nestled her head into the crook of his shoulder. Jos never could see signals or read body language. Jake was not having it. He rolled away, got up, and took off jogging around the block.

Jos could see that Jake was immune to her charms, so she tried harder, unaware how overbearing she quickly became. She asked him to skip his newspaper corner so they could go to the movies. During his folk-dance performances for the Heritage Weekends, she expected him to pick only her from the crowd for the audience participation dances. She wanted to volunteer for the folk-dance company; she wanted to work at the Lyric Theater; she wanted the two of them to go to a cabin like the one he talked about going to with Cal. She wanted to join Jake for his Tuesday night folk-dance sessions, but that would mean he had to give up his weekly tryst with Mark beforehand, which he was not willing to do. Jos was no longer simply annoying; she was a full-fledged pain-in-the-ass.

Finally, Cal came home and called Jake the first chance he could get. Jake was thrilled to hear his voice, and he talked quietly so their private conversation would not be overheard. Jos was lurking about, as had become usual, and she became instantly suspicious of Jake whispering into the phone. She strode up to him, grabbed the receiver out of his hand, and demanded of the unknown person on the other end of the line, "Who is this?"

"Damn it, Jos. Mind your own business."

"Is this a girl? Are you cheating on me?" She stood over Jake, looking like she wanted to hit him with the phone. She turned her attention back to her competition. "Who are you and what do you want with my boyfriend?"

Cal chuckled. "I'm Cal. I am not a girl, but I'm Jake's best friend."

"Well, I've never heard of you." Jake wrenched the phone

from her hand and screamed at her to go the hell away. Jos was taken aback by the tone of his voice. She had thought she was in charge of this relationship. She pouted and ran to the screen porch to cry into Betty's shoulder about how mean Jake was to her. Theirs was not a relationship, and it was quickly becoming not much of a friendship either.

Jake was relieved to have Cal back home, because he now had an excuse to ignore Jos. Since he had been gone for half the summer, Cal did not have a full-time summer job, but he picked up alternate shifts at the pool as lifeguard and swimming instructor whenever he could. Jake cleared his schedule so he could have every possible minute with Cal. They celebrated their eighteenth birthdays together. They went to the movies. They did everything they loved to do together. They never felt closer, but they had only a few weeks left before college.

21

Apogee

"The point in the orbit of the Moon or other satellite where it is farthest from the Earth."

For two years, they had debated the merits of going to college. Jake wanted to be a professional actor doing nothing but musical comedies on stage. He had done several musicals, so he felt a little bit professional already. He had been singing since he was seven and dancing since he was ten. He got cast in roles without having any acting training. What else could a college musical theater program offer him? Jake's parents Jim and Betty were dead set against Jake wasting his college years on a theater degree. Betty, who had not even finished college, insisted that he had to have a fallback plan. Jim wanted Jake to pick a sensible career.

Cal had a big problem with that notion of a "career." What did that mean exactly? He felt it promised a lifetime of indentured servitude doing something that did not interest him. Going to college meant choosing a major to decide upon a career, so he could graduate with a degree and get a job, so he could make money and buy things. He was not interested in acquiring material possessions; he wanted to work outdoors and live a simple life. His parents, Zan and Leigh, wanted him at the very least to attend college to get the certifications he might need to pursue those outdoor activities professionally.

Cal felt that Jake did not need a degree to become an actor, because he already was one, but if he had to go to college, then he should pick a major in something he liked. Jake encouraged Cal to follow his heart and continue doing those things that fulfilled his need for nature and beauty. Neither ever told the other to consider security, earning potential, or supporting a family. The two of them were hoping for a life that made them happy, not necessarily rich. Jake applied to and had been accepted into the University of Arizona in Tucson for no more reason than his grandparents now lived there, and he could move in with them. Cal enrolled in the University of Louisville, so he could stay at home for the time being.

All the time that he and Cal had been intimate, Jake also had been having sex with neighbor Mark. Four years with Cal, four years with Mark. Jake knew what Mark was feeling because they always had pillow talk after sex, but Mark never talked about the specifics of his home life. Jake could not remember ever seeing Mark's wife Becca again after her initial hospitalization. He saw the grandparents in the yard playing with the kids; he saw Mark's sister visiting; he never saw Becca. He did not know if she was so ashamed of what she had done that she never showed her face. He did not know if they even lived together anymore. He did not know if they divorced. It was not a topic for discussion.

Jake and Mark still met every single Tuesday night, but they had not gotten together at Mark's house for a couple of years. Two days after Jake's eighteenth birthday, Mark invited him over to his house for a belated birthday celebration. It was just the two of them and his kids. They had pizza, played board games, and then Jake helped Mark put the kids to bed. Mark walked around the first floor, locking up for the night and closing the blinds. Waiting long enough until the kids fell asleep, Mark undressed Jake and pulled him onto the floor pillows in the den. It was a nice change from screwing on the moldy couch in Mark's office.

Jos had come over to the Davies' house, ostensibly to hang out with Betty but wanting to forcibly spend time with Jake. Betty mentioned that Jake was babysitting the Blakely kids across the street. Jos decided that she would surprise him, so she walked over. She tried the back door first to see if it was open. She jiggled the knob, but it was locked. She knocked on the door, waiting only thirty seconds before she started banging on it. She had seen Mark's car in the garage, so she knew someone was at home, so she started calling out. "Jake, Jake, where are you? Why don't you answer the door?"

Mark and Jake stopped what they were doing and hurriedly dressed. By then, Jos was ringing the front doorbell repeatedly, waking up the kids. Mark's little daughter started crying. Mark went up to calm the little girl, rocking her gently while standing at the top of the stairs. Jake had to deal with Jos and opened the front door. Mark looked down at this intruder, and Jos looked up the stairs at him. She tried to act innocently, sweetly saying, "Oh, there you are. I was knocking at the door, and you didn't answer me."

Jake was seething. "What the hell is wrong with you? You woke the kids." Jos became even sweeter but looked nervous and asked, "Didn't you hear me? Why didn't you answer? What were you doing in there?" Seasoned liar that he had become, Jake told her that Mark needed a hand with something. Jake heard Mark snort a laugh at that. Jake told her to get lost and closed the door in her face. He was in no hurry to go home, so after getting the kids back to sleep, Mark and Jake went back to what they were doing in the den.

Mark started to get up to signal the end of the evening, but Jake hugged him tighter and sighed. Mark felt Jake's tears as they dripped onto his chest. "You okay, buddy?"

"I don't want to go."

"I can't let you stay the night, Jake. The kids . . . "

"It's not that. I mean I don't wanna go away. I don't wanna go to college."

"Most people want to go to college. It's part of growing up."

"But I won't get to see you anymore or be with you."

"Jake, you're young. It's normal to feel scared. You leave your parents' home and go away. That's a natural process that we all must go through."

"I won't have you. I won't get to see my friend Cal."

"Again, you're young. You won't understand this now, but you will come to realize that you need to see the world, need to sleep with other people. Have sex, enjoy it. People come and go out of our lives. This is all part of that."

"I don't want to let go of you."

"You have to, Jake. It's time." Mark let Jake continue hugging him for a while longer until he had shed his tears. They dressed and moved into the kitchen. Before opening the back door, Mark gave Jake a long kiss and then a full, strong hug. They walked to the end of Mark's driveway.

Jake smiled as he looked at this man who taught him all about sex and his body. "Please don't tell my mom."

Mark laughed. "No, our little secret."

The next night, Jos came over, hoping to smooth over ruffled feathers, completely unaware that she kept messing up with Jake. They stood at the top of the driveway, trying to have a calm conversation, but Jake was angry. Mark was out on his evening jog and stopped when he saw them there. He walked right up to Jos and confronted her. "Young lady, I didn't like the way you tried to barge into my house. When Jake is over there, he has a job to do, so I don't want him distracted while he is watching my children. Do not ever do that again."

All sweetness and light, Jos profusely apologized. Mark turned to Jake. "I hope we get to see you at Christmas." He jogged the short distance to his house. The second that Mark was out of earshot, Jos said, "What an asshole. He seems like a real jerk. I don't see what's the problem with letting your girlfriend help you babysit. I love kids. I hope we have some of our own someday." Whoa, whoa! Kids? She issued a demand: "I don't like that man. I don't want you to ever go over there again."

"Jos, you do not control me, and you do not get to tell me one damn thing." Jos started sobbing again and ran into the house, looking for Betty. His mother was lying in wait for him in the dining room, demanding to know why he was being so awful to Jos. His father wandered in to hear the answer, because he was getting tired of Jos's constant emotionalism. Jake told his parents what she had done over at Mark's place the previous night and his firm response just now. Jos walked in the room and tried to rationalize her actions. When she could not do that, Jos resorted to sobbing again, heaving into Betty's bosom. Jim and Jake threw up their hands and walked away.

That should have been the end of their imaginary dating, but Jos never thought anything was ever her fault. She was back at the house the next night, determined to make Jake love her. The phone rang and Jos was closest, so she picked it up. A girl's voice asked, "Is Jake there?"

"And who the hell are you? This is Joslyn. I'm Jake's girlfriend."

"Oh, I'm glad it's you. I'm Nicole, Cal's girlfriend. The boys are such great friends that I thought it would be nice for the four of us to hang out tomorrow."

Jos smiled as she strode out onto the screened porch to tell Jake that they were going out with Cal and Nicole the next night. Jake was annoyed because he and Cal had planned to go out to the cabin instead, but the girls had ruined that plan. The girls thought they were out on a double date, while Cal and Jake treated this as a perfunctory task to placate them. They sat at a crowded booth in the back of Denny's. The boys scooched toward the walls since they knew the girls would have to get up and use the restroom several times.

Jos wore a lime green tube top, showing off her ample boobs but also her doughy midsection. Nicole went for perky, wearing a tight pink tank top and pulling her mousy brown hair behind her ears. Two older men seated a few feet away commented to one another how Cal and Jake were cuter than their dates. The boys made pleasant conversation, but Nicole had nothing to contribute, only wanting to know how cute Cal thought she looked. Jos blathered on about any thought that fleetingly crossed her mind, once again grabbing Jake and not letting go. The girls were utterly unaware that underneath the cramped table Jake and Cal had their legs entwined and were gently rubbing their knees against each other's crotches.

The girls went off to the restroom together. Cal asked, "Why do girls always have to use the toilet in pairs?"

"They don't want the other one gossiping about them while they are gone."

Cal rolled his eyes. "So, how's it going with your girlfriend?"

"She's not my girlfriend. Jos only thinks she is. And what about you?"

"Nicole is okay, but she never has anything to say."

"But do you and Nicole have fun together?"

"Not really. She doesn't do fun. She does cute."

"That sounds exhausting. If you don't have fun, then why is she your girlfriend?"

Cal thought for a minute, and he was not sure of the answer. "I don't know. It's what is expected of me, I guess. Everyone thinks we're supposed to be with girls. It's what we have to do. Right?"

"I don't care what anyone else thinks. I just want us to be happy. I know I'm happier with you."

Jos and Nicole got back to the table, and Nicole asked, "Have you been missing us?"

As one, both Jake and Cal responded, "No." Cal added, "Just talking about starting college." That subject cast a pall over the rest of their double date.

Jake had one last task to accomplish before college. Traeger had developed tumors around his anus and tail, and the dog would grunt or squeal every time he tried to sit or lay down. The vet had said he was probably in a good deal of pain. Jim felt that the dog would not get the same kind of love, care, and attention once Jake left for school, but he said it was Jake's decision to make because Traeger was his dog. Jake knew that if he did not decide, then his dad would the moment he left. With Jake's consent, his dad and big sister Ellie took Traeger to the vet and had him put to sleep. Upon their return, Ellie handed Jake the dog's collar, and he burst into tears. He put the collar on his wrist as a bracelet to remember his beloved pet. It felt like he was tying up loose ends.

Jos continued her dirty tricks, trying to interfere with Jake's final weekend with Cal. When she heard about his plan to go to the cabin for two days right before leaving, Jos demanded, "What are you going to do for an entire weekend? I think I should go with you, so you don't get bored." When Jake firmly rejected that bad idea, she called Nicole and tried to get her to work her charms on Cal so both could join the boys for a romantic weekend. Cal knew what the girls were trying to do and refused to invite them. Nicole pouted; Jos seethed.

On Friday night and all Saturday, Cal and Jake had fun doing all the things they loved to do. They skinny-dipped at the swimming hole; they canoed on the lake; they hiked nude through the woods; they sang nonstop; they gazed at the stars. As the sun started to set on Saturday, they got quiet, keenly aware that this was their last evening together. One would get emotional, and the other provided comfort, and then their roles switched, and then switched back again. Cal said, "I want us to try something. Someone told me this was a cool thing, and they said to do it with someone you care about."

Jake was game, as he was with anything his friend suggested.

Even activities that proved a little more dangerous than non-swimmer Jake would normally be willing to do. Cal knew that Jake would be thinking about that and assured him, "Don't worry. It's not dangerous. Just fun." He got the egg timer from the kitchen, opened the door to the porch, and motioned for Jake to join him. Cal took Jake's hands, telling him to do everything he did. They stood with their feet a few inches apart, crossed their right foot over the left, and lowered their butts until they were sitting Indian style on the floorboards of the porch.

Cal instructed Jake to open his legs, as if moving into a split, so he could scooch in closer. Cal draped his legs over Jake's, crossing them behind his friend. Jake did the same, like two links in a chain, so their crotches were pressed together and their faces just inches apart. With light from the living room hitting one side of their faces and moonlight shining down on the other, Cal said, "I want us to memorize each other's face. I'm going to set the timer for five minutes and we can't talk. Just look at each other." Jake could look at Cal forever, so he nodded his agreement. Cal turned the dial on the timer.

At first, the two of them felt a little self-conscious, so there was nervous giggling. They went silent for a while, and then they smiled broadly, which led to uproarious laughter. They got quiet again, with the most serious expressions on their faces. Both blinked away tears. They let the emotion overtake them and soon they were sobbing. They cried, they smiled, they laughed again, they went quiet. The egg timer dinged. Neither moved, unwilling to break that bond. Then Cal caressed Jake's face, and Jake pulled Cal closer, so their bodies were pressed fully together in a tight hug.

Cal instructed Jake, "Now look at the moon and put my face right in the middle of it." The moon was nearly full; Jake found two gray areas on the moon's surface onto which he could superimpose Cal's eyes. The rest of his face then came sharply into focus. He looked away from the glowing orb in the sky, but when he glanced back, he could still see Cal's sweet face looking toward him. He kept turning his attention elsewhere, and every time he looked, Cal was the man in the moon. Cal asked, "Memorized?"

Jake smiled and cried, "Forever." Cal told him, "Same here." In the morning, they did not take their usual morning hike. Instead, Cal led him down to the lake, so they could go out on the water. When they climbed into the canoe, Jake looked for a life preserver, which they had left up at the cabin. Cal said, "If you fall in, I will save you." Jake knew he would. They paddled close to shore for more than an hour. They did not talk at all, instead enjoying the sounds of their paddles dipping in and out of the water. Finally, Cal said quietly, "I love it out here. Will anyone want to share this kind of life with me?" Jake responded in almost a whisper. "I will." Jake would have spent the rest of his life with Cal.

Dropping Jake home, they got out of the car and faced each other. Trying to keep it together, Jake said as calmly as he could manage, "Well, I guess this is good-bye." Cal quickly told him, "No, never good-bye, just see you later." Jake pulled Cal into a hug, and they just held on for dear life. Both tried to remain stoic about this farewell, but they could not deny what they were feeling, and the loss they were about to feel. As they moved into a long, sweet kiss, Jim walked out the kitchen door into the garage and watched them as they clung to each other, unwilling to let go. Jim got emotional seeing them in their overwhelming sadness. He came in close, putting a reassuring hand on each boy's shoulder, finally saying very gently, "Okay, that's enough. It is time to go."

Jake sobbed as he said, "Thank you for being the best friend ever." Cal looked crestfallen as he responded, "Be brave, be happy. And don't forget to look to the night skies." Cal sobbed in the car all the way home. Jake was on the red-eye flight to Tucson late that night. He came to the painful realization that he was not going to see the two people he cared about most in the world. For the tenth time that day he started sobbing. He wept for Mark and his best friend, but mostly it was for Cal. To go off to college felt like leaving him behind. This did feel like good-bye forever.

22

Eccentricity

"The measure of how much an orbit deviates from being circular."

Jake landed in Tucson, Arizona, stepping off the airplane into what felt like a blast furnace. It was 110 degrees that day. His grandparents met him at the airport. It was an awkward drive from the airport on the far southwest corner of town to the eastern edge of the city where they lived. Like most kids, Jake did not really know his grandparents. They were these nice old people he saw on holidays. Here he was moving in with these senior citizens, who nervously tried to make conversation with the teenager who would now be living with them.

The house was a nice three-bedroom, two-bath ranch house, with a small side patio and back desert garden enclosed by a cinder block wall. It was not a mansion; it was just a nice, clean house to call home for a couple of years. He should have had the hall bathroom all to himself, but his grandfather took a long time in the master bathroom. So if Grandma had to use the toilet, then she took her sweet time in the hall bath. Jake found a secluded corner of the back garden that had no windows looking out onto it, so he could run outside and pee secretly if ever he needed to, which was quite often in that house.

Jake had a week to kill before classes started. One of the first things he did was to start jogging again. He was a gymnast and dancer, so he was well acquainted with his body, but he marveled at how much looser and freer he felt as his legs stretched into a rhythmic stride. He woke up at dawn to go running. The city limits ended just to the east of his grandparents' house, so the streets were not paved beyond that point. It was all desert landscape and gravel roads. He hugged the side of the street and became distracted by a roadrunner. He focused so intently on the odd bird he had never seen before that he almost did not see the rattlesnake ten feet in front of him. He was not sure yet if he was going to love this place or hate it.

Jake got to use his grandparents' second car, a fire-engine red Ford Pinto, so he would have transportation to school. They lived far east of downtown, and the buses did not come out that way. Jake's dad gave him a credit card to pay for gas and upkeep. That first month, he used a lot of gas driving every square inch of his new city. He explored campus; he drove into the desert; he went up in the foothills to check out the expensive mansions.

Tucson was surrounded on all four sides by small mountain ranges. The Santa Catalina Mountains to the north were the most impressive, rising to 10,000 feet. To the east, the Tucson Valley ended at the Saguaro National Monument and the Rincon Mountains. The Tucson Mountains to the west were a scattershot range of dusty, tall bumps rising from the ground. The Santa Rita Mountains to the south were too far to see from the house or campus. In the heat of summer, the city settled into odd schedules, with businesses closing during midday and reopening late afternoon to stay open longer into the cooler evening.

Jake felt weird being there. It was hotter than he had ever experienced, the landscape was strange, and even the air smelled funny, a mix of perfume and dust. As soon as classes started, he was happily surprised to discover they had a folk-dance group. He joined right away and did his first performance within the week. He made friends quickly, among them Lauren, a naïve, heavyset girl with a coloratura soprano voice. Lauren always imagined herself playing the iconic leading ingenue roles of musical theater, but she had a figure more suited to playing the ingenues' mothers.

Jake quickly discovered that Lauren was a classic fag hag. When she was seven years old, her fallopian tube strangulated her left ovary, so she'd had a partial hysterectomy. Three years later, it happened again on the other side. Her mother, who was Southern Baptist, walked into her recovering daughter's hospital room and said, "Now you will never be a real woman." Her own religious beliefs mirrored those of her mother. Unable to have children, she believed sex was only for procreation and therefore she never could have sex with a man. And yet, she still wanted to feel love and to have a boyfriend, so she become enamored with almost every homosexual she met, because they would never try to fuck her.

Jake and Lauren met a luscious-locked, tall, dark, handsome operatic baritone and swooned. Free of any commitments and separated from Mark and Cal by 1,700 miles, Jake was horny as hell, and here was this big, strapping 6'3" slab of man meat. They wound up in bed together on the first day they met. His unintentionally hilarious name was Ken Dahl, soon to become Ken Doll when he started sleeping with blond-haired Jake, who by association became known to their friends as Barbie. Lauren hung around the Drama Department a lot and befriended Ken about the same time Jake did.

Lauren was sweet, pleasant, complimentary, even fawning, so she made friends easily. She and Ken chatted between classes, met at a fast-food place for lunch, and even went to the movies on occasion. She started telling everyone, "My boyfriend Ken and I had a lovely date last night." She implied that they had spent all night together. The true story was that after their platonic date, Jake was the one who was satisfying Ken's sexual appetite. Her delusion turned the reality of Jake's relationship with Ken into a lie. Having spent years lying to hide his affair with his neighbor Mark or his friendship with Cal, Jake did not want to do that anymore.

Ultimately, he did not have to say or do anything, because all their friends realized what was going on. At the folk-dance performances, Ken would attend, and it was clear to everyone that he was there to see Jake, not Lauren. When Ken did a musical, Lauren and Jake went to see his shows and greeted him backstage afterward. Somehow, her mind could not register that he was giving Jake a long, passionate kiss and a full body hug, while she got the cursory pat on the back. Jake had to endure sharing Ken with delusional Lauren until the end of his first semester, when Ken transferred to a music conservatory and left Tucson.

Jake thrived in the relative freedom of college, despite staying with his grandparents, and he loved Tucson. Meanwhile, Joslyn was bombing out at her women's college, somewhere in the Midwest. Jake could not remember where and did not care. Always the drama queen, Jos did not focus on her studies, but pined away for Jake and wallowed in the teenage melodrama of her dormmates. She also had a persecution complex and felt the other girls were out to get her. Her grades had been awful. As Jake flew home for Christmas, Jos dropped out of college.

Her mother reacted as expected, saying that Jos was worthless and would never succeed at anything. Her father was not happy about the money wasted on her schooling.

Jos's emotionalism got the best of her. She said she hated them as she stomped into her bedroom, slamming the door and locking it. She called Jake's mother Betty on the phone to say her parents were threatening to have her committed to a mental institution until she came to her senses. Betty, being a good friend but not thinking this through clearly, told Jos, "Get out of there." Louisville had a rare snowfall that week, so Jos threw her clothing and most cherished personal effects out into the snow.

Betty ordered Jake to go pick up Jos. Jake sat inside the car as Jos took several trips to the snowbank under her window to retrieve her belongings and put them in the trunk of the car. Jake could see both of her parents watching this scene with much amusement from the living room window. Jake asked, "What now?" and Jos demanded, "We're going to your house." When they arrived there, Betty was waiting at the kitchen door. Jos exploded into tears, collapsed into Betty's arms, and then whimpered, "Can I stay here?"

Betty instructed Jake to take all of Jos's stuff up to his bedroom. He asked, "Where the hell am I supposed to sleep?" Jake believed that Jos hoped the two of them would be sharing his room. Betty told him that he could sleep in the basement family room. "For how long?" Betty replied, "For as long as needed." He hoped it would be a night or two, but it lasted the entirety of his Christmas break. Since she would be staying over Christmas, Betty bought Jos gifts, so she too would have something to open on Christmas morning. Betty marked all those gifts as being from Jake.

Firmly ensconced in their house, Jos never left Jake alone for even a minute. In frustration, he snuck out to take a nighttime walk around the neighborhood whenever she was preoccupied. On one of these walks, Jake saw Mark jogging. Completing another lap around the block, Mark stopped to say hello. There was no hug, no kiss. He told Jake how handsome he had become, as he had finally grown to a height of 5'10". Mark asked about college; Jake inquired after his kids. He ended their brief conversation with "Merry Christmas, Jake" and jogged over to his house. He made it very clear in that moment that they would not be resuming their affair. Jake was sad, but in a way, he felt relieved that he could move on to the next thing in his life.

He went to Cal's house, hoping to see surprise him, but he and his family were not there. He called Cal, but no one picked up the phone. He kept riding his bike over to his house several times, and no one was ever there. They must be taking a trip for the holidays. It was another disappointment. He looked forward to Christmas, family time, and playing cards and board games, but Jos was always there to take the fun out of it. She was terrible at games, and she was a sore loser. If she got the lowest score two games running, she would announce she was going up to "her" room. If Jake did not follow her, she came back down and whined that he was not paying enough attention to her.

She had not insinuated herself into the Davies family so much as she established her overwhelming physical presence in their house. Everyone was at a loss with how they were supposed to treat her, because Betty would remind everyone repeatedly how awful Jos's parents had been. Jos might as well have taken scissors and emasculated Jim because he said nothing. Jake's siblings just thought she was exhausting. Betty beamed stupidly at her. Jake was the only one to get snippy with

Jos, because he was tired of being mauled all the time. Privately, Jake called her "the octopus" for always wrapping her tentacles around him.

Jos sat next to Jake at the dining room table, so underneath she could move her hand up his leg to rest on his crotch. He got so tired of trying to prevent her from doing this that he just gave up and let her grope. On the couch, she sidled up next to him, put her head on his shoulder, and then rolled herself onto his lap so he had to hug her. If he did not respond further to this obvious move, she would raise herself up closer with their faces inches apart. One time he was trapped underneath her and could not fend off her kisses, so he pushed her onto the floor. This prompted a loud crying fit that everyone had to endure for an hour.

When Jake went down to the family room to take a nap, she followed him downstairs to lay next to him on the mattress. He stopped taking showers upstairs and began taking them in the open stall in the basement by the old maid's room. Jos came downstairs, undressed by the furnace, and tried to join him in the shower. Jake yelled, "Goddamnit Jos, get the fuck out of here." She had not seen him naked before this and he had no interest in her nude body. Jim heard the commotion, and Jos barely managed to get dressed again before he came downstairs.

Since her obvious ploys to get Jake to love her were not working, she switched her tactics to Betty, who was practically hypnotized. Out of nowhere one night while everyone was quietly reading and listening to the stereo, Jos started wailing that she hates her family. She sobbed into Betty's bosom on one corner of the couch. Jake was seated barely three feet away on the other end, trying to concentrate on a book. When Jos wished that she could be part of this family, Jake heard Betty, in her badly modulated whisper, say to her, "Well, there is a way." In making Jake's mother her ally, Jos turned her into his adversary.

With still a week of vacation left, Jake was miserable, so he went to talk to his father. Jake asked if he could go back to school early. Jim was open to the idea. He felt that it would be easier on everyone if Jake was not there, because all of Jos's antics centered around him. Jim got him on a flight the following night. Jos shifted between anger, grief, misery, fear, and humiliation with lightning speed. She started screaming, "No, don't go. Please! How will I live without you?" In exasperation, Jake said, "Figure it out, Jos." Jake told her that she needed to move out and find somewhere else to live. She ignored that request.

He had a week of peace before he started classes. He spent most of the time in his bedroom reading books or listening to cast albums. He went for jogs in the mornings and sat out on the side patio late at night to look at the stars. His heart ached, because he did not get any time with Cal at Christmas, and even Ken Doll had left for another school. Cal and Jake had exchanged phone calls at least twice a month during his first semester, but they quickly ran out of things to say to one another. The calls became less and less frequent. The few letters they sent also dwindled. Clearly, the two of them were developing separate lives.

Jake spent a lot of time at the college library just sitting on the sofas and looking out at the mountains. He wondered how and when he was going to tell Jos that he was a homo. He knew she was going to get very ugly about this. For all of her "gee, everything is wonderful" gushing, he had heard her call guys in high school "faggots," and not in a joking way. She had called Jake's Junior Prom date Laura a "dyke" with considerable venom. How would she react when she found out the truth about him? Was she going to call him a faggot too?

At this point, he did not care. Jake wanted Jos out of his life. The entire semester, he refused to write or call her. He kept so busy on campus that he was almost never home in the evenings when she would usually call. Whenever he would call home, he wanted to talk to his parents, but Jos always grabbed the phone or chattered away in Betty's ear the whole time. Jim knew that Jake was always home on weekend mornings, so he drove to his office to use the Watts line at work to call, whenever he needed or wanted to talk with his son. Jake asked, "Um, how's it going with Jos?" Jim grunted, "Let's not talk about her."

With one semester under his belt, Jake scheduled an appointment with an assigned counselor to talk about choosing a major. Vincent Gordon was certainly a character who challenged and unnerved him. He was a tall hippie type prone to wearing short shorts, tight-fitting tank tops, and flip-flops, with his long, light brown hair in a ponytail down his back. He had a pleasant face, if not particularly handsome, but Vincent had a chiseled physique. He shook Jake's hand and asked him to wait while he answered a phone call. Waiting for him to finish, Jake stared up at a poster on his wall of two naked men clasped in a full body hug. It was a sexy poster, but Jake kept averting his eyes because he did not want Vincent to notice his interest. He noticed. He said, "Isn't that hot?" Jake stammered a bit and mumbled, "Yes, it is."

Vince then said it was nice to have other fags in the department, meaning Jake. Again, he fumbled for a response, and Vince mentioned that he had seen him a few times in Tucson's one and only queer bar, which he frequented with Ken Doll. He talked like a confidant about sexuality, and it was a discussion that Jake had never had with anyone before this. Vince called himself a militant fag who worked toward achieving equality for "gay" people. The term "gay" was only just entering the lexicon, and Jake was not sure how he identified. Bullies had called him sissy, fairy, queer, queen, faggot, nelly, and fruit, but Jake did not know that "gay" was quickly becoming the accepted term.

Vince recounted his coming-out story and asked when Jake knew. Jake said he was ten when he knew but did not include specifics about his early fumblings with other boys. Vince was so open that he did not hesitate to ask questions that no one else had asked Jake. Even so, Jake was a little shocked when Vince came right out and asked, "Have you had sex yet?" Jake told him that he had, so of course he asked at what age. Jake told him that he was just fourteen and that he had had sex with this older man for close to four years. Vincent was the only person that Jake ever told about Mark. He asked if Jake had wanted that relationship, and Jake revealed that he initiated it. He asked, "Did you like it?" Jake responded, "I loved it." He smiled and said, "That's hot!" He said "hot" a lot.

Vincent was never inappropriate at the office, but Jake felt just a little uncomfortable around him because he always spoke openly and honestly about sexuality. Jake was unaccustomed to that. He encouraged Jake to become comfortable with that part of himself. Very quickly, he became a good friend, inviting Jake over to his house for dinner. At eighteen, Jake was the youngest person in the group by a full decade. The other guests were Air Force sergeant Roy, medical technician Jose, and engineer Harris. They didn't treat Jake like a kid or even a student. He was just another friend.

They ate and polished off a few bottles of wine under a gazebo in Vince's backyard with only the illumination of candles. Vince suggested they move to the hot tub, but Jake said he had not brought a swimsuit. Vince said, "So? No one did." He pulled off his shirt, dropped his trousers, and stepped into the hot tub, and the three other guys followed. Jake stood there, holding his glass of wine, and smiling nervously. After a few minutes, they started to tease and tempt him. "Come on in, you know you want to get naked with us."

They cheered at Jake's shedding of clothing and sliding into the hot tub. Vince and the handsome black guy, Harris, were to Jake's left, and the hot military guy, Roy, sat next to beefy Latino Jose on his right side. The two couples started making out, with Jake in the middle, feeling like a fifth wheel and wondering what he was doing there, until all of them started leaning in to kiss him. After a half hour of foreplay, Vince stepped out of the hot tub and opened the French doors to the master bedroom. The other guys got out to join him. Jake was still in the water when Vince said, "You're invited too." Jake was not shy about his body or about sex, but he put his clothes back on and left by the side gate.

A few days later, Jake went to see Vincent in his office to thank him for inviting him over for a nice evening. Vince said, "I'm sorry we scared you off." Jake reassured him that he had not, and he was just working through relationship stuff. Vince put on his counselor attitude and asked if Jake needed to talk. Jake declined for the moment, saying he was trying to figure out what he wanted. Vince said, "Okay, I'm here for you. And maybe another time." The next dinner party was that weekend, and this time Jake did not put his clothes back on. The five of them had so much fun that they got together every Friday and Saturday evening. Jake dubbed it "Boys' Night."

Jake's freshman year came to an end the week of Memorial Day, and Jim wanted Jake to come home for part of the summer. He would only be in Louisville for six weeks, though, because he needed to fly back to Tucson by July 15 to meet with the university office that decided on residency status. With three kids in college, Betty having started courses to finish her own degree, and youngest son Shaun coming up on college in two years, Jim needed to save money wherever he could. He needed Jake to get Arizona residency so he could pay cheaper state tuition. Jake did not mind because it meant less time spent near Joslyn.

23

Limb

"The edge of a celestial object's visible disk."

The red-eye flight landed early in the morning, and Betty picked Jake up at the Louisville airport, with Jos in tow. Jos launched herself onto Jake, and it's a good thing he had a strong back from dancing because she was not a petite girl. Once Jake pushed her off, the octopus wrapped her tentacles around his chest so he could not even hug his mother. Walking down the airport concourse, Jake could hardly move forward, because Jos would not let go, trying to kiss him. Who was this show for? Betty took them to breakfast at Denny's and Jos was practically sitting in Jake's lap. He had to push her off and ask her to "give me a little breathing room." Betty just smiled stupidly at them.

Jos was still encamped in his bedroom, so once again Jake had to make the basement family room his bedroom while home. It was hardly private because Jos followed him whenever he went down there. From Jake's first moments home, Jos attached herself to him like a tick. He was glad she had a job because he could get a break for several hours from this onslaught of nonstop fawning. When Jos came home from work, Jake found somewhere else to be in the evening. His folk-dance group had changed location and moved to Thursdays, so he popped in to see everyone. He biked over to Cal's house, but his mother Leigh said, "I'm sorry, honey. He's away this month, taking kids on a rafting trip."

Jake tried to see if Mark Blakely was around. He had not seen Mark jogging his normal route through the neighborhood, so he rode his old bike to Mark's office, where they used to meet every Tuesday before folk dance. No luck for Jake, as Mark was not there when he stopped by. Jake went to the movies; he climbed the maple tree by his driveway—anything to put off having to go inside. When he walked onto the screened porch, Jos jumped up from the glider to kiss him, saying she had missed him so much since morning. Jake put her at arm's length and said "Omigod, please ease up. You always slobber all over me. Just stop." Jos dissolved into another one of her fits of hysteria, which brought Betty running.

Jim let Jake take one of the cars after he mentioned wanting to visit a friend. Instead, Jake drove to the only homo bar he knew existed in Louisville. The bar was on Third Street in Old Louisville, the downtown neighborhood with historic Victorian-era buildings. The ugly, squat, narrow building was nondescript from the outside with just a small neon sign that read "bar," a stubby mansard roof with asphalt shingles, and a black door. Inside, the décor suggested that people came in here to hide their sexuality, not flaunt it. The music from the jukebox emphasized male crooners and female chanteuses of an earlier era. It was dark as a tomb. There was nothing to even suggest this was a homo bar, except only men came here.

The bar took up most of the room, with stools along the entire length of it, with several two-seater tables along the side wall. Someone had just vacated a barstool, so Jake sat down quickly, awaiting the bartender to notice him. He did not have much experience in such bars, having only been to one in Tucson, so he was a little nervous. It did not help that his stool was underneath a dim pendant light which illuminated his blond hair. People stared at him because he was yet again the youngest-looking person in the place. The bartender called him Skippy, took his beer order, and checked his driver's license, announcing to the entire bar, "he's legal, folks," which prompted a round of applause.

The guy to his right was laughing, so Jake thought the guy was making fun of him. He had not really looked at him when he first sat down, but now glanced side-eyed at him. He was a very large man, towering over Jake. He was six-foot-seven, and all muscle. His neck was as thick as a telephone pole, and his biceps were the size of Jake's dancer thighs. When the bartender brought his beer, Jake stood up off the stool to get his wallet, but this man did the same thing to pay for his drink. Standing next to him, Jake had to crane his neck to finally take a look at his handsome face. It was Ranger Rick.

"Omigod, it's you. I'm so happy to see you."

Rick smiled. "Hi, cutie. You've grown up. How old are you now?"

Jake was still six weeks away from his birthday, but he said he was nineteen to make himself seem more mature. Jake thanked him for buying his beer and they started chatting like they were old friends. Rick put his strong hand on Jake's shoulder and rubbed gently as they talked. Jake finally found out a little about this huge man, who had been so kind to him two years earlier at the hospital and afterward. Rick was thirty-nine years old, an investigator rather than just a beat cop, and Cuban American, having moved to Louisville from Havana when he was twenty years old in 1958, the same year that Jake was born.

After a half hour of chatting and a second beer, Rick asked Jake to come home with him. The bar erupted into hoots and hollers as they left together. Several men were jealous that this kid had landed the hot cop, while others envied the cop for snagging the cute teenager. Rick assured Jake that his car was safe where it was parked on the street, so they walked the half block back to his place. He lived in a vintage house that had been subdivided into one-bedroom apartments. He lived on the first floor and the apartment retained a lot of the old building's original charm. There was a center hallway with a dining room and the kitchen on the right side and the parlor room and bedroom on the other side, all with old French doors off the hallway. The bathroom was at the back.

The bedroom was large, with an enormous bed, which Rick had to have custom-made for his height and his size. In old homes like this one, closets were usually tiny or nonexistent, so a late 1960s renovation had added an entire wall of closets, which had mirrors on the sliding doors. It was fun having the mirrors there, because it was the first time that Jake ever got to watch himself having sex not to mention watch this massive, muscular man in action. After a few hours, Jake worried about overstaying his welcome, but Ranger Rick said it was awfully late and he should stay the night. Jake did, but they did not sleep much.

Early in the morning, Rick invited Jake to come back the next night. Jake drove home and the house was quiet. When Betty woke up midmorning, she yelled at Jake for hurting Jos's feelings. She grilled him about where he had been all night and who he was with. He said he had been with a friend. She demanded, "Who is she?" Jake told his mother that the person's name was Rick and said that he had been a friend in high school, which was not exactly a lie, but hardly truthful either.

That night, Jake waited until Jos had to use the bathroom before he called Rick, who was coming to pick him up. Jake left the house before Jos could get back downstairs and stop him from leaving.

Jake had even more time with Rick that evening and spent the night with him again. Rick was a beast in bed, very dominating and even a little bit rough, and his huge body engulfed Jake's taut dancer's build. He loved it. The next morning, Betty complained again, and Jake reminded her that he was an adult. Her response was "Oh no, you're not, as long as you stay in this house." Jake laughed at that, which only made her madder. Every night that Rick did not have to work, Jake called him to come and get him. They spent the night together four times that first week. Jos was angry that Jake kept disappearing on her.

She would not have known this if she had not moved in with his family. Jake offered neither an apology nor an explanation. On those nights that Rick had to work, Jake stayed home, and he insisted that Jos leave him alone occasionally. She sat chastened on the couch, but she could not last more than a few minutes before she had to scooch over closer and start touching him or trying to fill the dead air with her incessant prattle. He kept shushing her and pushing her hand away. She cried and wailed, and Jake yelled at her to stop it. He told her these hysterics were why he was staying with a friend.

It was at that moment that he yelled at her, "Damnit, I'm not your boyfriend." He had never made any romantic moves toward her in high school. He thought of her as nothing but a friend, and not much of one at that. He knew she was not a virgin, and he did not care, because he had no interest in her sexually. He had heard talk that she had slept around a lot. A lot of different sources at high school provided intimate details of her sexual exploits which only corroborated the comments made by others. For all those rumors about Jos, though, there were probably as many about Jake being a homo. Why did she pick him? How did they get to this crazy point?

The truth is she did not pick Jake. Jos picked his mother, seeing Betty as someone that she could manipulate easily. Although she wanted to be a great painter, Betty was defined by her role as wife and stay-at-home mother. Her prolonged absence from the family in the summer of 1972 was an attempt to find a new purpose to her life, since her kids had grown up. Betty was a bit lost and needed a project. Jos wanted to become that project for her. Unfortunately, Jake got sucked into Jos's intrigue. She had almost discovered Jake having sex with neighbor Mark the previous summer, and Jake felt she was always shadowing him after that. He always wondered if she had told his mother about that night or her suspicions.

Betty and Jos had been plotting all spring. Betty had been working part-time and had saved up some cash and decided to fly Jos out to Tucson with Jake when he went back for his state residency meeting. His grandparents were taking a car trip back east and would not be there for a couple of weeks. Jos knew they would be gone; Jake did not. Betty had decided that Jos was going to take Jake's virginity that summer. There is no way either of them could have known that he lost his virginity almost five years earlier.

Jake did not mind that Jos was coming on the trip, because they could have fun whenever it was just the two of them. She became unbearable whenever she was putting on a show for Betty's benefit. They laughed during the flight, but once again she had to be overly demonstrative in front of the flight attendants, draping herself over Jake so he could hardly move in his seat. They took a taxi from the airport to the house, and Jake gave her a tour of his new world. They got home in the early evening, ate dinner that Jake cooked, drank a glass of wine, and sat out on the side patio to watch the sunset against the Catalina Mountains. He did not want to stargaze with her, as he reserved that activity for Cal alone.

Jos seemed disappointed that she could not sleep in Jake's room, because he only had a twin bed. She gestured to the double bed in the guest bedroom where she would be sleeping, but he told her good night. He should have locked his door. An hour later, she came into his room stark naked after he had fallen asleep on top of the sheets. She saw Jake's nighttime boner, straddled him, and took a ride. Jake was already inside her by the time he woke up and realized what was happening. He was not wearing a condom. He tried to push her off, but she was an ample girl, pushing all her weight down on his hips and shoving his shoulders into the pillow. Before he could find a polite way to get her to stop, he had already blown his load inside of her.

Having had intercourse, Jos now expected this would become a regular thing. She was back in Jake's room every night that she was there. Jake had learned that sometimes with Jos it was easier to just give in than to keep beating her off with a stick. But he would not consider sleeping the whole night together in the double bed. That was too much like a commitment. This was just sex, and Jos had to let Jake know as loudly as possible how devastated she was to be going home without him. Jake was glad to put her on a plane and be rid of her.

—ಊ—

Residency done and pretend girlfriend dispatched, Jake now had seven weeks to kill before he started classes again. He called his gal pal Paula Jean in Los Angeles. She had graduated college right after Jake's first semester and started work at a major Hollywood studio. She had extended an open invitation to visit anytime, so he could audition for films, TV shows, and commercials. Jake had money in savings, so he bought a round-trip Amtrak ticket for twenty bucks and took the slow twenty-four-hour train ride to Los Angeles.

Paula had a modest one-bedroom apartment near Studio City, and Jake planned on sleeping on her sofa for the next month-and-a-half. He repaid her hospitality by making her dinner, cleaning her apartment, shopping for groceries, and even doing her laundry. She started referring to Jake as her own personal houseboy, even introducing him like that to her friends. Jake became popular at the studio parties. Here was this fresh-faced, fit eighteen-year-old blond dancer-gymnast a few weeks away from his nineteenth birthday, so he got a lot of attention. He did not let it go to his head, but he always took a deep breath to calm himself seconds before diving into any of these social situations. At times he was intimidated by all the famous people he was meeting; other times he was overwhelmed.

One night, Jake and Paula arrived at a luxurious home in the Hollywood Hills, with a lot of guests' fancy cars parked along the long, curving driveway. Approaching the front door, Paula fished a little wire-ring notepad and a pen out of her purse and handed them to Jake. She had written her phone number on the front cover and told him to give that out if anyone asked for his contact information.

The moment they walked through the door of this palatial mansion, a scantily clad woman with huge breasts barely restrained by her bikini top shoved a glass of champagne into Jake's hand. A couple of handsome men zeroed in on him from the moment they entered, but Paula kept her arm linked through his. She was not laying claim to Jake as hers; she was protecting him from the wolves. Jake worried that at just eighteen years old he would not have much to say to any of these people, and that they probably wouldn't be interested in anything he had to say either, so he just smiled a lot. But his looks were enough. Paula was blond too, and together they turned heads.

Right away Jake also noticed large bowls of what looked like powdered sugar strategically placed in corners, under the cabana, even on top of the toilet tank in one of the bathrooms. Paula pointed and shook her head no. Jake assumed it was drugs and had no interest.

The host was an independent film producer named Allen, flamboyantly dressed in an embroidered purple caftan to hide his girth. Paula was working with him on two films, so he signaled her to come over. He air-kissed her and then told her to loosen her hold on Jake, which was her cue to get lost. Allen grilled Jake, excited to learn he was a singer and dancer, all the while he was aggressively fondling his ass and backing him into a corner. Natalie Wood viewed this interaction and came to rescue Jake, saying, "I just have to meet this cute boy." Allen was not going to say no to the three-time Oscar-nominated star, so she took Jake's arm, walked him back to Paula, and told her, "Now would be a good time to get him out of here." Jake could not believe he just met Natalie Wood.

Before they left, Jake spent an hour talking with an older actor and gave him Paula's number. Later that evening, he called Paula's apartment and invited Jake out to dinner. This Former Child Star was sweet, funny, smart, and surprisingly sexy. Jake spent the next two days in the actor's bedroom. When he left for an out-of-town film shoot, another call came in for Jake. The Leading Man had flirted with Jake at that same party, and he was a little less gentlemanly in his invitation, telling Jake simply, "Let's fuck." They spent five days together, until Leading Man dumped him for a bleached blond muscled surfer. The famous movie star was a sweet man, and everyone liked him, but sexually he was a pig who slept with anyone who had a penis.

The phone in Paula's apartment rang off the hook for Jake. None of the calls were for potential jobs or auditions; most were requests for dates. Some of the more brazen calls asked how much Jake charged for sex. One man even wanted to "represent" him in that regard. Why did people think he was a prostitute? He did not understand it. He never wore revealing clothing or tight shorts like some of the guests did at these summertime parties. And it's not like he walked into a room, wiggled his ass, and threw his legs up in the air. Jake did not think he was even that handsome, maybe nice looking, but never as stunning as all these movie stars. He decided it was his blond hair. Or maybe it was his youth.

At a fundraiser that Paula dragged him to, Jake stood by an overlook past the swimming pool, gazing at the astounding view of the city below him. Someone came up beside him and said, "Hey, kid. Not much for parties?" Jake looked at the man and felt his heart leap up into his throat and started to go weak in the knees. He had watched this TV Cowboy's Western series in reruns when he was a little kid. Paula had coached Jake how to remain cool when faced with a famous person. She had told him to take a deep breath, pause, and then act like that person was just normal, like a neighbor or friend. No talk of being a fan, no showbiz chat, and definitely no fainting. Just small talk.

Inside, Jake was screaming "Omigod, omigod, it's him. I've loved him for years." Instead, he said slowly and as calmly as he could manage, "I'm visiting from out-of-town, don't know anybody, and not sure I fit in here."

He smiled at Jake. "Kid, I feel the same way. I should introduce myself. I'm Rob. Only my real friends know to call me Rob." He had used his real name, not the Hollywood celebrity name he adopted.

Jake hesitated, thinking he had mistaken this guy Rob for the TV Cowboy, so he hesitated but took a gamble. "I will make sure to call you by your real name then, so that we can be real friends." Rob loved Jake's casual response, so he stood at the railing talking privately with the kid for an hour. They talked about nature, horses, wildlife, swimming, hiking, and a shared love of the outdoors. When he said his good-bye, Rob smiled, shook his hand, and started to leave. He turned back and asked, "Wanna come see my ranch?" Jake spent the next six weeks with Rob. Despite a thirty-four-year age difference, they got along famously.

Unlike Child Star and Leading Man, who identified themselves as Hollywood homos, Rob was confoundingly mysterious about his orientation. There had been countless rumors of him with other actors, fueled in no small measure by being one of agent Henry Willson's manufactured "boys," whom he had taken from obscurity, refined their looks, and given them manly monosyllabic new names. His movie star name came from Willson, but it was never a moniker that he liked. Rob told Jake, "In Hollywood, you have to decide what you want, what you are willing to tolerate, and then you always have to be true to yourself."

Rob was being true to himself, which meant sometimes he liked women, and right now, he liked Jake very much. When Jake needed to go back to college, Rob asked him to stay. Jake was tempted, because this man had been one of his childhood heroes and one of the most beautiful men in Hollywood. He still was, and his deep voice was a major turn-on for Jake. However, Rob did not invite him to move in or offer to support him. He just wanted him close so the two of them could continue to have sex. Since coming to L.A., Jake had slept with fifteen men, including the three famous actors, all much older than he was. If he stayed, he could guess what his life and career might turn into. Sadly, Jake said good-bye to Rob and took the train back to Tucson and college.

24

Occultation

"When the Moon or a planet passes directly in front of but never completely obscures a more distant planet or star."

Starting his sophomore year, Jake tried to get back in the groove of classes, but he was distracted. And his mood was not helped by a life-threatening experience he had in the campus parking lot just three days after the start of the semester. Since Jake lived off campus, the University assigned him a regular parking space. Jake would drive the ten miles from his grandparents' house to his parking spot on the east side of the football stadium. In the morning and early afternoon, his car baked in the hot desert sun. By 2:00 p.m., though, the double-decker stadium shaded his parking spot.

After finishing up his classes, Jake walked to the red Pinto, opened the driver's door first, then popped the back hatch to let the heat out and walked around to roll down the passenger side window. He threw his backpack onto the seat, closed the hatch, started walking back around to the driver's side, and moved to step into the car. He had gotten his right foot safely inside when a rattlesnake slithered out from underneath the car and stopped three inches from his left foot. Jake was wearing only flip-flops. His first instinct was to try to yank his foot out of the way quickly, but the snake's head started moving from side to side, its rattle going furiously. Jake instead pushed both hands down onto his knee to keep his leg from shaking.

He was terrified; he'd hated snakes ever since that garter snake wiggled between his legs when he was a kid. Jake did not want to look at it, but he knew he could not take his eyes off it, lest he accidentally move his foot. He was crying in panic and sweating in the summer heat. He sat there, half in and half out of the car, for half an hour until the guy who was parked next to him started walking around to *his* own passenger side. Jake pleaded, "Don't come any closer. There's a rattlesnake by my foot. Can you call someone?" This guy did not like snakes either and ran off to find help.

Within a few minutes, two police cars came screeching into the parking lot, and the guy pointed out Jake's location. One cop looked at the snake and assessed the situation with a simple "oh, shit." Initially, there were only four cops, but then several more police cars showed up, with more than a dozen police officers milling around trying to decide how to handle this. Jake just had to keep still and wait for them to figure it out. Finally, one cop got into the other guy's car and moved it out of the way. A young officer slowly handed Jake a bulletproof vest through the passenger window. He instructed Jake to "very slowly, and I mean slowly, slide this across your lap."

Another cop, who was a crack shot, stood ten feet from Jake's driver side, looking directly at Jake and his target. The shooter warned, "You're going to hear a loud bang. Try not to move until I've killed it." Jake did not have a second to prepare himself and yelled as the explosion went off. Something sharp hit his big toe and Jake started screaming, "It bit me; it bit me." But the sharpshooter's aim had been true, hitting the rattlesnake square in the head. The bullet kicked up a chunk of asphalt, which is what slashed Jake's big toe. The cops took him to the University Hospital emergency room to make sure that he had not been bitten and sew up the wound.

Jake wished he could have been braver and more like Cal, who'd had his own run-in with a rattlesnake on his big kayaking trip a year earlier. Cal had recounted the incident to Jake before they went off to college. Cal and his kayak buddy Kurt had gotten separated after going through some rapids, so Cal pulled his kayak onto the shore. As he climbed onto the muddy bank, he stepped close to a rattlesnake, which Cal quickly decapitated with his oar. He decided that he did not have to hunt for their dinner that night, and Kurt took a photo of Cal holding the dead rattlesnake in his hands, pretending to bite into it. Jake thought it a quintessentially Cal thing to do, but he hated looking at that photo.

It had been a full year since they had last seen each other. Jake tried to not think about Cal too much, because it made him too sad, but now Cal came roaring back into the forefront of his thoughts. He wrote a letter telling Cal about the snake ordeal and his Hollywood adventure but leaving out all the sex stuff. He received no reply. He called Cal's house, only to ever get the answering machine. One of his calls even became a little desperate, pleading with Cal to phone him back. He heard nothing, not from Cal, not from his parents. It felt like Cal had ceased to exist altogether, at least for Jake. He could not understand why, and it wounded him deeply.

Jake needed to talk with someone, so he called his counselor Vince, who invited him to come have dinner at his house on Friday. That was usually their Boys' Night, and Jake wanted to talk privately, but Vince assured him that their little group of friends was taking a break for a few more weeks. Sergeant Roy had military exercises out of state, while engineer Harris was working on a highway project in Phoenix. His trips to Louisville and then Hollywood had taken Jake away for the entire summer, so Vince hugged him warmly at the front door. He was genuinely happy to see his young friend. Throughout dinner on the patio, Jake was quiet, not saying much about his summer, and fighting back tears.

Vince gave Jake's shoulder a squeeze. "I hope you know that I'm a good enough friend now that I can tell when something is not right with you. You can say anything to me."

Jake nodded but he did not know where to start. "I'm sad. I think I'm disappointed in myself. I'm disappointed in how things are turning out. I don't know what to do." He told Vince about his random hookups in Hollywood, and the movie stars who liked him and were only too happy to indulge his sexual interest. Vince might not have believed anyone else telling this story, but he knew Jake to be an honest young man. He shook his head in wonder as Jake recounted his trysts with the three stars, but he was truly flabbergasted when Jake produced nude Polaroid photos of himself posed, in succession, with the three famous actors.

"Well, it looks like you had a good time. A really good time."

"I guess, but I didn't feel good about a lot of it."

"How so?"

Jake pondered a bit because he did not want to sound stupid. "I don't know. I felt like maybe I wasn't doing the right thing."

"Oh, please. What is the right thing? Who gets to decide that?"

"I felt like maybe I shouldn't be doing all that stuff. Like people wouldn't approve."

Vince was visibly annoyed, not at Jake but at this type of thinking. "Of course certain people won't approve. You're a homo. There are always going to be those who expect you to act in a certain way or that tell us what we can and cannot do. Fuck 'em. Are you supposed to not do something because someone you don't know doesn't approve of love between two men?"

"I don't think this was love. I mean, these men liked me, but they only wanted to get in my pants."

"And how is that a problem? Look, you're judging yourself. No one else is judging you. I'm not. What you did all summer was claim your power."

Jake was confused. "What power is that?" Vince often talked in grandiose platitudes, especially when it came to matters of sex, so Jake often felt like he needed an interpreter.

"You were owning your sexual power. You were confident. You went in there and said *this is what I want, what I need*. And people responded to that sexual authority. Shit, Jake, you fucked with three big movie stars. Not many people, if any, will ever be able to say that. But you can. So, yes, you were being powerful."

"Maybe. Mostly, I felt used. They didn't care about me. I just happened to be there, and I was eager to please. I feel so stupid."

"Jake, I don't know much about Hollywood. It's not my world, but I do know that showbiz is not exactly known for its kindness. Probably more for its casual disregard for individuals. So, maybe you are not a person to them; maybe you are a commodity to use as they see fit. But you are always totally in control. You can always say no. And if you don't want to say no, then go have a little fun and don't worry about what anyone else thinks."

"I do worry about what some people think. I wonder what they would think about what I'm doing. It's like I've forgotten them." Jake then told him all about his neighbor Mark and his best friend Cal, and how he had spent four years being intimate with both at the same time. He talked about his one-semester liaison with Ken Doll, the opera student. "I haven't forgotten them, but all of them seem to have forgotten me. Everyone always leaves."

Vince dismissed Ken Doll as unimportant. "He was only temporary. You two had fun for a few months and now he's gone." As for Mark, Vince might have thought him a predator had Jake not stated that he had been the instigator of that relationship. His only comment about Mark was, "I'm glad you had someone to guide you kindly into sex." Jake did not care for Vince's assessment of Cal. Vince said, "From what you've told me about him, it seems like he couldn't decide whether he liked you in that way. Maybe you scared him."

Jake resisted that characterization. "No, we were best friends. We were the same person. We loved each other."

"Did you ever tell him?" Sheepishly, Jake admitted that he had not. "Did he ever say the words to you?" Jake shook his head and looked away.

Vince continued, not reading the cues that he had slipped into lecturing Jake. "What you felt was lust for each other, or it was curiosity about your bodies. Love is such a hetero construct. Why should we want that? We don't have to be tied to that idea of getting married, raising a family. We get to be free."

"What if I want to be loved?"

"You're young, Jake. You'll learn." Vince went into the master bedroom to turn down the bed, thinking Jake would be spending the night as usual. Jake left by the side gate, angry that Vince did not understand or appreciate what he had had with Cal. He got back to his grandparents' house and sat on the patio to look up at the night sky. He could still see Cal's face in the moon, but he did not look for him every night as he had promised. The more time that passed, the harder it was and the longer it took to conjure Cal's face.

As Christmas break approached, Jake began negotiations with his father about how long he would be back in Louisville. He did not want to have to change plane tickets like the previous Christmas, so he reminded his father that Jos got weird and ridiculously emotional whenever he was there. Jim would not allow Jake to come home for just a week, but he agreed to let Jake go back to school a week early. First thing, Jake went to Cal's house, but there was no sign of life inside. No one answered the door. Where was Cal? Why could he never find him? Jake might as well have gone back to Tucson that minute.

Jos was still living with Jake's parents after a full year. She got home from her job and threw herself into his arms, crying and kissing him all over his face. She tried to French kiss him in front of the entire family, as they were just sitting down to the dining room table. Jake turned his head and suggested she sit her ass down so they could eat dinner. Conversation was a challenge, because every time his parents asked him a question about school, Jos interrupted with some declaration of her love. He might have listened to her if she ever had something to contribute, but her gushing was insipid and tiresome.

Since that first night they had sex in Tucson, Jake made sure to have condoms with him whenever he was around Jos. He did not want her getting pregnant. That first night home, the family stayed up late playing cards around the dining table, having drinks, and laughing a lot. Jake's dad, sister, and brothers said good night and went to bed, and finally Jos proclaimed that she had to go to work in the morning. Jake talked with

Betty for half an hour before he went down to his mattress in the family room. As he stripped off his clothes and lay down naked, Jake could hear Jos come back downstairs to talk with Betty in the living room, which was above the family room.

Moments later, the door to the basement opened and the stairs creaked as Jos tried unsuccessfully to tiptoe downstairs. Without asking, she took off her t-shirt, bra, and panties and knelt beside him. It seemed that he was going to have to endure this again. He preferred sex with guys, but he was a normal teenager, so arousal was always instantaneous. Why was he allowing this to happen? Why was his mother okay with this? Jos tried to mount him, but he made sure to block her until he could put on a condom. He was a reluctant participant, so he lay back and just let her do her thing. She never noticed that he never looked at her and could not care less if they did this or not. His perpetual boner told her otherwise.

Betty used the family room as her artist's studio to paint, but she stayed away while Jake was home for the holidays to allow Jos a chance to be alone with her son. Jake had to laugh at their silly intrigue, because both his mother and Jos thought they were being so clever and sneaky. Jake was not stupid. He knew they had arranged this together, hoping to ensnare Jake into a situation he could not stop, to ensure that Jos became a permanent part of the family. Jake should have stopped this before it had gone this far, but he never thought about breaking up with someone he did not consider his girlfriend. Jos now had this expectation that they were a couple.

Jake's only weapon against Jos was Ranger Rick, with whom he spent most nights. Jos was jealous, thinking he was sleeping with another girl. Truly, she did not know him at all. On those nights when he stayed home, he refused to have sex with her. He installed a heavy dead bolt on the inside of the door to the basement, so she could not come downstairs. Discovering that she was locked out, she rattled the doorknob and pulled hard against the door so that it was banging against the door frame. Worried she would break something, Jake ran up the stairs, unbolted the door, and threatened to never speak to her again if she did not stop. She stomped upstairs and slammed Jake's bedroom door so the whole house shook.

The next evening, Jake asked Jos to take a walk with him. It was cold outside, and she did not want to go. He put on his coat and walked out. Within two minutes she ran after him. He waited at the top of the driveway. She grabbed his right arm and squeezed tightly, resting her head on his shoulder as he tried to move. Jake told her, "No, just walk." They did not get past one house before she wanted to hold hands. He stopped, turned to her, and insisted, "No, we need to talk, and I don't want you grabbing at me."

He started walking and she ran to catch up. She grabbed his arm tightly again. He shrugged off her hand roughly this time and told her, "Just keep your hands to yourself. Can we please just take a goddamn walk?"

She pouted. "You've been so mean since last summer."

"You've been so clingy since then," he replied.

She started the waterworks, sobbing, "You're my boyfriend and I love you." He asked her how she had concluded that they were dating, when there had never been anything romantic between them.

"How can you say that, Jakey? We dated all through high school."

"That's not true. We hung out for just a few weeks. We never dated."

"We spent all those romantic nights together."

"At Denny's?"

She grasped for fond memories. "You took me to Elton John and Heart."

"Because you begged me too."

"Our prom was so romantic. You kissed me so tenderly."

"Jos, we had a fight because you wouldn't stop trying to kiss me."

She was confused. "Why did you become my lover then?"

"Because you sat on my dick."

"You must have liked it. You got so hard."

"I'm always hard."

"You wanted me so bad."

"No, Jos. It was the other way around. You wanted me. I didn't want to sleep with you."

"You show me how much you want me every time we make love."

"I don't have much choice in the matter. Haven't you noticed that I never ask you for sex?"

She started to sniffle for dramatic effect. "Why don't you want me anymore? I've been your girlfriend for four years."

"Stop lying. You have never been my girlfriend."

By now, her tears were flowing. "Why can't I be your girlfriend? Is there a girl back in Tucson? Tell me who she is."

"There is no girl, Jos."

"What do you want then, Jake?"

"I don't want a girl."

"I feel like I'm losing you."

"You can't lose what you never had."

"Why don't you love me anymore?"

Jake stopped to look at her. "You aren't listening to me at all, are you?"

That's how it always went with Jos. She had this scenario set in her mind about how things were supposed to go her way.

If life did not match her fantasy world, she would deflect onto Jake how he was somehow at fault for not living up to her expectations. If that did not work, she got clingy, as if he would be stunned into submission by her soft fleshy body. If clutching failed, she resorted to weeping. If that tactic did not pan out, she wailed. The harder she tried to make Jake love her, the more she repulsed him. He did not just resent her; he started to hate her and wish they had never met.

Before heading back to school, Jake took the dead bolt off the basement door. He had a heart-to-heart chat with his father on the way to the airport that quickly turned into a lecture. When Jake mentioned his frustration, Jim said that Jake was going to have to "be a man about it" if he wanted to break up with Jos. That comment felt like a slap. Jim suggested that soon Jake would need to put aside his childish pursuits, meaning his performing, grow up to become an adult, and start working toward making a living that would someday support a wife and a family. Jake was only nineteen years old, and Jim was already telling his son how the rest his life was going to go. Jake understood that that is what his father had done, but he did not want those same things for himself.

Jake was going to have to figure out this problem for himself. He had the luxury of running back to school, while Jim was still stuck having Jos in his house. Anything he might do to get her out would only make his wife Betty furious, and he ascribed to the notion of "happy wife, happy life." Jake offered a suggestion. "Grandpa makes me work for my room-and-board. I help clean and fix up his rental properties. Make Jos pay rent." The day after Jake left, Jim brought up the topic of rent to her, and Jos knew her time was up. She moved out two weeks later. She moved back in with her parents for a while before that proved untenable again and she finally had to get her own apartment.

25

Inclination

"The angle between the plane of a celestial body's orbit and a reference plane, such as the Earth's equator."

Jake felt that everyone was pushing him toward something he did not want, and that concern only intensified once he arrived back in Tucson. Betty called her father only once a month, but suddenly she was calling him every week. Jake often saw Grandpa glowering at him when he was on the phone with her, and he knew his mother was checking up on him. His grandparents usually left him alone to do his own thing, knowing that a college student had a lot of class requirements, school commitments, and social activities. Jake could come and go as he pleased, but now Grandpa started interrogating him about every moment of his day.

Picking Communications for his major, Jake worked at the PBS television station that the university operated. He often had late-night studio setups, which required him to stay until 3:00 or 4:00 in the morning. He drove home, entered the house through the garage, locked up, and quietly went into his bedroom to sleep. Now his grandfather disapproved of everything Jake did. His late nights at the TV studio began to be a topic of concern for him, that perhaps he was leading too wild a life and not concentrating on more important things. When he tried to explain exactly how difficult and time-consuming work at the studio was each week, Grandpa launched into almost the exact lecture that his father gave him driving to the airport. Jake knew his mother was behind this.

He tried to explain his TV studio work in terms that Grandpa could understand. His grandparents loved watching *The Tonight Show* with Johnny Carson, so he gave a lengthy explanation about how NBC most likely put on that show every night. Grandpa was interested at first, impressed that Jake seemed to know his stuff and could convey that information to him, but he then dismissed this kind of work. He said, "Well, that's just playtime. That's not a real job." He had developed his own company and had become an executive, all through his own ingenuity, ambition, and hard work, so that was the only kind of career he understood.

Grandpa disregarded everything Jake was studying, what he was pursuing, his performance activities. He was particularly critical of Jake spending any time working in the arts, calling it "an utter waste of time, a distraction to living in the real world." Jake had thought they were becoming close, but that clearly was not true. His grandfather did not know and did not care about his dreams and goals. He did not even care to hear Jake's opinion on any topic that they discussed. He just wanted to mold Jake into a version of himself, into what he thought a man should be.

Grandpa had this odd notion that becoming a Shriner, like him, would do the trick. Jake asked for more information about the Shriners, and Grandpa could not give him a satisfying answer, saying only that it was a charitable organization. Jake went to the university library to find an old newspaper article, stored on microfiche, that documented the long, convoluted history of Freemasonry. It was a boring article that made the organization seem equally dull. The Fraternal Order of Shriners was not a charitable organization, but rather a fraternity based on fun, fellowship, and the Masonic principles of relief, truth, and brotherly love. It sounded kind of faggoty to him.

Grandpa thought that Jake would be well suited for the branch of the Shriners known as the DeMolay Society, for young men between the ages of twelve and twenty-one of "good character." That was code, meaning young white men. The older Shriners served as mentors to the younger DeMolay members, and Grandpa felt it important for Jake to have a strong male role model. The Society's seven cardinal virtues were Reverence for sacred things, Patriotism, Filial love, Courtesy, Cleanliness, Comradeship, and Fidelity. Jake was not religious; he had no interest in American fervor; he did love his parents; he was always polite, and he showered every day. The last two, Comradeship and Fidelity, made him laugh. Jake was certain the group would contribute nothing to his life.

But out of respect for his grandfather, Jake agreed to attend a ceremony of the Shriners, in which a lot of older white men shed their dull daily business attire for rainbow-colored, bedazzled robes and festooned fezzes. For an organization that he promised would make Jake a man, there sure were a lot of sequins in that gymnasium that night. Grandpa looked expectantly at Jake for his opinion, saying, "You love theater, and this is a type of theater." Jake's response was hardly enthusiastic: "I'm already working in theater. Why would I want this instead?"

On the ride home afterward, Grandpa told Jake this group had purpose, so Jake asked what that might be. Grandpa said fund-raising for worthy causes. Jake said it would be easier for these rich men to simply donate to those causes, instead of spending all this money on fancy robes and fezzes, colorful banners, and a big processional ceremony. Grandpa persevered, extolling the Shriners' community and strong male camaraderie. Jake challenged him, "Couldn't you guys just go out for a beer?" Jake was not trying to being confrontational or even a smart-ass. He wanted honest answers to some basic questions. Grandpa did not care to give him those answers; he just wanted to make it so that Jake could not say no to him.

His grandfather insisted that Jake go to at least one meeting for the DeMolay. Dressed in a suit and tie, Jake went to a church to join twelve other white guys his age for this gathering. The man in charge that night was someone Jake had met previously when he had come over to the house to work with his grandfather on a committee. He was much younger than Grandpa, probably Jake's father's age. This pillar of his community tried groping Jake in a toilet stall during a break that night. Jake wagged his finger at him and warned, "Naughty, naughty." That man never extended an invitation for Jake to join the DeMolay, so he was off the hook.

For all this familial concern about his manhood, Jake never felt more like a man than when he was in bed with another man. No one can please a man the same way that another guy can, because they know what feels good. Jake was irritated that some people thought that a homosexual wanted to be a woman. Nothing could be further from the truth. Jake was never more aware of his penis, his ass, his biceps, his pecs, his muscles, his back, his shoulders, his waist, his legs, everything that made him male, than when he was with another man. The exhortation to "be a man" was a challenge for Jake to be something that others believed he was not. He had proved to himself that he was a man a long time ago. Vince had been correct. This was about Jake proclaiming his power.

Inclination

After completing his sophomore year, Jake returned to Louisville for the summer. The first thing he did, as always, was to look for Cal. Jake suspected that perhaps Cal's parents Leigh and Zan felt their friendship was too close. He checked at the gym where Cal worked with Coach Williams, at the JCC pool, at all their usual haunts around town. No luck, so he caved and finally went to Cal's house to ask his parents. They greeted him warmly but told him that Cal was out of state working as a counselor and activities director for an adventure camp. Jake was disappointed once again but not heartbroken, as he was now very familiar with Cal's habit of vanishing for months at a time.

He was not nervous about going home because Joslyn had moved out, and he would not have to deal with her every second of every day. In fact, he did not see her for the first week of his summer vacation. He spent several nights over at Ranger Rick's apartment before finally agreeing to meet with her. He was trying to keep her at arm's length, setting the boundaries for the upcoming summer. He arrived at her apartment in the Hikes Point area, near the crazy convergence of the Watterson Expressway, Taylorsville Road, and Breckinridge Lane. Jake hoped the bad traffic in her area would provide an additional excuse for not spending every single evening with her.

They went to Denny's and had a nice time chatting over burgers, fries, and a soda. Jake made sure that they were seated at a table with separate chairs rather than at a booth, so she could not sidle up to him. She talked about her apartment hunt, her secretary job, her continued struggles with her parents. He told her all about his semester that had just ended. She looked sad because she did not get to gush and fawn and grope. He liked her better this way, and this was probably the only way that they could remain friends.

Jake got a summer job working for the Louisville *Courier-Journal*. His former manager, Bob, from when he had the newspaper corner, had come to buy a painting from Betty that he had seen at a local art fair. Bob hired Jake to turn around one district, where a previous supervisor had not kept up with taking payments from the newspaper boys for the daily papers they delivered on their routes. Jake got all the routes paid up to date in just a few weeks, and even had to deliver a few routes when boys quit, until someone else could take over. Very early one Sunday morning, Jake fell asleep at the wheel while driving between paper routes and ran into a ditch, destroying the car's undercarriage and requiring several weeks of repair. No car meant no more job.

Jos started spending more time once again at Jake's house, because they were getting along, without the romantic foolishness of last Christmas. They even spent a day at King's Island amusement park in Mason, Ohio, but Jake got horribly nauseous eating a piece of pizza and nearly vomited. He felt worse as the day progressed, so Jos had to drive all the way back to Louisville, and Jake hated when she drove. For days, he had no energy, felt sick to his stomach, and noticed that his urine had turned brown.

Betty took Jake to the doctor, who ran tests that came back positive for mononucleosis, jaundice, and hepatitis B. The doctor ordered him to drink lots of fluids, get plenty of rest, and stop all physical activity. Jake thought he would be better in a few weeks; the doctor said it would take probably two months or longer. On top of that, the doctor told Jake no sexual activity of any kind because he could get someone else sick.

That diagnosis would keep Jos off him, so that was the upside. He also had to call Rick to let him know that they could not meet for the rest of the summer. Rick was disappointed, but his main concern was for Jake's health.

Jake moved into his sister Ellie's old bedroom, because it had the private half bathroom so he could easily run to the toilet, which he did every few minutes. Betty was his nurse, and Jos started coming over on her lunch hour to help and then would visit again every night. Jake was barely conscious most of the time, so he hardly noticed whenever someone walked into the room to take his temperature or give him more chicken broth or tea to drink. Jake loved his father's visits most of all. Jim sat on the edge of the bed, rubbed Jake's arm, and quietly repeated, "Get well, buddy." He sat in the desk chair for hours, reading a book so he could be close to him in case he needed anything.

Due to his condition, Jake had not had sex with Jos since the first week of his Christmas break six months earlier, and that was fine with him. Since he was incapacitated, Jos took advantage of the situation. Whenever she could be sure no one would interrupt, she locked the bedroom door, got naked and straddled him. He was hardly aware she was doing this because he slept most of the time, barely conscious for an hour or two each day. He had a vague awareness of getting erections, but most of these seemed like fevered wet dreams. When he started feeling better, Jos confessed that they had been having sex the entire time he was sick. She said she used a condom every time, but that was small comfort to Jake.

By mid-August, the doctor still had not cleared Jake to go back to school. Jos was thrilled, but Jake was desperate to run away and start his junior year. Jos forced the discussion of commitment, saying she was tired of waiting. They ought to get married. Jake said that they could talk about it, but only discuss, and only after he had finished college. She did not agree. In her usual conniving way, she twisted their conversation into something approaching a marriage proposal. Jake thought, "I'm too sick right now. I will deal with this later." Big mistake. Jos told everyone that Jake had proposed.

Jim came up to Jake's room to have a talk. He came right out and asked, "You want this?"

"It's what I'm supposed to do, right?"

Jim pressed his son a little harder, "Are you sure about her?"

"No, but if not her, who then?" His sister lived with a boyfriend. His brothers had girlfriends. Jake had watched as most of his high school and college friends dated, became attached, and got engaged. Even his beloved Cal had gotten himself a girlfriend. Everyone expected him to do the same thing. In late August, the doctor finally cleared him to go back to school. Betty and Jos hoped that he would take the semester off from school to fully recover, but Jake had to get out of there. With the doctor's admonition to take it easy, Jake escaped to Tucson just a few days before classes were set to begin.

His fall semester was dull and uneventful because he still felt lethargic. He could not go to folk dance; he could not take dance classes; he could not stay up late at the TV studio; he could not jog; he did not have energy to do anything but go to lectures and sleep. He felt pathetic, like he was mindlessly sleepwalking through life without a purpose. With so much free time and the inability to do the things he loved, he kept thinking of Cal, who seemed to have had a very clear vision for his future from a very early age. Why couldn't he be the same way? All Jake wanted to do was to run away, take a nap, hide, and waste

Inclination

time. It seemed like everyone was telling him how to live his life. Just for once, he wanted to have some fun.

By Halloween, Jake had blood work done and learned he was fully recovered. The Tucson doctor told him it was okay to have sex again, so long as he did not overdo it. Jake called Vince and told him to invite the others for Boys' Night. He wanted to make up for lost time. Jake loved these weekend trysts with Vince, Roy, Harris, and Jose. No one was shy, and they were comfortable with one another. In between bouts of their various couplings, they often stood around naked in the kitchen getting a bite to eat, or sipping some wine, while one of the others might light up a cigarette. They had indoctrinated Jake into this cult of cock. Jake wanted to have fun before his fun days were done. And sex was fun.

Vince thought that Jake looked down and grilled him in his usual unrelenting way to find out what was wrong. Jake revealed to them that he had somehow gotten engaged to marry a girl. He explained how he had met Joslyn, how she became a gal pal, and how that friendship changed when his mother became close to her. They asked questions about how and why Jake came to have sex with her when he knew that he was a homosexual. Harris deemed Jake's mother Betty as evil, but Vince, with his psychology background, proclaimed her only a clueless dupe to Jos, who was the true villainess.

Then Jake revealed how Jos managed to have sex with him all summer, despite his illness and without his consent. Vince observed, "If the roles were reversed and you were the girl, that would be rape. But you were unconscious and got fucked, so that's still rape." Jake cried and apologized for ruining the evening, but all of them were loving and supportive. And they were angry too. Jake shared with them the pressure he was getting from his parents and his grandfather. Even Jake was feeling that he had to conform to what society determined was normal. He was beginning to feel like he was doomed to have an unhappy life.

Always the smart-ass, Jose joked that Jake's dick might still get a workout with a wife for at least the first year of marriage. Jake countered, "It gets enough of a workout with you guys." At the end of their evening together, Jake wound up with Roy, the Air Force sergeant. Jake liked all the guys, but he felt differently about Roy, a little more intense, both sexually and emotionally. Jake cried a little while in Roy's arms. Roy whispered, "It's not so bad. I'm married too." That admission jolted Jake. Roy continued, "It's what guys like us have to do. You find ways to make it work." Jake spent the night with Roy in the guest bedroom, while the other three had noisy sex all night long in the master bedroom.

Jake returned to Louisville for Christmas. Again, no Cal; this time he was kayaking with friends in the Florida Keys. At least Jake had Ranger Rick to fill his lonely hours. Jake was livid to learn that Jos had had their wedding date moved up an entire year, from after his college graduation in May 1980 to July 1979. Her only reason was "I'm not going to wait anymore for us to get married. It's this, or else I walk." Jake prayed that she would, so he told her, "Go ahead and do it." Jos pretended that she did not hear that. Even saying it out loud, Jos was oblivious to anything that did not fit her fantasy narrative. Jake did not know what else he had to do to end this charade.

Jake attended Pre-Cana classes with Jos, because she wanted them to marry in her parents' Catholic Church. He did not like anything about religion, so he could care less whether any kids they might have would be raised Catholic. Pre-Cana was supposed to be a six-month course of instruction, but they only had two weeks before Jake went back to school, so they attended class every night. So as not to raise any red flags about his scorn for religion, he learned very quickly to simply say "yes" to every question the deacon asked.

Their only time spent together was at these marriage classes, which prompted many disagreements, so they fought about everything. After every class together, Jos arranged activities to keep Jake all to herself, never asking what he might want to do. Since she did not care about his opinion, Jake did not care if he spent any time with her. He merely acknowledged that he had heard her and then went out and did his own thing, which usually meant going to see Rick instead. He spent every night at Rick's apartment.

Betty thought Jake was out screwing a bunch of girls, so she worried that he would be incapable of committing to Jos. That struck Jake as completely ridiculous; he had never shown any interest in girls his entire life, and that included this girl. Rick had two nights off, so Jake skipped the Friday night Pre-Cana to be with him. Jos was devastated that Jake had stood her up for this most important event in their journey as a couple. She got Betty riled up at his insolence. The next morning when he walked into the house, Betty was lying in wait for him. "Your father and I want to have a talk with you."

26

Panspermia

"The hypothesis, first proposed in the fifth century BC by the Greek philosopher Anaxagoras, that life exists throughout the Universe, seeded by space dust, meteoroids, asteroids, comets, and planetoids."

Betty grabbed his T-shirt and pulled him into the master bedroom, where Jim was working at his desk. Jim and Betty motioned for Jake to sit in the desk chair, while they faced him, like a jury, from the edge of their bed. Betty jumped in right away. "You stay out every night. Who is keeping you away from home?"

"His name is Rick."

Betty was already fuming. "Who the hell is that? I've never heard his name before."

"Yes, you have. I told you about him last Christmas."

"You should be spending time with Joslyn. Not some stranger."

"He's not a stranger. He's a very dear friend who I care for a lot."

"He's nobody to you. Jos is the only person in your life who should matter."

"No, Mom. She's the only person who you think should

matter. I can't stand her anymore. Can we stop pretending that I want this?"

She walked to the door and looked to Jim. "Talk to your idiot son. He's going to ruin this."

Jake always thought of his father as a kind, thoughtful parent, but he did not know Jake any better than his mother. Jim expressed their concern that Jake might be doing drugs and that this Rick person was leading him astray.

"Wow. If you think I might be doing drugs, then you haven't been paying attention all these years. And you don't have to worry about Rick. He's a cop. He's the same man who came to interview me at the hospital. You should remember him."

"I don't remember him. Sorry. But who is he to you?"

Jake paused and took a deep breath. "Dad, he's my boyfriend."

Jim did not know how to react. He paused just a little too long for it to be a matter of finding the right words to say. He was stumped. Jake filled the void by admitting, "Dad, I like guys," and promptly burst into tears. Jim thought Jake's crying meant he did not want to be a homo.

"Do you want to talk with someone?"

"What? You mean like a shrink? No, I don't need a shrink. What I need is to stop pretending I'm something else."

"What about Joslyn?"

"What about her? I never wanted this. Mom wanted this."

Sadly, his father had no words of wisdom for his son, so he passed the buck. "You better go talk with your mother."

His mother was sitting in the living room. Betty was very short, less than five feet tall, so sitting on the couch meant she would have had to heave herself off the cushions if she got upset at him. Instead, she had seated herself in the high-backed chair, from which she could easily push off the chair's arms and stand up quickly. Clearly, she was expecting a confrontation. She demanded to know, "What the hell is going on with you?" Jake relayed to her the exact same information that he had just given his father. Betty launched herself from the chair and smacked Jake hard across the face.

She was furious. Jake was going to ruin her plan to have Jos become a part of her family. Jake did not hold back, now just as eager to hurt his mother as she had just hurt him. "Mom, I have no interest in Jos. Never have. I'm a homo."

"No, you are not. No! You just have cold feet before the wedding." Jake tried to make her understand that he did not want to get married, and that she and Jos were railroading him into this. Betty raised her hand to slap Jake again, but he grabbed her arm before she could. When he was eleven, Jake had lipped off to his mother and she tried to smack him with a belt, but he was bigger than her even then and had taken the belt out of her hands. She cried at that, and she cried now.

He packed his suitcase, walked out of the house, took a bus downtown to Rick's place, and waited for hours outside his apartment in the cold. Jake spent the next five days there, not going to Pre-Cana classes and not calling his folks. He was a mess, but relieved to have finally told his parents the truth. Now he had to tell Rick everything, about the annoying and undesirable girlfriend, the engagement, the upcoming wedding he did not want.

"I should let you know this, Jake. I was married once too." In almost the exact words used by Jake's buddy Roy in Tucson a few weeks earlier, Rick said, "It's what we have to do." Jake had no idea what he wanted. Out of the blue, Rick asked if Jake wanted to move in with him instead. Jake had not expected such an offer. He liked Rick; he lusted after Rick; maybe he loved Rick. He was handsome and so sexy. They had fun together; they had great sex together. Jake had mentioned that he felt that he was wasting his time in college, but Rick was now suggesting that he drop out and move back here to start a life with him.

Being twice Jake's age, Rick was set in his ways, and being a cop, he might always want to be in charge. Jake had already established a pattern of having dominant personalities around him. He let neighbor Mark be the controlling force in his teenage life for four years. His friend Cal was a gregarious, warm-hearted guy who drew people to him, while Jake was content to let him have the spotlight. The opera student Ken Doll cut an impressive figure, and Jake had seemed merely his sidekick. His counselor Vince was this grandiose mentor and sexual guru, and Jake was his acolyte. Then there was Jos the octopus, the bulldozer, the pain-in-the-neck.

When was it ever going to be his turn to stand out, to take charge of his own life? Jake did not turn down Rick's offer, but he asked him to be patient. Jake promised they would discuss it again when he came back in May. For the next few days together, they just decided to have fun, which meant they hardly ever got out of bed. Rick drove Jake to the airport, got out of the car at the departures drop-off, physically lifted him off the ground in a big hug, and gave him a long kiss on the curb in front of everyone. He did not care if anyone saw them, and neither did Jake. He was mad at Jos, mad at his parents, mad at Catholics, mad at Pre-Cana, mad at married people, mad at the world. To hell with them all.

Rick and Jake did not have any kind of agreement. Most of the time, they were 1,700 miles apart from one another. Jake assumed Rick had other lovers, and Jake was sure Rick realized the same thing about him. Jake spent his last five days in Louisville sleeping with Rick. He spent the next six days back in Tucson sleeping with Vincent. When Jake finally showed up at his grandparents' house, Grandpa called Betty to let her know that he had arrived safely. Jake would not speak with her. During their first game of backgammon, Grandpa gave Jake the old lecture about maturity, adult responsibility, and the usual nonsense about being a man. Jake kept his mouth shut.

Jake decided to strike out on his own for the last months before his wedding. He moved out of his grandparents' home into a boarding house immediately west of campus. He rented a long, narrow bedroom off the kitchen and next to a full bathroom that no one else used. His door opened into a back hallway, but he also had an outside door that caused him concern. It was not very secure, as it was just a hollow interior door with a flimsy doorknob lock. He worried someone could break in easily, so he went to the hardware store to buy metal kickplates, crossbars, and two strong deadbolts to reinforce the door.

Jake was back to folk dancing and performing, doing late nights at the TV studio, and hanging out with classmates at food joints and bars around campus. By not living with grandparents, he finally got to experience what college life was really like. He liked the boarding house's upstairs wraparound porch from which he could stargaze and talk to Cal. He did that less frequently now, but to stop entirely would feel like giving up on the dearest friend he ever had. A housemate, Brandon, a cute, compact freshman, caught Jake talking to the moon and teased him about it. They started sleeping together that night.

In addition to his daily trysts with Brandon, Jake still reserved Friday and Saturday nights for going over to Vince's house for Boys' Night. As Roy was married, he had family responsibilities and often could not join in. Harris had another interstate highway project he was managing, so he too was gone. That spring, it was just Jake with Vince and Jose, but even Jose stopped coming for a while because he preferred the whole group dynamic with all five of them together. Jake thought about inviting little Brandon to join their group. However, he was this Mormon kid from Utah who had made disparaging remarks about blacks and Latinos. Jake could not have Brandon be a part of their group, so it became just Jake and Vince, and that suited the two of them just fine.

Jake was twenty and had already been sexually active for six-and-a-half years, and he'd had some wonderful lovers so far. Mark taught him everything he knew about sex. He and Cal shared an intense intimacy that he'd felt with no one else. Ranger Rick was this astounding, gargantuan physical specimen of raging manhood, who nearly drove Jake insane with lust and then made him swoon with tenderness. Vince, though, was simply the most remarkable lover he ever had.

Vincent could be adventurous, inquisitive, verbal, uninhibited, open-minded, enthusiastic, sensual, spiritual, political, animalistic, raunchy, nasty, rough, raw, or gentle. He turned sex into an art form, and it was also a political statement. A great part of it was his willingness to talk openly about sex, sexuality, desire, lust, physical need, and emotional want, and to communicate all of that during sex. He challenged his partners to think, not just thrust. Above all, he felt that there should be no shame associated with sex or the body, and that fucking should be fun and joyous. He and Jake laughed a lot. Even though he was renting a room, Jake lived only four blocks from Vince, so he spent most nights over there.

The semester flew by too quickly, and Jake dreaded what awaited him back home. He went back on a one-way plane ticket, just seven weeks shy of the wedding. He still compared his upcoming wedding to standing before a firing squad. With words of support from Roy and Rick, he decided that this was indeed "what guys like us have to do." He made peace with his decision to go through with it and tried to think about all the positive aspects of being married. He could not come up with any. His parents had conveniently forgotten Jake's admission, made over winter break, to being homosexual.

Jake's first task was to find Cal. He needed to talk with his best friend, to find out why they had not seen each other in two-and-a-half years, to see if he ever missed Jake. He debated whether to invite him to the wedding. Jake was not sure that he would be able to go through with it if he saw Cal sitting in the church while he swore to "love, honor, protect, while forsaking all others." Jake felt that would be the ultimate disloyalty. In his search, he learned that Leigh and Zan were not in Louisville that summer, instead taking a long-planned trip traveling across Europe. He could not find Cal at home, at the gym, or at the cabin.

After a week of searching to no avail, Jake was despondent. Betty, acting so concerned at his sadness and disappointment, chirped, "Why the long face? You should be celebrating this new chapter of your life." When he explained how he could not find Cal, Betty informed him that she had taken care of that problem. "Oh, he kept lurking around the house, always asking for you."

"Omigod, when was he here?"

"Every time you came home from school." Jake realized that he had tried so hard to get away from Jos that he was always hiding out with Rick for a couple years now. He had not been home all those times Cal came looking for him. This time, it had been him running away. He had always wondered why Cal never looked for him. He had been looking the whole time since they graduated high school, but he could not understand why Cal did not phone him back or write anymore. Maybe his parents had something to do with that. If his mother could do this to him, maybe Cal's had done something similar.

"When was the last time he was here? I have to know."

"It was last summer:"

"But I was here all summer sick in bed. Why did he never come up to see me? You had to know I wanted to see him."

"You were so ill that I thought it best that you have no visitors so you could get as much rest as possible."

"So, you decided that Cal couldn't come up, but you let Jos pester me all fucking summer?"

"Jos was helping me care for you."

"Goddamnit. She was forcing me to have sex with her the entire time. Did she tell you that? Tell me what you said to Cal."

"I told him that you were engaged, and you didn't need him anymore."

Jake was stunned, but mostly he wanted to strangle his mother at that very moment. "Why would you do that? You have no right to interfere in my life. Omigod, I fucking hate you." He stormed away from her, yelling, "You stupid, stupid bitch." It had been his mother who was keeping Cal away from Jake. How could he fix this? How could he get back those three years they lost?

Betty always took Jos's side over his. She thought that Jos's emotional manipulation and physical aggression toward him were somehow adorable. Jake blamed his mother for all of this. Upon meeting Jos for the first time, it was his mother who insisted that she come back to visit anytime. When Jos pulled that stunt throwing her belongings into the snow, Betty invited her to move in. When Jake showed no sexual interest in her, Betty engineered that trip to Tucson, where Jos first bedded him without his consent. Most of this nonsense with Jos could not have happened without Betty's willing participation. He would not be getting married if it had not been for his mother's interference.

Jake blamed himself for not having the strength of character to stand up to these two strong-willed women. The first thing he did was to call Cal and leave a message, apologizing for his mother's rude attitude toward him. Then he wrote a letter to Cal, riding his bike over to the house and putting it in the mailbox outside to make sure that he got it. In it, he wrote, "All I have ever done these past three years is think about you. It was never my fault that we didn't find each other. I have tried and been devastated by not having you in my life. Please contact me as soon as possible. I need to see you. I miss you. All my love, Jake."

For six weeks, he did everything he could to avoid speaking to his mother. He stayed away from the house. He refused to go out with Jos. He stayed with Rick, hanging out at his apartment even when he was working for the day. When Jake did come home, Betty acted like nothing had happened between them. Jake rebuffed her attempts to hug him or to talk with him. She never apologized. On Thursday of wedding week, Jim threw a bachelor party for Jake, with only his brothers, a few relatives who had come for the wedding, and Jim's closest work partner. Jim did not think to ask Jake if he wanted to invite anyone.

The night before his wedding, Jake spent the night with Rick, having their usual contortionist, backbreaking sex. As Jake left, Rick pulled him into one of his body-engulfing hugs.

He gave Jake a long kiss and whispered, "Bye, my baby boy. You know where I am. Let me know when you're single again."

The family started to gather. Jos and her mother had ignored Jake's request for a small, simple wedding. They turned it into this costly Catholic High Mass for the Louisville social set. If the Cathedral had been an ocean liner, it would have capsized and drowned everybody, because Jos's family guests numbered in the hundreds; Jake's family had just twenty guests on their side of the church.

Jake looked like a twelve-year-old in his all-white tuxedo. Jos looked exactly as she had at their senior prom, except with the addition of a bridal veil. Jake sleepwalked through the day, hardly remembering the photography session, the wedding itself, or the reception. As they drove away to spend their wedding night at the brand-new Hyatt Regency Hotel, Jos wanted to talk about their favorite moments from the day. Jake could not remember any. Jake's parents threw a party afterward for family at the house. In front of everyone, Jim offered his assessment of Jake's marriage and their chances for happiness, announcing, "I give it a year."

After their single night at the fancy hotel, the newlyweds moved into the Motel 6 on Bardstown Road for the next six nights. It was located across the street from the old diner where Cal and Jake used to hang out, next to the Showcase Cinemas where they had worked together, and a mile from Cal's house. Their first night there, Jake waited until Jos had fallen asleep to leave the motel room and walk over to Cal's house. He hoped that the odd time of day might be the trick to finally finding him at home. The house was dark. No one was there. Jake was dejected walking back to the motel. Here he was supposed to be paying attention to his bride, and all he could think about was Cal.

When it came time for the nightly ritual of Jos wanting him to impregnate her as quickly as possible, Jake would go into the bathroom to masturbate so there would be nothing left for her. When it was her turn in the bathroom to get ready, Jake put on a condom on himself without her seeing it. He had to practically jump her bones the second she came out so that she was too surprised to think to take it off him. There was no way he was letting her get pregnant any time soon, or hopefully ever.

27

Retrograde

"When an object moves in the reverse sense of normal motion, appearing to backtrack in the sky because of the changing viewing perspective caused by Earth's orbital motion."

Jake and Jos spent all week boxing her clothes and belongings and packing them, along with cast-off furniture from Jake's parents, into a small hauling truck. If truth be told, Jake packed everything. Jos sat and watched. Their plan was to drive back to Tucson for Jake to start his senior year at college. He wanted to do the trip in three days, but Jos did not want to sit in a truck for ten hours a day, trying to cover six hundred miles at a time. She asked that they spread it out just a little, spending no more than eight hours covering four hundred miles. Jos did not ask; she demanded.

Jake had to drive the entire trip as Jos had shown herself to be a distracted driver most of the time. He did not trust her behind the wheel. Jake saw it as an adventure; Jos thought it an ordeal, so she complained about being hot, bored, and uncomfortable the whole way. The trip could have gone faster, and Jos wanted it over as soon as possible, but she was the one causing all the delays. They had to stop every hour so she could get out, go pee, and stretch her legs. Instead of grabbing a sandwich at a delicatessen and eating in the truck, Jos insisted that they stop for sit-down meals, even if it was only a pancake house.

At night, they stayed at cheap motor lodges, where they could park their truck right outside their room. Jake waited until Jos went into the bathroom for her nightly ritual of showering, combing, flossing, brushing, douching, powdering, and primping. Then he would walk out past the parking lot to the kid's playground. There he sat on a park bench and looked up at the stars. He found the moon and conjured Cal's face, so he could talk to his friend. He asked for forgiveness in betraying their bond by getting married, by not looking for him harder, by going away to college in the first place. He had so many regrets when it came to Cal. He wanted them to start over from scratch and change their futures. It was too late for that now.

"Who are you talking to?" Jos scared the hell out of Jake, as he was lost in his private reverie with Cal.

"Nobody. Just talking out loud."

"It sounded more like a conversation with someone. So, tell me who."

"Just a good friend that I miss."

"What's her name?"

"Jeez, this again. You really are kind of stupid. There is no girl, never has been. I was talking to my friend Cal."

Jos had forgotten who that was. "No, you are stupid for talking to someone who's not here. You might as well be talking with ghosts."

Jake acted like she was not there, continuing his conversation with Cal silently, although she could see his lips moving. She asked questions; he gave no answers. She blathered about her favorite moments sightseeing that day, even though they never left the interstates. She grabbed his arm and nestled her head into his shoulder, expecting a squeeze or cuddle in response. He kept looking overhead, not paying attention to her, which always drove her crazy. Finally, she acted like she enjoyed stargazing as well. She looked up, scanned the skies quickly without really looking, and sighed dreamily.

"This is so romantic." She nuzzled his neck more vociferously, then kissed it several times. Jake kept his attention focused on the moon. She pulled his chin toward her so she could kiss his lips. He did not kiss back but returned his gaze overhead. Getting no response from him, she did that thing he hated, where she rolled across his lap so he would have to support her weight while she attempted to slobber all over him. He pushed her off as gently as he could, stood up from the bench, and walked away from her, never talking his eyes off the moon.

Jos was stymied that her attempts to let him know who was boss in this relationship were not working. "Come in soon?" Although her voice made this sound like a question, it was a demand. Jake ignored her, not looking at her, not saying a word to her. She did not exist in that moment and would not until he was done spending time with his faraway friend Cal. She grunted in frustration and stomped back to their room, putting the chain across the door so Jake could not get back in. He slept across the seat of the truck that night.

The next morning, Jos took her time getting ready and strolled out to the truck like nothing had happened. She made it known that she was ready to go that very minute, but Jake walked into the room, put the chain on the door, and took his time to shit, shower, and shave. He made Jos wait in the truck for half an hour before he climbed up into the driver's seat. Jos was irritated, but she was smart enough to know that she would not win an argument if she started one first thing in the morning. She was quickly learning that Jake was not as easily manipulated as she would have liked. He simply ignored her when she tried. The trip took four days, but it felt like weeks.

Jake thought of Jos as kind of useless. Jake packed the truck in Louisville; he unpacked it in Tucson. He had found an apartment for them ahead of time and paid the first and last months' rent and damage deposit out of his savings. He set up all the furniture and rearranged the apartment, with her offering intrusive instructions that were no help at all. He cooked dinner every night. She took time off and did not look for work right away, saying she wanted to get acquainted with her new city first. What she wanted to do was sit out by the pool every day, swim, read a book, and nap. Jake worked tirelessly to make this their home. She did nothing to help.

Sex between them was perfunctory at best. Jake felt it was his husbandly duty to perform, but this was not about satisfying Jos's desires. She wanted to get pregnant as quickly as possible, probably because she saw it as the only way to hold onto him. Every time they ever had sex, Jake got up to take a pee afterward and watched as Jos pulled her knees up to her breasts and held that position, as if willing his almighty sperm to fertilize her eggs. It was so calculating on her part, and they had not even discussed having children yet.

Jos liked routine, so Jake learned quickly that there was always a certain time of day she wanted to have sex. He would anticipate the daily coupling and made sure he went into the bathroom, ostensibly to use the toilet but really to masturbate furiously a couple times, so he would be drained of the potent sperm. Being an actor, he convinced her that he had reached climax by thrusting a little harder and a little faster, grunting audibly as if spent, and then collapsing his head onto her shoulder. When he got up, he watched her hitch up her hips and grab her knees, before closing the bathroom door and laughing at her. It turns out men could fake an orgasm too.

Two weeks after returning to Tucson, Jake started rehearsals for *The Music Man* with the light opera company in town. He had auditioned in late May before going home for the summer and found out that he had been cast as Tommy Djilas, the lead dancer. On his first day of rehearsal, he arrived early before most everyone else. Walking into rehearsal, he saw a cute guy across the room, sitting on the floor with his back against the wall. He had the same smile as Jake's neighbor Mark, the same lean build as Cal, and a face as handsome as Ranger Rick. His name was Will, and like Jake, he could do gymnastics. Jake thought, "Oh boy, here's trouble."

For four weeks, Jake had only been with Jos and had tried not to think of men. He could fool himself that he was finally heterosexual, until he started spending every evening at rehearsal with Will. Nothing sexual ever happened between them in the four months they worked together, but all Jake wanted was to spend time with him. They huddled together during rehearsals and whispered stupid comments that just made themselves chuckle. They stayed together at breaks; they ate meals together on full rehearsal days. They lingered longer at the end of the evening, so they could have a few more minutes together before going home.

They said good-bye at the end of each rehearsal at first with a pat on the back, then a quick hug, then an embrace, then with a quick brushing of his lips against Jake's cheek, then a full kiss. As they got to know one another, Will learned Jake was married to a woman, and Jake learned that Will was living with a much older man. Jake wanted to know everything about his new pal's relationship, what their arrangement was, how it worked or did not work. Jake did not ask about their sex life, but Will could tell he wanted to know and so shared all the steamy details. Jake told Will about sex with the men he had known. Jake wanted what Will had. He did not want what he had. Jake's marriage seemed doomed.

The long rehearsal schedule led to just a single week of performances. After the final show, the cast packed up their personal effects from the dressing rooms. Neither Will nor Jake was in a hurry to get out of the theater because they wanted to say good-bye to one another. Will revealed that he and his lover were moving to Miami. As they gave each other a last hug and kiss, Will gave Jake the paperback he had been reading. It was Andrew Holleran's novel, *Dancer from the Dance*, about two young, handsome men who meet briefly, fall in love, and go their separate ways, trying to find happiness. The book felt like a call to action, and a warning.

Jake's sense of moral obligation was sorely tested in the first six months of marriage. His parents had been married for twenty-five years, and he always assumed they were happy. However, being his parents, he never saw them as sexual beings, despite needing to be to have had children. Jake saw them as this chaste, loyal couple, and now Jake wondered how anyone could get married, live together, and not want to murder one another. For half a year, he had tried to not have sex with another man, but this experiment with Jos was just not cutting it for him. He missed his friends Vince, Roy, Harris, and Jose and their weekly romp.

Jos worked as a secretary at a small law firm, and one of the legal aides, Doris, invited Jos to join the other girls in their weekly get-together. They met every Friday after work for drinks, dinner, and sometimes a movie. No men allowed. When Jos told him that she was going out, Jake was over the moon, instantly calling Vince to tell him he was coming back to their group. Jake worried about being unfaithful to his wife only momentarily. He rationalized his decision by reminding himself that he never wanted this marriage, got railroaded into it, and never had a say. Although she was completely unaware, Jos had her Girls' Night Out, while Jake had his Boys' Night.

The light opera choreographer Carlan thought Jake was a good dancer and a very quick study, but he was concerned that Jake had not done any ballet training since high school. Jake could not afford dance lessons, because Jos spent most of their available cash to buy new dresses, shoes, stockings, and purses for her secretarial job. Carlan had his own dance studio, so he offered Jake free classes if he would clean the studio and dressing spaces at the end of each day. Carlan was not only his choreographer, but also became his dance teacher, his mentor, his friend, and the first person to get Jake thinking long-term about his career.

With two light opera shows under his belt, Jake had rehearsals for his third show every weekend and most weeknights, and now he was gone from home even more, working at the dance studio. Jos was not happy, because her husband was not there to attend to her. Jake reminded her that this was part of the trade-off for getting married before he had graduated college.

Jake was getting class credit for doing these shows and for working at Carlan's studio, which allowed him to audit out of most of his required class credits to earn a minor in dance. Jos did not care and demanded that Jake not do any more shows. He told her no and let her know of his intention to audition for the next show.

Jos figured the only way to thwart her husband's indifference to her demands was to invade his territory once again. Without telling Jake, she showed up for the *My Fair Lady* auditions. Jos had a pleasant soprano voice, if not particularly well-trained or disciplined, but musical director Rona needed some good singers for the show's more legit sound. She cast Jos in the chorus. At first, Jake did not mind, because he thought Jos might be a little less possessive, but she quickly reverted to old form and started clutching him through every rehearsal. She had to let the other women and the homos in the company know that Jake was already taken.

Jos went up to the director Eric and told him that she and Jake had to be paired together in every scene. Eric thought Jake was too good a performer to waste on partnering him with an amateur, so he laughed at her and told her to fuck off. She thought he was joking. He was serious. He hated her. Jos disliked the long rehearsals and the complicated process of bringing together the separate disciplines of acting, singing, dancing, and production into a cohesive whole. She only did the one show, and she complained that Jake went on to do three more in a row without her that year. She had had enough of theater and felt Jake should get to that point as well. For her it was a hobby, but this was his career.

Coming home from rehearsal, Jake found Jos in a rage, yelling that theater was his mistress. He walked through the front door of their apartment and had to duck. She had removed several of his Broadway cast albums from their sleeves and was now throwing them like frisbees to shatter against the living room walls. He tried to grab her arms to stop her, but she started screaming. He picked up her favorite wedding gift, a crystal bowl with silver handle, and threw it to the side of her head, exploding into hundreds of tiny glass shards. She uttered a guttural growl and launched herself on him, slapping his face and head and biting his arms. The neighbors came out of their apartments to see what the commotion was.

The building managers called the cops to report a domestic altercation. Jos was seriously injuring Jake, and he could not get her to stop. He slung her over his shoulder, flung open the front door, walked ten steps to the pool, and threw her in. The cops arrived to find the scene quiet. Jos had waded to the shallow end of the pool and just stood there. When the cops asked if she needed assistance or wanted to file charges against Jake, she did not say a word and did not look at them. She climbed the pool steps, walked into the apartment followed by the police, who saw her climb into bed sopping wet. When the cops saw Jake's bruises, bite marks on his neck, and nail scratches on his face, they asked if he wanted to file charges against Jos. He declined.

Knowing that *Damn Yankees* auditions were coming up next, Jake's folk-dance friend Lauren brought over a theater student, Brian, so he could ask Jake about the light opera company and listen to the show's cast album. Jos and Lauren became fast friends, while Jake pegged Brian as another homo from the moment he walked in the door. He was a good-looking kid, with very dark hair, prominent eyebrows, a nice toothy smile, and a warm baritone voice. Jos played the gracious hostess, while Lauren imagined the four of them were on a romantic double date. Meanwhile, Brian and Jake huddled together, talking in depth about the company and the show, sharing their love for musical theater.

Brian and Jake became friends, but Brian did not end up auditioning for the show and Lauren was not cast. But Jake's enthusiastic talk about *Damn Yankees* had convinced Jos to audition again, so he was stuck doing another show with her. Jos was cast in the female chorus; Jake was cast as one of the baseball players, the high tenor in the show's most famous song "Heart," and the mambo dancer partnering with the female lead on "Who's Got the Pain?" The mambo number was sheer nonsense, a dance specialty designed for the show's original star Gwen Verdon. It was meant as silly fun, not overtly sexual, but Jos thought otherwise. She hated that Jake was onstage bumping and grinding with another woman.

Jos never wanted to socialize with the cast after rehearsals, but one night she announced to Jake that they were joining everyone at Denny's. Jake and Jos got boxed into the back of a huge booth, where she decided to pick a fight with him in front of everybody. She was jealous that his mambo dance number with Lola was so sexual; she wanted him to give it up. Everyone gaped in astonishment at this dumb request. She pressed on, making a scene about how Jake was her husband, so he should not be doing this with another woman. Jake was mortified. When she would not shut up, Jake wriggled under the table, crawled out, left her there to face the scorn of the others, and walked home.

The next day, director Eric pulled Jake aside to talk before rehearsal. He said, "You know, we all love you, but everyone hates Joslyn." Jake had heard several cast members refer to her as "the bitch," while one of the other women even called Jos a "cunt." Eric continued, "If you are going to insist on having Joslyn do the shows with you, then it might be better if you weren't part of the company anymore." Jake replied, "Eric, you're the one who cast her, not me. I don't want her here." He laughed and said, "Oh, thank God. She's terrible and I hate pairing you with her." Jos finished this show, and Eric never considered casting her again.

28

Nebula

"A debris cloud of dust and gas in space, usually illuminated by one or more stars."

Jos had discovered the self-help workshops "est" through an acquaintance at work. Doris invited Jos to attend one of their meetings. She came home excited to share with Jake this life-changing opportunity. She was immediately hooked by the message "to transform one's ability to experience living so that the situations one had been trying to change clear up just in the process of life itself." Or some such thing. She had signed up for the training, which would take two weekends, and cost several hundred dollars.

Once again, Jos showed no concern for money and did not blink at the cost. Jake was shocked at how much it was, so she stated that she would pay for it out of her salary as a secretary. She did not seem worried that Jake's two jobs would have to pick up the financial slack and pay for more of the household bills, which she already did not help with much. The "est" standard training program consisted of two-weekend workshops with extra evening sessions during the intervening week. The seminar organizers locked you in a hotel ballroom with 199 other soul-searching individuals and demanded no talking until called upon. They allowed no food or toilet breaks, even though the sessions lasted for hours.

Jos signed up for the training and convinced Lauren from the folk-dance group to do it too. Months later, Jake finally caved and chose to do the training along with a few theater friends. Jake could not say what value Jos derived from the seminars, because she adopted the airy-fairy psychobabble that all "est" participants used, which made no sense to Jake. Jake knew that the training gave him the absolute certainty that he wanted to be a musical theater actor full time, and that was not a career his wife was ever going to allow him to do. He also came to realize that having what he truly wanted meant not having Jos in his life.

They did a couple of ancillary workshops after the training. They first did the About Money course, which of course cost a lot, so the first step in getting over any money concerns was to simply sign up and fork over a lot of money to do it. From this workshop, Jake learned he was too careful about money and sometimes he should come from a condition of abundance, rather than survival, to achieve what he wanted. What Jos took away from it is that money did not matter, so she should spend as much of it as she could. Jake found the teachers especially irritating, because they had this type of double-speak that seemed to twist his every consideration into justification for why he needed this course.

Then they did the About Sex workshop in the fall of 1981. Jos was trying to act like she was sexually liberated and talked constantly about the wonderful sex life she had with her husband. She was so determined to convince everyone about the depth of their passion that she never noticed how people rolled their eyes, smiled politely, and quietly wandered away from her rhapsodic monologues. There were clearly some swingers at these classes, and Jake wondered if they came here every week not to become enlightened but merely to hook up with someone new. A couple of women and several men gave Jake their phone numbers.

Jos was not fooling anybody at these classes. She turned out to be just another repressed Catholic school girl who had hang-ups about her body, intimacy, and nudity. Her body language was defensive, with a large purse usually clutched across her body and her arms folded tightly against her breasts. She was particularly nervous the week that they showed clips from a gay porno flick to see how people reacted to a usually taboo topic. It was at this session that Jake heard the instructor say that the word "gay" was increasingly accepted as the least offensive term for homosexuals. Jake quietly rolled the word around his tongue to see how it felt. "I'm gay. I'm gay. I'm gay." Yeah, he could live with that.

Jake's unflappable response to the gay porno proved even more troubling to Jos. Why did he seem so calm about it? Why was he not grossed out about sex between two men? Jake kept his opinion to himself, which infuriated her. Honestly, it was no big deal to Jake, because there was nothing in those clips that he had not done with other men a few hundred times already. They split the class into smaller discussion groups of ten people, and Jake wound up in the same group with Jos. When they got into a philosophic discussion about the nature of sexuality, Jake's comments about exploration and being free from inhibition shocked Jos.

She apologized to the group for her husband's behavior, meaning he had an opinion she did not share. She then tried to negate his comments. The others jumped all over her for trying to control Jake, which only made her fight back harder and prompted even more heated condemnation. She wanted to make a show of leaving in a huff and demanded Jake come with her. He refused because he felt challenged by the conversation in the same way that Vince had always challenged him. One of the women, who had chastised Jos, made a peace offering a few weeks later by inviting them over for a cocktail party at her house.

It was very similar to his Boys' Nights, in that a few guests snacked on canapes and drank wine before taking a dip in the hot tub. It seemed every hip homeowner in Arizona had a hot tub. No one brought swimsuits, so the hostess dropped her sun dress and oozed sensually into the bubbling water. She was followed by a bespectacled professor, a peroxided businesswoman, and a well-built silver daddy. Jos nervously chattered away, looking for Jake to make a quick exit with her, but he dropped trousers and climbed naked into the hot tub with the others. Jake sat between the two men, and the Professor and the Silver Daddy fondled him underwater.

When Jos finally doffed her clothes nervously to join the others, she asked if Silver Daddy might move so she might sit next to Jake. He smiled and said the open space between Hostess and Businesswoman was just as good. He did not relinquish his spot, nor did the Professor. She smiled as she sat down, but Jake could tell she was irritated. The conversation turned naturally to sexual matters, particularly fidelity and open relationships. The talk progressed then to gender roles, bisexuality, homosexuality, and lesbianism, and the Hostess put an arm around Jos's shoulders. She flinched but forced a smile. The Hostess told her to "loosen up a little, honey," and starting to caress Jos's curls.

The Businesswoman leaned in to give her a peck on the cheek, but Jos turned in her direction at that moment, so the peck turned into a kiss on the mouth. They all chuckled at that.

The Silver Daddy winked at Jake conspiratorially and started kissing him, complete with tongue. Jos was the one who had wanted them to do this About Sex course, but she was not so open-minded to tolerate her husband kissing another man. She stood up and threw her body between Jake and the Silver Daddy, trying to shove him out of the way. She whimpered, "I need to sit next to my husband." When Jake told her to relax, she went nuts, expressing a profound disgust for faggots and dykes. The Hostess stepped out of the hot tub, glared at Jos, and said, "Party's over. Time for you to leave."

At the next class the following week, the Professor, the Silver Daddy, the Hostess, and the Businesswoman were friendly toward Jake but gave Jos the cold shoulder. Jake and Jos finished the course, and Jake went off to do another musical with the light opera company. Jos took another "est" workshop by herself, becoming what people called an "est-hole" for making these workshops the entire focus of their lives. The new class brought her into close contact with Larry and Patty, who helped Jos overcome her rigidity about sexual norms. Jos traveled with them a few times for classes up in Phoenix, and during their overnight trips, Jos began a regular three-way with them.

The About Sex workshop advised participants that feelings of desire between classmates might develop, but there was a mandate that couples had to be honest with each other if one of them wanted to have an extramarital affair. Jos had made such a big deal before their wedding about taking Pre-Cana classes, which drilled fidelity, monogamy, and purity into their brains, then she broke that covenant when she had her ongoing affair with Patty and Larry. Jake found out about it from Larry, who thought Jos had been honest with her husband. She had not been. Jake was no better with fidelity, but he had never lied about Vince and the boys. He just never mentioned them, so technically he was not lying.

It was time for the two of them to have a serious discussion, so Jake took her for a drive. He drove into the foothills of the Catalina Mountains to a ritzy neighborhood of new mansions overlooking the city, and he found a quiet spot to park. She started crying, apologizing for lying to him, and he stopped her. "It's time to be honest. I can't be married to you. It's not fair to you." When she begged and pleaded for him to reconsider, he stopped her again because he could not let her dominate this conversation. He needed to be truthful. "Jos, I'm one of those faggots." She shrieked "no, no, no, no, no" while slapping his arm, shoulder, and face repeatedly and then dissolving into more tears.

The next morning, Jake moved out with only his clothes and his Broadway cast albums. He let Jos have everything else—dishes, furniture, books, TV, all their wedding gifts, the car. He stored his belongings in his old bedroom at his grandparents' house but spent every night sleeping over at Vince's house. After more than two-and-a-half years of playing straight, Jake did not have to pretend anymore. He and Vince had as much sex as they could manage day and night. Jake had graduated almost two years earlier, but Vince was still ruled by his college job. Anticipating his weeklong spring break, Vince invited Jake to go camping with him in the Spatizi Mountains of northern British Columbia.

They flew from Tucson to Vancouver and took a puddle jumper prop-engine plane to Terrace, where they rented a truck camper for a week. They drove the two hundred miles to the Spatizi Plateau Park to spend the next six nights hiking, camping, skinny-dipping, cooking over campfires, and screwing their brains out while communing with nature. Every night, Jake climbed a rock to look out over the valley, gaze at the stars, and talk to Cal. At that very moment, Cal was also in the Spatizi Mountains doing the same thing, talking to the moon, just two miles away from Jake's location. He was leading a camping group on a fishing and hunting tour. The boyhood friends had no idea how close they were to one another for the first time in six years.

Jake had become close friends with Brian, the cute gay guy that Lauren had brought to the apartment a year earlier. He and Jake started spending a lot of time together, lounging by the pool, going to the movies, going out to eat. Jake told him about his separation from Jos and his intention to move to the East Coast to work in theater. Brian was graduating in May, so he said, "I'll come with you." When Lauren heard that Brian was leaving with Jake, she panicked and announced that she wanted to work in musical theater too. Since it was cheaper for three people to live together than two, Brian and Jake invited her to join them. They made plans to leave Tucson at the end of May.

Jake and Brian talked at length about moving to New York City versus someplace else. Neither wanted to go to New York right away, become waiters to survive, and then never work in theater again. They needed to go to another city first and get some more theater experience to build up their resumes, so they decided to move to the Washington, DC, area, which had a big circuit of dinner theaters. Lauren's cousin Beverly lived there, and she said they could live in her empty townhouse until she managed to sell it. They only had to keep it spotlessly clean so Bev's realtor could show it at any time to a potential buyer.

Jake filed for divorce by mid-May. On his final day in

Tucson, Jake spent the night with Jos back at their apartment. They had dinner; they had farewell sex; they both cried. Jake did not hate Jos, but he never would have married her had she not become so close to his mother. He never had a chance to be honest with her and tell her that he was gay before they got married, because their friendship warped into something complicated by her need to be rescued from her dismissive parents and his mother's eagerness to meddle in their lives. The relationship was tainted from the start. It was not fair to Jos to believe that they were happily married. It was not fair to Jake to pretend to be something that he was not.

Jake called Drive Away Cars, which arranged for drivers to return automobiles cross-country for snowbirds who had driven out to Tucson for the warm winter but who flew back home. Drive Away had a Lincoln Continental that needed to be returned to Bethesda, Maryland, very close to where they would be living in Beverly's townhouse. Jake paid the $100 security deposit on the car and had a week to get it back east. The three of them had no furniture to take, but even with only their clothes and personal belongings, they still managed to fill up the trunk and half of the back seat. They set off cross-country on Wednesday, May 26, 1982.

They only drove four hours on the first day, from Tucson to Flagstaff, Arizona, where Lauren's parents lived, so she could say good-bye to her family. Lauren slept in her old bedroom, while Brian and Jake bunked in the family room on sleeping bags. They got an early start the next morning because it would be the longest part of the trip. They drove fourteen hours that day, passing through Albuquerque, New Mexico, and Amarillo,

Texas, before staying the night at a cheap motel in Tulsa, Oklahoma. On Friday, they drove nine hours through St. Louis, Missouri, until they reached Jake's parents' house in Louisville, where they would be staying overnight.

Before embarking on their trip, Jake had called Ranger Rick to let him know he was going to be in town for a night. Arriving late afternoon, Lauren and Brian only wanted to eat some dinner, watch a little TV, and go to bed early. Betty was angry that Jake was divorcing Jos, so she was not speaking to him. Jake drove to Rick's apartment at 5:00 p.m. Jake and Rick had not had sex for three years, since the night before his wedding, so Rick was tearing their clothes off before he had even closed the front door to this apartment. They spent the night together, and Jake did not get any sleep.

In the morning, Rick said good-bye, but Jake corrected him that it was only "see you later." He promised Rick that he would always keep in touch and contact him whenever he came back to town to visit his family. On the way back home, Jake made two stops. The first was the hill in Cherokee Park where he and Cal first met in the branches of the old White Oak tree that had been toppled in the tornado. He then swung by Cal's house to see if he could find his friend. No one was at home. Jake stood out front for several minutes, fighting back tears of frustration. He could not do this anymore; it hurt too much to search for Cal and never find him. He decided that this would be the last time. He was finally saying good-bye to his best friend. Jake stopped talking to the moon.

Since Jake got no sleep at all, Brian drove most of nine hours to Bethesda, Maryland, just outside of Washington, DC. They arrived at the address of the townhouse and waited outside in the car for an hour, until Beverly showed up to give them the keys. Brian, Lauren, and Jake quickly unloaded the car and did a happy dance in the empty living room because they were in a new city. They went shopping to buy groceries, paper plates, cups, plastic spoons and forks, a few cooking utensils, and toilet paper for the next couple of weeks. They ate dinner around a cardboard box on the floor of the living room that night.

Lauren took the smaller guest bedroom, while Jake and Brian shared the master bedroom. With no furniture, they put their sleeping bags on the floor. On Sunday, they went sightseeing in downtown D.C. On Memorial Day, Jake returned the Drive Away car to Bethesda. They had driven 2,500-mile cross-country in four days. It felt like the start of a very big adventure. For Jake, it was the start of a new chapter as a single gay man.

29

Space-Time

"A mathematical model combining the three dimensions of space and one dimension of time into a single four-dimensional manifold, used to visualize relativistic effects, such as why different observers perceive differently where and when events occur."

When they were young, Cal and Jake lived in different cities, but they began to understand the concept of time when they were both four years old. Little Cal learned that his two brothers and his sister had a few more years on him, and that gap in age would always remain constant. He also knew that he was not allowed to do some things around the house until he reached a certain age. For little Jake, he started learning his numbers and discovered that his mother was twenty-six years old. No matter how old he got, he always thought of her as twenty-six. Whenever he went home, he expected to see his young mother and was always shocked when he saw her wrinkled face and graying hair.

Time moved so slowly when they were kids. School let out and their summer vacation seemed to go on for an eternity. They could not know it then, but it was a matter of perspective.

As children, they experienced a three-month-long summer vacation as an extended period of time because it was. They had only lived a short time thus far and that span of three months every summer represented a huge percentage of their entire lives. As they grew up, that percentage shrank, and their perception of time seemed to speed up. Time was not moving any faster; they had just experienced so much more of it.

In high school, Cal and Jake first heard of the concept of "the line at infinity." In projective geometry, any pair of lines always intersects at some point, but parallel lines do not intersect in the real plane. However, if one shifts his gaze far off into the distance, to the horizon and to the edge of infinity in fact, the perspective changes. The parallel lines seem to tilt toward one another and meet at their furthermost point on the line at infinity. Cal and Jake found this concept so fascinating that they speculated on how it impacted them directly. While they shared many similarities, they believed their parallel lives might never have come together. Children's perspectives are always of an infinite future ahead of them, so in their world, their parallel lines had to converge.

It was probably nonsense, but as they grew older, the idea might have made more sense to them. As adults, they no longer saw their futures as endless, could no longer imagine infinity, and thus could not envision those lines converging, so their individual lives seemed to return to their parallel courses. Cal and Jake seemed destined to follow their own paths once more, always moving forward and never intersecting. As the years passed, time did seem to fly by, and their intense friendship faded further and further into the past. Jake did not forget about Cal; he just did not allow himself to think of him. Jake held onto the hope that they would see each other again one day, but he had to move on with his life.

Jake had a fulfilling, if very messy, life as an adult. He and Brian, who had traveled cross-country to Washington, DC, became a couple, so Brian became his first live-in boyfriend. Brian's Catholic guilt over being gay meant he broke up with Jake several times for a few weeks. Brian always wanted to get back together again until the next time his mother sent more religious pamphlets urging him to renounce the sin of homosexuality. Jake did not let any grass grow under his feet during these frequent estrangements, hooking up with whatever guy was interested and available. They broke up after three years when Brian, also an actor, got cast in a show out of town.

Jake first learned about AIDS when his theater buddy Robert got his diagnosis in 1983. A true renaissance man as an actor, director, costume designer, and teacher, Robert refused to let his diagnosis become a death sentence. He and Jake had a good cry over the bad news, ate homemade pasta, drank a few bottles of wine, and Robert announced that they would never talk about it again. They never did, and Robert defied the odds for years. Several of Jake's friends and lovers were not so lucky. Four lovers died while they were dating Jake. Seven former lovers died after their relationships with Jake were over, although their friendships never ended.

At the first memorial service for a dancer named Bill, Jake and Robert were the only two people at the funeral home. No other friends, no family. They made a pact then and there that they would never allow any friend to die alone or go unacknowledged. They each started a memory book honoring their fallen friends. In Jake's book, he listed the name, the birthday, the date of death, and then inserted a photograph and wrote an anecdote about the friend. In Robert's book, he added fabric swatches to bring a little color to what he started to call his death book. They went to every memorial service. In all, Jake memorialized over three hundred friends in his book, before he could not handle the immensity of such loss any longer and simply stopped adding to it.

Jake slept with an activist named Roman, who got him involved with ACT-UP to protest government policies and inaction in dealing with the AIDS crisis. Jake's few short months as a grade school baseball player came in handy when he lobbed a balloon filled with fake pig's blood into the face of an anti-gay senator. Jake and Roman broke up soon after because it was all a little too angry for Jake. He next coupled with Conrad, a wealthy businessman who came into town for two weeks every two months and lavished gifts, new clothes, fancy dinners, and theater tickets on Jake. They broke up when Jake learned that Conrad was married, had three kids back home in Denver, and had an expectation that Jake would always be his little mistress.

Jake met Alan, a handsome Denzel Washington look-alike, when the two of them were cast as stand-ins on a movie shoot together. They were friends-with-benefits, who never exactly dated. A year after they started seeing each other, Alan got his diagnosis of AIDS, a death sentence at that time. Jake came out of the shower to find Alan snorting cocaine. When Jake objected, Alan hit him. Alan blamed Jake for giving him AIDS, despite the negative test that Jake had received just two days earlier. Alan proceeded to beat up Jake, injuring him in much the same way that Herb Steig had done in high school. Jake had rhinoplasty to rebuild his destroyed septum, and Alan died of a drug overdose.

In May 1988, Jake's parents, Jim and Betty, decided to sell their big house in Louisville and downsize to a smaller place. Jake had just finished playing Fyedka in a production of *Fiddler on the Roof*, so he had a week off before he started rehearsals for his next show. He wanted to go home to see the old house one last time before his parents moved out. Jake also had unfinished business. He needed to see Mark Blakely before he would have no more reason to visit the old neighborhood again. Jake leaned against the maple tree at the top of their driveway and waited for Mark to take his nightly jog around the block. He stepped out into the light of the streetlamp and stopped Mark in his tracks, asking if they could get together to talk about a few things.

Mark had no interest in rekindling something with Jake, who reassured him that he wanted nothing and was not looking to make trouble. Jake just needed to talk with his old friend, "At the very least, you owe me that." Mark agreed reluctantly to meet over lunch at his office. Jake volunteered to bring burgers and fries. They did not hide in the office that was their trysting spot for years but ate their lunch on a park bench under a willow tree outside his office. They engaged in small talk for the first fifteen minutes, until Mark apologized for turning Jake gay. Jake laughed and assured him that he was going to be gay, no matter what had happened. Jake had instigated their affair, so he had to remind Mark of that little detail, exonerating him from any guilt.

"I don't need you to apologize. I just wanted to thank you."

Mark seemed stunned at that. Incredulous, he asked, "Why would you ever thank me?"

"For being my friend and being kind, when I didn't have anyone else." Jake got emotional and this affected Mark profoundly as well.

"Are you happy?"

"Yes, relatively happy, although I'm not seriously involved with anyone right now. Are you happy with your choices?"

Mark paused and decided that he was. He never admitted to being gay or having homosexual feelings. This thing between them had simply happened. He did not examine it any more fully than that.

Jake had one more thing to ask. "Did you ever do this with any other kid?

Mark was both embarrassed and stunned by the question. "Oh, no, no, never. You were special to me." When they got up to say their good-byes, Mark pulled Jake into a hug and whispered in his ear, "I loved you, Jake." Jake was honest with this old friend and his first lover, saying he felt the same way. That would be the very last time they ever saw each other.

Returning to D.C., Jake was faced with several funerals in a row. An unexpected consequence of AIDS was the pets left homeless by his dying friends. With the help of his next-door neighbor Spencer, Jake took in dogs and cats until he could find them new homes. At one point, Jake had two cats and five dogs sharing his small studio apartment at the same time. Jake loved confounding prissy neighbor Sheila by making sure to walk a different dog each time he knew she would be leaving for work. One day, it would be Jake with two basset hounds, the next a Great Dane, and the day after a Yorkie. Sheila would shake her head trying to figure out just how many dogs Jake had. In all, Jake fostered fifty-three dogs and cats in a seven-year period.

Over the course of his nine and a half years in Washington, Jake had worked on TV commercials, done industrial shows, and did stand-in and extra work for films and television series. He had done many productions of musicals, most of them in dinner theaters, performed in musical revues, and did seven different one-man cabaret shows. He also performed in a few operas and ballets, as well as a couple of legit plays, but he did not see much more advancement left for his career. His pal Tim had bought a vintage bungalow in West Palm Beach, Florida, and invited Jake to move in with him so he could try the Florida film market. Jake got cast at a theater doing six musicals in a row, did two commercials, and worked a lot of catering jobs. He hated Florida and left after two years.

With nowhere else to go, Jake called his father to ask if he might move home for a short while. Jim thought Jake could help, as Betty was set to have spinal compression surgery and Jim could not take any more time off following his own recent cancer procedure. Jake intended to stay for four months at the most, while asking his friend Robert, who had since moved to Chicago, about potentially staying with him for a while. Jake worked as a host at an Italian restaurant, singing Happy Birthday and opera arias in Italian. Toward Christmas, he rushed to the mall to do gift shopping and grab a bite to eat before going to the restaurant.

Jake bought a bag of sunflower seeds for his dinner, eating husks and all. Within two days, his stomach blew up as his digestive system tried to break down the fibrous bulk. On Christmas morning 1993, Jim found Jake unconscious on the bathroom floor. He rushed him to the emergency room, where a nurse commented that it looked like he had swallowed a basketball. Jim corrected her, "No, my son is a dancer and gymnast, so he's very lean." The doctors at first misdiagnosed Jake with colon cancer, which Jim had had a few years earlier, then rediagnosed it as an impacted colon from the undigested sunflower husks clogging his intestines.

Jake had two surgeries, was in the hospital for thirteen days, and racked up a $35,000 bill with no medical insurance. He had to file for bankruptcy and stay in Louisville for another four months until he could save a little money to move to Chicago. Having such a long stay in Louisville meant Jake got to spend that much more time with Officer Rick Rodriguez. Their sexual dalliance had continued unabated for the past seventeen years. Ranger Rick had been okay with seeing Jake only when he came home for family visits, but he asked Jake a second time to move in with him before he could run off again. Jake was very fond of Rick, but they had never talked about love once in all those years. Jake was not sure that great sex was a good enough reason to make him stay.

Just as Ranger Rick had been his lover since 1976, Jake also continued to see his college counselor, Vince. Being a university professor, Vince had summers off and worked for nonprofit organizations. Vince followed Jake to Washington, picking up an annual summer stint doing fundraising for the National Endowment for the Arts. Rather than rent a sublet for three months every year, Vince stayed at Jake's studio apartment. If Jake was dating someone whenever Vince showed up, Jake would tell that guy to go away and come back after Labor Day. Vince then spent two summers with Jake in Florida and his first two summers in Chicago.

Jake's love life needed a datebook and a social director. Jake left Ranger Rick in Louisville and started sleeping with brawny hospital administrator Diego in Chicago the very next week. Then a young theater friend, Christopher, came to town and stayed with Jake for a month, rekindling their sexual affair from a few years earlier, until he could find his own place. Then Vince came to stay the summer, and Jake was juggling him with Diego, depending on who was working when. Somewhere in there, Jake managed to find time to work his various part-time survival jobs. While he had a fun summer, Jake was almost relieved when it quieted down to just three nights a week with one man, Diego, by the fall.

Moving to Chicago in 1994 was coming full circle for Jake, who had left the area with his family when he was just eight years old. It felt like home right away. He was not having much luck restarting his acting career. He auditioned for everything and got callbacks frequently, but when it came to casting, the companies always picked the more familiar local actor they already knew rather than the newcomer. Part of the problem was his blond hair, which always made Jake look much younger, and no one could figure out his age. At thirty-six years old, Jake looked more like he was twenty. A balding, heavyset agent said, "Wow, you're thirty-six? I hope I look as good when I'm your age." Jake thought, "Too late." The agent was twenty-eight. Jake thought he looked fifty.

To pay the bills, Jake did office temp work and marketing research, waited tables, bartended, and did catering work. He was not picky; he just wanted to work and not have to sponge off an older man to survive. There were plenty of those who were willing to fill that role for Jake, but that is not the life he wanted. After four years of not getting cast, Jake retired from his showbiz career at the age of forty. He lucked into doing some writing for a Chicago-based magazine and became its full-time film critic within two months. It was not exactly the performance career he wanted, but it had an oblique connection to the arts that he liked.

A year and a half after moving back to Chicago, Jake met businessman David at a Halloween party. David was lean, bordering on skinny, with light brown hair and piercing blue eyes. Mutual friend Gavin invited them over for cocktails at his place before heading over to the Halloween party. Jake dressed as a beatnik poet, complete with battery-operated bongo drums and bad poems he had written for the occasion. David went as a sailor. Jake knew where the party was but did not have a car. David had a car but did not know where to go. Gavin paired them to drive over together. They had a nice chat in the car, but they headed in opposite directions as soon as they walked in the front door.

David was a smoker, and Jake was not, although he was a cocktail smoker whenever he drank. After two hours mingling, Jake found David outside on the front stoop smoking a cigarette. Jake asked to bum one from him. David said, "I'm about to leave. It's my birthday, so I'm meeting some friends. Do you need a ride?" David drove Jake back to his apartment and asked, "Can I come up and change? I don't want to look ridiculous when I meet my friends." They got out of their costumes and stayed naked for a few hours. They exchanged phone numbers, playing the waiting game to see who would be the first to call the other.

Neither called, but they bumped into one another on Michigan Avenue two weeks later. They made a date for that Friday night, and Jake ended up spending the weekend. Within ten days, they were spending all their time together. As they started to get serious about one another, David made it very clear that he was not looking for a monogamous relationship. Since Jake had shown himself to not be very good with fidelity anyway, that was alright by him. David traveled a lot for his business, and he did not want to feel constrained if he wanted to have a little fun on the side. Jake was certainly not going to play the cuckold and sit at home waiting for him. If David was going to have his fun, Jake would too.

Jake had visited his parents in October for two weeks right as he met David, so he had his usual dalliance with Rick. Although Jake had turned down his offer to live together, Rick felt strongly that he and Jake were meant to be together. He asked if Jake would reconsider and move back to Louisville. Rick knew every little sexual trick to drive Jake crazy and he employed them all, hoping to make it impossible for Jake to say no to him. It began to feel a bit like an interrogation and coercion. As a cop, Rick would always have to remain closeted, so he could never acknowledge Jake as a boyfriend or partner. Jake would have to continue to pretend to be something that he was not. He would have to continue living in the shadows as a man passing for straight.

Jake did not give Rick an answer. He knew David was taking a business trip in January, so Jake made plans to visit Rick again for a full week then. Two months later, Jake, as promised, drove home to visit his parents but mostly to see Rick. He showed up at Rick's apartment at the appointed time, but no one answered the door. Jake waited for half an hour until he saw two college girls come up to the building and walk into Rick's apartment. Jake rang the bell so he could ask the girls if they knew where he could find Rick. Neither knew who that person was. They had moved into the apartment just a week earlier.

Jake went to the old gay bar down the block from his place. It was now a convenience store, and the gay bar had relocated two blocks further south. None of the bartenders or regulars had seen Ranger Rick for weeks. Jake went to his police precinct, trying to pass himself off as a family member to get information on Rick. The desk sergeant just looked at the lean, young blond man and knew he was in no way related to the dark, tall, muscular Cuban. There was nothing more Jake could do. He did not know if Rick left the city, got reassigned, or died. They had met at the hospital when Jake was recuperating from his assault. They started sleeping together two years later and continued to do so for eighteen years. Jake was surprised how upset he was over losing Rick. He may have loved the man after all.

Jake's lease on his studio apartment was coming up at the end of April 1996, and David's platonic roommate was moving out. After much discussion, they decided to move in together. Both figured it might last a year if they were lucky, but every year that their relationship endured, they were kind of amazed at themselves. Neither thought they could make a committed relationship work. Theirs was not always an easy union, with David's traveling for work, and a lot of rocky times. They did keep at it, until it seemed nothing could break them up. Jake should have warned David that he would not give up easily, that his friendships and sexual alliances tended to last for years and years. David was stuck with him.

In August 2000, Jake's longtime friend Robert finally succumbed to AIDS. Robert could get combative about almost anything, and he got mad at Jake for being so annoyingly hopeful all the time. Robert was not feeling well, and he hated that Jake always tried to cheer him up. Sometimes, Robert just wanted to wallow in his pain and sadness. They stopped talking for a week. During that time, Robert had a massive heart attack and died. A cleaning woman found his body when she came to clean his apartment five days later. He was fifty-two, and he and Jake had been good friends for eighteen years.

Four months later, Jake got a phone call from Vince. The last time they saw each other was on his summer-long visit to Chicago five years earlier. Jake hoped he and Vince could have a reunion very soon. Vince's voice sounded raspy and weak, and the conversation was short. "I'm sick. I've finally gotten it. I love you, Jakey boy." He hung up. Jake looked for flights to Tucson, but before he could buy the plane ticket, he got word that Vince had died. He was fifty-four years old. Vince had been his sexual guru for nineteen years, but mostly he was a dear friend. Jake was overwhelmed. "Everyone always leaves me."

30

Quasar

"An unusually bright object caused by vast amounts of energy that are found in the most remote areas of the known universe."

On the day that Jake flew off to college, Cal cried so much that he developed a painful bout of hiccups that lasted for hours. But he did not allow himself to fall into a prolonged funk. Whenever something upset him, he never allowed time to experience the grief or pain; he simply started moving and never stopped. He bought books to get ready for college; he set up weekend adventures with Brent; he worked out in the backyard stretching and doing his gymnastics. The only time he stopped to think of Jake was on his nightly stargazing from the tree platform out in his backyard. He talked to the moon, saying everything he could never say to Jake in person.

His girlfriend Nicole tried to coax him out on a date, but Cal was annoyed at her persistence. He rebuffed her as gently as he could, but she kept at it. Cal had started dating her a year earlier when they were lifeguards together at the JCC pool. It was alarming how quickly she latched onto him. She wanted to monopolize all his time, plan every activity they did, and regulate who he could see if he was not going to be with her. Nicole did not like Jake because she thought two guys should not be that close to one another, but now Jake was gone and no longer her problem. Her concern was getting Cal to make some sort of commitment to her.

She decided that, after a year of dating, it was time. Cal's idea of a date was simply hanging out together, going to the mall to see a movie and walk the stores, or doing something physical like hiking. She wanted something more romantic, like a proper date with dinner at a nice restaurant followed by cuddling on a couch in front of a fireplace. She knew about the Kuliks' cabin and thought that would be the perfect place, but Cal had never invited her to see it. He did not want to go to the cabin just now because he thought of it as his special place he shared with Jake. He needed more time. He pointed out that she had fancier tastes, and the rustic cabin would not suit her. "You'd hate it." She did not argue.

Nicole's mother and two sisters had all gotten married young instead of going to college. She made that her goal as well, and Cal was her target. When he left for three months to kayak the Fraser River in Canada, she complained about him being gone too long. When he skipped out for a weekend kayaking or canoeing by himself or with Brent, she got snippy. When she discovered those getaway jaunts would always be a priority for him, she put her foot down and told him, "No. You're not going to do that anymore."

"Excuse me. You don't get to tell me what to do. We have no agreement."

"We should. I am getting tired of waiting for you to always come back from play time. You should be thinking about settling down and starting a family."

"That's not going to happen right now. I'm only eighteen. We're too young. There's a lot of things I want to do first."

Nicole smiled. "We'll see." She was confident that she and Cal would soon marry, but her feminine wiles were no match for Cal's wanderlust. The following summer, he organized a camping and canoeing trip for inner-city schoolkids on Lake St. Clair, which straddled the U.S. and Canada border just east of Detroit. Cal did not ask permission and did not even tell her he was going. He was gone for three months. She broke up with him on the day he returned to Louisville. He was relieved to no longer be facing the prospect of an early marriage that he did not want, but it still hurt to be dumped. He felt like everybody left him.

Cal took his parents' advice and went to school to get the basic certifications he needed so he could do the activities he loved professionally. He raced through his four sessions to become certified as an Emergency Medical Technician. He became the youngest EMT in Kentucky history, achieving that feat just a month after his nineteenth birthday. His friend Brent, who got him into kayaking and canoeing, convinced him that he should next go for certification by the Coast Guard, so he could captain boats and sailing ships for a living. It was the Lake St. Clair canoe trip, though, that changed his focus. The adventures he planned could just be a tourist thing, or they could also change people's lives.

Cal loved kids and loved working with them, because he reasoned that he was still a big kid himself. He loved their fearlessness in trying new things, whereas adults often gave in to their fears and general laziness. If his father, Zan, could teach him how to fish and hunt and camp and survive in the wild, then Cal could be that person for other kids who did not have the same kind of influence in their lives. He started out as a counselor for outdoor wilderness camps, quickly moving up to nature educator. He went back every summer that he was free.

He returned to British Columbia several times, working for an outfitting company as a guide for fishing and hunting tours deep in the wilderness. He saw the casual slaughter of animals by tourists looking to shoot a stag just so they could brag about it to their friends, so he tried to teach all his clients about sustainable hunting. He preached hunting not for the sport of it, but solely as a means of survival. Whenever someone caught a fish, Cal made that person hold the fish as its lifeforce was leaving its body and thank the fish for providing sustenance. When he had to kill a deer or a moose for food, he showed clients how to responsibly carve up the carcass, leaving behind the carrion for the bears, wolves, and birds. Every living thing could benefit from a kill. Nothing was wasted.

In the fall of 1982, Cal went to Australia to work as an environmental instructor at outdoor training camps. As a teenager, he had seen Nicholas Roeg's movie *Walkabout* and always dreamed of having a similar experience. While there, he took the opportunity to explore the Outback. He met several Aboriginal leaders and they shared with Cal their lifestyle and their beliefs about interacting with the earth. His guide, Jiemba, told Cal how his people were careful observers of the stars, which served as the homes of ancestors, animals, plants, and spirits. The stars also served as calendars and a system of rules and laws that informed all aspects of their daily life and culture.

Jiemba recounted a legend. "Long ago, two boys paddled out in a canoe to fish. The elders warned them not to go onto a sand spit where a big dangerous shovelnose ray, the Dhui Dhui, lived. The boys fished there anyway. The ray bit their fishing line, but the boys would not cut loose. The ray towed them around the ocean until they disappeared into the horizon. When the boys still had not returned after dark, the elders looked south after sunset to see the Southern Cross rising, which was the Dhui Dhui, followed by two pointer stars, the two boys in their canoe." Cal liked to think that he and Jake were those two boys darting across the heavens together.

On his travels, Cal saw up close the impact that mankind was having on the planet. Rather than being able to just appreciate the beauty of the world around him, he spent as much time picking up paper wrappers and soda cans off beaches and scooping garbage out of the ocean. He became a committed environmentalist, making sure that on every one of his adventures, his clients carried their trash out with them and left nothing behind. On ships or camping trips, on islands or in forests, his philosophy was "You consume it, then it is your responsibility to dispose of it responsibly."

In January 1984, he traveled to Peru, backpacking with a hiking buddy along the Inca Trail to Machu Picchu. They climbed into the Andes Mountains up to the snowline, but without proper equipment, they could not reach the 20,000-foot summit. Cal wanted to try anyway. While that might have been enough excitement for anyone else, Cal then built a balsa log raft and floated down two hundred miles of an Amazon River tributary. He wanted to see the impact that logging and invasive farming were having on Indigenous tribes along the river. He was an outsider, but he charmed them when he borrowed a wooden flute to play "What's Love Got to Do with It." They had never heard of Tina Turner.

Possessing the skills of a geographer, biologist, and anthropologist, Cal loved all his cross-cultural trips, but he loved the water most of all. He started working as a charter boat captain and sailing instructor. During the summers when hurricanes threatened, he moved yachts and masted schooners into safe harborage before the storms hit. On occasion, clients hired him to do ship deliveries from the Caribbean islands back to ports as far away as Maine and Nova Scotia when they decided to fly instead of sail back home. He started out in the Virgin Islands, but resort hotels were swallowing up the islands and influencing political decisions, which made sailing there an annoying sea of red tape.

He shifted his attention to the Gulf of California between Baja California and the mainland of Mexico. Conditions were comparable to the Caribbean, although less beset by hurricanes. It was drier and hotter, but the Gulf of California felt more like virgin territory in terms of tourism. Cal could build a reputation on his own terms there, rather than trying to fit in with the corporate travel system in the Caribbean. He was a seasoned sailor, who had sailed the length and breadth of the waters on both sides of Central America. He felt at home there.

Cal worked with a boat broker who brought him clients that wanted to hire a motor yacht or a sailing ship for a weeklong cruise. The broker would hire Cal as charter captain, who then had to find his own cook or chef to make the meals for the guests. Cal always hired women to be this support person on the vessels, and all became his girlfriends. Never allowing much time for a personal life, he often spent weeks at a time on these boats and never dated. With the captain and the cook being in close quarters for a prolonged period, it seemed natural that the two of them would become attached to one another.

The first chef, Alyson, disliked humidity, and in the cramped confines of the galley, it felt like she, not the food, was baking in an oven. She lasted three cruises. The next cook Renee lasted just two weeks, after being miserably seasick the entire time. The third chef Kelly was the one who answered the employment ad, and yet somehow, she thought Cal was taking her on a cruise rather than hiring her to work on one. She lasted all of one week. With the help of one of the female passengers, Cal ended up doing a lot of the cooking that week, in addition to everything else he had to do. It was so hard to find good help.

The fourth cook was a real find. Genevieve Marchand, nicknamed Jenna, was a great cook, did not mind the stuffy confines of the galley, and in fact found the challenging conditions inspired her to make memorable meals. She was pretty, energetic, and had almost as much love as Cal did for adventure and nature. Cal thought that this is the type of girl he could marry. And he did, after traveling together for five weeks. Cal did not propose so much as admitted that they seemed a good match for one another. Jenna agreed, so they went to find the nearest dockside minister at their next port of call. They had lunch at a sidewalk café so Jenna could have a margarita to celebrate; their wedding night was on the boat with a family of six to feed and entertain.

The marriage day was the last congenial moment they shared. In typical fashion for Cal, he was not forthcoming with personal information. He never mentioned that a company merely contracted him to captain these vessels. Jenna thought Cal so confident in his command of this ship that she assumed that he owned it. Learning the truth, she demanded he quit and go back to the States to find a better career, so he could make enough money to buy them a boat of their own. They hardly spoke to one another after that. When the sailing season ended in mid-May, Cal returned the ship and ran away to Canada. He spent the summer kayaking solo along the Yukon River. The marriage lasted seven weeks.

The following January, Cal returned to Baja and had a few weeks before his first charter. He decided to test his ability to do celestial navigation and sail the four-hundred miles from Santa Rosalia across the Gulf down to Mazatlan on the mainland in an eighteen-foot catamaran. Using only a sextant, he and his high school kayaking friend, Brent, survived a capsizing at night in the open sea, which forced a landing in the tiny fishing village Las Piedras for minor repairs. After three days of sailing, Cal and Brent reached Mazatlan, establishing a beach camp outside of town and then exploring the highlands to the east.

A few years later, Cal began to explore Guatemala and Belize, establishing contact with Mayan Indian groups there. Through one of his adventure camps, he began bringing American students to Central America, where they lived with host families for a few weeks. Several years after that, he explored Costa Rica, living for several months on the Peninsula de Nicoya taking tourists on kayak trips of the coastal areas and hiking into the rain forests. Cal was always adding to his bucket list of all the beautiful, far-flung places he wanted to visit someday.

A committed environmentalist, Cal lived a minimalist life with few possessions. His life was rich in experiences and challenges, and he valued people and relationships, not things. He resided in an outdoor camp built under a huge banyan tree, using reclaimed materials. Besides his professional sailing skills, Cal seemed to do everything perfectly. He was a gymnast, canoeist, kayaker, rafter, backpacker, rock climber, mountaineer, scuba diver, snorkeler, fisherman, sailor, and gun and bow hunter. Even better, he did these things in more secluded areas, where he could doff his clothes. Everyone knew how much Cal liked to be free of clothing, like an animal in the wild. He was living his dream life.

In August 1994, Cal was finishing at a wilderness camp in Indiana when he started feeling very fatigued. His skin was itchy all the time, and a restlessness in his legs kept him up at night. He woke up exhausted, had no stomach for food, and developed a scary purple bruise after banging his shin on a pulley for the ropes course. His entire body ached. He called his parents, and they recommended he see their old family doctor in Louisville. The doctor thought he knew what the problem was when Cal relayed his symptoms. Blood tests confirmed his suspicions when the results came back, showing that Cal had developed hepatitis C.

The doctor said there was no way to know exactly when he had gotten infected. Cal wanted to know how he had gotten it. They discussed the risk factors, but he did not seem to fit the profile of any of them. Then the doctor told him that the infection spreads when blood contaminated with the virus enters the bloodstream of an uninfected person. He then asked Cal, "Are you gay?"

Cal denied that vehemently. "Could I have gotten it from a woman?" Cal decided that it had been his ex-wife Jenna who had given it to him.

"It's not very likely. The woman would have had to be menstruating and some of her infected blood would have to enter your penis and travel up your urethra to enter your bloodstream. The odds are astronomically high against that being the cause."

"Could I have caught it in South America or Mexico?"

"Cal, let me repeat this. Infected blood from another person would have to enter your bloodstream. There is no other way unless you shoot up drugs, and you don't seem the type."

"No, I've never done drugs. I don't even drink."

"That's good to know. Let's stop focusing on how it happened. Let's concentrate on how we treat it."

The doctor wrote "gay" on Cal's chart and then prescribed Interferon, which Cal would have to inject under the skin into a muscle or vein. To start, a nurse would administer the injection to get Cal on a regular schedule. After a brief period of observation, Cal could start to give himself the injection, if he remained consistent. Side effects could occur, and Cal developed those immediately. He started having colitis, low blood pressure, and lethargy. Since he had no energy to work, he could not afford to pay his bills. A month past his thirty-sixth birthday, Cal had to move back in with his parents, who now lived in North Carolina.

Leigh and Zan thought his being back home might be a good thing for him. They could cook meals, watch out for him, and offer love and assistance whenever he might need it. Then Cal's mental state started to deteriorate. In rare cases, patients on Interferon could start exhibiting aggression and obsessing about death. Cal got frustrated and would start to scream at his parents for no reason. He had enough self-control to redirect that uncommon anger elsewhere and started punching the walls of the house. Another time, he smacked his head repeatedly against the brick fireplace until his father could wrench him away before doing more serious harm to himself.

Cal began to exhibit signs of bipolar disorder, a condition uncommon in his family. He was calmly sitting on the couch in the living room when he suddenly started pacing the floor wildly. When he could not contain that nervous energy, he ran out of the house, jumped on his bike, and rode straight into the nearest intersection against the traffic light hoping a truck or a bus would plow into him. He found a payphone and called home, saying, "Well, I didn't die. I guess I'll come home." Leigh and Zan were scared for their son, but they were also becoming scared of him. His mother called several of his kayaking friends to come for a visit, hoping they could cheer him up.

Leigh did not tell Cal of his friends' visit until the night before their arrival. Considering this an ambush, Cal threw some clothing into a backpack and fled the house. He did not wait to see his friends, and he did not tell his parents where he was going.

31

Wormhole

"A speculative structure, based on a theory of Einstein's field equations, linking far-flung separate points in space-time, visualized as a tunnel with two ends."

Jake did not talk with his ex-wife Joslyn often. When they filed for divorce in 1982, he left Arizona for the East Coast to work in theater. Jos stayed behind in Tucson, and she could not let anyone think she had anything to do with the dissolution of her marriage. It was all Jake's fault. He was a faggot and misled her, tricking her into marriage. She trashed Jake's name to all the close friends he had made in the six years he lived there. Jos was exceptionally good at maligning him, and not one of his friends ever spoke to him again. Jos proved she was not his friend, so he did not feel the need to be friendly with her.

Whenever she attempted to call him, she acted chummy like nothing bad had ever happened between them. Jake never pretended that he was happy to hear from her. He did not engage in small talk and cut to the chase. "What's up?" She launched into whatever litany of woe that bedeviled her at that moment. She complained about politicians; she railed against pro-life zealots; she fretted over government legislation that went against her beliefs. Mostly, she called to complain about her parents.

Jos had been adopted as an infant when her parents could not get pregnant after many attempts. More than a decade later, they finally managed to conceive and give birth to their own child and stopped caring about their adopted daughter, at least that was how Jos perceived it. She'd had an angry, constantly combative relationship with them since she was a teenager. It was because of this rift that Jos finagled an invitation from Jake's mom Betty to move into the Davies' house. That is when most of Jake's problems and unhappiness began. For more than a year, Jos worked her toxic magic on Betty, so that Jake hated going home to see his own family.

Suddenly, Jos acted distraught that her father was dying. Jake did not want to talk with her, but he was not insensitive. Jake had lost his own parents a few years earlier. His father, Jim, succumbed after eighteen years of cancer, and his mother, Betty, died two years later after a series of strokes. Jake had long before forgiven his mother, but Betty had never forgiven Jake for divorcing Jos. Over the years, Jake had called his parents every single week. His dad always answered, chatting with Jake for ten minutes or so before handing the phone to Betty. Jake could hear his mother ask in her very loud whisper, "Who is it?" When Jim told her who, Jake heard her say every single time, "I don't wanna talk to him." Jake never really regained a loving relationship with his own mother. It was another reason to resent Jos.

Jos's dad was very old, had grown infirm in his later years, and now had congestive heart failure. She sobbed about how he was such a great man and how her life would never be the same without him. Jake was happy that Jos could not see him roll his eyes. This was the man Jos said she hated, who she said hated her, who she said wanted to have her institutionalized for not finishing college. She had used this man's bad attitude toward her as an excuse to move into Jake's house.

Jake was not stupid, and he remembered everything she had said. It was okay for Jos to lie to herself or lie about her family. Jake would not tolerate her lies about him, because her revisionist fantasy of a happy marriage ignored Jake's reality. She tried to turn his life into a lie, so she could perpetuate her rewritten version of history. She set the tone for the conversation, but she was going to be disappointed that Jake did not play along. She said, "Jake, I must tell you that our marriage was the happiest time of my life. It was wonderful, wasn't it?"

"No, Jos, it was not. I was miserable. I never wanted to marry you."

"How can you say that? It hurts me that you want to deny those three years together."

"It was actually six years from prom through the divorce." They had a long discussion and disagreement about what they went through and what they felt. Jos could not know Jake's side of the story, but she really did not care to hear it. She only wanted to pour out her heart. This prompted Jake to finally tell her everything. He told her about messing around in the bushes with his grade school friends, the adult neighbor, Cal, the rapes, the assault, the hospitalization, the woods behind the Collings Estate, his college counselor Vince, Ranger Rick, and on and on. He had known he was gay for a very long time.

It was all news to Jos, but it seemed like he had finally pierced her fantasy, if only just a bit. She said, "I'm sorry for all the bad stuff you went through in high school." She seemed genuinely concerned for his trauma, but then she managed to bring it back around to herself, as she always did. "If you knew you were gay, why did you lie to me?"

"I never lied to you. You just never let me get a word in edgewise."

"But you always asked, 'Why does everyone think I'm gay?' So that was a lie on your part."

"No, Jos. You got that wrong too. You called my friend Billy a faggot, and I was mad at you and asked, 'Why does everyone think being gay is bad?' That's what I said to you. But of course, you wouldn't remember that, or you only want to remember your version."

She tried to laugh it off, to make light of the tense moment, but then she got serious again. "I really got the bad deal out of this marriage. What hurt me the most was that you just left Tucson without saying a word to me." Again, she was sticking to an imaginary narrative in her head.

Jake was stunned. "Jos, this is nuts. You really don't remember? I drove us up into the foothills so we could have the big talk. I said it out loud to you, 'I'm gay' and you started screaming and slapping me. We then spent our last night together back at the apartment. That was obviously a good-bye. Is any of this ringing a bell?"

"I don't remember that at all."

"That's convenient for you to not remember anything. Jos, we divorced in 1982 and it has been thirty-five years now. It's time to stop lying to yourself. I don't lie to myself, and I won't allow you to keep lying about me any longer. If you can't be honest, I don't want to talk with you anymore."

She then dropped a bomb. "Fine. By the way, Mark Blakely died." She hung up. At first Jake thought the comment was weird. Why bring him up? Then he remembered that he had just told Jos everything that he went through in high school. He specifically mentioned an adult neighbor. Her comment confirmed his suspicion that she had figured out their relationship the night she tried to barge into Mark's house. He was quiet for a few minutes, thinking of Mark, and he started crying. They probably should not have done what they did together, but Jake had made peace with it years ago and in fact had been the one who started it. That sweet man, Mark, had been such a big part of his development as a budding gay boy, and now he was gone.

Jake's husband David asked why he was crying. Jake's response was a garbled goulash of tangled words, emotions, and tears, and it made no sense. For three days, Jake burst into tears every time he thought of Mark. He kept trying to tell David, but the tale sounded even more ridiculous each time he tried to tell it. David seemed a little more intrigued by the process by which a fourteen-year-old boy started having sex with an adult male, rather than the emotional impact of that connection. Jake wondered himself if he remembered how it transpired, so he pulled out his journal to try to make sense of it all. Jake wrote for a full week and had composed forty pages about Mark, but also fifty pages about Cal. It was natural that he wrote about them together because they shared the same period in Jake's history.

Jake had tried not to think of Cal in the forty-one years since they graduated high school, but here now he had written down whatever he could remember about him. He cried again, but it was no longer over Mark. "Oh, Cal. Where are you?" Social media, cell phones, and even the internet did not exist when he went to college. Now he hoped to use them to find Cal finally. A web search revealed nothing, and Cal did not have any social media profiles. Although it was unlikely Cal's parents would have online profiles because they would be in their nineties now, Jake checked for them next. No luck. He found a social media profile for Cal's sister Natalie, but she did not keep it current.

Finally, Jake thought to try contacting the Lyric Theater in Louisville that Cal's parents Zan and Leigh had cofounded. Maybe somebody there would know how to reach the Kulik family. It was a former nurse, Marsha, now pushing eighty years old, who revealed that Zan and Leigh had sold their cabin in 1981 and then sold their house about six months later, before moving to New Bern, North Carolina. Jake told Marsha that he was specifically looking for their son, Cal. After a long pause of several minutes, Marsha's next text read, "I'm sorry to tell you this, but something bad happened to him. He disappeared many years ago. You need to talk to Lily, who's still close to Leigh and Zan. Lily would know."

He talked with Lily on the phone, and Jake learned that Cal had gone missing in the Pacific Ocean on June 1, 1999. His body was never found. After a month, authorities ended the search for him, stating that he was "presumed dead." She helped fill in some of the blanks of Cal's life, as best she could. Jake was happy to know that he fulfilled his dream of working outdoors. He shared stories of Cal as a teenager, while she let him know a little something of his later years.

Unfortunately, their hour-long conversation left Jake with more questions than answers. Who had he become as an adult? Had he continued to play the flute? Had he still walked on his hands like they did together? Had he still giggled whenever he found something funny? What did he learn from his worldwide adventures? Had he remained the same happy, exuberant guy? Had he loved someone and been loved in return? Had he still had those moments of deep introspection that often bordered on melancholy? Would he have even remembered the blond kid that also played the flute and could match him in the gymnastics moves, and yet put him up on pedestal?

Lily gave Jake the number of Cal's sister Nat, as well as the names of several people he could contact to learn more about Cal. Jake fell down the rabbit hole into the wonderland of Cal's life since high school. He called two of the girlfriends who served as cooks on the sailing charters. He contacted Brent Cooper's family, who had been close to Cal. He wanted to talk to anyone who knew him. The phone call to Cal's ex-wife Jenna did not go well. When Jake asked if she would be willing to talk briefly about Cal, she said, "That faggot?" She hung up on him. Otherwise, everyone wanted to talk about Cal and his impact on them.

Jake finally got up the courage to call Nat. He did not want to upset her, but he thought she might appreciate the chance to talk about her brother. Nat did remember who Jake was, although they had never had any interaction with each other. She was older than Cal, and as such had already gone off to college by the time Cal and Jake started spending all their time together. They talked several times, and Nat sent Jake a large packet of Cal's papers. She had to find a home for Cal's stuff, as her parents were old and might not be around much longer. She felt that Jake would not simply throw it all away.

Jake was grateful for the materials and felt like he had found a treasure chest. He gazed fondly at Cal's smiling face in the photographs, as he stood at the helm of a ship, hoisted his prize catch of two lobsters, chopped a coconut, or smiled for the camera while on his favorite beach. Jake read every travel journal Cal wrote. In reading Cal's musings about nature and his world, Jake could once again hear Cal's voice in his head. He had not been able to remember what his voice had sounded like for decades. The years fell away and it was almost like having Cal right there, whispering in his ear.

Nat sent a few more packets in the mail, giving Jake a far more in-depth glimpse into Cal's adult life than he could have ever hoped for. Even chats with friends and family could not provide this much detail, and all of it was in Cal's own words. The first letter he pulled out had an address on Gresham Road, and Jake yelled out loud. He ran to the computer to do a search. That address was right behind his parents' house. Cal had rented a room in a house that was literally five hundred feet away. He found two more letters with the same address, so he determined that Cal lived there for eighteen months from 1982 to 1983. Jake had gone home three times during that period. How did they never bump into each other? If his parents had known, Jake blamed his mother for not telling him.

Jake found Cal's letters home to his parents the most intriguing. He wrote at length about his various girlfriends, but that label of "girlfriend" came with a caveat. Jake found a letter corresponding to each one of the five women his family claimed he had dated on the ships. Cal wrote his parents about every single one of them: "I'm not sexually attracted to her. That has to be part of a relationship, right?" He kept looking for what he described as the "perfect partner." In none of his letters did he ever write wife, girlfriend, or woman. He always used the word "partner."

Maybe in choosing to write that, he was finally being honest with himself. Perhaps more importantly, in that term, he could convince himself that he was not lying to his parents. If anything, it was an omission that gave him the space to not have to come out as gay, and yet not be so specific as to what he truly wanted. He wanted a "partner," whatever that meant to him. If Cal had truly been straight, he would have just written "girl" or "woman" in all those letters.

Several times, Jake found that Cal wrote the line, "I miss my friend." Can that have been Jake he was referring to? Jake did not want to engage in stereotypes, but Cal seemed the epitome of a gay boy. He was sensitive and loved the arts. He was sweet and loving. He was kind to his friends, or at least to the people who were kind to him. He never shied away from sharing his feelings, and he was the most touchy-feely person Jake had ever known.

Jake realized that it was just six weeks away from June 1, what would be the twentieth anniversary of Cal's disappearance. He decided to go to the Peninsula de Nicoya in Costa Rica to honor the memory of his boyhood pal. Jake asked his best friend Christopher if he wanted to join him on a week-long trip, and Christopher agreed to lend his emotional support. They flew from Chicago to San José and drove a rust-bucket rental car the one hundred thirty miles to the Peninsula. That first evening, Jake walked to the beach, the place where someone last saw Cal, to scope out the spot for the memorial the next day.

A little before sunset, Jake and Christopher walked to the spot. They sat quietly and Jake started sobbing. Chris held his hand. Jake shared his favorite memories of Cal with Chris until the sun started to slip below the horizon. Jake sang a song to Cal and cast flowers into the surf. Together they cried for this lost friend. As it grew dark, Jake sat on the sand, looking out over the Pacific, and thought on Cal's final moments at this very place.

Cal left his parents' house before his old friends could descend on him and try to cheer him up. There was nothing they could do for him. He felt the hepatitis had ruined him, made him unable to do those things that defined him. He felt weak and useless and despaired that he would never regain his strength.

His relationships lasted no longer than a few months, so he felt that no one loved him. Being tired and depleted, he thought he looked ugly, no longer the picture of robust health he had always been. He felt there was no place for him in this world anymore.

He slept on the floor at the Wilmington Airport and boarded a 9:00 a.m. flight to Charlotte, connecting to a direct flight through to San Jose, Costa Rica. He landed in the early afternoon and hitched a ride from the airport with a couple who were heading out to the same coastal town of Samara. Upon arriving at the Peninsula de Nicoya, Cal spent the rest of the day killing time, strolling the beachfront. He loved this town because it still did not have the big chain hotel resorts that were taking over natural areas, another sign that the world was changing, and not in a way he liked. Finally, he walked a half mile down to the south end of the beach to a secluded spot shielded from view by boulders and bougainvillea trees. He stood on a rise looking out over the Pacific Ocean.

Cal walked to the edge of the water and stood ankle deep in the waves. He allowed tears to flow as he watched the sunset. He turned and looked overhead to the east as the stars came out. It was a new moon that night, so it was barely visible. He mumbled a few words to himself and to the sky and then heaved a big sigh. He turned toward the west and watched the last seconds of light as the sun vanished for the day. He started walking into the ocean. Once he got to the small reef, his feet could no longer touch bottom, so he started to breaststroke.

There was nothing beyond the rocky knob of Isla Chora but open ocean. Cal settled into an easy stroke through the water. Fifteen minutes after starting out, he felt something brush against his leg. He stopped to tread water and look back toward land. He could no longer see it. He turned back to the west, swimming headlong again. A few minutes later, something brushed up against him again, this time more forcefully. He pushed himself forward, without hesitation. His powerful strokes through the water disturbed tiny plankton, creating bioluminescence all around him. The twinkling lights in the water mirrored the stars overhead. Cal swam onward into the void, into infinity where the sea meets the sky.

32

Zenith

"A point directly overhead from an observer."

Everyone experiences loss, so no one can claim that theirs is any greater than that of anyone else. Some losses, though, just hurt more than others. As a gay man, Jake survived the AIDS era, losing lovers and many friends. Both of his parents had died; several very dear friends succumbed to cancer and heart attacks. And yet, for Jake, no loss hit him as hard as learning about Cal's disappearance. He last saw Cal forty-three years earlier, but he had only just learned of his disappearance the previous year, so it felt like he had just died. He could not talk about Cal without bursting into tears.

Cal inspired such love and devotion amongst his friends. He was that unique, that extraordinary, and that beloved. He represented the promise of the whole wide world. He was everything that Jake hoped that he would be, everything that he was not, everything that he never became. He wondered if they would have remained friends all this time, because Jake worried that he might have been a big disappointment to Cal. Jake just could not comprehend that his friend was no longer in this world to bring happiness and joy to everyone's lives. It was no wonder that Jake could not put his memory aside.

If Jake had it this hard accepting the news, his family would always have to hold this loss in their hearts, even twenty years later. Jake had to see Cal's parents. If he could not tell Cal directly, he wanted Zan and Leigh to know the impact Cal had upon him. Jake asked Nat if he could visit their parents. She said, "Come soon. They're old now and might not be here much longer." Jake flew to Wilmington, North Carolina, armed with only a head full of memories about Cal and a couple of photographs from the mid-1970s of him and the two of them backstage during one of the shows they did together. When he first walked in, they smiled at him, not yet comprehending who he was.

He showed the photographs, and they recognized themselves, but it still did not register how he knew them. He shared some stories with them, which made Leigh smile, but they still did not remember him. As he sat down to visit with them, then it came to Leigh, "Oh, you're Cal's friend." That just about broke Jake's heart, and he fought back tears. They exchanged pleasantries for an hour, as they asked about Jake's life and career, and Jake praised their midcentury modern home. He loved the wall of glass looking out to the weeping willows beside the marsh, and their immaculately groomed yard.

When he began to share his memories of Cal, Jake sensed some confusion from the couple. Was he sharing too much personal information or talking about something taboo? He had thought very carefully on what he wanted to say to them, and he tried to keep their conversation in generalities rather than specifics. He did not want to upset them in any way. Perhaps some of his memories were too exact to him and Cal, so it might have sounded like fanciful stories to them. Gradually, they warmed to Jake, pulling photo albums off the bookshelves for him to see.

There were so many childhood photos of Cal leaping and bounding over furniture, running across his backyard, on vacations, doing handstands, hanging upside down from a tree branch, playing his flute. Jake felt like time had folded back on itself and Cal was in the room with them. In every childhood photo, he could see the Cal he knew. He told them that he only ever had one photo of the two of them together. This photo was taken by Zan at the cabin one summer. In it, the boys had their shirts off, looking young, fit, and beautiful, with big grins on their faces and their arms draped over each other's shoulders. Jake had enlarged that photo and framed it. They looked so happy, like they were the closest of friends.

As the years passed, Jake looked at Cal's smiling face in that photo on his wall and wondered if Cal would even remember who he was. He knew that Cal was more important to him than he ever was to Cal. Jake did not know if he would have survived high school without him, his attention, his kindness, his support. That photo traveled with Jake from Louisville to Tucson, to Washington, DC, to West Palm Beach, Florida, and back to Louisville. At some point during all those moves, he misplaced the framed photo. He no longer had it by the time he had moved back to Chicago in 1994. Jake grieved the loss of his photo as much as he grieved not ever finding Cal again.

Jake found his family's recollection of Cal's life spotty at best. They could not remember the names of the various girlfriends. Nat said Cal had never married, while Zan said he did. His parents believed Cal might have gotten engaged to an older woman he knew in Belize. They remember him being with her for five years, but Cal's letters show he was there for a much shorter time, several months spread over a couple years' time. When Jake tried to establish a timeline for all of Cal's adventures, no one had a clue when he did what. How could his own parents not know of their son's whereabouts or relationships? It showed how Cal was secretive with everybody.

Jake was not willing to bring up Cal's disappearance, but a newspaper report in their scrapbook prompted their reminiscences. The women in his life knew the Interferon injections caused emotional problems for Cal, and they all thought he was depressed and may have taken his own life. The men could not accept he might have committed suicide, seeing it as a sign of weakness, so they preferred to say that Cal was a risk taker and got caught in a strong rip current. Jake felt that was wrong. Jake did not swim, and it was Cal who taught him how to float. Cal always said to him, "If you ever get in trouble in a current or tide, just relax, turn over, and float." Cal was a world-class athlete and swimmer, so he never would have gotten caught in a strong current.

Jake was trying to complete the puzzle of Cal's adult life, while Zan, Leigh, and Nat were like toddlers running off with the pieces. He listened to their conflicting thoughts on everything Cal did. Jake took it in but did not know what to believe. What did ring true were their observations that Cal was the happiest child, always smiling, without one mean bone in his body. He laughed and smiled all the time; he loved to give hugs to everyone; he jumped up and down when he got excited. He was a bundle of pure kinetic energy and joy. Jake knew that to be the truth because that was his experience of him. That seemed to translate to Cal's life even as he got older.

Where did you go, Cal? Did you really die in the ocean, or did you simply run away to that deserted tropical island you always hoped to find? Jake wanted to believe that he was still out there somewhere. But could he have been so cruel to let his family and dearest friends believe he died? Cal was a gentle, tender soul, but he seemed tortured too. Jake wondered if his upbringing, societal pressure, and his own expectations made it impossible for him to express his own true self. For Jake, that seemed to be the explanation for Cal's life. In a way, he was always running away from himself. Jake would never know for sure.

Zan and Leigh needed a nap, so Nat invited him to see Cal's old bedroom. "His clothes are gone now, but there are a few items of his still in there." The bedroom had been built behind the garage as a guest space with only a sliding door onto the covered back patio as an entrance. The only way into the house from that room was through the hall bathroom. Jake walked past the toilet into the bedroom and saw a photo of Cal at age ten with a swimming medal around his neck. His favorite kayak paddle was mounted on the wall. The room was dim with no direct light coming in and much of that shielded by the porch roof.

He walked to the corner next to the sliding door and looked at the books Cal had read, which still filled the shelves. Right next to the bookshelves, Jake looked at something hanging on the wall. He stared at it for the longest time, and it did not register in his brain what it was. It could not have been any odder than if he had seen the *Mona Lisa* hanging in a gas station restroom. This thing did not make sense and should not have been there. Nat came up behind Jake. "Oh, wow. I always wondered who that was. Now I know. It's you."

Jake knew this photo. He and Cal had been hanging around on the Belvedere between dance sets at the last Heritage Weekend before college. They lived in the era before cellphone cameras were a thing, so they did not have a lot of photos of one another. On this day, though, Cal had his little instant snapshot camera and captured his best friend Jake, after a performance, smiling sweetly and looking happy. They were happy then, and Jake was overjoyed in this moment. Cal had never forgotten him and kept this photo to always have him close by. Nat patted his shoulder as he cried happy tears.

Jake said his good-byes, hugging Leigh and Nat and turned to Zan who handed him a photo album and several folders. "I want you to have these as mementos of Cal. You boys loved each other so much."

"Yes, we did. Thank you for sharing your son with me. He was the best." He hugged Zan and turned to the door out to the garage. Zan called after him. "Don't be sad for Cal. He had a very full life. He did more in his time than most people could do in three lifetimes."

Jake smiled back at him but wondered if that was true. He may have had a full life, but Jake questioned if he was happy. He felt that Cal's life was mostly solitary. There was no evidence that he had had a great love in his life. That made Jake sad. He drove his rental car thirty miles from the house to the Cedar Wildlife Refuge, where Cal would go to look out over the Outer Banks for stargazing. The sun had just set, and the skies were getting darker by the minute. Jake sat on a concrete bench next to a low bush with purple flowers. The scent of the flowers was sweet, and the night breeze was warm and gentle.

He closed his eyes, took a breath, and then looked up. He took in the vast canvas overhead and smiled as a shooting star streaked across the sky. The moon was full, so Jake found two gray spots on the surface and superimposed Cal's eyes onto them. Then the rest of his face came into focus. For the first time in decades, Jake began talking to the man in the moon again. "Hi, Cal." He had never gone away; he had never left him. He had been right there all the time, shining down on him.

Jake lived a very long life. He always remembered a doctor friend's advice given to him years earlier. The doctor had said, "Pay attention to what's going on in your body and never let down your guard." It was wisdom to live by. Jake did not smoke, never took drugs, and always kept his consumption of alcohol or wine to the barest minimum. He watched what he ate, and he was active every day. As he grew older, he adapted his routine to fit whatever phase he was at in his life at that moment. He continued to dance and do his gymnastics stretching for as long as he could, until he started to worry that some of the acrobatic work might be dangerous at his older age and cause him injury.

By the time he had turned seventy-five, he was still walking five miles every day, but he transitioned his exercise to gentle yoga stretches. He had outlived his cats; he had outlived his husband. By the age of eighty, he had outlived his siblings, lovers, and his dearest friends. He worked his brain every day by continuing to play his flute and sing show tunes, committing new music and songs to memory so those brain synapses continued firing at full strength. Media technology had changed in his lifetime, so he stopped buying films on DVD and music on CD and making physical copies of sheet music. He transferred his entire library to the cloud.

Not wanting so many physical possessions any longer, he had yard sales to divest himself of kitchen equipment, furniture, clothing, books, and knickknacks. He was compressing his lifestyle to the barest minimum, so he no longer needed the large condo he owned on the northside of Chicago. He wanted to move to a smaller town, so that city lights would no longer obscure his view of the stars. He got a great deal on a ramshackle eight-hundred square-foot bungalow in Manitowoc, Wisconsin, but the foundation footings were not up to code.

Carpenter ants had eaten away at the wall struts, and the roof was caving in. Part of the structure collapsed before he had a chance to move in and fix it up.

It was cheaper to demolish the house and put up something newer on that piece of property. He bought a used shipping container for just two thousand dollars, and he found a company that converted those containers into small homes. The designer and contractor kept trying to upsell Jake on premium finishes and features he did not want. Jake insisted on keeping this last home he would ever live in as simple as possible. He did not even use the entire twenty-foot-by-forty-foot space, finishing only four hundred square feet and turning the other half into a glass-enclosed four-seasons room and covered porch overlooking Lake Michigan. The total cost to construct his new, unadorned, tiny house was just $20,000.

He had the contractor paint the ugly dirty container a deep forest green so that it might disappear into the landscape. It was small with just enough space for a queen-sized bed, modest closet, basic bathroom, and a small living area that had room for only a little kitchen, two easy chairs, and a small bistro table. He did not need much space because he no longer owned much. When he finally moved in, he brought just a large suitcase for his clothes and a small box of possessions containing a few toiletries, some cooking items, his flute, a laptop, and a cellphone. He wanted to take up as little space in the world as he thought necessary.

Every morning he walked the Mariner Trail along the lake and then returned home through town, stopping in the shops to say hello to his neighbors. He lived alone but he was never lonely. He dozed in his recliner after lunch and spent most of the late afternoon reading a book in his four-seasons room. He stood on the porch overlooking Lake Michigan and played his flute for an hour in the early evening, imagining that the crystalline notes rolled down the bluff and floated across the water to the east horizon. Each day as dusk came, he poured his single eight-ounce glass of red wine, raised a toast to the skies, and said his private benediction to the stars and moon overhead. That was his daily routine for twenty-five years.

His blond hair had at some point in the last few decades given way to a full head of white hair. He still only wore reading glasses. In his last years, he still required no prescriptions despite doctors' repeated attempts to get him to start taking medications he did not need. He was in perfect health, but in his last month of life, he thought he might need to get his hearing checked. He began to perceive music on the air. At first, it was just a single tone, and he assumed it was a wind chime. Then it was clearly a sequence of pitches forming a musical phrase, simple and not specific to any song or piece of music he knew. Soon, he understood that it was a flute played in its middle register, with soft tones that soothed him.

On the last day of his life, he took his usual morning walk, but he was tired and came home early. He could not stay awake, drifting off into several short naps. He awoke suddenly and glanced at the wall clock that read 1:23 p.m. He realized in that very moment he had turned one hundred years old. He dozed all afternoon and realized that his time had come. He made three video texts to the manager of the senior citizens' home where he played flute and sang show tunes once a month, to the library where he volunteered, and to the Coffee House Bake Shop where he liked to socialize with neighbors. The message was the same: "I'm slowing down today. Please check on me tomorrow. Thanks."

He fell asleep again on the chaise outside and awoke to find that the sun had already set. He struggled to get up but gathered the energy to grab his flute and pour his wine. Walking to the porch railing, he raised his glass, said his nightly invocation to the skies, then began to play. He did not know what he wanted to hear; he just wanted to make music at this moment. At first, he played just the single note he heard on the air a few weeks earlier. He played it several times before trying the short musical phrase that followed it. He repeated that musical line until he could hear the tones shimmer in the air around him.

He improvised a few random sequences of notes, runs, trills, and arpeggios. He started playing whatever piece of music he plucked from his memory—radio hits, songs he sang in shows, show tunes he loved, Disney songs. Finally, he settled on Edvard Grieg's "Morning Mood" from *Peer Gynt*, a piece of music he committed to memory eighty-five years earlier. He played the first few lines of the piece until the place in the score when the flute has a call and response with the full orchestra. He lowered the flute from his mouth, but the music continued, wafting toward him on the evening breeze. It was another flute. He played his next line, paused, and heard the musical response from the air.

As he resumed, the two flutes played the music in unison for a few lines until the ethereal instrument shifted to a harmonic third below Jake. As he played, Jake looked to the skies, found the Ursa Major constellation, and witnessed a momentary shift. The two pointer stars of the Big Dipper, Dubhe and Merak, and the North Star Polaris seemed to go nova, pulsing in greater magnitude before returning to their normal brightness. The starlight then luminesced and ejected from their source, merging with the energy of other stars as it streaked across the sky. The pulsing light vanished when crossing the path of the evening's half-moon, visible only as a shimmering distortion.

The starlight then plummeted toward earth, with the glow of every star seeming to coalesce into it, and a shape began to take form. The twinkling object dropped down to the surface of Lake Michigan, rocketing toward Jake at the same time it seemed to slow down. As it drew closer, he recognized it for what it was. Here then was Mandjet, the solar barque known as the Boat of a Million Years. The ship of stars floated to a stop, with the elevated bow resting against his railing. A figure walked up the steps of the bow and made the small hop from boat to porch.

He looked different but still the same. Jake recognized the curly hair, the leanly muscled body, the broad grin on his face. His brown hair had plenty of gray in it. This must have been what he looked like when he disappeared into the ocean all those years ago. Jake did not know if they were talking or somehow communicating silently with one another. Jake transmitted his thought to his long-lost friend, "You got gray." Cal conveyed to Jake, "You got tall . . . and old."

Jake laughed and started to cry. "I've missed you so much. I always thought about you. I searched for you but couldn't find you again."

"I'm here now." Cal reached out his hand to Jake. In the instant that they touched one another, Jake left his corporeal form. He looked over his shoulder and saw his wizened body still on the chaise, now at peace. He had passed with a smile on his face. When Jake turned around again, Cal was now standing on the bow of the ship, waiting for him. He looked up and hesitated. "But you're still so beautiful. And I leave the world an old man."

"Heaven is what you make it." Suddenly, Jake was on the bow of the ship standing next to Cal. They hugged and were rejuvenated into the manifestation of their former selves, when they were just eighteen, when they were happiest together and yet saddest at separating, when they were at the peak of their physical perfection, when they were most hopeful. Their lives over, they now faced eternity together, and so their parallel paths forever merged on the line at infinity.

The ship floated away from Jake's home and tacked toward the eastern horizon. Jake looked nervously toward Cal, who smiled broadly and nodded his reassurance that everything would be okay. The boat soared off into the cosmos, trailing a thousand shooting stars in its wake until it blinked out of sight. The stars and moon are constant, and so are Cal and Jake.

Acknowledgments

This book is a work of fiction, although it is very much based on my personal experiences as a teenager. Real people that I have known in my lifetime inspired the characters in this novel, but they are not those people I knew. How then can I call this a work of fiction? Would it not be closer to autobiography or memoir than a wholly created story? It is fiction, because the complicated process of writing—getting the story out of my brain and onto the page, finding the structure, organizing the stories, refining the timeline, streamlining connections, merging characters, and in many instances, inventing dialogue—is all part of the act of creation. As a writer, I get to take my own true story and give it the shape and the outcome that I wish it had had in my youth.

By its very nature, writing is a solitary pursuit. The author is the one who comes up with the idea and spends a vast amount of time hiding away from other people, ignoring all distractions, defiantly protecting the writing sanctuary, shooing away the cats at certain times while cuddling them during pensive moments, and getting down to work every single day. However, our lives are populated with many other people, and no one ever goes through this process entirely alone. It has been no different for me during this yearlong adventure. First and foremost, I must thank my husband Dan for giving me the space, the time, and the freedom to write this book, which has amounted to ripping off a bandage, cutting open old wounds, treating them, and allowing them to heal finally.

I have several people to thank for their contributions to this book. Michael Unger, M.D., helped me understand some medical issues, particularly hepatitis C, providing general information on its causes and treatment, the side effects of Interferon, and the stress often caused by the diagnosis of such a serious ailment. My dear friend Edward Kuras is a therapist, with whom I chatted for hours and hours about the real people and their fictional counterparts. I wanted to make sure that my characters remained consistent throughout, but he reminded me that people are not consistent and rather more complex. Without giving me advice, Ed gave me the best advice I could have gotten (and that is what good therapists and good friends do). That freed me to write the characters as not simply black or white, but with all the shades of gray in between.

I am indebted to graphic designer Jonathan Hahn for my cover art design and the interior layout of the book, making it look so good. My editor Allison Felus was a true champion in my corner, always encouraging, cheering me on, providing valuable feedback, trimming the fat out of the narrative, correcting some silly mistakes, and helping make this story the best that it could be. I want to also thank my brothers Jeff and Greg for always encouraging me to remember the best parts of our youth.

My sister Janice Lewis Grasch gets a special shout-out for providing me with the reason for writing this book. I was visiting her in Louisville, staying at her house, when I discovered that the childhood friend, who was the inspiration for Cal, had moved into a house across the street from our parents and lived there for a year-and-a-half. I was stunned that we still never managed to reunite despite my three visits back home during that period. Trying to provide some words of comfort and wisdom, Jan said to me, "Well, it wasn't meant to be." I realized then that it wasn't a matter of "we weren't meant to be" but rather that "we weren't allowed to be" who we truly were. And that is when I knew I had to write this story.

I must thank another sister, that of my childhood friend, who gave me access to some photos, letters, and journals that gave me a glimpse into the man he became but that I sadly never got to know. She also gave me permission to write the version of him that I wanted to write. While I hope the character of Cal is true to his spirit and personality, Cal does not even come close to representing the entire reality of him. How can any of us know someone else fully? I knew a part of him, a part that he may have kept hidden away from his family and friends, but it is not the entirety of him.

Finally, I will forever be grateful to that sweet, silly, jubilant curly haired boy who saved my life both literally and figuratively. I don't think I would have survived high school without him. I always considered him the other half of my soul. He gave me the sun, the moon, and the stars, but he stole my heart. It is still his face I see when I gaze at the moon. If he could have read this book, I can only hope that he would know it as the love letter to him that I always intended it to be. I hope instead that it can be a love letter to all the Jakes and Cals of this world.

Jonathan Lewis, November 1, 2022

CPSIA information can be obtained
at www.ICGtesting.com
Printed in the USA
BVHW071848110123
655992BV00009B/673